My Sister's Bones

My Sister's Bones

NUALA ELLWOOD

VIKING
an imprint of
PENGUIN BOOKS

VIKING

UK | USA | Canada | Ireland | Australia
India | New Zealand | South Africa

Viking is part of the Penguin Random House group of companies
whose addresses can be found at global.penguinrandomhouse.com

First published 2017

001

Copyright © Nuala Ellwood, 2017

The moral right of the author has been asserted

Set in 13.5/16 pt Garamond MT Std

Typeset in India by Thomson Digital Pvt Ltd, Noida, Delhi

Printed in Great Britain by Clays Ltd, St Ives plc

A CIP catalogue record for this book is available from the British Library

Hardback ISBN: 978–0–241–97727–9

Trade paperback ISBN: 978–0–241–97815–3

www.greenpenguin.co.uk

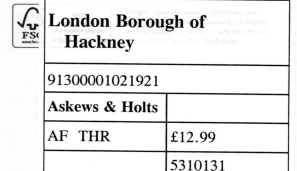

This novel is dedicated to my father – a 'great good' man.

'When the dumb Hour, clothed in black,
Brings the Dreams about my bed,
Call me not so often back,
Silent Voices of the dead'

Alfred Tennyson

Prologue

She is safe now. Free from her demons. Her final resting place is still and tranquil, a little watery pocket of calm. She would have liked that, I think to myself, as I watch a pleasure boat sail into the dock. She would have thought it appropriate.

It is hard to believe that after such a violent death she could ever find peace, but I hope she has.

My sister. My beautiful sister.

'Go safely,' I whisper. And as I scatter her ashes into the water I breathe a deep sigh. Perhaps this is the end.

The boat fills up with tourists and their excited voices fill the air as we stand here, three broken souls, saying our last goodbyes. But as I watch her go I am struck once again by the thought that's been haunting me ever since she died.

Of the two of us, how is it possible that I am the one who survived?

PART ONE

I

'Would you like me to repeat the question?'

The doctor is speaking, but it's hard to hear her over the voices.

'Kate?' The doctor shifts in her seat.

'Sorry, can you repeat that?' I try to focus.

'Shall I close the window? It's quite noisy out there.'

She goes to stand up, but I put my hand out to stop her. She flinches and I realize she may have mistaken my gesture for aggression.

'No,' I say as she sits back down awkwardly. 'It's fine. I just thought I heard . . . nothing. It's nothing.'

I mustn't tell her about the voices.

She nods her head and smiles a half-smile. This is familiar territory. Auditory hallucinations; voices in the head. As a clinical psychologist, this will be heaven for her. She takes her notepad and points her pen at a fresh page.

'Okay,' she says, and a glint of silver grapples with the rays of the morning sun as her pen swipes across the paper. 'These things you can hear, Kate, can you describe them to me? Are they discernible voices?'

'I don't know what you're talking about,' I reply.

'You find them difficult to make out?'

'Look, I know what you're doing here,' I say tersely. 'But you won't succeed because I'm not what you think I am.'

'What do I think you are?'

'A mad woman who hears voices, who sees things, imagines things. You think it's all in my head.'

But as I speak they're back, fading in and out like a radio between frequencies. Shaw says something but I can't hear for the screams. The old woman wailing; the young father running through the streets holding the blasted body of his baby girl in his arms. My old faithfuls, the ones that return to me whenever I am under stress.

I can't help myself. I put my hands to my ears and hold them there. The voices dissolve into a low hum, like the sound you hear when you place a conch shell to your ear. I see my mother, her cheek pressed against mine. *Listen, darling, can you hear it? That's the ocean talking to you.* And I believed her. I believed that the sea lay hidden inside the shell, though what I was hearing was really just the air bouncing off the curved cavity. I believed her because I needed to. She was my mother and she never lied.

'Kate?'

I see Shaw's lips move. She's saying my name. I stare at her for a moment and she stares back. Her eyes are a dirty green, the colour of the winter sea inside my head. It's getting louder now, the waves pounding on the rocks.

'Kate, please.' Shaw starts to get up. She's going to get help.

I force myself to take my hands away from my ears and clasp them together. The peridot bracelet that Chris gave me on our eighth anniversary ripples down my arm and gathers in a spool at my wrist. I run my finger along the surface, rubbing the stones like the genie's lamp. *Make a wish*, I think to myself. I remember the night Chris gave me the bracelet. We were in Venice. It was carnival time and as we weaved our way through the misty streets marvelling at the elaborate costumes of the revellers he slipped something into my pocket. 'To the next eight years,' he whispered, as I clasped the bracelet on to my wrist. I close my eyes. *Please bring him back.*

'How's your sleep been recently?' asks Dr Shaw. 'Any nightmares?'

I shake my head and try to focus, but all I can think of is Chris and that trip to Venice. The smell of Venetian canal water lingers in the air.

'It's very pretty,' says Shaw, gesturing to the bracelet.

'Apparently the peridot stone protects against nightmares,' I whisper.

'And does it work?'

I carry on rubbing the stone with my finger and thumb. It is strangely comforting.

'Does the stone work, Kate?'

She's not going to let this go. I take a sip of water from the plastic beaker they gave me an hour ago. It is tepid and smells of chemicals, but anything is better than the stench of the canals.

'I've had the odd bad dream,' I reply, wiping my mouth with the back of my hand. 'Who wouldn't? It's been a rough few weeks.'

As Shaw continues to write I stare at my feet and for a second I see body parts congealed in mud, like some macabre jigsaw puzzle. She asked me about nightmares but where do I start? Do I tell her how I've stood in shallow graves and felt my feet sinking into the earth, my toes drenched in body fluids? Do I tell her about those endless black nights when I have woken up begging for noise, for chatter, for anything but the incessant silence of the dead? No, because if I do I will only confirm her suspicions. I have to stay focused and stay one step ahead of her or it's all over. I rub the peridot for protection as Shaw stops writing and looks up.

'And would you say these bad dreams have got worse since you've returned to Herne Bay?'

I put the beaker back on to the table and sit up in my chair. I have to stop letting my mind wander; I have to be alert, careful. Every word I say here can be used against me.

'No, they haven't got worse,' I say, trying to keep my voice steady. 'They've just become real.'

2

Sunday 12 April 2015

One week earlier

I shiver as I step off the train and stand on the deserted platform. The sea air whips angrily around my face as I pull my bulky rucksack on to my back and make my way towards the exit. The station clock reads 11.59. I feel uneasy as I walk through the blistering silence. Have I made the right decision? I pause, and contemplate climbing back on to the train, but the engine has stopped and a guard in a fluorescent waistcoat is opening the doors to let the cleaners do their work. This is the last stop, the end of the line.

I pull my thin jacket tighter, chastising myself for leaving my heavier coat packed at the bottom of my bag. I'd forgotten how cold Herne Bay can get at night, even in April. My mother used to call it bone-chilling weather.

As I walk towards the steps I look around for any sign of life but there is nothing. I am the only person here. I hope he got my message. Of all the terrifying situations I have found myself in over the years, none has made me feel as uncomfortable as this. Herne Bay. Where darkness comes early and life is as predictable as the tides. It will take all the strength I have left to get through these next few days.

As I step into the half-lit ticket hall my phone vibrates in my pocket and I pause by the red glow of a vending machine to answer it.

'Hello. Oh, that's okay. I'll be right there.'

A light rain begins to fall as I step out of the station and spot the silver saloon car parked in the empty taxi rank. I wave to the man sitting in the driver's seat as I stride towards the car, my heavy rucksack digging into my collarbone. My brother-in-law waves back but doesn't smile. He knows that my presence in Herne Bay will cause trouble. Still, I'm grateful that he came to collect me. He's the only member of my family who still wants to speak to me.

'Hi, Paul,' I sigh as I open the door. 'Thanks for coming out at this hour, I really appreciate it.'

'No problem,' he replies. 'Stick your bag on the back seat. There's more room.'

I want to stick myself on the back seat as well, and pretend I'm in London in some anonymous taxi, going home to my own bed. Still, the drive from the station to my mother's house is a short one, I tell myself, as I toss my rucksack into the back and climb into the passenger seat. Clicking the seat belt, I lean back and close my eyes. I am home, whatever that means.

'Are you sure you want to stay at your mother's?' asks Paul as we pull out of the car park. 'I mean, you're more than welcome to bunk at ours for the week.'

'Thanks, Paul,' I reply as familiar landmarks pass by the window. 'But I really don't want to put you out.'

'You wouldn't be putting us out,' he says. 'It would be a pleasure.'

'Oh, come on,' I say. 'I doubt it would be a pleasure for Sally. I can just imagine her face if I rock up at the door.'

'Fair enough,' he says. 'What about a hotel then? There's a new one opened up on the seafront, nice and plush, you'd like it.'

'Honestly, Mum's house will be fine,' I say firmly. 'I'm only here for a few days and, anyway, after everything that's happened it'll be good to spend some time there; give me the chance to take it all in.'

'Okay,' he says. 'But the offer's there if you change your mind.'

'Thanks, Paul.'

He is silent for the rest of the journey and I look out as we drive through indistinct residential streets, the names of which blur in front of my eyes like ink dissolving in water. My stomach growls and I suddenly feel light-headed. This always happens when I come back here. It's like I'm allergic to the place.

'Do you mind if I open the window?' I ask Paul, praying I don't throw up over his immaculate dashboard.

'Go ahead,' he says, gesturing to the button by the door handle.

'That's better,' I sigh as a flurry of cold air hits my face, though the pungent fishy scent doesn't help.

I put my hand in my pocket and run my fingers along the reassuring smooth surface of my lucky pen. The pen – a beautiful silver fountain pen inscribed with my name – was a gift from Chris on our first anniversary. It has been everywhere with me – Syria, Afghanistan, Iraq. Whenever I touch it I know I'm safe.

'It's so quiet,' I whisper, tucking the pen back into my pocket as the car crawls up the hill towards Smythley Road.

I'd forgotten the blanket of silence that descends on the town at night. As I look out I imagine the inhabitants of Smythley Road cocooned in their beds, like the characters in the Edgar Allan Poe stories I devoured as a child, lost in their 'little slices of death'. It's hard to believe that this had once been my home; this silent world.

'Here we are,' says Paul as he stops the car.

His voice makes me jump and I look up at the house we have parked outside. Number 46: a lifeless 1930s semi with greying pebbledash that had once been sparkling white. I still remember the telephone number – 654345 – and my childhood mantra: *My name is Kate Rafter and I live at number 46 Smythley Road with my mummy and daddy and my sister, Sally*. My eyes moisten but I blink the tears away, reminding myself that the first step is always the hardest.

As I open the door and step out on to the pavement my lungs contract, like the prelude to a bout of coughing, and I have to steady myself by placing my hands on the car bonnet.

It's just a week, that's all, I tell myself. A few days of sea air and signing Mum's papers then back to work, back to normal.

'You okay?'

Paul is standing behind me. He lifts the rucksack from my shoulder and guides me towards the house.

'I'm fine, Paul, just tired.'

'Are you sure I can't persuade you to book into a hotel?'

'No,' I say as we walk up the drive. 'I just need a good night's sleep, that's all.'

'Well, you'll get one here, I'm sure,' he says breezily. 'It's nice and peaceful. Don't know how you manage it, jumping from one hellhole to the next. I'd be wrecked.'

I smile ruefully. That's all that matters to most people – getting a good night's sleep. I imagine Paul in Homs or Aleppo, snoring his head off while all around him people fight to stay alive.

I stand on the doorstep staring at the door. It still feels inconceivable that my mother is not behind it, the smell of baking wafting in her wake. My mother *was* this house; it was the only world she knew.

'I'll leave you to it,' says Paul, interrupting my thoughts. 'Here are the keys. Chubb's for the front door, mortice for the back. Thermostat's in the kitchen above the kettle if you're cold. I'll pop over in the morning to see if you're okay.'

'Thanks,' I reply, taking the keys and rubbing the sharp metal between finger and thumb. 'And give my regards to Sally, won't you?'

He flinches at the sound of her name.

'She's still my sister,' I tell him. 'Despite everything.'

'I know,' he says. 'And deep down she knows that too.'

'I hope so,' I say, the cold air sending shivers down my back.

'You get yourself in,' says Paul, patting my arm. 'It's freezing out here.'

I follow him down the gravel drive and watch as his car disappears into the shadowy folds of the bay, putting off going into the house for a few more moments. Once I open the door it will all become real. My mother's death will be confirmed. It is almost too painful to bear. But I have to do it, I tell myself, as I reluctantly make my way back to the house, or I will never move on. As I approach I see a light in the upstairs window of the house next door and I pause. It is a reassuring sight, a sign of life amid darkness and death, and I feel comforted as I put the key in the lock and open the door.

Inside, I fumble around trying to find the light switch, tripping over my rucksack as I run my palms across the glossy woodchip walls. When I eventually locate it the dim glow that ensues brings a knot to my stomach. I'd forgotten: my mother always abhorred bright lights. Light was not to be trusted. It revealed too much. And so my mother had installed low-wattage bulbs throughout the house and retreated to the shadows.

I walk down the hallway, thinking how the first eighteen years of my life had been spent in near-darkness, terrified of what lay hidden in the corners. I go from room to room, flicking switches, my heart sinking as each dull bulb splutters impotently to life.

I stop at the kitchen. It looks different. Paul and Sally have obviously set to work getting the house ready to sell. The dark red walls of my childhood have been painted magnolia and the lino replaced with an insipid beige carpet. But it's all good, I tell myself as I step inside. However boring it may be, beige is what I need right now; its dull neutrality will keep me from hurtling down the hole of memory.

I walk into the pantry and see that Paul has stocked up ahead of my visit. There are new packs of coffee and tea, a fresh loaf of white bread, tins of soup and baked beans. Opening the fridge, I see full-fat milk, butter and eggs and a packet of smoked bacon: things I haven't eaten for years. Still, I'll be grateful for them in the morning.

I see he's also left a couple of bottles of white wine. I take one out and pour myself a large glass. I know I shouldn't. After all, until the events of the last couple of months, I barely touched alcohol. I vowed never to turn out like my father and Sally. But since Aleppo, a drink seems to be the only thing that will settle my nerves.

That and my sleeping pills.

I pat my pocket and pull out a pack. I swallow two with the rest of the wine and make my way upstairs, praying that they will work fast.

But as I reach the landing I stop. My throat tightens, and I stand for a moment looking at the closed door of my mother's bedroom. It's still there. An ancient foot-shaped gash in the wood panel. I find I am trembling. It's like being back there, thirty years of distance gone in a flash. Why on earth did she never replace it?

I will myself not to go in, to wait until morning when my brain will be ready, but it's no use, my hands are already pushing at the door. I breathe in sharply. My father's anger permeates the space and it feels like any moment now he is going to come charging at me, ask me what the hell I think I'm doing snooping around like this. But all is silent as I step into the gloom.

Nothing has changed. I stand incredulous, looking at the collection of dusty furniture. The same mahogany chest of drawers; the same heavy velvet curtains; the same horrid brown wallpaper with spiky dandelions threaded through it. I see my mother's head hitting the wall over and over again, my father's hand holding her hair while he smashed her into the golden flowers. The room smells of damp fabric and cheap air freshener. Paul has obviously tried his best to spruce it up but my mother's blood is all over this room. Even if the visible marks are gone I can still smell it in the air: a musty scent of fear.

I close the door and step out on to the landing. A framed picture of the Sacred Heart looms ominously in front of me. The bearded Jesus holds his hand out towards me, a blazing heart pulsating in his chest. I hated this picture as a child, couldn't bear to look at it. For me it symbolized everything that was wrong with my family: blind faith in the face of violence and adversity; submission to a greater good. 'Blessed Jesus pray for us,' I read aloud as I stand in front of the faded picture. Underneath those words in spindly blue handwriting my mother has written the names of her children – two living, one dead – her husband and, finally, always last, herself.

'What good did you ever do us?' I shout and my voice echoes through the empty house.

I glare at the beatific man in the frame. What kind of God takes a child's life away? I read my little brother's name again and wonder for a moment what it must have felt like to drown, to gasp and flounder and call out for a mother who never came. I think of another child who didn't make it and I close my eyes, trying to keep the images at bay. Enough, I tell myself, and with a sweep of my hand turn the picture over to face the wall.

I am delirious with sleep as I open the door to Sally's old room. Someone – most likely Paul – has made the bed with freshly laundered sheets and there is a large fluffy towel neatly folded on the chest of drawers. The thought of a long hot bath is tempting, but I know it is not a good idea with strong sleeping pills in my system. Still, a shower might help.

I take the towel and make my way back across the landing to the bathroom. I turn on the light and am greeted by a sight so horrifying it makes my toes curl: my reflection in the full-length mirror. Here I am, looking all of my thirty-nine years and then some. My face is lined and puffy, my hair a thick ball of greying wire wool. I make a mental note as I turn on the shower to check in with Anton for a full head of highlights as soon as I get back to London.

The water burns my skin and as I scrub my face I smile at the futility of worrying about my appearance. What are a few grey hairs compared to the horrors of the last few weeks? My life has imploded and all I can think of is a cut and blow-dry.

But then I remember my lovely friend Bridget Hennessey, one of the most fearless journalists I have ever known and my mentor when I started out. She had just come back from reporting on the war in Kosovo when we met and had endured a mock execution at the hands of a rebel gang. For ten days she was held hostage with a sack tied over her head while the sound of gunshots rang out from the room next door. They told her they had killed her driver and cameraman and that she would be next. The psychological torture she endured would have sent most of us mad but she held herself together until she was released. I remember watching her in the newsroom as she calmly typed up the account of what had happened, her perfectly manicured fingernails tapping at the keyboard. I sat there with my unkempt hair and bitten fingernails and wondered how she could have gone through such a terrifying ordeal and still think it necessary to get her nails done.

'But that's the whole point, Kate, my dear,' she said when I asked her about it later. 'Real life can't stop – it mustn't stop, otherwise those bastards have won.'

I step out of the shower and wrap myself in the large white towel. Warmth envelops my body and I close my eyes, imagining I'm in our favourite hotel in Venice and Chris is waiting for me in the bedroom. I can feel his rough warm skin next to mine as I walk along the corridor; his fingers working their way inside me; the taste of mulled wine on his lips. But the bedroom is empty and cold and the feeling dissolves as I slip under the polyester sheets and close my eyes.

Moments later I am in a shop filled with dust. It swirls around the room, seeping into the cavities and crevices like poisonous gas. As I step further inside, the dust thickens and I can't see. My mouth is dry with fear but I must keep going.

This shop was once full of customers, full of life. Piles of travel brochures and black-market cigarettes lined its shelves and a small boy ran down the aisles telling his stories to anyone who would listen, but now all is silence as I walk through the mounds of rubble.

The ground is different here, slick and wet, and when I look down I see my boots are covered in dark red stains. I'm no longer walking on rubble but trudging through thick, glutinous blood.

I hear a camera click and its flash illuminates the room. The shock of the light makes me lose my footing and I fall, face down, into the fluid. Looking up, I see a pile of stones, a small shrine amid an ocean of blood, and I crawl towards it, sensing what lies beneath. I feel his heartbeat vibrating beneath my hands and I begin to dig. I am a burrowing animal as I pull away the rubble, clawing at it with my fingernails. Spots of crimson dot the stones and I realize it is coming from my hands though I feel no pain. Then I see him, lying on his back, eyes wide open, arms raised upwards; a baby looking for its mother.

I try not to look at his face as I bend down to pick him up. Behind me, the camera flashes and the boy is illuminated in a harsh white glare. I can't see him; he is dissolving into the light. Stop it, I cry to the man with the camera, you can't photograph this, and as my voice echoes against the shattered walls the ground shakes. The boy looks at me, pleadingly, and I try to grab hold of his hand but it slips through my fingers. He is dust and I watch as he returns to the earth. But in the final moments he calls out.

'Help me!'

It's the last thing I hear as the camera's flash blinds me and I blink myself awake.

I am lying crouched on the floor, scraping my nails against the carpet, and though I know that I'm safe, that it was just another nightmare, my mouth still tastes of dust. Hauling myself up from the floor, I see that the room is full of a cold, bluish light. I'd been so tired I'd forgotten to close the curtains.

I go to the window. The sky is clear and cloudless. Such a contrast to the polluted skies I see each night in London. I stand for a moment looking at the moon and the twinkling marine stars and I think of Syria. There, darkness came down fast. Like a guillotine, Chris used to say. And I feel myself disconnect. It seems as though all of that – Syria, London, Chris – is another life, and *this* life, this town on the edge of the sea, is the only one that exists. I'm no longer a fearless journalist, I'm a scared teenager crouching once more behind the curtains, scared of the nightmares that come when I close my eyes.

3

Herne Bay Police Station

10 hours detained

'Perhaps we should go back a bit,' says Dr Shaw, 'to when you first arrived in Herne Bay.' She looks down at the paper in front of her. 'I understand it had been some time since you were last here. What made you return?'

I sit and watch as Shaw crosses and uncrosses her legs, as she sips tea from a polystyrene beaker, wipes the dregs from her mouth and places the cup on the floor beside her feet. The large, oval clock that hangs on the wall behind her head ticks rhythmically as we sit in silence, one pondering the question, the other awaiting its answer. An answer I am sure she already knows.

I will be forty years old in a couple of months and as I sit in this tiny, strip-lit room I see a cake with lemon icing and buttercream filling. I see my mother flitting about in a tiny kitchen, cracking eggs into a bowl that is as big as her head. And I see myself, four years old, balancing on the edge of the kitchen counter watching her every move. 'I want a cake the colour of the sun,' I had told her. And my mother grants my wish, for after everything we have suffered together she can't bear to let me down. If I want a sunshine cake then she will make sure I get one.

I hear Shaw clear her throat and I look up, my mother's face disappearing into the woodchip wall.

'I fancied a bit of sea air,' I reply.

Shaw leans forward and takes a cardboard file out of her bag.

'We've spoken to Paul Cheverell,' she says, taking a piece of paper from the file. 'He's your brother-in-law, yes?'

I nod my head. My chest tightens. What has Paul been telling them?

'He told us that you came back because there'd been a family bereavement,' she says, reading from her notes. 'It was your mother, I believe?'

'Yes.'

I stare at the wall behind Shaw's head, desperately trying to erase the image of my mother's grave from my mind, but it's all I can see.

'Were you and your mother close?'

I look back at Shaw and tell myself that the sooner I answer her questions the sooner I can get out of here. I shall pretend this is work, that I'm sitting in a meeting room not a police cell, and the subject under discussion is someone else: an abstract mother; a person who doesn't make cakes or call her daughter 'lovey' or cry at Elizabeth Barrett Browning poems. If I imagine this other person and not my real mother then I can get through this.

'Yes, we were,' I reply, smiling. *Smile at the difficult ones, get them onside.*

'You visited her often?'

'Not as much as I'd have liked.'

'Why was that?'

'Well, my job means I'm not often in the UK for more than a few days at a time, and when I *am* here it's non-stop.'

I know how lame it sounds as the words come out but I can't tell Shaw that I found it all so difficult; that the thought of seeing my beautiful mother in a nursing home, her mind gone, was too much to bear.

'She was suffering from dementia?'

'Yes.'

I try to hold on to the image of the abstract figure, the hypothetical mother, but it fractures and I see Mum bending over the kitchen table with a pile of scrap paper, trying to find out where she'd written my aunt's phone number. Those scraps of paper were her memory, her lifeline, but then she would lose them and get even more confused. At one point I sent her a Dictaphone and I remember her sitting on the sofa trying to work out the buttons, confusion etched on her face. She had no idea what to do with it.

'How long had she been in the nursing home?'

'Not long,' I reply. 'Just a few months.'

'She must have deteriorated rapidly.'

'Yes,' I say. 'Though Paul has told me since that it was peaceful; that she died in her sleep.'

'She'd had a stroke, is that right?'

'That's what they told me,' I reply with a shrug. I want to change the subject.

'Your brother-in-law said you couldn't get back for the funeral.'

Shaw's voice is cold and dispassionate and it cuts through me, reinforcing my grief, my guilt.

'That's right.'

'Why was that?'

Her words are bullets and I have to force myself to stay in my seat when every part of me wants to jump up and fight back.

'I told you, my work keeps me overseas sometimes for weeks on end. I was in Syria.'

'And you couldn't get back?'

'No. I wanted to but . . . it was difficult.'

'So you missed your mother's funeral. That must have been tough?'

'Yes. It was.'

I try not to think of that afternoon, of the men and the blood and the child crying out for me, and instead I think about the journey back to the UK. Sitting there waiting for the plane to take off, I felt something inside me break; I even thought I heard it snap, somewhere in my chest. It hurt, it physically hurt, like when you stretch an elastic band to its limit and it breaks in your hand. And in the midst of my grief for my mother was a gnawing guilt; the knowledge that I was running from an atrocity that I had played a part in creating. I had done something terrible, something I could never forgive myself for.

But I don't want to tell Shaw any of this, it's none of her business.

'It must have been strange coming back to Herne Bay after all that time.'

Shaw's voice brings me hurtling back to the present.

'Yes.'

'I understand you've been staying in your childhood home,' she continues.

I nod my head and instinctively start to pick at my arm. The cuts are beginning to scab and they sting. I close my eyes and imagine painkillers and a large glass of Chablis, knowing that neither will be forthcoming. Shaw notices my rubbing and frowns at the lacerations that zigzag up my arm.

'That looks painful,' she says.

'It's nothing,' I say, folding my arm into my chest defensively.

'How did you do it?'

'I said it's nothing.'

She looks at me for a few seconds, then seems to make the decision to carry on.

'And your father, is he still alive?'

She must already know this too. 'No,' I reply. 'Thankfully not.'

'Why thankfully?'

'Because he was a violent drunk,' I reply. 'I hated him and he hated me.'

'Why did you hate him?'

'Because he treated my mum like a punchbag.'

I pause. I've said too much again.

'Look, I appreciate the therapy session but what's this got to do with anything? I understand how this works, Dr Shaw. I interrogate people for a living. But the issue is not with me – it's with *her*.'

'Kate, I just need you to be honest,' she says, folding her arms across her chest. 'These questions will help us get as clear a picture as possible of what has led to your being here. Do you understand?'

Reluctantly, I nod my head.

'We can take a break at any point,' she says lightly, as though addressing a recalcitrant toddler. 'Just say and we can pause.'

'No,' I snap. 'I'm fine. Let's just carry on.'

'Okay,' she says, shuffling in her seat.

She looks flustered for a moment and this pleases me. For a few moments I am the one in control.

'You said your father was violent and that he hated you. Why did he hate you?'

'I have no idea,' I reply. 'Maybe I reminded him of my mother who he also hated. Look, my parents had lost a child, my little brother, and it broke them. My mother dealt with her grief by cosseting me while my father just got angrier and angrier. He blamed my mother for my brother's death. He was an alcoholic and when he was drunk he would lash out.'

'Why did he blame your mother for the child's death?'

'I have no idea. It was his way of coping, I guess.'

'How did your brother die?'

'An accident,' I reply brusquely. I've had years of practising this response whenever well-meaning people ask. 'He drowned.'

'And your mother was with him?'

I hear screaming. From the corridor? I'm not sure. I look at Shaw but she hasn't heard it. My heart is racing and I try to remember what they told me the last time this happened. Breathing. I have to focus on my breathing.

I close my eyes and slowly exhale, aware that Shaw is waiting for me to answer.

'Kate?'

I open my eyes and take a deep inhalation of clammy air.

'I'm sorry,' I say as I breathe out. 'I'd rather not talk about that. It was a long time ago and it has nothing to do with why I'm here.'

'Okay,' says Shaw. 'What about your sister, Paul's wife Sally – did your father hit her too?'

I shake my head.

'No.'

'Why not?'

'How should I know?'

'Are you and your sister close?'

'No, we're not.'

'Why is that?'

'Oh, I don't know. Is anyone close to their sister? Are you close to yours?'

'I'm an only child,' says Shaw.

'Lucky you,' I reply snarkily.

'I was asking about *your* sister, Kate.'

'Okay, okay,' I exclaim, shaking my head. 'Why aren't we close? I have no idea. I guess our lives are just very different.'

Shaw nods her head and scribbles something down. As I watch her I think of the last time I saw Sally, her face contorted as she yelled at me. *You swan in here when I haven't seen you in years and think you can start telling me what to do? We're not kids any more, Kate. I make my own decisions now.*

'In what way?' continues Shaw. 'In what way are your lives different?'

'In every way.'

I think of the email that landed in my inbox as I sat huddled in a Syrian basement: *Mum's dead. Thought you should know.*

One line. That's all Sally could give me. One terse line that told me my mother, who I loved beyond words, was gone.

Bitch.

'What was that, Kate?'

I look up at Shaw, the memory of that email coursing through my head. Did I say that out loud?

'My sister is not a particularly pleasant person, Dr Shaw,' I say. 'We don't get along. Can we just leave it at that?'

4

Monday 13 April 2015

Paul stands on the step with a beaming smile. He's holding a carrier bag.

'Fish and chips,' he says. 'Herne Bay's finest. I bet you missed them.'

I haven't but I feel strangely upbeat as I lead him through the passageway. For the first time in ages, I have woken with a clear head. The voices are silent. For now.

'I wangled myself an extended lunch break so I thought I'd pop to Tellivers. I bet you're dying for some real food after being in – where were you again?'

'Aleppo,' I tell him. 'It's in Syria,' I add, noticing the blank look on his face.

'Yeah, well I bet they don't have food as good as this out there,' he says as he puts the carrier bag on the table.

It's a fucking war zone, I think, as I stand in the kitchen doorway watching Paul set the table. There's barely any food and the people are fighting to survive. The last thing I was thinking about in Aleppo was bloody fish and chips.

'Actually, Paul, I'm not that hungry,' I tell him. 'I've only just had breakfast.'

'Oh, come on,' he says, patting the wooden dining chair next to him. 'It won't kill you and you could do with feeding up a bit. You're all skin and bone.'

He's only trying to be friendly I tell myself as I reluctantly join him at the table.

'There you go,' he says as he piles my plate with fat chips. 'Tuck in.'

I put a chip in my mouth and chew slowly. It tastes surprisingly good.

'I've spoken to your mum's solicitor in Canterbury and she's booked us in for one o'clock on Wednesday to sign the papers,' says Paul. 'It shouldn't take long. Oh, and you'll need to bring some ID with you. Have you got a passport?'

I stare at him incredulously.

'Paul, do you think I could do my job if I didn't have a passport?'

'Oh, sorry,' he laughs. 'Of course you have. Forgive me, my head's full of work stuff.'

He goes to the kitchen cupboard and brings out a dusty bottle of malt vinegar.

'Want some?'

I shake my head and watch as he drowns his chips with the pungent brown liquid.

'Will Sally be coming?' I ask.

'No,' he says, putting his fork down. His face looks grave.

'What is it?'

'Well, it's just Sally. She's not feeling too good.'

'You mean she's drinking again?'

'She's had a few setbacks, yes,' he says, picking up a chip and twisting it distractedly between his finger and thumb.

'Have you tried AA?'

He shakes his head. 'She won't hear of it. She doesn't think she has a problem. I wish you would speak to her. You might make her see sense. She won't listen to me any more.'

'Oh, come on, Paul, she told me very clearly the last time we met that I wasn't welcome. She practically pushed me out of the door.'

'I know, but that was a long time ago and you know how sensitive she is about the Hannah situation. She thought you were blaming her.'

'I was trying to knock some sense into her,' I say, pushing my plate away. 'I don't care if she was offended, she needed to know the truth. If she'd been sober, Hannah would still be here, it's as simple as that.'

'I know,' says Paul. 'But at least Hannah's okay. Thanks for your help with finding her, by the way. It really put our minds at rest.'

'She's my niece,' I reply. 'I had to see for myself that she was safe, which is more than can be said for Sally.'

'Look, I know you're angry with her,' says Paul. 'But Sally's really deteriorating. Can't you put this silly feud behind you and make up?'

'I'm sorry, Paul, I just think there's something odd about a mother who gives up like that,' I say, taking my plate and scraping the fish and chips into the bin. 'I mean, does she even care?'

'Come on, Kate, that's not fair,' he says, wiping his lips with a piece of kitchen paper. 'Of course she cares. Hannah's leaving destroyed Sally. Her drinking got worse, she lost her job. She was in bits. She knows deep down it was her behaviour that drove Hannah away – the drinking, the arguing – she knows that and it's eating her up inside.'

As I stand at the bin I see my sister's terrified face all those years ago in the maternity ward. She was so young, just fourteen when she had Hannah, still a child herself. I remember sitting by the side of the bed, the baby in her little plastic cot, and Sally looked at me and said: 'What do I do with it, Kate?'

'They loved each other really,' says Paul, his voice interrupting my thoughts. 'You should have seen her the first Christmas without Hannah, she was beside herself. But then you couldn't have seen it, cos you were never here.'

He picks up his plate and takes it over to the sink. 'She's your sister, Kate. She needed you then. And she needs you now.'

'I tried,' I say, watching him as he skitters about the kitchen like a large confused bird. 'But she wouldn't listen to me.'

'No, you tried being the big reporter,' he says. 'Investigating and phoning contacts. Which was great, because you helped us find Hannah. But Sally didn't need to be interrogated; she just needed you to be her sister. She needs you now, Kate.'

'Okay, Paul, but one thing at a time,' I say, standing up and opening the back door. The house stinks of stale vinegar and I need some air. 'Let's sort out Mum's affairs first and then, well, I'm not promising anything, but I'll think about it.'

'Thanks, Kate. It would mean so much to Sally and to me if you buried the hatchet,' says Paul, grabbing his jacket from the kitchen counter. 'I better get back to work now. But listen, I was thinking, you haven't seen your mother's grave yet. I can take you tomorrow in my lunch hour if you like.'

The words 'mother' and 'grave' sound strange and I want to shake him and tell him he's got it all wrong, that my mum's just gone to the shop and she'll be back in five minutes.

'Kate, are you okay?'

My eyes cloud with tears but I don't turn round. I can't let him see me cry.

'I'm fine,' I say, blinking. There's a solitary pink rose at the far end of the garden. If I stare hard at it the tears will stop.

'But I would like to see the grave,' I say, still staring at the flower. 'If you're sure it's not too much trouble.'

'No trouble at all,' he says gently. 'I'll pick you up tomorrow. Twelve thirty?'

'Perfect,' I say, turning from the door. 'And thanks, thanks for all you're doing. I do appreciate it.'

'Not a bother,' he says. 'See you tomorrow.'

I hear the door shut behind him and I sigh with relief. At last I can be alone with my thoughts.

Stepping outside, I look at the garden. It's a mess, a tangle of weeds and broken plant pots. My mother was a keen gardener. She'd grown up on a farm and I think part of her still yearned for the countryside. The vegetable plot she cultivated here was her little haven; a reminder of her childhood. She would spend hours in this garden tending to the potatoes and carrots and runner beans that she grew. Sometimes in the summer holidays I would join her and we would weave in and out of the beds, munching raw beans. 'One for the pot and one for us,' she would say, her eyes shining with relief that for a few hours at least she was free of him. While he was at work she could be herself; she could laugh and sing and be a young woman again. Sometimes she would bring out her poetry books and we would sit on the patio and read together. It was my mother who I got my love of words from. She'd been all set to become an English teacher but abandoned her dream when she met my father and fell pregnant with me. 'Back then careers and children didn't mix,' she once explained to me. 'You had one or the other. Never both.'

I kneel down next to the spot where the rose bed had once been and place my hand on the gritty, dry soil. My mother had drenched the garden in flowers: tea roses with rag-doll heads, sweet peas that grew like clusters of fragile butterflies curled around teepees of twisted willow; nasturtiums with giant paw-shaped leaves that spilled out of an old tin kettle; candy-cane-striped peonies. And all along the path tall delphiniums that gave the garden an element of Edwardiana, of girls in white dresses and men in boaters. They were certainly an uncommon flower in suburban Herne Bay but that was probably why my mother liked them. It set her apart from the neighbours.

But now the flowers are gone and all that remains is a mess of weeds and dry soil. This rose bed has haunted my adult life. I see it when I'm walking down the street in Soho or holed up in some bombed-out hotel. I see it when I close my eyes and pray for sleep. It's the bitter-sweet symbol of my childhood and as I kneel here I touch the ground and remember how it felt beneath me as I lay shivering in the cold.

I was thirteen years old and my crime had been to intervene in one of my father's tirades. Mum had cooked a chicken pie and he had come home drunk and made a fuss, saying it was dry. As usual I had stepped in to defend my mother while Sally just sat there like the doting daughter, agreeing with him. 'Yes, Daddy, it *is* a bit dry.' God, she was unbearable. He really laid into Mum that night and I just saw red. I remember lunging towards him, putting my body between my terrified mother and his coil of rage.

He stopped then and I thought for a moment that I'd helped, that he was seeing sense, but instead he grabbed me by the arms and marched me through the kitchen. After hitting me around the legs with his belt he opened the back door and shoved me out into the night. It was late November, bone-chilling weather, and though I was fully dressed it was still no weather to be out in. There was an empty compost bag by the fence and I fashioned a shawl out of it by ripping it down the middle and pulling it round my shoulders. But it was still so cold I could feel my teeth chattering. I hammered on the door, begging him to let me in. I called out for my mother, for Sally, but no one came. It seemed like hours as I watched the lights go off, one by one, in the house and I curled up on the softest spot I could find, my mother's rose bed.

Then a strange thing happens. As I stand in the garden all these years later a memory comes back to me, so vivid it almost knocks me off my feet. A small shadow in the window. Sally. As I lay shivering in the flower bed that night I'd looked up to see Sally standing at her bedroom window. I'd waved my arms and called out to her.

'Come down and let me in,' I'd begged. 'Please, Sally, open the door.' She wouldn't have been able to hear what I said, but she knew I needed her help.

She'd continued to look at me but her face was expressionless.

'Please, Sally.'

But she just shook her head, stepped back and closed the curtains. A few minutes later I heard my father unbolting the door. He'd made his point and I was allowed back inside. It took me hours, huddled in every item of clothing I possessed, before I felt warm again. I see Sally's face at the breakfast table the next morning, staring at me like I was a ghost; like she couldn't quite believe that I'd survived.

I shudder as I walk back into the house to fetch bin bags and a garden brush. How can a memory lie dormant like that for so many years then spring forth unbidden? But I can't let myself think of it. Not now. The memory is just that, a memory, a fragment of the past that has no place in the here and now.

Instead I try to concentrate on the task ahead. I know little about gardening but I can weed and clear and that will be enough to while away a few hours and get the garden into some kind of order. I grab the bin bags from the cupboard underneath the sink and locate an old wooden brush in the pantry. The day is warm and I feel brighter as I make my way back out into the garden.

It feels good to be in the fresh air, and the work, though laborious, is cathartic. The more clumps of tangled weed I drop into the black bag, the lighter I feel. After a couple of hours it looks like a different garden and I feel better too, though horribly hot and sweaty.

I am just depositing the last of the bin bags into the wheelie bin by the wall when I hear a child laughing. It's a warm sound and it flutters through my body as I walk back up the path. It sounds so much like . . . I walk towards the sound, and as I reach the rose bed I see him lying on his front reading his favourite comic; an old one that he's read a hundred times. And he's laughing, belly laughing, at the silly jokes. He had such a beautiful laugh.

I look up and see a woman sitting in the garden next door. She is young, in her early thirties, and she wears a blue scarf over her hair. It is patterned with red roses and it makes me smile as I draw closer. My mother had one very similar that she used to wear across her shoulders when she went to church. Her rosy scarf we used to call it when we were kids.

'Hello,' I call as I peer over the fence.

She looks startled for a moment and puts the drink she is holding on to the grass next to her.

'I'm Kate,' I say brightly. 'I'm staying here for a few days.'

'You are Mrs Rafter's daughter?' she says, getting up from her chair.

'Yes, that's right,' I say as she comes to the fence.

'My name is Fida,' says the young woman. 'Your mother talked about you lots.'

'That's nice to hear,' I say. 'I miss her so much.'

'I miss her too,' says the young woman, looking beyond me towards my mother's garden. 'She was kind. She used to give me . . . I can't think of the word. They were pastries? Round with jam . . .'

I can smell the doughnuts as I watch the young woman grappling with her words. My mother was a prolific baker and bread-based dishes were her speciality. She would always make doughnuts after my father had beaten me, and to this day I can't eat them for they taste of both my mother's guilt and my own sorrow.

'Doughnuts,' I say. 'Jammy doughnuts.'

'Yes,' shrieks the woman, her face beaming. 'Jammy doughnuts, that's it. They were good. She would leave little boxes for me on the front step like . . . like Santa Claus.'

'And your child, does he or she like doughnuts?' I ask, craning my neck to see if the little one is still there.

The young woman's smile drops and I wonder if I've said the wrong thing.

'Only I heard a child just now. They were laughing. It was lovely.'

'I don't have a child,' says the woman and I see a familiar pain in her eyes. 'You must have heard children out the back. Sometimes they take a shortcut, the children from the school, they take the path by the fields.'

'Either that or I'm hearing things.' I giggle, trying to lighten the mood.

The young woman laughs but her eyes are sad.

'You live alone then?' I ask, unable to quash the journalist in me.

'Sometimes,' she says. 'My husband, he is away a lot.' She gestures her hands up to the sky.

'He works abroad?' I venture.

'Yes,' she says. 'Abroad.'

'That must be tough,' I say. 'Being alone so much.'

'It's fine. I'm happy,' she says, though she doesn't sound it.

'Where are you from, if you don't mind me asking?'

'Iraq,' she says, her voice lightening. 'Fallujah.'

'Oh, I know it well,' I say. 'I was there in 2004.'

She nods her head and looks off into the distance. It is a look I have seen countless times before on the faces of people who have been forced to flee their homeland, a mix of sadness and confusion.

'2004,' she whispers. 'So you were there during the Battle?'

'Yes, I was,' I reply.

'I left just after that,' she says, folding her arms across her chest. 'My cousin was leaving and my parents they said go with him. Said it would be for the best . . .'

She trails off, and a fat tear falls on to her dress. She hastily wipes it away.

'I'm sorry,' she says.

'It's okay,' I tell her. 'I understand. For me Fallujah was a work assignment but for you it was home. It must be so hard for you.'

'Iraq is not my home any more,' she says quietly. 'This is my home.'

She smiles but her eyes are still sad. There are so many things I would like to ask her but I know that this isn't the right time.

'Iraq will always be your home,' I tell her. 'It's part of you. Like this place is a part of me even though I left Herne Bay years ago.'

She nods her head. 'Sometimes I dream of Fallujah,' she says. 'How it was when I was young and I wake up wishing that I could go back but I know it would not be the same now.'

I am about to tell her about a recent article I wrote on the city when a loud crash stops me in my tracks.

'What was that?'

I look at the woman. Her smile has faded and her hands are shaking.

'I have to go,' she says hurriedly.

'Is everything okay? Can I help with anything?'

'No, please, everything is fine,' she says, her voice trembling. 'I have to go.'

She pulls her scarf up so that it almost obscures her face then half walks, half runs towards the house. I stand for a moment looking at the empty space she has left behind and wonder what it was that made her react in such a way. But as I turn to make my way back to the house I see my mother reading in a threadbare armchair as my father's key turns in the lock; I see her face turn from happiness to dread; and I think of the young woman next door, the fear in her eyes, and a shiver courses down my spine.

5

Herne Bay Police Station

13 hours detained

'How long have you been taking sleeping pills, Kate?'

I am standing by the tiny square window tracing an oval shape on the glass with my fingertip. I can hear Shaw breathing somewhere behind me. She's annoyed that I've got out of the chair, that I've removed myself from her gaze.

'Not much of a view, is it?' I remark as I look out on to the small strip of car park. 'It must depress you, all this grey concrete.'

'Kate, could you answer my question?'

Shaw's voice remains steady though I know she is losing patience.

'Sorry,' I say, turning to face her. 'Could you repeat it?'

'I asked how long you've been taking prescription sleeping pills.'

'Fifteen years,' I reply, too exhausted to lie.

Shaw's eyes widen infinitesimally. I've been trained to notice these things.

'That's a long time.'

'Listen, Dr Shaw,' I say slowly, as though addressing a small child. 'Have you ever tried sleeping through a mortar attack?'

She shakes her head then writes something in her notebook. I smile as I imagine her neat handwriting swirling across the page: sleeping pills, mortar attacks . . . diagnosis.

'It's not just the bombing,' I continue. 'It's the jet lag and the deadlines. There are times I've gone forty-eight hours without sleep and then when I try to my brain won't shut down. We all take sleeping pills, Dr Shaw. It's as much a part of the job as a flak jacket and a good translator. It's normal.'

'What about other medication?'

She puts her pen down and stares at me. I turn back to the window and watch as an overweight copper struggles to get into his car.

'I don't take any other medication.'

Shaw clears her throat.

'So you've never been prescribed anything to deal with hallucinations? No antipsychotics for instance?'

I turn round and see that she is reading from a sheet of headed notepaper.

'What's that?' I ask, a feeling of dread creeping through my bones.

'Antipsychotics?' she says, looking up. 'They are a type of drug used to treat a range of conditions. Mainly schizophrenia but also bipolar, depression . . .'

'No, I know what they are,' I say as I come back to the chair. 'I'm talking about the paper in your hand. Where did you get it from?'

Shaw tucks the document back into the blue file and folds her arms.

'Kate. I will ask again,' she says firmly. 'Are you taking any other medication besides sleeping pills?'

I look at her; try to read her face. Does she, like me, just want this all to be over? Does she just want to get home in time for tea with her husband and kids, put her feet up, watch the telly? Of course she does. I decide to come clean. Anything to hasten my release from this place.

'I was prescribed something a few months ago,' I tell her. 'Though it seems you know that already.'

'Right,' says Shaw. 'And are you still taking them?'

'Yes,' I lie.

'Do they help?'

I flinch as I remember hitting the pavement, the taste of blood in my mouth and the feeling that my head was on fire. I see the frazzled doctor at A&E handing me a box of pills as though they were sweets and the weird sense of weightlessness as I lay on my bed waiting for them to kick in. The side effects of those drugs were worse than any hallucination, any nightmare. I couldn't think straight, could barely construct a sentence, let alone write a report or conduct an interview. In the course of a couple of weeks I was reduced to a marshmallow. All I wanted to do was sleep and eat and not think. Eventually, I flushed the pack down the loo. The voices came back the next day but after weeks of nothingness they were like a welcome friend.

'Oh yeah, they help,' I tell Shaw.

'And the hallucinations? Have they lessened since you started taking the medication?'

'Yes,' I reply. 'Completely. Though I took the pills more for anxiety than anything else.'

As if to taunt me, the old woman chooses this moment to scream and I jerk forward in my chair. The room falls silent. Did Shaw notice? She stares at me blankly as she delivers her next question.

'Would you say that your job and the things you've seen have, perhaps, contributed to that anxiety?'

'Of course,' I reply. 'I'm not a robot. I couldn't do my job if I wasn't moved, wasn't affected by the things I've seen.' *Show you have feelings, that you're human . . .*

Shaw nods her head. I stare at her, trying to read her expression, but she is giving nothing away.

'Now,' she continues, looking down at her notes again. 'You've been back and forth to Syria how many times in the last two years?'

'Oh God, I don't know,' I reply. 'Eight or nine times.'

'Eight or nine times,' says Shaw. 'And while there you have witnessed some extremely distressing things, yes?'

'Yes,' I reply. 'But so have all the other reporters and the aid workers and the people living there. My experience is not unique.'

'No, but it's pretty extreme,' she says. 'Going in and out of conflict zones with such frequency must take its toll on your mental health. I'm sure it would affect me if I had to work like that.'

'Maybe I'm tougher than you,' I spit. Her tone is beginning to annoy me.

'These assignments,' says Shaw, ignoring my comment. 'How long on average do they last?'

'It depends,' I say. 'No assignment is the same.'

'Well, for instance, your last assignment in Aleppo. How long were you there for?'

'Three weeks.'

'And you stayed with a family there?'

I nod my head.

'Three weeks in the same place,' says Shaw. 'Under extreme conditions. Long enough to build up a connection, a strong bond with the people you were staying with. Would you agree?'

I know now where this is heading and I can't bear it. I shake my head, but she continues.

'In your last report you spoke of a young boy,' says Shaw. 'What happened with him in Aleppo affected you deeply, didn't it, Kate?'

The blood drains from my body. Why this? Why can't we just go back to the cuts? They are easier to explain. I look at the door and see the shadow of a policeman on the other side. I have no choice; I'm trapped.

'Kate. Could you tell me about him? His name was Nidal, wasn't it?'

She leans forward in her chair and I catch the scent of her perfume; something sugary and cheap, like everything in this town. It sticks in my throat and I can't breathe.

'I'm sorry,' I say, standing up. 'This is getting silly. My head is throbbing and I need to get home.'

'Kate, as I told you when we began, you've been detained under Section 136 of the Mental Health Act.

43

We're allowed to keep you here for up to seventy-two hours until we reach a decision on your mental state.'

'I can't be kept here for three days.' I try to control my voice but it comes out as a yell.

Shaw sits deathly still as I stand up and start to pace the tiny room. Her impassiveness makes me want to slap her face, to knock some sense into her. I shudder as I remember my father saying the same thing as he went at my mother, his fists raised. I take a deep breath and sit down. Anger is not going to help the situation. I need to keep calm.

'Kate, would you like to take a break or are you happy to carry on?'

'I'll carry on,' I say. 'But I have nothing to say about Syria. Nothing at all.'

6

Monday 13 April 2015

I slump to bed at nine thirty, drowsy with pills and a two-hour TV documentary on Margaret Thatcher. The Iron Lady's voice is the last thing I hear as I collapse into bed, curled up like an ancient fossilized creature, my knees touching my chest, my chin buried deep under the covers.

'Where there is discord, may we bring harmony. Where there is error, may we bring truth. Where there is doubt, may we bring faith. And where there is despair, may we bring hope.'

The bed smells of 1979. The year Sally was born. The year I was given a 'big girl's bed'. My miserable childhood is embedded in the wood, in the springs of the mattress, in the blue velvet headboard, and as I close my eyes I follow the scent and find myself tumbling down the rabbit hole. I am four years old again, sitting on the sofa beside my mother and the new baby while my father inches his armchair closer to the television, turning up the volume so he can hear every word the new prime minister has to say. I go to speak but he shushes me. 'Keep quiet, you little pest. I'm trying to hear what she's saying.' Sally starts crying to be fed and the screams obliterate Thatcher's voice. My mother jumps up to soothe her but it's too late, he's missed her words and someone is going to pay. 'Useless bitch,' he yells as he comes at her with fists raised. 'Lazing on the sofa when you should be looking after the baby. You're not fit to have kids.'

I hear my mother's screams as I crawl deeper into the hole. I cover my ears as the air grows warmer and I smell a familiar smell. Death dust. I'm back in Aleppo. I know what lies ahead: a deserted street, blood and rubble, piles and piles of rubble that I must dig through to get to him. My penance.

'*You're not fit to have kids.*'

My father's voice, thin and reedy, bleeds through the air pocket that connects the past with the present; a warped present, an infinite series of moments that I find myself living through night after night. I try to shout at him, to tell of the legacy he left us, a world of guilt and pain, but my anger has no outlet. My adversary looks back at me with hollow eyes. The dead can't fight back.

His voice grows fainter as I reach the darkest point of the tunnel. I'm back in the shop, the first shot has just been fired and there is still time. If I go quickly I can get to him but each time I try something alters. Tonight the street is filled with water and, as I plunge into it, relief soars through my body. I'm a strong swimmer and the water is washing away the dust and the blood. I can do this; I can get to him in time. His skin is warm when I reach him and a spark of hope fills my heart . . . *where there is despair, may we bring hope* . . . But as my hands take hold of him, a noise punctures the air, a terrifying cry that seems to come from inside me.

I let go and feel myself rising up, up into pale moonlight that trickles into my eyes. Stillness hangs above the room like a thin membrane, time is suspended; outside, the suburbs are holding their breath and I hold my breath too, waiting for the film to be punctured.

Nothing. I turn over and begin to count. I've been told that counting helps ward off anxiety attacks.

'One, two, three, four . . .'

The scream comes again, sharp and unbidden, and I sit bolt upright in the bed, my hands shaking. It sounds like a wounded animal fighting for its life and it is coming from outside my head.

'Who's there?' I call out.

I get up from the bed and stand at the window. Light is coming up on the horizon, casting a pink haze on to the empty garden. I look out into the neighbours' gardens. Nothing. Then, just as I'm about to close the curtains, I see it: a shadow. It's coming out of the shed in the garden that belongs to Fida. Slowly it takes shape and in the light of the fragile morning sun, I see what it is.

It's a man. He is dressed in black, a peaked cap covering his face. I lean closer to the window and watch as he makes his way up the darkened path. I need to alert Fida.

Then I see her.

She's outside the back door in her dressing gown. The man hands her something then they make their way back into the house together. But as she goes to close the door she stops and looks up at my window. Instinctively, I jump back. Did she see me? Possibly, but I don't care. I haven't done anything wrong. As I climb back into bed I remember the husband who works away. He must have come home. Everything is fine, I tell myself, the woman next door has her husband back, he has come home to her where he belongs. Tonight she will sleep curled up in his arms.

But as I close my eyes those screams are still echoing in my head, and as I slip off into sleep I'm no longer sure where they come from.

7

17 hours detained

It is getting dark in the interview room and I watch as Shaw flicks a switch and the room fills with a sickly yellow light.

'That's better,' she says as she walks back to her chair. 'It hurts my eyes to read in the half-light. Now, Kate, I'd like to ask you a few more questions about your work.'

She smiles a weak, anaemic smile. I don't return it.

'I told you,' I say, raising my voice above the buzz of the strip light. 'I don't want to talk about Syria. I made that very clear.'

'Yes, you did,' says Shaw, looking down at a fresh bundle of notes. 'But this isn't about Syria. I'd like to ask you about your last day at work. Something happened in the newsroom, didn't it, Kate? Would you like to tell me about it?'

My heart freezes as she flicks the pages of her notes. How does she know all this? Who has she been speaking to? Harry? Rachel? I go to speak but my voice catches in my throat and I start to cough. Shaw looks up.

'Are you okay?' she asks, getting to her feet. 'Would you like a glass of water?'

I nod my head and watch as she walks over to the water cooler. She pours a cup and brings it to me.

'Thank you,' I whisper, taking the cup and sipping the tepid liquid. It tastes of plastic and I wince as I swallow it.

'Are you happy to continue?' asks Shaw as I place the cup on the table next to me.

'Yes,' I mumble, looking at the clock above her head. I need to get out. I need to get back to him.

'You'd had a long lunch that day?'

'Longish,' I reply.

Shaw nods then writes something in her notebook. I look down at the floor but all I can see is Chris, his face a fragmented collection of parts, broken pieces like the bodies he exhumes. I see his beautiful mouth, the top lip curled, his stubbled jaw, his dark, close-cut hair, his blue, almond-shaped eyes, but I can't put the parts together. I need to put them back together.

'Somewhere nice?'

'Yes, a restaurant in Soho,' I reply as the street unfolds before me. I see familiar landmarks I have walked past a thousand times before: Bar Italia and Ronnie Scott's, the Dog and Duck, all my old haunts. And there he is. I see him through the window of the restaurant, his hands clasped in front of him, waiting, preparing his speech.

'What time did you get back to the newsroom?'

Shaw's voice is sharp, a knitting needle stabbing at my brain.

'I don't know . . . Just after five I suppose.'

'So a very long lunch,' says Shaw, smiling patronizingly. 'Was it for work or pleasure?'

I stare at the wall, remembering that day. I see us sitting there like two strangers.

I look up at Shaw. 'Work,' I reply. 'It was a work meeting.'

'But you had a couple of drinks, yes?'

I nod my head and remember the wine that tasted like acid. The first drink I'd had in years. Glass after glass as I sat in my club after saying goodbye to him on Frith Street.

'Would you say you were intoxicated?'

'No.'

'Really?'

'I'd only had a couple of glasses.'

'Your colleague Rachel Hadley says that you were decidedly the worse for wear and in no fit state to be working when you got back to the office.'

She is reading from her notes. I shake my head incredulously. Rachel bloody Hadley. She would do or say anything to get to me.

'Why are you shaking your head?'

'Because the person you've just mentioned is a parasite, a silly little girl who wants my job.'

If only she hadn't been the first person I saw, I could have got through the rest of the day, finished my article and left without any drama. But there she was as I walked to my desk, standing like a checkpoint official, blocking my way, asking: 'Long lunch, Kate?' in her whiny, nasal voice.

'That's Rachel Hadley,' says Shaw. 'The woman you assaulted?'

'Yes.'

The shame is still as strong now as it was a few weeks ago and I feel my cheeks burn as I remember what happened next.

I tried to edge my way past to get to my desk but she put her arm out to block me and announced in a loud voice that I was unsteady on my feet and would I like her to make me a black coffee. Then she put her arm on my shoulder and after that everything went hazy. All I could see in front of me was a blockage, an obstacle to overcome.

Shaw is looking down at her notes. It will all be there, every last detail of that wretched day.

'You hit her across the face,' says Shaw.

I stare at the table.

'And your colleagues had to intervene?'

'I believe so, yes. I was upset.'

I was aware of the others rushing to her aid but they were like ants, tiny dots on the periphery of my consciousness.

'Harry Vine says you are one of the finest journalists he has ever worked with.'

I look up at her. So she has spoken to him. Harry, my editor.

'He speaks very highly of you,' continues Shaw. 'Despite your actions that day.'

'Yes,' I stammer. 'He's a good man. One of the best.'

As I speak I try to order my thoughts. Harry knows I'm being held under the Mental Health Act. My life is over. My career is over. What will I do?

'You've known him a long time?'

'Around fifteen years.'

'Fifteen years,' says Shaw, raising her eyebrows. 'The same length of time you've been taking sleeping pills.'

I smile ruefully.

'Yes,' I reply. 'I hadn't thought about that before.'

'What did Harry say to you in the office after your outburst?' asks Shaw.

I wince as I recall Harry's face as he brewed a strong coffee and handed it to me. His hands were trembling and he looked, for just a moment, scared of me.

'He . . . he just asked if I was okay.'

I don't tell her that he threatened to suspend me and that I begged him not to on account of my upcoming assignment to Syria. I was lucky. His hands were tied. He knew I was the only person who could get into Aleppo. He had no choice.

'Rachel Hadley could have called the police.'

I look at Shaw and it is then I notice how similar she and Hadley are; the same blonde bobbed hair, the same sibilant voice. They could be sisters.

'Yes, she could,' I reply. 'But she didn't.'

'Harry says he told you to take the rest of the week off.'

'Yes, he did,' I say. 'And he was great about it. I'm sorry, truly sorry for what happened to Rachel. I don't like the girl but I shouldn't have hit her. I do know that.'

'And can you tell me what happened when you left the office?'

I look at the papers in her hand and my mouth goes dry. She can't know. It's not possible.

'Kate?'

'I'm sorry . . . My head is spinning. I just need a second . . .'

I jump up from my seat and walk to the tiny window, placing the palm of my hand on the glass. Behind me Dr Shaw shuffles in her seat and as I watch the light fading over the car park I try to blink away the memory of that night.

'Kate, are you okay?'

Her voice merges with the others in my head and as I stand looking out at the grey expanse of concrete and the bleak sea below I think of my mother and how she implored me to get out of this town and make a better life for myself. And I did it. I got away, as far away as possible. But now I'm trapped in its clutches again. And I know that this time there is no escape.

8

The graveyard is deserted when we arrive and I hang back while Paul walks on ahead of me through the ornate wrought-iron gates.

'It's this way,' he calls as I stand on the path, clutching a posy of irises to my chest.

'Yes, I know,' I reply, and as I step inside the gates my stomach grows heavy with dread.

'I hate this place,' I say, catching up with Paul. 'Always have.'

He smiles and pats my shoulder.

'We don't have to stay long,' he says, his voice upbeat. 'Whenever you want we can get out of here.'

'I just want to see her,' I reply as we weave in and out of the gravestones. 'I want to see my mum.'

There are so many graves. It is hard to imagine the town producing enough people to fill the vast space, but here they are spreading out in front of us, the great and the good of Herne Bay from the nineteenth century to the present day.

I shudder as we pass the church, squat and unremarkable in its neat grassy plot, remembering how, as a child, the smell inside that place would make me feel sick. Every part of it, from the clammy troughs of holy water at the entrance, contaminated by strangers' hands, to the claret carpet that snaked its way from the aisle up to the altar, felt like it was closing in on me. When the priest finally uttered the words, 'Go, the mass is ended,' I would clamber across the parishioners, clutching my chest as I ran for the door. Sitting in that church was the closest thing to being buried alive that I could imagine. Yet, for my mother, it was comfort and salvation; the place where her grief could be soothed with incantations threaded along the beads of her stark white rosary. I never understood that.

Paul catches me looking up at the ugly building.

'I used to bring your mum here,' he says. 'Before she went into the home.'

'She couldn't get enough of the place,' I reply with a half-laugh. 'Used to bring us here every week when we were kids. Never on Sundays for morning mass like most people, but Saturday night, because that was when the priest heard confessions.'

'Yes, it *was* always Saturday night,' says Paul. 'I'd wait for her in the car and she would be hours in there. I used to wonder what terrible sin she'd committed to make her confess every single week. I mean, your mum was one of the gentlest, kindest women I've known. What could she have felt so guilty about?'

I shrug my shoulders.

'Who knows, but she'd had a lot of grief to deal with. Maybe talking to the priest helped.'

'Yeah, maybe,' says Paul.

We walk on as row upon row of headstones open out before us. I recognize the older ones, the ones crumbling and caked in lichen that date back to the 1800s.

'I don't know about you,' says Paul, frowning as we step through them, 'but when I go I want to be cremated. A nice neat dispatch.'

'Me too,' I say. 'I've already stipulated it in my will.'

'I should do the same,' says Paul. 'Then there's no confusion.'

We walk through the older graves and my stomach contracts when I see a familiar name.

'Alexandra Waits,' I say, stopping at a moss-covered stone. 'Still here.'

'What are you talking about?' asks Paul. 'Who's Alexandra Waits?'

'She's the girl with angel wings,' I say, pointing to the ornate sculpture atop the grave. 'When I was little I used to scare myself by imagining I could see ghosts in this graveyard. I particularly liked this stone because of the wings and the fact that the little girl was my age. I used to sit here and talk to her, tell her my problems.'

'That's a bit weird, Kate,' says Paul, laughing awkwardly.

'It was probably all the gothic stories I was reading,' I say, running my fingers over the gnarled wings. 'But, seriously, I always felt calm when I came and sat with Alexandra. It felt like she was really listening.'

'Like your mum and her priest,' says Paul.

'Yeah, I suppose so. I used to hide out here while the mass was going on. Sometimes I even had a sneaky cigarette.'

'Always the rebel,' says Paul.

'Hardly.'

'How old were you?'

'About eleven,' I reply. 'I would sit for hours and imagine what kind of life Alexandra had lived, what she looked like. I guessed she would have had dark hair like me and that she liked writing, but because it was the 1800s and she was just a girl no one took her seriously. So she threw herself into the sea, because if she couldn't be a writer then it was no use living any more. That's the story I came up with anyway.'

'It's a good story,' says Paul. 'Though she probably died of TB like everyone else in those days.'

'Yeah, I guess,' I say. 'The last time I visited her I got scared out of my wits. I was being silly and trying to summon her by repeating her name over and over: "Alexandra Waits, Alexandra Waits." And I heard someone say my name. My full name.'

'You serious?' says Paul, frowning. I can tell he's uncomfortable with all this.

I nod my head and look back at the angel wings, remembering the terror of that evening and how I ran all the way back to the church, looking over my shoulder to see if Alexandra was chasing me.

'That's really creepy,' says Paul, shuddering. 'I hate anything like that. Makes me go all funny.'

He stumbles as we leave the old graves behind and I smile. I didn't realize he was so easily scared.

'There's no need to worry,' I say as we head towards a cluster of new graves. 'Sally told me, years later, that she'd followed me out of the church and hidden behind a tree. It was her voice that scared me half to death.'

'Doesn't surprise me,' says Paul quietly. 'She's still scaring us half to death, isn't she?'

I nod my head as we go on, names and ages flashing in front of my eyes: Helen Stamp, 56 years; Judy Turner, 78 years; Morgan Hyatt, 6 months; Ian St Clair, 30 years. Some of the gravestones have photographs on them and ones where babies are interred are festooned with balloons and pictures of cartoon characters. A halogen Minnie Mouse floats in the breeze above a white head-stone, its smiling face bearing down ominously on to the graves.

'Look at that, eh,' says Paul as we pass the tiny grave-stone. 'Six months old. No age to die that, is it? No age at all.'

I shake my head and try not to think of that terrible night but as we cross the path I'm back in the lift, falling through space. I put my hand on Paul's arm to steady myself and as I look up I see the mulberry tree and I know that Mum is near. She's come to save me from falling further.

'Bury me beneath the mulberry tree,' I whisper.

'What's that?' asks Paul.

'Oh, nothing,' I say. 'Just a memory of Mum.'

It was something she had written at the back of her Sunday missal. I never knew what it meant but the line stayed with me over the years. Now it all makes sense. She wanted to be buried next to her baby son.

'It does that to you, this place,' says Paul. 'Brings back all sorts of memories.'

'Yes,' I reply, walking past the stones that lead to the tree.

Past Rita Mathers who has been 'sleeping peacefully' since 1987 and Jim Carter who has been 'one more angel in Heaven' for the last thirty years, until there it is. A simple rectangular piece of granite, slim and unobtrusive, marking the final resting place of my parents and brother.

As I look at my father's name I go cold. Why would she want to be buried with him? But then I think of the mulberry tree. David is here. There is nowhere else my mother would want to be.

'Here we are,' says Paul, standing back so I can get a closer look. 'The stonemasons got it finished in time for your visit, thank goodness.'

'Yes,' I mumble as I stand holding the sweet peas tightly in my hands.

The flowers that must have been placed there on the day of the funeral lie shrunken and brown on the grass by the stone. I pick them up and set them aside then place the fresh sweet peas on the ground. The air smells of soil and the delicate scent of the flowers as I crouch by the stone and read the inscription. Here it is. Mum's life and death neatly summed up in three lines.

Gillian Louise Rafter
14th November 1945 – 26th March 2015
Forever in our hearts

I skim over my father's inscription and read the writing at the bottom of the stone.

In Loving Memory of
David Robert Rafter
18th January 1977 – 23rd August 1978
Sleep in the arms of Jesus, little man

I close my eyes and try to imagine what my brother would have looked like as he grew up; what kind of a life he would have led. But like Alexandra Waits, he is just a name inscribed on stone. If only I could remember him. I let myself sink down on to the grass as the smell of sweet peas wafts across the air, and I trace his name with my finger.

But as I go to stand up, someone screams.

'What was that?' I say, looking up at Paul.

He is standing above me, his face blurred by the sun. 'What?'

'That . . . noise,' I say, holding a finger to my lips. 'Listen.'

'I can't hear anything,' says Paul. 'Unless it's your friend whatsherface.' He laughs nervously.

'It was . . .' I begin. 'It was nothing. Probably a seagull.'

But I know what it was. It was the old woman. Why won't she leave me alone? I kneel down by the grave again.

'Sally told me a bit about your brother,' says Paul, coming to kneel next to me.

'What did she tell you?'

'Not much really, just that she had a brother who died before she was born. That he'd had an accident.'

'That's right,' I say. 'I don't remember him. I was only three years old when he died. He was just a toddler. Mum had taken him to the beach one day and he got into the sea. She tried to rescue him but the waves were really strong and they carried him away. That's as much as I know. Mum never liked to talk about him.'

'It must have been devastating for your parents.'

'It was. They never got over it. Sally and I spent our childhood trying to put them back together. It didn't work.'

'It's tough being a parent,' says Paul. 'Or step-parent in my case.'

'Yes, but it's not really the same, is it?' I say. 'You know that one day you'll see Hannah again. But for your child to die, well, it's just . . .'

I swallow the words. This place is starting to get to me.

'Have you never wanted to, you know, do the whole family thing, settle down?' he asks.

I shake my head.

'So there's no one on the scene at the moment?' he says jokily. 'No fella back home in your swish London pad?'

'Oh, give it a rest, Paul,' I say as I stand up. 'You know I'm a terminal singleton. Now, tell me more about the funeral. Did many people come?'

'A few,' he says.

'Really?' I press.

'Yes,' he snaps. 'I didn't let your mum down, okay? We gave her a good send-off.'

He sighs and pushes a stray bit of hair away from his eyes. He suddenly looks exhausted.

'I'm sorry. That was insensitive of me. I know these last few weeks must have been hard for you and I really am grateful you were here for Mum at the end.'

I put my hand on his shoulder and he looks at me and smiles.

'It *has* been hard,' he says. 'But we coped. We got through it.'

I watch as he picks up the sweet peas and puts them in the stone vase by the grave.

'All the old crowd turned up,' he says, arranging the flowers. 'Your aunt Meg came down from Southend and a few of your dad's mates from the pub.'

'And Sally? Did she come?'

He rests his hands on the stone and closes his eyes.

'Paul?'

'She – she wasn't well enough,' he says. 'And then . . .'

'Paul, what is it? Come on, you can tell me.'

He gives up trying to keep it in. 'When she heard about your mum she just lost it. She's locked herself in the conservatory with a stash of booze and she won't come out except to buy more drink when I'm at work. She doesn't wash, she barely eats. I don't know what to do, Kate. I'm scared.' He buries his face in his hands.

I kneel down next to him and put my hand on his shoulder.

'It's okay,' I say soothingly. 'You're not on your own. I'll do what I can to help.'

'Will you?' he says, looking up at me. 'Do you mean that? You see, I've tried everything – kindness, tough love, I even tried forcing her to AA – but none of it's worked. She needs you; even though she pushes you away, she needs you.'

I stand up and look at my mother's name on the headstone. She would want me to do whatever I can to help Sally.

'I made sure they played all her favourite hymns,' says Paul softly as he gets to his feet. '"I Watch the Sunrise"; "Queen of the May"; and "Abide with Me" as they brought her in.'

As I stand listening to Paul's account of the funeral I close my eyes and imagine my mother's coffin sitting in front of the altar; a tiny casket, hanging there in the air like a frail bird.

Beside me, Paul starts to sing the opening lines of 'Abide with Me'. I look at that damned mulberry tree as Paul sings about the eventide and I wish my mother hadn't had to deal with such violence. She was a good person and she didn't deserve it.

Paul stops singing and looks at me.

'Sally chose the reading,' he says. 'Even though she couldn't make the funeral, she still wanted to have a bit of input.'

'What reading was it?'

'One from the Bible,' he says. 'She said your folks had it at their wedding. What was it again? "Love bears all things, hopes all things, endures all things." That one.'

My body goes cold and any sympathy I was beginning to feel for my sister dissipates. Why would she choose such a thing? It was nonsense, and a huge slap in the face to our mother, a woman who had endured more than she should ever have had to at the hands of that man.

'So you see, Sally did care,' says Paul. 'She still wanted to be involved.'

'Paul, you know very well that Sally couldn't stand our mother.'

'Oh, come on,' he says. 'I wouldn't go that far. Yes, they had their ups and downs but they loved the bones of each other really.'

'Which is why it was you who arranged Mum's care home and drove her to mass and ferried her to the shops,' I reply, feeling the anger pounding in my temple like a pulse.

'I cared about your mum, too,' he says. 'I didn't mind doing those things because she was a lovely lady. She welcomed me into the family so kindly, especially after my own mum died. I was happy to help.'

'I know you were,' I say gently. 'And you've been a great son-in-law. Better than either of us were as daughters. I just wish I'd seen more of her in her final years.'

As I stand here I have a sudden memory of Ground Zero, where I first met Chris. I see the forensic anthropologists in space-age suits hauling bodies from shallow graves. The perversity of that image, the 'wrongness' of a body coming out rather than going into its grave, makes me go cold.

'Come on,' says Paul, noticing the state I'm in. 'Let's get you home.'

He takes my hand and guides me back through the graves, past the Minnie Mouse balloon and Alexandra Waits, past the church holding my mother's secrets, but it is all too much and as we reach the gates I let go of his arm and sit down on the grass verge. The tears that I've spent the last few weeks holding in come springing forth and I put my head in my hands and cry for the mother I've lost.

9

Herne Bay Police Station

17.5 hours detained

'You've witnessed some terrible things in the course of your career, Kate, haven't you?'

I don't want to answer her. I'm tired of her questions. Instead, I look down at my bracelet and he's with me. I feel the warmth of his hand as he strokes my bare skin, his soft lips kissing the back of my neck, and I ache with longing for him. Human touch is a primordial need, I think to myself, as I watch Shaw flicking from page to page. It's not love that I miss, it's not even the sex; no, what I miss above all else is the reassuring touch of someone else's skin. His skin.

Chris's hands were rough and scarred, the legacy of twenty years exhuming graves. But the feel of his hands wrapping round me as he slipped into bed in the early hours of the morning, not speaking, just holding me close, was all I needed, it gave me the strength to pack my bags and head off to the next war and the next and the next. The memory of his skin, the promise of it, was what kept me going all these years. And now I will have to learn to live without it.

'Things that would have broken most ordinary people.'

Shaw's voice brings me hurtling back to the here and now. I feel exposed. But I know I have to stay focused and answer her questions. Even if I don't like them.

'But I didn't break or else I wouldn't have been much use,' I reply. 'It's the first rule of journalism: stay impartial.'

She writes something down and I wonder if in my effort to stay calm I'm starting to sound too cold and detached. Isn't lack of emotion a psychopathic trait? I decide to change tack, to soften my edges a little and keep her onside.

'The one that stays in my head is Layla. A little girl who lost both her legs when a shell hit her home.'

Shaw looks up, startled that I've begun to talk unbidden.

'She was so brave,' I continue. 'Still smiling despite the pain. I remember she took my hand and said something I didn't understand. She said it over and over again, so when the doctor came in I asked him to translate for me. He told me she was asking where I had put her legs and when would she be getting them back.'

Shaw shakes her head and sighs a long, deep sigh, the sigh of a mother who knows her children are safe at home.

'She was four years old and all alone in one of the most dangerous places on earth. The rest of her family had been killed in the attack. No one knows how she survived. I sat by her bed listening to her cries of pain.'

I take a sip of water and try to steady myself as Layla's moans fill the room. 'Painkillers were in short supply and they'd cauterized the stumps of her legs without anaesthetic. At one point I reached into my rucksack and pulled out three boxes of cheap Paracetamol. When the doctor came in I handed them over and he looked at me like I'd just come up with a cure for cancer. I looked at Layla and wondered what kind of future lay ahead for an orphaned child with no legs in a country seething with . . .'

The moans grow louder, obliterating my words. I put my hands to my ears, try to block them out, but they seem to multiply.

'Kate.'

Shaw's voice is muffled against the din.

'Please stop,' I shout to the voices. 'Please just stop.'

I feel Shaw's hand on my shoulder and I look up.

'What is it, Kate?' she says gently. 'Tell me.'

I shake my head. She can't find out.

'Are you okay?' she presses.

'I just . . .' I say, my hands trembling. 'I just need a break. Can we please have a break?'

'Of course,' says Shaw. 'We can take five minutes.'

She returns to her seat, collects her things and leaves the room. A moment later a stocky police officer enters to take her place. He stands by the door, frowning at me.

Meanwhile the moans grow louder and louder and as I sit under the policeman's gaze I am as helpless as little Layla, wondering where her legs have gone.

10

Wednesday 15 April 2015

No more voices last night. I suppose that is a good thing, but they have become such an integral part of me I've become strangely used to them. My sleep wasn't altogether restful though. I dreamt of Aleppo and it was the clearest of all the dreams I have had so far. So vivid that even now as I sit cradling a cup of coffee and looking out on to the damp expanse of my mother's suburban garden I still feel shaken. And as I close my eyes I can smell the mustiness of the bedroom and hear the gentle *tap*, *tap*, as a small boy drives his toy car up and down the corridor.

Nidal is in the corridor playing. As I step over him, he bombards me with questions.

'What is England like, Kate? What are the people like?'

'Oh, I don't know. Some are nice, some are a bit grumpy.'

'What is grumpy?'

I make a face and purse my lips. 'It's like this,' I tell him. 'Never with a smile.'

'Oh, unhappy,' he says, his face falling. 'Why are they unhappy?'

'Well, in England, people complain a lot. Often about things that aren't really important.'

'Like what?'

'Oh, like trains running late and poor service in restaurants, oh, and the weather, everyone in England complains about the weather.'

'Is it cold in England?'

'Sometimes. Though we complain when it's too hot as well as when it's too cold.'

'English people sound funny,' he says and his face breaks into a smile.

'Yes, they are. But you'll see it for yourself one day. You can visit me.'

'Maybe,' says Nidal. He shrugs his shoulders and turns away.

'What is it, Nidal? Tell me.'

I kneel down beside him and put my hand on his shoulder.

He turns round and his face is stained with tears.

'It is this,' he yells, gesturing to the dank hallway. 'I used to go to school. I used to play football and go on school trips. I did real things, fun things. Now I am trapped in here with this.'

He grabs his toy car and hurls it at the wall.

'I don't want to do pretend things, I want to do real things again. I don't want to be locked up inside like a prisoner.'

I take his hand. It is shaking.

'Nidal, I know you are scared but this won't last for ever.'

He bats my hand away.

'My aunt, she wants us to go with her to Turkey,' he says. 'She knows a man who can get us there but Papa, he says we can't. He says we stay here until all this is over; that he won't become refugee.'

Khaled is a proud man, I think to myself, though I wish with all my heart that he would follow the aunt's advice and head for Turkey.

'Mama says we should go,' he says, his voice cracking. 'She says that we'll be safe there and I can play football again.'

As I look at him, his eyes wide with hope, I remember the refugee camp I visited on the Turkish border six months ago. It was chaotic and disease-ridden and rammed full of desperate people whose dead eyes told me they had seen things that I could never imagine. It is not the paradise Nidal is imagining, but it would offer safety and shelter and a chance for Khaled and Zaynah to set about rebuilding their lives. But I know Khaled's mind is made up.

'Your father knows what's best for you,' I say to Nidal, trying to reassure him.

'You think this is best?' he cries, gesturing to the dank hallway. 'I can't stand it. I want to get out.'

'You will get out,' I say softly. 'And when you do you can come visit me in England and meet all the grumpy people I've been telling you about.'

He looks up at me. His face is swollen with tears.

'No,' he cries. 'Stop saying that. Stop saying they are not happy. They *have* to be happy. They live in England.'

'Nidal, sweetheart,' I say, putting my arm round his shoulders. 'Please don't get upset.'

But he can't hear me. His hands cover his ears and he shakes his head furiously.

71

'I don't want to talk to you any more,' he says. 'You say silly things. Just go away. Leave me alone.'

I touch his shoulder gently as I stand up and make my way out. As I reach the end of the corridor I look back and he is there, still shaking his head, and I realize how insensitive I have been. Why did I tell him that people were unhappy in England? Couldn't I see that, for him, a little boy trapped in a war zone, the idea of anyone being unhappy in a safe place like England was more than he could bear?

A hammering at the front door interrupts the memory and I stand up and put my empty coffee cup into the sink. It will be Paul, come to take me to the solicitor's.

I open the door and he hugs me.

'You look better this morning,' he says. 'Did you sleep well?'

'Yes,' I lie. 'Though the seagulls are rather noisy.'

'One of the drawbacks of living by the sea,' he says with a laugh as he steps inside. But something's not right. The lines around his eyes deepen as he stares back down the driveway.

'Is everything okay, Paul?'

'Yes, everything's fine,' he says. 'It's just I'm in a bit of a rush, that's all. We're short-staffed at work and I've told the lads I'll be two hours max.' He glances at his watch.

'Oh, you should have said. I would have got a cab.'

'Don't be silly, I wouldn't hear of it,' he says. 'Those lads are a bunch of pansies sometimes and I've put in enough overtime as it is.'

'If you're sure.'

'I'm sure,' he says. 'Now come on, grab your coat, chop chop.'

I take my coat from the hall cupboard and knock over my bag in the process.

'Dammit.'

'Here, let me help.' Paul crouches next to me and begins to pick up various items that have fallen on to the floor. He hands me a box of pills and narrows his eyes as I hurriedly toss them into the bag.

'Surely it hasn't come to that, love?' he says as we get to our feet. 'Those things are no good for you. In fact, they're dangerous. You could end up having an overdose.'

'I know what I'm doing,' I say as he opens the door. 'I'm a big girl now. No need for safety caps.'

'Yes, well, even big girls can get themselves into trouble,' he says, shaking his head. 'That looks like pretty strong stuff you've got there.'

'I'm fine, honestly, Paul,' I say as we step outside. 'You mustn't worry.'

But as I go to close the door I remember something.

'Won't be a sec,' I tell him, running back inside. 'Just need to get my lucky pen.'

'Lucky pen?' he calls from the front step. 'Blimey, I've heard it all.'

I go into the living room and look on the coffee table where I last had it, but it's not there.

'That's strange,' I say. 'I'm sure I left it here this morning.'

'Oh, come on,' says Paul, walking into the room. 'We'll be late. Look, I'll lend you my lucky Bic.'

He grins and reaches into his pocket, pulling out an old biro with a chewed cap. I take it and put it in my pocket. But as we head for the door I feel strangely uneasy. Where can it be? I can clearly remember putting it down next to the pad I was writing on.

'I don't know what I'll do if I've lost it,' I say to Paul as we head back outside.

'Oh, it'll turn up,' he says, locking the door. 'Things like that always do.'

I nod my head but as we walk to the car I have a bad feeling in my stomach.

'Retrace your steps,' says Paul, pointing the fob at the driver's side of the car. 'Always works for me.'

While he makes a fuss of adjusting the mirror and making sure his seat belt is properly secured I take my phone out and check to see if I've had any messages. There are none. I start to compose a text but there's so much to say I don't know where to begin. I delete the message and put the phone into my bag as Paul starts up the car.

'Anything important?' asks Paul as we slowly pull away.

'No,' I reply. 'It can wait.'

Paul turns on the radio and the car fills with the crackly voice of a DJ but all I can think about is my lucky pen. It's an omen, I tell myself. Maybe my luck has finally run out.

A lugubrious sun hangs in the late-afternoon sky. It casts a feeble light across the surface of the water as I sit on a bench watching the last of the fishing boats make their way into the harbour.

I'd asked Paul to drop me at the seafront on the way back from the solicitor's office where I'd spent an hour drinking tepid tea and reading the contents of my mother's will. When all the documents had been signed the solicitor, a pleasant young woman called Maria, had handed me an envelope: a letter from my mother. It was a shock. I never expected Mum to leave me a letter.

Paul offered to stay with me while I read it but I knew I would need to be alone to hear my mother's final words, so I decided to take myself and the letter to the benches at Neptune's Arm, the mile-long stretch of breakwater where my mother and I used to sit before Sally was born to watch the boats come in. It seemed fitting somehow.

The wind is icy and it whips around my face like an angry hand as I sit with the unopened envelope on my knee. Several feet below me the fishermen growl and bluster as they haul their heavy nets full of flounder and silver eels on to the shore and shoo away the seagulls who, following the scent of death on the air, whirl remorselessly above their heads.

The birds wail in tandem with the howling wind. It is a cruel, brutal noise that always makes me think of the vultures that descended on the death carts in Africa during the famine of 1984, pecking scant flesh from the emaciated bodies of children. I remember lying on the living-room floor watching the scenes unfold on the TV screen while behind me Sally played with her dolls, oblivious to the hellish images that were already boring into my memory. At one point she stopped and pointed at the screen where a little boy with emaciated legs and a swollen tummy batted flies from his face. 'Where's his mummy?' she asked and I told her in my matter-of-fact way that his mother was probably dead. 'How did she die?' Sally asked. And I told her that she had died from hunger; that the sun had dried the earth, that the rain had failed to come and the crops they needed for survival had shrivelled and died. 'Was Mummy starving?' she asked. 'When baby David died? Did our crops fail?' And I shushed her as I heard my father's footsteps coming down the hall and switched the channel to a quiz show where a man in a shiny suit was showing a crying woman what she could have won.

The sea below me thuds and the waves hurtling in and out sound like tiny explosions. *Boom*, pause. *Boom*, pause. I find myself lulled by the noise. It makes me feel safe. Finally I tear open the envelope and flatten the lavender-coloured paper on my lap, and as I see my mother's distinctive curled handwriting the waves fall in step with the pounding of my heart.

30th Sept., 1993

Dearest Kate,

I am writing this letter in our favourite spot: the big old green armchair where I nursed you as a baby and where you would sit as a young child to read your books. I can still see you there, like a statue, lost in your stories. It used to scare me sometimes, your silence, and I would have to call your name to check that you were still there, that you hadn't floated off to some distant land.

Your father's death has prompted me to get my affairs in
order and write my will, but I also wanted to leave you a letter
that will only be read after my death.

He is gone, Kate, and with his passing I want to ask for
your forgiveness. You saw things in your young life that no child
should ever see. We never spoke of what you witnessed and your
silence scared me more than his fists. I worried that it had
damaged you so deeply you would never recover.

But, Kate, though he was a monster there was a reason for his
anger. He had lost his child, his precious David, and though we
told you girls it was a tragic accident, that is not the truth. You
see, it was my fault that David died and I have lived with that
guilt ever since.

The words scramble as the wind blows the edges of the
paper and I have to squint to read it clearly. Here it is: an
ancient wound that never healed. Reasoning and pleading, guilt and sorrow, it is all here in my mother's letter;
decades of penance spelled out in petrol-blue ink.

We were at Reculver beach, as you know. You and me and
David. He had seen a boat. He kept shouting it: 'Boat, boat!'
And I saw it, a fishing boat way out across the water. I said,
'Yes, David, pretty boat.' But he'd forgotten about it ten
minutes later. He was making a sandcastle. You pottered
around my feet collecting shells. I was exhausted that day,
things with your father had been difficult. The day was hot and
I felt so tired I sat down in the shade by the rocks. I didn't
mean to fall asleep, I swear it, but I did, and when I woke up I
couldn't see David. I ran down the beach shouting his name
over and over.

77

I get up, still holding the letter in my hands. The edge of the breakwater is wide and exposed and I stand for a moment looking out on to the milky surface, trying to take in what I have just read. My mother fell asleep? My sensible, over-protective mother fell asleep while in charge of two toddlers. It doesn't make sense.

You were closer to the waves now. I ran past you as I headed for the water calling David's name. A couple of moments later I saw him. He was floating face down in the sea. I went to run to him but my feet wouldn't move. Everything seemed to slow down. I could hear you screaming and a man calling but still I couldn't move.

Next thing I knew there was a fishing boat and a man waving his arms. He'd got David. He'd got him out of the water. You were in the boat too. That man had done what I had failed to do. He had brought my children to safety. But as he reached the shingle he looked at me and shook his head. When he did that my feet started to work at last and I ran to the boat but it was too late. David was dead.

It was my fault, Kate. I fell asleep when I should have been looking after my children. I was a bad mother that day and I want to say sorry for all the pain and hurt you've had to experience as a result of my negligence.

I will be sorry for it until the day I die.

I read the last sentence in a daze.

I fold the letter neatly and put it in my pocket. The sky is covered in a jagged cloud that filters the light of the sun on to the fishing boats, temporarily erasing the names.

I grip the blue railings and scan the mottled horizon. The shoreline has taken on a new meaning since I read the letter; what was once a place of happiness and escape is now tainted. I look up the coast towards the twin towers of Reculver, the remains of the Roman fortress jutting out from the cliffs, and shiver as I remember my mother's insistence that, every Sunday, we visit the little strip of beach that runs below. As I grew older I assumed that my mother was using the Sunday trips as an excuse to escape my father's moods; now I realize that they were something much more unsettling.

I sit at the edge of Neptune's Arm, watching as my feet dangle towards the sea. What had I been expecting from my mother? Words of comfort? A warm drink to make the nightmares stop?

I ease myself further along the edge of the wall and take the letter out of my pocket. Below me an old fishing boat bobs aimlessly on the surface of the water. I look down at the empty wooden husk and try to think of my mother, try to summon the image of the soft, sparrow-like woman who gave me life, but she's not there. I can't find her.

I scrunch the letter into a tight ball and, lifting my fist, watch as the wind catches the paper and carries it high across the harbour wall, up and up like a gull, twisting and turning in the salty air.

As the sky clouds over and the marine light shifts, I see a deserted street at dusk and the shadows of two soldiers lengthening on the concrete, their guns raised. I am back in Aleppo staring numbly into an abyss. I put my hands over my eyes and start to count, willing the images to go away.

I need to get out of here.

I walk back to the seafront and wait by the bandstand for a moment to watch the fishing boats come in. A cluster of fishermen stand on the breakwater smoking cigarettes. One of them, a thickset man in a blue cable-knit sweater, looks up and sees me. He nods his head and I recognize him.

It's Ray Morris. Dad's old friend.

'Ray,' I call, waving my hand.

He stubs his cigarette out and steps across the shingle towards me.

'It's never Denny's girl?' he says. 'Little Kate. How are you?'

His skin is dewy and pink and his eyes, reflecting the last rays of the late afternoon, are pale grey and glassy. He takes off his hat and shakes my hand. His hands are raw and calloused as if he has spent a lifetime immersed in salt water. The last time I saw him was the night before I left for university. He'd come to deliver some fish and Mum invited him to stay for dinner. We'd avoided sitting round the dining table since my father's death the previous year; too many bad memories. But that night my mum made an effort and set the table with the best china. It was the first civilized meal we'd had in years. And my last in that house.

'I'm fine,' I reply, suddenly feeling like a child again.

'What are you doing back?' he says. 'Last thing I heard you were in the middle of some war.'

'I'm just here for a few days,' I tell him. 'Sorting out Mum's things.'

'It was terrible to hear about your mother,' he says, looking out towards the horizon. 'Terrible. She was a good woman.'

'Yes,' I whisper, trying not to think about the letter. 'She was.'

'I'm sorry I didn't go to the funeral,' he says, putting his hat back on. 'Only I . . . well, I've never been one for churches and all that.'

'Don't worry,' I reply. 'I didn't go either.'

'Oh,' he says.

'I was in Syria.'

He nods his head.

'We all read your stuff,' he says, gesturing to his mates out on the beach. 'But must take its toll, eh?'

He smiles and it's all I can do not to cry. Something about his voice reminds me of my mum.

'It's nice to have a break from it for a bit,' I say. 'Have a bit of normality.'

'How's that sister of yours?' he says. 'Sally, weren't it? Has she moved away too?'

'No,' I reply. 'But she keeps herself to herself these days.'

'She used to work in the bank on the high street, didn't she?'

'Yes, she did,' I reply. 'She left a few years ago. I think she fancied a change.'

'Don't blame her,' says Ray, frowning. 'I don't think I'll be doing this much longer. It's getting on for fifty years now. You get less for murder. Still, it's given me a decent living.'

'Which one's yours?' I ask, gesturing to the boats that are lying upended on the shingle.

'That one over there by the rocks,' he says, pointing to a small black and white vessel.

I strain my eyes to read the squiggly writing on the side but I can't make it out.

'What's it called?' I ask.

'*The Acheron*,' he says, a slow smile creeping across his face.

'The river of pain?' I exclaim. 'That's rather dark.'

'Yes,' he says. 'Appropriate, though. People forget how forbidding that sea can be.'

He stops and I watch him as he looks out at the water. His whole being is rocky and solid as though he was carved out of the sandstone cliffs centuries ago and left to weather in the salty air.

'It must be a tough job,' I say.

'It has its moments,' he replies. 'The thing to remember is that, no matter what, you can never tame that beast.' He points towards the sea. 'It will always have the last word.'

I go to answer but the wind swallows my words. One of the fishermen calls Ray's name and he puts his hand up.

'All right, Jack!' He turns to me. 'I'm needed,' he says. 'It was good to see you, love.'

He pats my shoulder and smiles.

'You too, Ray,' I say, suddenly feeling very small.

'Mind you pass on my best to Sally, when you see her,' he says. 'And you two look after each other. Now your mum's gone you need to stick together. Most important thing in the world, family.'

He looks at me for a moment then nods his head and goes to join the others by the boats.

Ray's words ring in my ears as I make my way back along the seafront.

Most important thing in the world.

I pass a group of children casting crab lines over the edge of the pier. Two little girls start to bicker over a twisted line, but the older one takes charge and begins to detangle it. And as I walk on I know what I must do. I take out my phone and hastily type out a brief text:

I'm coming over.

Then I put the phone in my pocket and flag down a taxi. I know it won't be easy but I need to talk to her. Ray is right; she's all I have left.

I I

'Would you like a glass of water?'

I turn from the window and try to compose myself.

'No thank you, I'm fine,' I reply, but as I return to the blue plastic chair images flit through my mind like a film on fast-forward. My head pounds but I try not to show my discomfort to Shaw. I have to seem to be in control or I'm finished.

'Okay,' says Shaw, clasping her hands together. 'We talked a little about your last day in the newsroom. Am I correct in thinking that you left for Aleppo two days later?'

My stomach twists but I try to stay calm. This is an interview and I am a journalist. This is not beyond me. If I keep on my toes I can do what I have always done with tricky subjects and second-guess her.

'Yes, that's right.'

'It was a very risky assignment,' says Shaw. 'I understand you were smuggled across the Syrian border via Turkey.'

She's not going to let this go. Though every part of me wants to avoid talking about Syria I know that I am

84

going to have to. But I will only tell her what I want to tell her; nothing more.

'How do you know that I was smuggled into Syria?'

She goes to speak then looks down at her notes. She shuffles through them for a few moments then looks up.

'Harry Vine told the officers when they contacted him,' she says, holding up a piece of paper. It's a print-out of my last dispatch. Harry must have sent them it.

'Seems like Harry has been very useful,' I say with an empty laugh. I keep eye contact with her for as long as I can. She must not know that I'm falling apart here.

'The district where you were staying was under siege I believe,' she says, holding my gaze. 'And being heavily bombarded.'

I nod my head.

'And most nights you were holed up in a basement which belonged to a shopkeeper and his family.'

'Yes.'

'The shopkeeper had a young child,' she continues. 'A little boy.'

I want her to stop. I want to shout at her, but I have to stay calm. I must.

'You grew rather attached to the boy, didn't you, Kate?'

I see his little face looking up at me from the door-way, a scrap of paper in his hands. *I've brought you a present to take back to England, to cheer up the grumpy people.*

'I was there to work, Dr Shaw.'

It's called the book of smiles. See.

'But children are different,' she continues. 'They are more vulnerable than adults. They need protecting.'

85

Mama said you were sad. I'll make you happy.

I clear my throat and his voice subsides.

'Yes, they do.'

'You focus on children quite a lot in your work, don't you?'

'Yes,' I reply.

'Why is that?'

'Because they're the victims, the innocent bystanders,' I reply. 'When you meet children who have lived through war you see how futile it all is. Children don't see borders or divisions. They aren't bound by tribal loyalties or politics, they just want to play, to go to school, to be safe.'

Shaw is silent for a moment then she smiles at me, her head cocked to one side.

'Do you have children of your own?'

'No. You must know that.'

'Yet it's clear you have an affinity with them which is remarkable when you're not yet a mother.'

'It's not about being a mother, Dr Shaw,' I reply. 'It's about being a human being.'

'Would you like to be a mother?'

'No.'

My voice stays steady though I want to scream and shout it hurts so much. Make her stop. Please make her stop.

'And you're not married?'

I shake my head.

'In a relationship?'

'Christ, what has any of this got to do with why I'm here?' I snap. Then reining myself in, I lower my voice.

'Why aren't you taking me seriously? I know I have some . . . some problems – but you need to search that house.'

'Please just answer my question, Kate. Are you in a relationship right now?'

'No,' I say, sitting on my hands to stop them from shaking. 'No, I'm not in a relationship.'

12

Wednesday 15 April 2015

I arrive at Sally's house just after three. The street is deserted. She lives in one of those new-build estates where every house looks identical. It's in a cul-de-sac and Sally's is tucked right in the centre of the curve with two houses leaning in from either side. I feel like a thousand eyes are on me as I knock on the door and wait.

There's no reply but I know she's in there. She has to be; according to Paul she never goes out. I knock again, harder this time, but still there is no response. Eventually I bend down and shout her name through the letter box.

'Sally, it's Kate. Will you let me in?'

The hallway is silent and there's no sign of life. I shut the letter box and as I stand up I see a woman coming down the driveway of the neighbouring house.

'She won't answer,' she tells me as she draws near. 'You can bang on that door and make all the racket you want but she won't come.'

I look at her. She's a large woman with neat grey hair cut short. Her brightly patterned blouse reminds me of one my mum used to wear but this woman has none of Mum's gentleness. She folds her arms across her chest as she stands there weighing me up.

'I'm her sister,' I tell her. 'She knows I'm coming. I can wait.'

'She only comes out at night when it's dark,' continues the woman. She shakes her head and sighs as if going out at night is a mortal sin. 'She sneaks out when she thinks no one can see her,' she goes on. 'But I see her. Dreadful state she gets herself into. Dirty clothes and hair all over the place, and she drives, though I'm sure she's in no fit state to do that. They say she spends the whole day drinking. And I've had words with her partner, what's his name?'

'Paul,' I say, not taking my eyes off the door.

'Paul, that's it,' says the woman. 'But he's hardly here so he doesn't see what I see. Says she's got depression but he doesn't see her lurching back in the car with bagfuls of bottles. Depression? There was another word for it in my day and it didn't end well. You're her sister, you say? I haven't seen you around here before.'

'I live in London,' I explain, trying to disguise the contempt that is rising in my voice. 'And I work away. Look, I'm sorry I disturbed you with the knocking but everything's fine. I'm going to go round the back and see if she's in the garden.'

But the woman isn't finished. She starts telling me what a state the garden has become in the last few months.

'Look, I'm sorry but you'll have to excuse me,' I interrupt her mid-flow. 'My sister needs me.'

I hear her mutter something as I walk down the drive and open the side gate. I gasp as I enter the garden. The woman was right. It *is* a state. The grass is patchy and overgrown with weeds and there are bits of broken furniture tossed here and there. Why hasn't

89

Paul done something about it, I wonder. He lives here too. Surely he can't feel comfortable with it? But it sounds like Paul is keeping away. I remember his face when he turned up to take me to the solicitor, pale and exhausted. Now, seeing this detritus, it all makes sense. This is no home.

I can just about make out the path that curves round the back of the house and I follow it up to the doors of the conservatory. That's when I see her. She is sitting on a chair, bolt upright, staring out at the garden.

She looks so different it startles me. It has been several years since I last saw her and she has deteriorated. Badly.

After a second I raise my hand.

When she sees me, her mouth drops open.

'Sally,' I call, knocking on the window. I gesture to her to let me in but she doesn't move. She just sits there staring at me as if she can't trust what she is seeing. I rap on the glass again and finally she mouths back at me: 'It's open.'

A deeply unpleasant odour hits me as I enter the house, a mix of over-ripe apples and sweat. Sally sits on a grubby white wicker chair in the corner of the conservatory. Her blonde hair has grown very long and it hangs greasily round her shoulders. She is wearing a dirty pink dressing gown and as I draw close it becomes clear that she is the source of the smell.

'What are you doing here?' she asks as I close the door.

'I've come to see you,' I reply. 'I've just been to the solicitor . . . about Mum.'

90

'Mum's dead,' she slurs, staring past me towards the window. 'He take you, did he?'

I assume she means Paul so I say, yes, he drove me there. 'He took me to see her grave as well and told me all about the funeral,' I add.

'He always had a soft spot for her,' she says coldly. 'Don't know why. She said she couldn't stand him, but then she hated anything that I loved, didn't she?'

'I don't know about that, Sally,' I reply. 'Mum loved Hannah.'

At this she lets out a snort and pulls her knees up to her chest.

'Oh, here we go again,' she sighs. 'Is that why you're here? To give me another lecture on parenting? You're so deluded, Kate. You always were, even when we were kids.'

I choose to ignore this slight and look around for somewhere to sit but there is nothing except an old, chipped coffee table. My stomach cramps as I bend down to sit on the edge of the table. I'm still feeling delicate and the smell inside the house is making me light-headed.

'You must have known that she didn't have long. Why didn't you let me know sooner, Sally? Why just send that email? You could have called me and I would have got home in time.'

Sally just shrugs. We sit in silence for a minute or so before she speaks, her voice low and slurring with the remnants of her morning pick-me-up.

'I didn't call you because you were off in bloody Timbuktu or wherever. I only had your email address.'

'Syria,' I snap, feeling all our old resentments bubbling to the fore. 'I was in Syria.'

'Syria. Oh, I do apologize,' she sneers. 'And no, I didn't know she was about to pop her clogs so I couldn't have warned you in advance. Anyway, I knew you wouldn't make the funeral so what was the point of going into detail? You haven't been back for years. Only time I hear from you is when I see your name in the papers.'

'That's unfair, Sally,' I reply. 'Yes, my job means I'm away a lot, but if I'd known Mum was failing I would have dropped everything to get back to see her. You know I would.'

She nods her head and I can see in her eyes she knows she's gone too far. The drink makes her spiteful but it's wearing off and soon she will be full of remorse. It's always the same.

'Anyway, how are you?' she asks at last. The room has grown heavy with my silence and she's trying to win me over. She'll probably ask me to buy her a drink in a minute. 'You don't look too well.'

And I look at her then, my baby sister, the person who I spent our childhood protecting, and for a moment have the urge to tell her. The words burn inside me, but then I see her trembling hands and I think better of it.

'I'm fine,' I say. 'Just had a bit of flu.'

'It's all these strange places you go to,' she says, her lip curling. 'God knows what diseases you might pick up. I see it on the news all the time. What's the latest one? Ebola? You want to be more careful.'

I take a deep breath and try not to let her rile me. The smell in here is really overpowering.

'I'm not ill,' I say. 'Just a bit tired.'

She shrugs her shoulders and we sit in awkward silence for a few moments.

'I need another drink,' she says, getting up out of her chair. 'Do you want one?'

'I'd love a glass of water,' I say. 'If it's not too much trouble.'

I'm trying to keep my voice friendly to avoid any confrontation but my words come out sounding harsh. Still, Sally doesn't seem to have noticed.

'Come through,' she says as she walks to the door.

I follow her out of the conservatory and into the living room. It's tidier in here; there are vases of fresh flowers on the mantelpiece and a small pile of paperwork on the arm of the sofa. It's clear that the conservatory is Sally's den, the place where she hides. The rest of the house seems to be Paul's domain and as I sit down and sink into the folds of the soft armchair I feel a pang of pity for him. How lonely he must be in this big house with no child and a ghost for a wife.

'Have you heard from Hannah?' I ask as Sally comes back with the drinks. I already know the answer but still I feel I need to ask. She hands me a glass of water, takes hers – a mug of something that smells suspiciously like wine – and sits down on the sofa opposite me. Her hands shake as she puts the mug to her lips and gulps the drink down.

'There's only one reason Hannah would get in touch or come back,' she says, cradling the mug in her hands. 'And that would be to see Mum. Now Mum's dead, Hannah may as well be too.'

'But Hannah won't know that Mum's dead,' I tell her. 'How could she?'

'It's the first thing she said to me when she rang that time,' Sally continues bitterly, ignoring me. 'How's Gran? Not "How are you? Sorry I worried you." No, the only person she was bothered about was her bloody gran.'

'They were very close,' I say. 'It's understandable. She should know what's happened. Mum would want her to know.'

Sally shakes her head.

'I wish you'd known the woman I knew,' she says. 'We seem to have gone through life with different mothers. She made my life hell. Nothing I did was good enough. But then you were the one who passed all your exams and then became a famous reporter. You were the golden child in Mum's eyes. Whereas me, all I was good for was having a kid and, according to her, I made a great big mess of that too.'

'You've still got Paul,' I tell her. 'He's a good man.'

'You don't know the half of it,' says Sally. 'Me and Paul? We're over. He's never here these days. Can't stand the sight of me.'

Her self-pity is too much for me. 'Can you blame him, Sally? It's not easy living with an alcoholic. You, more than anyone, should know that. There are places that can help, you know?'

'Oh, give me a break,' she says, standing up from the sofa suddenly. 'You swan in here when I haven't seen you in years and think you can start telling me what to do? We're not kids any more, Kate. I make my own decisions now.'

94

She takes the mug and goes into the kitchen. I hear her pouring out another drink and my heart sinks.

'What about Hannah?' I say as she comes back into the room. 'If you tried to get back in touch, hold out an olive branch, then maybe you could sort things out.'

'Ha,' she says, with a grin on her face that is so much like my father's it makes me go cold. 'You think Hannah gives a shit about me? That's a joke. She couldn't stand me. Said I'd ruined her life. The last thing I need is that girl coming back making trouble. All I want is to be left in peace.'

'But she's your daughter,' I say, taking a sip of water to calm myself. 'Surely you want to know she's okay?'

'Oh, here you go again,' she cries, banging her fist on the arm of the sofa. 'She's fine. Off sunning herself on some bloody island. We know she's okay because you did your big investigation, remember? Honestly, you're such a nosy cow, Kate.'

I sip my water again as we sit in silence. She's right, I did look into things when Hannah left because, unlike Sally, I was concerned. Hannah could be a handful but she was still only sixteen and not particularly worldly wise. I needed to find out where she was, to put my mind at rest. Sally wouldn't listen to me so I asked Paul to dig around, ask her friends if they knew where she'd gone. At first none of them would speak to us – like most teenagers they were afraid of landing her in it – but then one of them saw sense and gave us Hannah's address. She was living in a squat in Brixton, so I told Paul that I would go and meet her, check she was all right. When I arrived she looked rather dishevelled and had put on quite a bit of weight, but she assured me she was happy, that she was living with friends and that she needed space away from Sally. I couldn't blame her for that. I gave her a hundred pounds and told her to keep in touch, but that was the last I heard from her. I went back to the squat a couple of times but they seemed to have moved on. Just as I was beginning to worry again I got a letter in the post from Hannah telling me she was off to Ibiza to work as a rep.

'But still you couldn't help putting the knife in, could you?'

I look up at Sally. The drink is kicking in and bits of spittle flick from her lips.

'Telling me it was my fault, that I drove her away with my drinking. You're just like our bloody mother. Self-righteous hypocrites the pair of you.'

She stands up suddenly and goes to the kitchen. Perhaps I should leave. I look at my watch; it's coming up to five o'clock. Paul will be home soon.

'Mum said it was all me,' she says as she comes back into the room, clutching a refill. 'That I'd driven her darling granddaughter away; that I didn't know how to be a mother. Ha, that's a laugh. I told her I'd learned everything I know from her, a woman who let her kid drown. I told her that *she* was the disgrace and that I would never speak to her again for as long as she lived. And I didn't.'

'How could you? David's death broke her,' I say, watching as Sally slumps back on to the sofa. 'In her letter –'

'What letter?'

'The one from Mum,' I reply tentatively. 'The solicitor gave me it.'

96

'Oh, really? How nice,' she slurs. 'And did they have a letter for me?'

'I don't know. I suppose if they haven't given it to you then no.' I take another sip of water, wishing that Mum could have just done the decent thing and left something for Sally, anything.

'Well, why doesn't that surprise me,' she says. 'Christ, even in death she puts you first. The woman was unbelievable.'

She pauses to take another gulp of her drink.

'So what did she say in this letter then?'

'She said she wanted to explain everything,' I say, my hands trembling. 'About David's death and the fact that it was her fault. But I don't understand why it was just me she wanted to explain it to. Why not write a letter to both of us?'

'Because you were her favourite,' says Sally, watching me over the rim of her mug. 'And she wanted your sympathy. She didn't care what I thought about her. I was the disappointment; the teenage mother. You were this bloody beacon of light; someone who could do no wrong. Everything she wasn't. Christ, her precious Kate would never let a child die.'

She stares at me so hard it's like she knows.

'Mum was a liar,' she says. 'And I know that for a fact. She was also a rotten, neglectful mother.'

As she takes another drink of wine I put my head in my hands. I can't take much more of this.

'Oh, sorry,' she says. 'Am I upsetting you?'

'It's just unnecessary, Sally,' I say, looking up at her. 'All this animosity and vitriol. Yes, Mum made a mistake, but my God she paid for it. She had years of Dad beating her up, night after night, and you just sat there saying nothing.'

Sally leans abruptly forward on the sofa and shakes her head.

'Why are you shaking your head?' I say. 'It's true. I was the one who stood up for her, who fought back, and what did you do? You just let it happen, you stayed silent, and that to me is unforgivable.'

'You know what?' she says, her voice low and menacing. 'You think you're so perfect, this great fucking saint who runs into war zones and saves people. What a joke. You see, Kate, I know things about you. I know what you're capable of.'

'What are you talking about?'

She slumps back and closes her eyes.

'Sally, tell me what you're talking about.'

'Get out of my house,' she mutters without opening her eyes.

'But –'

'Leave me alone. Do you hear me? Piss off.'

'Okay,' I say as I stand up and make my way out of the room. 'I give up. At least I can tell Paul that I tried.'

I open the front door and stagger down the driveway holding my bag across my stomach like a shield. I can't breathe. I need to get out of here, get far, far away from Sally and her poison. I try to clear my head of her, try to think pleasant thoughts, but her voice is ringing in my ears, getting louder and louder until it feels like my head will explode and all I can hear are those words:

Kate would never let a child die.

13

Later that afternoon

I arrive home to a pile of post lying on the doormat. I pick it up and flick through as I walk to the kitchen. *Reader's Digest*; a letter from Cats Protection; a circular from a life insurance company offering a free silver pen to anyone who takes out a policy in the next ten days. That is it, the remnants of my mother's life.

As I walk into the kitchen I try not to think about Sally and the argument but I can't shake off her bitter words. *Deluded.* That's what she called me. Am I? I look down at the post in my hand and think of my lucky pen and Chris telling me that he loved me. I believed in both of those things; I believed that a pen could keep me safe and that Chris and I were soulmates destined to be together for ever. I held on to those beliefs and threw common sense out of the window because I didn't want to face up to reality. Maybe Sally is right, I think to myself as I put the junk mail in the bin, maybe I am deluded.

My head aches as I take off my coat and open the cupboard in search of painkillers. I can hear the old woman. Her screams are faint for now but I know they'll get worse as the evening progresses. I need to do the deep-breathing exercises I read about, the ones that are supposed to help with anxiety, but I feel too tense. I just want to go to sleep before she can get any louder. But it's still early; hours to go before I can take a sleeping pill. Instead I fill the kettle and swallow a couple of painkillers as I wait for it to boil. The pills stick in my throat so I run the cold water and put my head under the tap, taking a long glug. As I lift my head I'm aware of a presence, something moving outside the window. I look up and see a figure by the back fence. Someone is in the garden.

Shaking the water from my hands, I run to the door and open it. My body goes cold. The door is unlocked. How can that be? I was sure I locked it when I left earlier – but then I was so distracted with losing my pen.

But as I step outside all is quiet, eerily quiet; like the silence you get just before a bomb explodes. I walk gingerly down the path, peering through the weeds, my heart pounding.

'Hello,' I call, making my way to the end of the garden where a pile of broken plant pots lies stacked against the far wall. 'Who's there?'

But there is nothing. Whatever or whoever was there has gone. I stand on an old brick and peer over the wall. The back alley that cuts behind the houses is empty save for some abandoned wheelie bins a bit further up.

I jump down and as I make my way back to the house I toy with the idea of calling the police – but the sight was so fleeting they would have nothing to go on, no description. I'm not even sure whether it was male or female.

No, best not to bother with the police, I think to myself, best to just get back inside and make sure everything is locked up. It was probably kids. But as I reach the back door my shoe catches on something. I look down and see a marble. It's just like the ones Sally and I used to play with as kids. I remember I kept a huge stash of them in an old Bovril tin. I bend down to pick it up. It's a nice one and the child in me marvels for a moment at the milky blue eye suspended in glass. As I stare at it my phone buzzes in my pocket.

I take it out and see Paul's name on the screen. It's a text. Clicking on it, I read:

Heard you've been to see the patient ☹ Thought you might be in need of a drink! I'll be in The Ship on the seafront at 8 if you fancy joining me. And thanks for trying, Kate. I know your visit will have meant a lot to Sal even if she doesn't show it. P x

I take the marble and the phone inside, locking the door firmly behind me, and wonder whether I really want to join Paul for a drink. He'll want to talk about Sally and there's nothing more to say. But then I think of the long evening ahead of me in this wretched house and it suddenly seems like a good idea to get out. I put the marble in my bag and head upstairs to find something suitable to wear. I've had enough ghosts for one day. A glass of cold wine, a friendly face and a few hours of ordinary life will do me good.

Paul is sitting at a low wooden table with his back to the room, his head bent as he drinks his pint of beer. I cross the warm, dimly lit bar and tap him lightly on the shoulder.

'Hello,' he says, swivelling round on his stool. He stands up and places a dry kiss on my cheek. 'What are you having?'

'No, it's okay,' I say. 'This is my shout.'

Paul smiles and returns to his seat, and as I walk to the bar to buy the drinks I can sense him watching me. He'll be thinking about Sally, wondering what we talked about and he'll be worrying. I know he will.

He looks pensive when I return to the table with our drinks.

'Don't worry, I'm not going to down it in one,' I say as I sit down with a bottle of white wine. 'Just always seems to work out cheaper if you buy a bottle rather than go glass by glass.'

I pass him his pint of beer.

'It's fine, Kate,' he says, watching as I pour the wine. 'You don't have to explain yourself. Some of us can handle the booze, and others, mentioning no names, take it to excess. Anyway, cheers.'

'Cheers.'

Paul swallows some beer then puts the glass down.

'This is nice,' he says, rolling his sleeves up as he leans forward.

'Yes,' I say, taking a sip of the wine. My legs feel all tingly. Probably the sea air earlier.

As Paul lifts his glass again the light catches his arm. Angry red welts cover it, jagged, like someone has taken a knife to him. He notices me looking and quickly rolls his sleeve down. I decide not to ask him about them.

'Strange to be back here,' I say, looking beyond him to the rest of the bar. 'It hasn't changed a bit.'

The low ceiling and dark beams make me feel as if I'm sitting in a hermitage deep below the earth. The Ship is the oldest building in Herne Bay; it dates back to the Napoleonic wars when it offered sanctuary to sailors fleeing the French. I imagine them hiding amid the dark crevices, a temporary escape from their violent, grog-stained world. My father used to drink here. I think of him sitting at the bar every Sunday; his muscular arm, honed from hauling animal carcasses, curved round the pint glass while a few minutes away his wife and daughters played out an old ritual on the beach. This had been Dad's hiding place, I think to myself, as the barmaid lights a thick wax candle behind us and places it in the window. His mausoleum.

And then I see Ray. He's standing in Dad's spot, at the end of the bar, his back to the wall. He nods at me and raises his pint glass. I smile and wave my hand.

Beside me, Paul is watching.

'Who's that?'

'Oh, just an old friend of my dad's.'

Paul narrows his eyes. 'Never seen him before,' he says. 'Is he from round here?'

'Yes, he's a fisherman,' I say. 'Been a regular in here for years.'

Ray has turned his back on us and as I watch him chatting to the young barman I get a sharp pain in the pit of my stomach. Why couldn't Dad just love me, I ask myself, why did he hate me so much?

'Do you want to talk about it?' says Paul, interrupting my thoughts. 'The meeting with Sally? She was terribly agitated when I got back.'

'There's nothing to say,' I reply, glad of the diversion. 'I tried to get her to talk about her drinking but she wasn't interested. She's just full of anger and bitterness. I don't think I'm the right person to get through to her.'

He sighs and I can tell he's disappointed. I feel for him; I really do. Getting involved with this family was more than he bargained for: our grief and our addictions; our guilty secrets.

'You know, when I met her she was great,' he says, turning to me and smiling. 'Full of energy and up for a laugh. I loved how outgoing she was. It was good for me because I've always been shy. She brought me out of myself.'

'Yes, she was a force of nature,' I say, remembering Sally's loud voice ringing through the house as she clattered in from school. 'And so optimistic; always seeing the good in people, even my dad. Well, especially my dad.'

Paul nods his head.

'Yet she never talks about him,' he says. 'Not once. Whenever I broach the subject she just clams up.'

'They were very close,' I tell him. 'And she was distraught when he died. That's when she started going off the rails. It was only a few months after his death that she got pregnant.'

'She's had a lot to deal with,' he says with a heavy sigh. 'Having a kid when you're just a kid yourself is tough. She puts up this hard exterior but I can see through it. I know her more than anyone, I really do, and I can see that she's damaged. My old mum used to say to me that when I was a nipper I was forever trying to fix things, make them better, and it was the same with women. I've always gone for the ones who need putting back together.'

Someone drops a glass and the noise makes us both jump. Paul holds his hand to his chest, breathing hard. For once I don't feel like the weak one.

'It's okay,' I say, putting my hand on his arm. 'It was just a glass.'

'I know,' he says, pulling his arm away and rubbing it. 'I'm a bag of nerves at the moment. I'm sorry.'

'You don't have to be sorry,' I say, taking a sip of wine. 'I understand what you're going through.'

'Thanks, Kate,' he says. 'Thanks for coming back. You know you're all she has left now.'

'She still has Hannah,' I say, putting the glass down. 'And no matter what, she can't give up on that girl. That's why she has to get better, not for me or for you, but so she can reconcile with her daughter.'

The colour drains from his face.

'I'm sorry, Paul. It must be hard. I know you were close to Hannah too.'

'Ha. As close as you can get to a feisty teenage girl.' He laughs hollowly. 'She was thirteen when I got together with Sal. Do you remember, they were living with your mum?'

'Yes,' I say, smiling. 'I remember Sally called me and said she'd met this gorgeous guy over the garden fence and I thought she'd lost her mind because the only person I remember living next door was this bloke called Mr Matthews and he was about ninety.'

Paul laughs.

'Your parents had bought it, hadn't they?' I ask.

'Yeah. Old Matthews was put in a home and his son sold it to them,' he says. 'That was in 1994, just after you left. They had a good few years, then they died within a few months of each other.'

'I'm sorry.'

'Nah, they'd had a good innings,' he says. 'Still, it was a blessing and a curse them leaving me that house. I'd never really liked Herne Bay. I always found it depressing. My folks would drag me here on holiday every year and I just wanted to stay home in Bethnal Green and hang out with my mates. But Mum and Dad loved it. They always said they would retire here and they got their wish.'

'It seems strange that you stayed here when you hated the place,' I say, pouring myself another glass of wine. 'You could have just sold the house. What made you settle here?'

He leans forward and smiles, his eyes glazed with the drink and the lights.

'Sally,' he says quietly. 'Sally changed everything. I'd decided to rent out the house and the plan was to stay in my flat in London but then when I was showing the estate agent round the garden I heard a whistle. I turned and there she was. All my plans went out the window.'

He takes a sip of beer. I can see this is hard for him.

'She was so excited,' I tell him. 'Said you looked like a short Liam Neeson.'

Paul splutters on his drink then wipes his mouth.

'Liam Neeson? Was she having a laugh?'

'Just happy, I guess.'

'Yeah, we were happy,' he says. 'But I could see right from the start that she had her hands full with Hannah. Boy, did that girl give her some stick. I remember the first day I came round for Sunday lunch. We got as far as the second course and an almighty argument broke out between the pair of them. I can't remember what it was about, too much gravy on her spuds, I don't know, but I was taken aback. I know if I'd called my mum the names Hannah called Sal I'd have been given a good hiding. But she wasn't my daughter; it wasn't up to me to discipline her.'

'Do you think the drink played a part in their problems?'

'Possibly,' he says. 'Though it was more of a social thing at that point.'

'But drinking can make people short-tempered,' I say, remembering how my father's rage would be magnified when he'd had a skinful.

'Looking back, I probably was a bit blinkered,' says Paul. 'I think I just wanted to see the best in Sally.'

'We all did.' I drain my glass and, without thinking, pour myself another.

'It was your mum who finally told me about Sally's drinking. I think she thought I should know,' says Paul. 'She said that when Hannah was a kid Sally used to drag her to the pub and make her sit outside while she got drunk.'

I nod my head, remembering my mum's frantic phone calls, her terrified voice telling me that Sally and Hannah had gone missing again. Then the follow-up call to let me know they'd been found and that Sally was just a bit under the weather.

'But that was before she met me,' says Paul. 'And I convinced myself that I'd fixed her and she wouldn't slip into her old ways again. But it helped with Hannah. When I found out about what she'd been through as a kid I started to cut her some slack. And I told Sally to go easy on her too. After that things were better. I got on well with Hannah, we started to do things as a family. It was wonderful.'

His voice breaks and he squeezes his hands together.

'I moved them out of your mum's place and we bought the house on the Willow Estate. Sally was still working at the bank so there was plenty of money coming in. But then it all went pear-shaped.'

'What happened?' It suddenly hits me that I've never actually asked Paul for his side of the story. The only version I had was Mum's.

'Well, Hannah started asking questions about her real dad but Sally was having none of it. I think she was worried that Hannah would get hurt. But I told her it was only natural she'd want to meet her dad. If I was her I'd want to know who my father was. I thought things had settled down then one night I came home and found Hannah in a right state. Apparently Sal had found her searching her father's name on the internet. She'd gone mad and shouted at Hannah, said some terrible things.'

'What things?'

'Oh, you know Sally once she gets going,' he says, raising his eyebrow. 'She told Hannah that this bloke, the dad, had wanted her to have an abortion. It was probably true but she shouldn't have said it. Hannah was devastated. I mean, no one wants to find out that their dad wanted to abort them.'

'He was just a kid,' I say. 'Same age as Sal, barely in his teens when it happened. His family moved away soon after. I think it was his parents who were pressing for the abortion.'

'Sound like a nice bunch,' says Paul, taking a sip of beer. 'I mean how spineless can you get?'

'They probably thought they were doing the right thing,' I say. 'As I said, he was just a kid. Anyway, they left no forwarding address so Sally had no way of getting in touch when Hannah was born. I think the chances of Hannah finding him on the internet were pretty slim.'

'Yeah, but it scared Sally,' says Paul. 'She got paranoid that Hannah was going to find her dad and leave her. It made Sally really jealous. She started drinking heavily again and that's when her other side started to come out.'

'Her other side?'

'It was like she was two different people,' says Paul, his voice heavy with drink. 'One minute she'd be telling me how much she loved me, and then suddenly, whoosh, she'd just go mental.'

'You mean violent?'

'What? No, not really,' he says brusquely.

'Paul, I need you to be honest,' I say, leaning towards him. 'About Sally, about what's happening to her. Look, I saw your arm. Is that something to do with her?'

He puts his head in his hands and sighs.

'Paul, please.'

'Okay, yes,' he says, lifting his head. 'Yes, she did it. Are you happy now?'

'Of course I'm not happy. This is horrific.'

'Well, how do you think I feel?' he says. 'I'm a man. I should be able to look after myself.' He looks down at his drink, not meeting my eye.

'What happened?'

'It wasn't her fault,' he says, lowering his voice, aware of the other men in the room. 'It was a few weeks back. She'd run out of wine and I caught her with the car keys in her hand, just back from the off-licence. I grabbed the keys and said she was crazy, that she could have killed someone driving in that state. She was so drunk she dropped the bottles, and then she went ballistic. She grabbed one of them and came at me with it, would have got my face if I hadn't put my arms up to defend myself.'

'My God,' I gasp. 'Why didn't you tell me?'

'I thought I could deal with it, but truth be told, after that night I was scared. I still am. I just don't know what she's capable of when she's drunk.'

I think about my visit to Sally earlier, the venom in her eyes when she talked about Mum. That awful grin on her face.

Paul drains his glass and I can't help looking at his arms and wondering what else he isn't telling me.

'Paul, do you think she ever hurt Hannah? Physically hurt her?'

He puts his glass down and stares at me for a moment. 'Be honest.'

'I don't know,' he sighs. 'If you'd asked me that question a year ago I would have laughed at you, told you there was no chance Sally would have laid a finger on her child. But after that night with the wine bottle . . . she was like a different person, Kate, like a monster. The anger, it was like nothing I've seen before.'

I nod my head. He may not have seen it before but I have. He might as well be describing my father. I think of those nights when I would cower in my room after a beating and have to listen while my father kicked the shit out of my terrified mother. It would go on for hours and hours. And the next day I would ask Sally if she'd heard it and she would look at me as though I was talking nonsense.

'You need another drink,' I say to Paul, putting my hand on his. 'Same again?'

When I return from the bar he is gone, though his coat is still on the back of the chair. I put his pint down and take another long sip of my wine. The bottle's nearly finished. Funny how after years of abstinence drink can so quickly become a habit again. I think of Sally and tell myself that after tonight I'll go back on the wagon. I look up and see Paul weaving his way through the bar.

'Sorry about that,' he says as he sits down. 'Call of nature.'

'Cheers,' I say, lifting my glass.

'Cheers,' he replies. 'And thanks for the pint.'

I drain the glass and pour myself another. I feel quite tipsy. Tomorrow I'll stop, but tonight I'm going to enjoy this warm fuzzy feeling. It feels like I'm holed up in a cocoon where nothing can get me, no nightmares, no voices, no images of him.

Paul is talking about his work but I'm not really listening any more. I catch snippets of words – Calais, paperwork, migrants – and I make sympathetic noises as he tells me about the upcoming forty-eight-hour strike by the French lorry drivers.

I swill the wine in my glass, and feel the bar spin slightly. I rather like it.

'It's going to cause chaos . . . Have to work late that week.'

As his story continues I take another gulp of wine, then another and another until his voice forms a strange snake-like coil around my head, binding me to the past. I'm aware of Ray watching me from the bar and suddenly I'm seventeen years old again, sipping Vermouth and lemonade with some unsuitable lad while Dad's friend keeps an eye on me. But somewhere in the centre of my consciousness I know why I'm drinking. I'm thinking of him.

'Where are you, Chris?' I whisper to the swirling room and for a moment I think I see him over by the bar, standing next to Ray, but the image disintegrates and Paul is back, telling me that if the strike goes ahead he might have to 'stay over in Dover'.

'Ha! Over in Dover. That rhymes.' My voice is jagged and I feel the words tensing against my teeth as I speak. 'Over in Dover. That's brilliant.'

I go to grab my glass to make a toast to Paul and the lorry drivers' strike and the delights of Dover but I miss my target and warm liquid seeps underneath my arm.

'Whoa, careful! Time to call a cab.'

I hear Paul's voice through the clanking sound of a bell ringing somewhere on the edge of my consciousness. Then a hand clasps round my waist, a gust of cold air whips into my face and I am on the ground, shuffling on my belly towards the men. I feel blood in my mouth, congealing and thickening as I try to breathe. Then the sound of gunshot pummels the air. I put my head down, close my eyes and start to count, and when I open them I see his face.

14

'Did you sleep well?'

I look up at Shaw as she waits for my reply. She looks refreshed. Her navy trouser suit has been replaced with a cream skirt and black polo neck jumper. She will have slept in her own bed, next to her husband. She will have eaten breakfast at her own table, showered in her own bathroom. She is a free woman. As I sit here in yesterday's clothes, the smell of the police cell embedded in my hair and skin, my back aching from the hard mattress I spent the night on, I try to remember what being free feels like. It seems like I've been held here for ever.

'What do you think?' I shoot back. 'It's not exactly the Ritz, is it?'

Shaw smiles awkwardly then begins.

'Can you tell me about the incident in Soho, Kate?'

I look up at Shaw again. She is reading from a new set of notes.

'What incident in Soho?'

'The Star cafe on Great Chapel Street?'

My body tenses. She knows.

'What about it?'

'You went there the day after the incident with Rachel Hadley, didn't you?'

She looks at me unblinkingly, her face a mask.

'Yes,' I whisper and as she prepares to ask me more questions I see myself that evening, fresh out of hospital and pumped up with painkillers, walking and walking like a zombie through the streets of Soho.

'Can you tell me what happened?'

'I was going for a coffee.'

'But you didn't quite make it to the cafe, did you?'

I look down at the linoleum floor, remembering the big hole outside the Star that was blinking and groaning at me like some great sea monster.

'What stopped you from going inside, Kate?'

'I was looking at the hoardings.'

Shaw looks confused.

'They're extending Tottenham Court Road Tube station and digging up Soho left, right and centre. They've dug a great big hole outside the cafe.'

'And the hoardings?'

'The hoardings are meant to hide the hole, make the whole thing look more attractive. They show the time-scale and blueprints for the new station.'

'What made you look at them?'

'I don't know,' I reply. 'I think it was the mammoth bone that caught my eye.'

Shaw frowns.

'It was a photograph,' I tell her. 'Of a mammoth bone they'd excavated the previous month. It was the developer's way of saying that all this disruption was for a greater good. Look, we're not just ripping up ancient streets and destroying Soho, we're giving something back, something of historical interest. Here's a mammoth bone.'

It is clear that Shaw has no idea what I'm going on about. I don't think she's ever even been to Soho.

'I'm sorry,' I say. 'Things like that just make me angry.'

She nods her head and writes something down in her notebook.

'So you were looking at these hoardings,' she says. 'And then what happened?'

I close my eyes and remember the sensation I felt that night. It was like the ground was moving beneath me and I was being pulled down. And then the noises started up. Screams. They were gentle at first but they grew louder and louder until I had to cover my ears with my hands. Then suddenly, *bang*, the explosion, everything flying up into the air: a head, a foot, an arm, a torso; raining down on me in a bloody twisted mess.

'Kate,' says Shaw, interrupting my memory. 'What happened?'

'I fell over. And, er, this girl tried to pull me up.'

'Rosa Dunajski?'

How does she know her name?

'Yes, I think so.'

'She's a waitress at the Star cafe?'

I nod my head.

'She came out because you were making a bit of a disturbance, shouting at people to run for cover.'

'No, that's not true,' I say, my voice shaking. 'I just fell and this girl started fussing and grabbing at me.'

'And then what did you do?'

'I – I pushed her away.'

Shaw looks down at her notes and begins to read.

'You pushed her so hard that she was knocked on to the ground, hitting her head on the pavement.'

'I didn't mean to – I explained all this later – she just gave me a shock, that's all.'

'That's what you said later to the police,' says Shaw. 'The manager of the cafe called them and you were questioned but Rosa didn't want to press charges. It seems she had a soft spot for you.'

'There was no need for the police to be called,' I say, my hackles rising. 'The manager overreacted. Rosa knew it wasn't my fault. The police could see it was just a mis-understanding. Christ, there are more serious crimes being committed in Soho than that, Dr Shaw. They didn't want to waste their time on something as trivial as a woman falling over.'

'I think you lashed out at Rosa because you were scared,' she says, putting the notes on the floor beside her feet. 'That's what happened, isn't it, Kate? You didn't fall over, you had a hallucination, isn't that right?'

Why is she doing this? Why won't she just let it go?

'It was a momentary thing, just a memory,' I say. 'Nothing serious.'

Shaw nods. 'And have you had anything like this since? Any more hallucinations?'

'No,' I reply, making sure to hold her gaze. 'I can assure you, I haven't.'

'Are you being honest with me, Kate?'

'Yes.'

She picks up her notebook and turns to a fresh page. I look at the clock and wonder how many more questions Shaw has waiting for me; how much more of my life I have to expose to her. As long as we don't go back to Syria, I tell myself – as long as we don't do that – then I can cope with anything.

15

Thursday 16 April 2015

The sheets are hot and moist against my skin as I come round. The room is dark. It's still night. I try to remember how I got home but my brain is mush and the only thing I recall is sitting in a bar talking about striking lorry drivers. After that, all is a terrifying blank.

My eyes are stinging and I have a raging thirst but I can't lift my head from the pillow. As I lie here, immobile, the events of the evening come back to me in fragments. A large glass of wine gulped down in one . . . an empty bottle . . . How can I have got so drunk on just one bottle of wine? Or was it two? I try to think clearly but I can't.

The room spins and as I sit up the pain starts; thick, jagged pain that stabs at my temples. I need pills. I get out of bed and feel my way towards the door, stubbing my toe on something sharp. Looking down, I see the shape of my handbag lying on the floor, the contents scattered all around and the thick silver buckle that ought to be clasped shut undone. I turn on the lamp then kneel down gingerly to check everything is there. Mobile, pills, purse. The zip of my purse is open and coins and notes spill out of it. I don't think I've lost any of it though. I pile them back in and see a crumpled bit of paper amongst the twenty-pound notes. Unfolding it, I see the words 'Marine Taxis' and a fare for £3.50.

Paul must have bundled me into a cab for the five-minute journey home. I try to picture his face but my thoughts are liquid and I can't get a hold on any one thing. Yes, it must have been Paul who helped me get the taxi; it has to have been.

Maybe I should call him, I think, as I close my purse and put it back into the handbag. I could explain myself; tell him that it was a one-off incident brought about by exhaustion; that I don't drink excessively, that a large glass is usually my limit. But then I change my mind. The poor man's probably had enough of me for one night.

The pain in my head intensifies as I get to my feet. I go down to the kitchen and take out two painkillers from the box in the cupboard, washing them down with a glass of water. As I stand at the sink I am startled by the sight of a gaunt skeletal woman glaring at me from the window. I jump back then realize that it's me. Jesus, I look a state. I need to rest otherwise I'm going to make myself ill.

Back upstairs I pop two of my sleeping pills into my mouth, swallowing them with the remainder of the water. Then, turning off the light, I get back into bed.

But as my head touches the pillow I am dragged back by a piercing scream. It sounds like the noise a cat makes when you step on its paw. I sit up in the bed and listen. Another scream. This time softer, a pathetic resigned yelp that dissolves into a series of low moans and sobs. Foxes, perhaps?

I climb out of bed and open the curtains. Flocculent night clouds drift across the sky and the lights from the distant pier trickle through them like thin golden arteries. The noises have stopped and all seems calm. *Get some sleep, Kate*, I tell myself, stepping away from the window. But as I go to close the curtains, I see something.

A small figure is crouched in my mother's flower bed.

My stomach contracts. This can't be happening. I'm awake. The nightmares don't come when I'm awake.

I blink my eyes. But, no, the figure is still there, right in front of me. This is no hallucination; there is a child in my mother's flower bed.

I stand at the window looking out. For once I have no idea what to do. The child isn't moving and, for a moment, I think it may be dead. But then the figure looks up, right up, at the window, and I gasp. In the glow from the moon I can see that it's a boy.

I pick my phone up from off the floor.

'Hello, yes,' I say when I finally get through, my hands shaking. 'I need to report a case of child abuse. He's the child of my neighbours and he's . . . he's in my garden. He's there right now. He must be freezing. I heard a scream a few moments ago then I looked out and . . . Sorry? My name? It's Kate Rafter, 46 Smythley Road, and as I said the boy is the child of my neighbours, they live at 44 Smythley Road. Yes, he's alone as far as I can tell. Where am I? I'm standing at my bedroom window looking out and he's huddled up in the cold. Thank you so much. What? Oh gosh, I'm afraid I can't remember the postcode right now . . . it's my mother's house, she died and I'm . . . er, it's Smythley Road by the . . . Okay, that's great. Sorry? Why do you need that? Okay. It's 16.06.75. Yes. And please do hurry. He's not moving . . .'

I can't wait any longer – I slam the phone down and run downstairs. On the way I go to the cupboard on the landing and take out a thick blanket. It smells of dust and mothballs but it will be warm. He'll be so cold out there.

Before I can get out of the back door I hear a noise at the front and run to the window. The police have arrived. I open the door to two police officers, a thickset older man and a pointy-faced young woman with a heavy fringe that nearly covers her eyes.

'Mrs Rafter?' asks the woman. She looks shocked. They obviously don't get many calls like this in Herne Bay.

'Yes, come quickly,' I say. 'He's out there . . . I was just going . . . he's in the flower bed . . .'

I march them through the house and into the kitchen. My head feels woozy and I hear the female officer sigh as I struggle with the back-door key. Finally it yields and I beckon them outside.

'He's this way,' I say, keeping my voice low so as not to scare him. 'He's . . .'

My legs buckle as I stand looking at the empty flower bed. He's gone.

'He was here,' I say, turning to the police officers. 'I don't understand. He was here just moments ago.'

'Mrs Rafter,' the male officer begins.

'It's Ms,' I say, still staring at the flower bed. 'I'm not married.'

'Ms Rafter, you told the operator that the child you saw lives next door, is that right?'

'Yes,' I say, my heart lifting. 'Yes, he's their child. I don't know his name . . . she's called Fida . . . they're from Iraq. You have to go next door and search for him. He was trying to get my attention. Please, you have to find him.'

The two officers look at each other and nod. They're taking me seriously, I think, as I lead the way back into the house. Maybe the boy is known to them; perhaps he's on some sort of 'at risk' register. Oh, please let them find him.

'Okay, Ms Rafter,' says the male officer as we open the front door. 'We'll go and see what's going on.'

'I've heard screams,' I say as they step outside. 'I've heard him screaming every night. It's horrendous. You have to stop them.'

The female officer nods her head and I watch as they make their way down the driveway.

'Please,' I say to myself as I close the door and go into the living room to wait. 'Please God let him be all right.'

Finally, after an interminable wait that seems like hours, but can only have been minutes, the doorbell rings. I jump out of the chair and run into the hallway.

'Oh God,' I say as I open the door and see their grave faces. 'Is he . . . Please tell me he's . . .'

'Ms Rafter, may we come in?' asks the male officer. He puts his arm out as if calming a flighty gelding.

'Yes,' I say. 'But please tell me he's okay.'

I lead them in through the dark passage into the kitchen. Their radios splutter and tinny disembodied voices trail in their wake. Panic rises in my chest as I gesture to the chairs but the officers stay standing. The woman looks around the kitchen. She still has that odd expression on her face and I notice her eyes rest on the box of sleeping tablets that I've left on the kitchen counter. She catches my eye then speaks in a slow Kentish drawl.

'Ms Rafter, we've been next door and the woman who lives there tells us she doesn't have a child.'

'What?' I exclaim. 'Then she's lying . . . she must be.'

It's then that I smell it: a strong, stale odour of wine. It clings to my clothes and my breath tastes sour. I step back towards the sink, hoping the police can't smell it too.

'She's talking nonsense,' I say. 'I've seen him and heard him several times since I've been here. He was out there on my mother's flower bed. I saw him. Did you search the house? What about the loft? She might have hidden him in there.'

My head spins as I talk but I have to tell them everything; they need to know how serious this is.

'That woman next door,' I continue. 'She's all very nice, chatting to me and smiling, but I know what she's up to. I know what I saw, officers. It was a boy . . . a little boy.'

The officers look at one another awkwardly and then the man speaks.

'Mrs Rafter –'

'I've told you, it's *Ms* Rafter.'

'Sorry, Ms Rafter, I just want to reassure you that we've done all we can this evening based on what you told us on the phone. We haven't found anything next door that concerns us. There was no sign of any children there. No toys, no child's bed . . .'

'Well, there was certainly a sign of him when I woke up,' I reply. My brain is jumbled with wine and the words lie heavy on my tongue. 'There was a scream . . . a child's scream. It sounded like he was in terrible distress . . . I looked out of my window and he was there as clear as you are now, curled up on the flower bed.'

'So you'd just woken up when you saw him?'

The female police officer looks up from the notepad in which she is recording my account. My brain creaks like an old wheelbarrow as I try to think.

'Yes, I'd just woken up,' I reply. 'But a couple of nights ago there was another scream and the day before that I heard a child laughing in the garden. But when I looked, there was no child there. You should put an alert out on your radios: tell your colleagues to keep an eye out for a small child with dark hair. You know, the first few hours are crucial in missing child cases. I know what I'm talking about, I really do. I'm a journalist.'

It all comes out in a stream of words and I feel breathless. I lean back against the counter to steady myself.

'What time did you go to bed?' asks the male officer. He smiles condescendingly. It makes me angry. It's like they are dealing with a confused old woman.

'I can't remember,' I reply. 'I got back to the house sometime between eleven and midnight.'

'So you've been out tonight?'

'Yes,' I say. 'Just for a couple of hours.'

'And have you been drinking alcohol?' The woman's face is rigid as she asks the question.

'I had a couple of glasses of wine, yes,' I reply. 'But that doesn't make any difference to what I saw tonight.'

The woman raises her eyebrows and glances at her colleague. I want to yell at them. All I have done is report a serious incident and I am being treated like the bad person.

'Okay,' says the male officer. 'There's nothing more we can do here tonight. We're happy that there's no child next door but I do appreciate you were concerned and you did the best thing you could in calling us.'

I shake my head. 'You're both looking at me as though I'm some sort of – of fruitcake and that really bothers me,' I say, trying to stay composed. 'I know what I'm talking about, believe me, I have experience in these situations. I – I . . .'

My brain freezes and I cannot find the words I need. I pound my head with the heel of my hand, trying to dislodge the words, but they are stuck fast.

'As I said,' continues the officer, raising his voice above the chatter of noise from his radio. 'You did the right thing in calling us and nobody is questioning your judgement. But if I were you I'd make myself a milky drink and try to get some sleep.'

I want to scream at them, tell them that I'm not mad, that the boy was real. But instead I compose myself and smile politely at them. What else can I do?

'I'll see you out,' I say and as I follow them down the hallway I notice they exchange glances. I hurriedly open the door and usher them out into the damp air.

'Goodbye, Ms Rafter,' says the male officer. 'We've made a record of our visit. Do get in touch if you have any further concerns but I would strongly advise you to get some rest. You've had a long night.'

He smiles and turns away and I watch as he follows his colleague down the driveway to their waiting car.

I'm not giving this up, though. I'll go next door and talk to the woman, tell her that I know what's going on. I'll ask her about the screams; I'll tell her what I told the police: that I can hear the screams every night.

I go to fetch my coat, but in the hallway I catch a glimpse of myself in the mirror; the image that greeted the two officers. I gasp. My eyes are caked in thick black mascara that runs in watery spirals across my eyelids to my temples; my hair, styled into a neat chignon earlier in the evening, has collapsed and wisps of it stick to my forehead. I am still wearing the floral wrap dress, tights and cardigan I had worn to the pub and the clothes reek of stale white wine.

I see myself as they saw me: a drunk with a sleeping pill habit. If I were in their shoes I wouldn't believe me either.

I walk slowly outside and look up at the house next door. All I see is drawn curtains and darkness. What was I thinking? The police found nothing. It must be nothing. I step back inside and close the door.

In the bedroom I peel off my clothes and climb under the covers. As I lie here I try to piece it all together. He was definitely real – the boy – I can see him now in my head, a small boy with dark hair. He was there and then he was gone. It just doesn't make sense.

My head hurts with it all and anger wells up in my chest. What is happening to me? Why won't it all just stop? I think of my mother's letter and Sally's words. Was she right? Am I just a nosy cow? I don't know. I can't make my brain stay still long enough to think clearly. I just want my old life back, my old bed and my beautiful, beautiful Chris. I take my phone and press redial. But it goes straight to the messaging service and a disembodied voice tells me that Chris O'Brien is not available. I throw the phone across the room and flop my head on to the pillow. And as I try to get to sleep I think of all that I have lost. This is what life is going to be from now on, I tell myself. This is what is left. One long nightmare punctuated by voices and screams.

16

Thursday 16 April 2015

I'm clearing up the breakfast dishes when I hear a knock at the door. My heart races as I wipe my hands on a tea towel and rush into the hallway. Maybe it's the police, I think to myself; maybe they've found something.

I fiddle with the latch, my head aching from the drink last night. Never again, I tell myself, as I finally get the door open.

'Oh,' I gasp. 'Hello.'

'Hello, love,' says Ray. 'Can I come in?'

'Yes . . . yes of course,' I say, flustered at this unexpected visit. 'Come through.'

I lead him into the kitchen, my head pounding. I really need some painkillers.

'Sit down,' I say, gesturing to the table. 'Can I get you a cup of tea?'

'Yes please,' he says, pulling a chair out. 'Milk. Two sugars.'

'Well, this is a nice surprise,' I say as I take a cup from the cupboard and pour some tea from the pot. 'What brings you here?'

He takes his cap off and puts it on the table. He looks preoccupied.

'What is it, Ray?'

'I just wanted to come and check you were okay,' he says as I put his tea down in front of him. 'Last night . . . in the pub. You were in ever such a state.'

Last night? The pub? I try to order my thoughts. And then I remember: Ray was there. What did he see?

'Oh, that,' I say, smiling nervously. 'Just had a bit too much to drink, that's all. Nothing for you to worry about.'

He frowns as he takes a sip of tea.

'I was just coming out of the pub when I saw your sister's fella putting you in the taxi,' he says, placing his cup down. 'You were shouting and yelling; making a right scene. At first I thought he was hurting you or something but then I saw the state you were in. I thought I'd better check on you, see if everything was all right.'

I suddenly feel light-headed. I pull a chair out and join Ray at the table.

'Honestly, Ray, it was just a one-off,' I tell him. 'I don't normally drink. I'm a lightweight.'

I laugh awkwardly.

'It's no good for you,' says Ray. 'I've seen many a good man ruined by drink.'

'Me too,' I whisper. 'Though I wouldn't describe my dad as a good man.'

'Ah, come on now,' says Ray. 'He'd suffered a hell of a lot.'

'We all did,' I say, my voice hard. 'You know he knocked my mum around, don't you? And me?'

Ray shuffles in his seat uncomfortably.

'We heard talk of it,' he says. 'In the town. But it weren't our place to –'

'Get involved?' I snap. 'Help? What's the old saying? All that's necessary for the triumph of evil is that good men do nothing?'

He looks wounded and I immediately regret being so harsh.

'I'm sorry, Ray,' I say, my voice softening. 'It wasn't your fault what happened with Dad. I just get so angry when I think about it, that's all. Especially what he did to Mum.'

'It's understandable,' says Ray. 'Though I saw another side to your father. A softer side.'

'Oh yeah?' I say. 'I find that hard to believe.'

'You know how we met, don't you?' says Ray, fixing me with his grey, rheumy eyes. 'Your folks and me?'

I shake my head. I'd never asked how they met. As far as I was concerned Ray had been in our lives for ever, or as long as I can remember anyway.

'That terrible day they lost your wee brother,' he says, his voice cracking. 'Well, I was the one who found him.'

'You . . . you were the fisherman?' I stutter, the words of my mother's letter coming back to me. 'The one who brought him back to shore?'

He nods his head.

'Oh, Ray,' I gasp.

'I've never got over it,' he says, his hands trembling. 'That tiny little boy just floating there . . . I tried. I tried with all my might. Gave him the kiss of life; went through all the first aid I knew, but it was no use. He was dead.'

My eyes fill with tears as we sit in silence. My little brother fills the room. There is so much I want to ask Ray but I don't know where to start.

'But you see,' says Ray finally, 'if it affected me like that, just think what it did to your father?'

'He wasn't there,' I say, wiping my eyes with the back of my hand.

'Precisely,' says Ray. 'And you know what? In the years that followed when we became mates, when we sat at the bar in The Ship and nursed our pints, he would quiz me over and over again on what happened that day. He wanted to know every little detail. He said he'd let the little lad down; that he should have been there.'

'Yes,' I say. 'But that doesn't excuse what he did to Mum and me. Why did he have to take it out on us?'

'It was the drink,' sighs Ray. 'Many's the time I'd pop in for a quick pint and your dad would already be on his third and it was not yet six in the evening. I'd drink mine and leave him there. God knows how many he knocked back each night.'

I flinch, remembering the feeling of dread as we waited for him to come home.

'But don't you see?' says Ray, putting his hand on mine. 'It was the drink that made him angry. If only he'd have dealt with that then maybe things would have been different.'

'Maybe,' I say, though I don't believe it. Dad hated me even when he was sober.

'I'm sorry,' I say, taking my hand away. 'I know you were friends but the day that man had a heart attack and died was the day my life and my mother's changed for the better. I'm sorry if that sounds harsh but that's the way it is.'

He nods his head and sighs.

'You know my sister's an alcoholic?' I say. 'That was another of Dad's legacies.'

'Yes,' he says. 'I'd heard she weren't doing too well. It's such a shame. She was a sweet little girl. Always chatting away nineteen to the dozen and such a pretty thing too. It's funny but whenever I think of you two girls I see you there on that beach with your mum. She would always be taking you for picnics.'

And as he talks I am blindsided by a memory. We're at Reculver beach. I'm searching for shark's teeth while Sally builds sandcastles and my mother sits on a towel reading a novel.

I'm digging in the sand with my fingertips, waiting for the touch of jagged tooth, but instead my hand rests on something thick and hollow. I pull it out and sit back on the shingle to examine my find. The object is black and has a complex criss-cross pattern indented into its surface. I run my fingers along it, delighting in the rough, sandpapery feel. It is my treasure, my secret, and I sit for a few minutes holding it to my chest like a sleeping baby.

'What are you doing?'

My mother is yelling at me. She grabs the object and runs towards the sea.

'Bring it back,' I shout but she doesn't hear me and I can only watch helplessly as she throws my treasure into the waves.

'You could have been killed,' my mother gasps breathlessly as she returns to the beach and slumps down on to her towel. And then she explains that the precious object I'd held to my chest was a tiny bomb – it was most likely a remnant of the famous bouncing bombs that had been tested on Reculver beach during the war.

'Bombs explode,' my mother tells me, 'and God help you if you get in their way.'

A few seconds later my mother has resumed her position reading her novel, while Sally finishes building her sandcastle. The incident is forgotten. But I can't move. All I can think of is the bomb and as the years pass I will ask myself over and over again how it can be that something so beautiful and small can cause so much pain.

'Such a shame,' says Ray, interrupting the memory. 'Is there nowhere she can go to get help?'

He's talking about Sally.

'We've tried,' I tell him. 'But she doesn't want help. I went round to see her yesterday and she was in a really bad way. I tried to talk to her but she wouldn't listen. She just got spiteful and started trying to make out she knew things about me.'

'Oh yeah?' says Ray. 'What things?'

'She wouldn't say,' I reply. 'But it won't be anything; it's just her way of deflecting attention from herself. My dad was the same. He'd always get vicious when he'd had a drink and start doling out the insults.'

'Hmm,' says Ray. 'You're right. Don't take it to heart. She won't have known what she was saying. It's very sad.'

He drains his tea and stands up.

'Well, I best be off,' he says, putting his cap on. 'I don't want to keep you. Just glad to see you're okay. I'm an old man and I worry.'

'I'm fine, Ray,' I say as we walk into the hallway. 'But thanks for coming over. With Mum gone I've no one else to worry about me.'

I smile as I open the door.

'Thanks for the tea,' he says, stepping outside. 'And give my best to Sally, won't you?'

'I will,' I say as I walk him to the end of the drive. 'Though I don't know if I'll see her again before I go.'

'Oh, do,' he says, pressing his hand in mine. 'Do try, Kate. She's your sister. You can't give up on her otherwise you'd never forgive yourself.'

I nod my head.

'Goodbye,' he says, taking his hand from mine. 'Take care now.'

'Bye, Ray,' I say and I watch him walk away down the hill.

As I turn to walk back towards the house I see Fida. She's coming from the other direction carrying shopping bags, looking like she hasn't got a care in the world. How can she be so blasé when her little boy is suffering? I feel the anger boiling up inside me as I watch her. I have to say something.

'Why did you do it?' I cry as she draws closer. 'Why did you lie to the police?'

She tries to push past me but I stand firm.

'Come on, Fida,' I say. 'This is silly.'

'No, what is silly is you,' she says. She takes her bags and marches up her drive. I watch as she unlocks the door and puts the bags inside.

'Fida, just talk to me,' I call. 'What is it you're so scared of?'

She shuts the door then turns and comes back down the driveway. She looks furious as she stands in front of me.

'Is it this?' she shouts, pointing to her hijab. 'Is that it? You think I'm up to no good? Well, you're not alone. There are many in this town don't want people like me here.'

'Don't talk nonsense,' I cry. I am horrified that she would think such a thing. 'I've spent my whole career reporting from the Middle East. I've worn a hijab myself. That's nothing to do with it. Now tell me where your child is.'

She closes her eyes and shakes her head.

'I don't know what you mean,' she says, throwing her hands in the air. 'I have told you I don't have a child. I've told police I don't have a child. What is it with you? You think if I had a child I would hide it? You think I'm crazy?'

'No, I don't think you're crazy,' I say, lowering my voice. 'I think you're scared. It's your husband, isn't it? He's the one doing this.'

'My husband!' she shrieks. 'Now you're blaming my husband?'

My head is splitting and I desperately need some more painkillers.

'I'm just saying I understand,' I say. 'I had to watch my mother go through a violent marriage.'

'Your mother was a lovely lady,' she says, her voice softening. 'Always kind and asking me about my homeland and what it was like.'

I try to speak but my words won't come out. All I can hear is Nidal's voice. It's been growing more insistent these last few minutes. He's calling my name; begging me to help him.

'Shhh,' I hiss. 'Just shhh.'

'Don't tell me to shut up,' cries Fida. 'Your mother would never have done what you did. She would never accuse my husband of wrongdoing and she would never call the police. Do you know what I have been through in Iraq at the hands of so-called police? Do you?'

'I can only imagine,' I mutter, a sinking feeling in my chest. It is all I can manage though I want to tell her that I know about Iraq, that I understand. I put my arm out and rest it on the wall.

'You don't look well,' she says, coming towards me. 'You should get back inside.'

'Yes,' I say and I let her guide me down the drive, back to my mother's house.

She settles me on to the sofa, arranging cushions around me as I lean back, my head a black void.

'I'll make you a hot drink,' she says and I watch through half-closed eyes as she disappears into the kitchen.

She returns with a mug of steaming sweet tea. I sip it slowly and it seems to help.

'Sugar is good when you feel . . .' She struggles to find the words so I help her out.

'Hungover?'

'Yes,' she says. 'Lucky for me I never feel that.'

'No, of course not,' I reply. 'Very wise too.'

I watch her as she rearranges her headscarf. She is very beautiful and so polite. She reminds me of my mother, always apologizing and overcompensating with smiles. That's what beaten wives do. But why would she lie about something like having a child? I realize as I watch her that I will have to tread carefully if I want to get to the truth.

'Fida's a nice name,' I say as I sink my head back into the cushions.

'Thank you,' she says. 'I was named for my grand-mother.'

'Me too,' I say. 'Though I never met her.'

She smiles and I notice that her hands are shaking.

'Fida, if there is anything you want to tell me,' I say, 'you know you can, don't you? You can trust me.'

'Ms Rafter, there is nothing to tell,' she says, flashing a smile that doesn't reach her eyes. 'Now, I'll leave you quietly. Try to get some sleep and no more calling police, okay? No more talk of children.'

As she gets up to leave I catch something on her face. What is it? Something like resignation, I think. I have to try one last time.

'I grew up with a man like this, Fida. I know how it works. They destroy you, up here.'

I tap my fingers against my temples as she stands in the doorway staring at me, her face now blank.

'You have to be strong for your child, Fida,' I continue. 'You owe it to him to be strong. My mother, God bless her, should have left my father but she didn't, she stayed silent and that silence allowed him to carry on.'

My voice catches in my throat and the smell of the hospital comes back to me, the thick, suffocating smell of blood and bleach.

'Ms Rafter, please. Stop this.'

'No, I won't stop this,' I shout, pulling myself up from the sofa and spilling my tea. 'I have a duty not to stop this. I hear your boy screaming *every* night.' I lower my voice, seeing her about to run. 'I know it must be tough for you to admit but you can get help. *I* can help you. There are people I know who can get you away from him: women's refuges, counsellors. You have to, Fida, for your child's sake, you have to do it.'

The exertion of spitting out the words is too much and I flop back on to the sofa.

'This is crazy,' she says as I turn on my side and bury my face in the musty material. 'You are not well. I will leave you alone. But, please, I ask you leave me alone too.' Her voice is full of barely hidden disgust.

I listen to her footsteps shuffling out of the room, then the front door slams shut and I am alone in the thickening silence.

'Are you dead?'

It's him. I recognize his voice even through my sleep-fogged brain.

'Oh, good,' he says as I open my eyes. 'You're alive.'

Nidal is sitting on the floor. His hair is matted with dust and grime.

'Hello,' I whisper. 'What time is it?'

'It's late but I can't sleep. The bombs have started again.'

His face is pale and the dark shadows under his eyes have deepened. He must sleep or he will get ill.

'Where is everyone?' I ask.

'They're sleeping. But I cannot.'

'You should try to rest, Nidal,' I say. 'You can't keep coming and waking me up like this. You have to sleep.'

He shakes his head. 'I will never sleep. You tell me a story. About England.'

'I can't, Nidal. I'm too sleepy. You tell *me* a story.'

'But you are adult and I am child. Adults don't need stories.'

'We all need stories, Nidal.'

'Okay, I tell you about Aleppo; how it used to be.'

I feel him shuffle closer to me then he rests his hand on my head. It is cool and soft just like Fida's was, and as I close my eyes he takes a deep breath and I'm there with him, walking through a beautiful city that no longer exists.

17

I can smell Aleppo when I wake up two hours later, my back aching from the springs of my mother's sofa.

'Nidal?' I whisper as I slowly come to. And then I remember where I am.

The dream had been so clear, so vivid, that as I stand up and make my way to the kitchen I can hear his voice in my head, the words he always left me with.

'*Tusbih 'alá khayr*, Kate.'

Goodnight, Nidal.

I need air, I tell myself, as I cross the kitchen and open the back door. If I stay in the house I will dwell on Nidal and Aleppo and then the nightmares will come. I have to get out.

I pour myself a glass of water and take it with me to the garden. Pulling a plastic chair over to the patio, I sit and watch as the sky darkens. It is chilly and I rub my arms to warm myself. And then I see something: a triangle of light showing through the fence.

I get out of the chair and go to take a closer look. One of the slats in the fence has come loose and is hanging at an angle.

'One more thing to fix,' I mutter to myself but as I go to return to the chair I hear something.

A voice. A very faint voice.

'Kate?'

I stand frozen to the spot. Fear ripples through me. The voice is coming from an unexpected direction. It is coming from a silent place, an empty place; it is coming from the house. Not next door – mine.

There is someone in there and I am out here alone. The hairs on my arms bristle as I hear footsteps coming closer.

'Oh, there you are.'

My shoulders sag with relief when I see him.

'Paul, what are you doing here?'

'You'd left the front door open. I was worried.'

He stands in the fading light of the patio. The kitchen behind him is dark and for a second he looks like a photograph that hasn't yet developed. I go to greet him and slowly his features begin to re-form.

'The door was open?' I exclaim. 'But it can't have been . . .'

I leave the sentence unfinished because there is no explanation for it. I heard the door slam when Fida left. I slept for a couple of hours and then I came out here. I haven't been anywhere else, have I?

'You got to be careful,' he says. 'There's been a spate of burglaries in this road. Not that there's much to steal in this old place.'

As I walk towards him I see that he is holding carrier bags.

'What's that?'

'Dinner,' he says, raising the bags to his chest like a set of dumb-bells. 'I thought you could do with a home-cooked meal. Tell me to sod off if you want; I'll understand.'

I wish he wouldn't feel the need to drop in and check on me all the time. I need space to think, to make sense of what is happening. But then I think of last night; my behaviour.

'No, it's me who should sod off,' I say, ushering him into the kitchen. 'I am so sorry about last night. I haven't had much sleep lately and I don't normally drink. I'm afraid the wine just went straight to my head.'

'It's okay,' he says, placing the bags on to the table. 'It's not a crime to have one too many, and anyway, you were very entertaining, especially your views on Dover.'

'What did I say about Dover?' I ask, trying to recall the previous evening's events. 'Oh, actually, on second thoughts, don't. I dread to think what I said. Really, Paul, I'm mortified.'

'Don't be daft,' he says with a chuckle. 'You were just merry, that's all.'

I watch as he slowly removes the contents of the bag. There's a cooked chicken, a bag of salad leaves, some cherry tomatoes, lemons, balsamic vinegar, olive oil, some sort of seed bread and two bottles of wine.

'Oh please, no more wine,' I groan.

'Come on, just a glass,' he says, unscrewing the bottle.

I smile awkwardly. I'd wanted to be alone tonight, wanted to clear my head, maybe even call Harry. I don't need to spend another night talking about Sally with Paul, it's just futile; but then I don't want to offend him either.

'Oh, I brought you this as well,' he says, throwing a bulky newspaper on to the kitchen counter. 'Thought you might like to catch up with what's going on.'

I see my employer's name in bold black type on the masthead and think to myself that it's the last thing I want, but I smile and thank Paul all the same.

'Right, let's have a drink,' he says.

I watch as he rummages through the glassware and emerges with a pair of old green-stemmed wine glasses. And as he pours the wine I think of Ray's visit earlier. I need to find out what happened.

'Paul,' I begin tentatively, 'last night . . . when we left the pub . . . did I make a scene?'

Paul finishes pouring the drinks then hands me a glass.

'You were a bit drunk, that's all,' he says, smiling sheepishly. 'Nothing to worry about.'

He's trying to protect me but I need to know.

'Please,' I say, taking the glass. 'Tell me.'

His smile fades and he has a long drink of wine before speaking.

'We were waiting for the cab,' he says, rubbing his finger and thumb along the stem of the glass. 'And you just went all funny. For a minute I thought you were going to faint or something. Your eyes went strange, and then you started to shake. You couldn't seem to hear me. It was like you were somewhere else.'

I go cold. He is describing what I go through each night. It's as though he has reached into my head and pulled out my nightmares. I take a nervous sip of the wine. So much for giving up.

'Then the cab drew up,' he continues. 'And I thought about getting in with you and taking you to the door but I knew I should be getting back to check on Sally.

144

So I spoke to the driver. It was a woman; that reassured me. She was nice, said she'd make sure you got home safely.'

As he speaks my hands start to tremble. I want him to stop now.

'But . . . well . . . it was what you said as you got in the cab that concerned me the most,' he says.

I look up, willing him to stop. But another part of me needs to know.

'What did I say?'

Paul puts his glass down and drums his fingers on the table.

'What is it, Paul? Tell me what it was that I said!' I can feel a familiar tightening in my throat. 'Please?'

He stops drumming then continues.

'It was probably the drink talking, I wouldn't worry . . . but as you leaned over to close the cab door you looked me straight in the eye and you said . . .'

'Paul, tell me what I said.'

He looks at the floor. 'You said: "I killed him." You kept saying it.'

I look down at the deep red liquid in my glass and wish I could disappear into its opacity. Who was the prince who chose to be executed by being drowned in a vat of wine? I can't remember but if ever there were a way to die, that would be it. I take a long sip and the taste mellows; I can feel the alcohol numbing my nerve endings one by one.

'What's going on, Kate?' he asks. 'Do you want to talk about it?'

No is the answer. I will never talk about it.

'I'm fine,' I say, reaching over to refill my glass. 'And you're right, hair of the dog was a good idea. Now, are you going to slice that chicken or will I have to do it myself?'

'Okay,' says Paul, his face all concern. 'I just want to say this and then I won't mention it again, but you know you can confide in me, don't you? You know that I'm here for you?'

'Yes, I do,' I reply briskly. 'Now somewhere in this sorry excuse for a kitchen is an electric carving knife. Remember those? If we can find it we can eat.'

An hour later we're sitting on the green fake leather sofa in the living room polishing off the wine. We've had a bit too much and are both slightly tipsy.

'I don't know about you but I'll be glad to see the back of this house,' says Paul, looking around at the grubby room. 'I've always had a bad feeling about it. God, listen to me, I sound like you talking to your friend whatshername,' he jokes.

'Alexandra Waits,' I reply and I tickle the back of his neck. 'Look, she's here. I think she likes you.'

'Get out of it,' he laughs, pushing my hand away. 'You'll spook me again and then I'll leave and you'll be all alone with Alexandra.'

'Sorry, I couldn't resist,' I say, laughing too. It feels good. 'But I know what you mean about this place. It's as though the walls have soaked up all the grief and violence that went on over the years.'

'If walls could talk,' says Paul.

'They'd say: could you get your father to stop bashing that woman's head against us please, he's damaging the plaster.' I laugh again, this time without humour.

Paul rubs my shoulder.

'I'm sorry,' he says gently. 'It must have been hell for you.'

His face is rather too close to mine for comfort so I sit up and reach for the wine.

'Anyway, enough about me,' I say as I refill our glasses. 'What was your childhood like? Did you get on with your parents?'

'It was okay,' he replies. 'I didn't really get on with my dad but I'm not one for analysing all that stuff. Shit happens and then you grow up, you grow some balls and get on with it.'

I smile.

'That's a good philosophy,' I say, taking a sip of wine. 'I should take it on board.'

'Well, it always worked for me,' he says.

'Speaking of your folks,' I say, putting my glass on to the table. 'What do you know about the people next door, your tenants? Fida and her husband.'

'Why do you ask?'

'Just curious, that's all.'

'They're all right,' he says. 'Keep themselves to themselves, pay the rent on time.'

'Do they have a child?'

'I don't think so,' he says. 'Mind you, I've never really spoken to them much. The letting agent deals with them. I think the woman's from the Middle East somewhere.'

'She's from Iraq,' I say.

'How do you know?' he asks. 'Have you been talking to her?'

'Yes, she was out in the garden. She asked me about Mum. Apparently they were good friends.'

'Were they? I don't remember that,' says Paul. 'Still, you know what your mum was like, she'd chat to anyone.'

'Yes,' I say. 'Listen, Paul, I think there's something odd going on in that house.'

'What do you mean?' he asks, leaning forward, his brow furrowing.

'Well, the other day just before she spoke to me I heard a child laughing in her garden but when I asked her she said she didn't have a child.'

'That's strange. Are you sure it was a child you heard? It couldn't have been, I don't know, a dog barking or someone's car radio?'

'Oh, come on, I know what child's laughter sounds like. I'm telling you, there was a child in that garden.'

'It does sound odd,' says Paul. 'But it's a busy street and I know there are kids on the other side of 44. Maybe it was them you heard.'

'Yeah, maybe,' I say, stifling a yawn. I know what I heard but I'm too tired to press it and, anyway, Paul is as much in the dark about the neighbours as I am.

'Do you know what you need?' says Paul, leaning back in the sofa.

'What's that?'

'Some fresh air,' he says. 'Look at you. You're exhausted. You've been cooped up in this dusty old place for days now. And before that you were in a bloody basement in Syria. You need perking up. How about we organize a day out somewhere nice, eh? You name a place and I'll take you.'

I smile at his attempts to cheer me up. I've had too much wine again, but the dull fuzziness in my head is rather soothing.

'Come on,' says Paul. 'Where shall we go?'

I close my eyes and hear my mother's voice: *Picnic time, girls.* And I don't know whether it's the wine or my own ghoulish tendencies but for just a moment I get an urge to go back there.

'Kate?'

I open my eyes and look at Paul. He seems different tonight, less frazzled than usual, almost attractive. The wine must really be getting to me.

'I'd like to go to Reculver,' I say, holding his gaze.

'The beach or the towers?'

'Both.'

'Okay, you're on,' says Paul. 'I haven't been to the towers for years, not since I was a kid. My dad loved them for some reason but then he always was a maudlin old bastard. They're haunted, aren't they?'

'Supposedly so,' I reply drowsily.

I take another sip of wine and close my eyes. I am so tired.

'Reculver it is,' says Paul, his voice muffled. 'We'll take a picnic. Kate? Are you asleep?'

He nudges me and I open my eyes.

'What time is it?' I grunt, stretching my stiff legs out in front of me.

'Nearly midnight,' says Paul.

149

'Sorry,' I say as I ease myself off the sofa. 'I should probably get some rest now.'

'Yes, you should,' said Paul, getting up. 'So do we have a plan?'

'A plan for what?' I say as I stumble towards the door. My head feels very odd and I wonder if I'm coming down with something. When did I last take a sleeping tablet?

'Reculver,' says Paul, following me out. 'This weekend.'

'Oh, I don't know,' I say, wishing I'd never mentioned the bloody place. 'Some things are better left in the past.'

'Go on. It'll be fun,' he says as he fumbles with the zip on his jacket. 'Just a few hours, that's all. It will do us both good.'

I look at him and think that he could probably do with the sea air more than me. Weekends can't be much fun in the Cheverell household. He deserves a break.

'Okay,' I say, unlocking the front door. 'You're on. Now get out of here and let me go to bed.'

He laughs then pulls me towards him and hugs me tightly.

'Thanks, Kate,' he whispers in my ear.

'Goodnight, Paul,' I say as we pull away from each other. 'Drive safely. You've had quite a bit to drink.'

'I'll be fine,' he says as he steps outside. 'It's not far. Oh, and I'll call the letting agent tomorrow, see if I can find out anything about the people next door. Now you go and get some rest, okay?'

'I'll try,' I call to him, watching him walk to his car. 'I really will try.'

I close the door and go back into the kitchen. The table is still laden with dirty plates. I take them and put them in the sink. They can wait until morning, I tell myself, as I pour a glug of washing-up liquid over them and run the hot water. The wine has made me fuzzy-headed and so sleepy that I wonder if my pills are necessary tonight. Still, better not to take chances. I slip two out of the box and swallow them with a mouthful of water. As I go to leave the kitchen I notice the newspaper lying on the counter. I unfold it, distractedly, and within moments I am wishing I hadn't.

SYRIA'S LOST CHILDREN

Exclusive: Rachel Hadley reports from the
Kahramanmaras refugee camp

Each word twists inside me like a knife. She's done it; the little witch has finally done it. After months of trying to undermine me, she's got her big assignment. I look at the accompanying photographs. There is Hadley simpering into the camera while holding a small child. I notice she's done her hair and has a full face of make-up. The child she is holding looks uncomfortable. It's a typical staged shot. *Dear God, woman, you're supposed to be a journalist.* I read the first couple of lines of her report, incredulous at her lack of impartiality. 'I'm so angry I can barely speak,' she bleats in the second paragraph. I turn the page and see that at the bottom of the report is a link to her Twitter page. 'For more updates from Rachel's exclusive story please follow @rachely88.'

I remember Harry imploring me to set up a Twitter profile so that readers could follow me and I told him in no uncertain terms that I didn't do social media, that readers could read my reports in the newspaper. I mean, Jesus, how are you supposed to update your social media page when you're trapped in a bombed-out city without running water, never mind bloody WiFi?

'Bullshit,' I exclaim, ripping the paper and Hadley's insipid face into pieces. 'All of it.'

I need to get back there immediately. I need to talk to Harry, tell him that I've recovered from what happened in Aleppo, that I'm ready to go back.

My heart is thudding so hard it feels like I may have another panic attack. I sit down in the chair, the remnants of the newspaper still in my hands, and try to catch my breath. And then I see it, a nice full bottle of red, on the shelf in the pantry. Good old Paul. I stand, pick up my empty glass and take it and the wine upstairs to bed.

18

The sky is raining blood as I crawl through the bodies. Where have they all come from? A few minutes earlier the room had been quiet, the only noise the steady hum of the refrigerators and the gentle ticking of the clock.

Explosions ravage the air above my head and with each detonation blood trickles on to my hair, my clothes, my skin, as more body parts drop from the sky like scraps of meat being flung into a lion's den. There is no sign of him, though I know he will be here somewhere, clutching his scrapbook in his hands and waiting to show me his favourite picture. I have to find him before the weight of the bodies suffocates him.

So I press on, flinging aside corpses to get to where he is.

'Kate.'

There. I can hear him, his voice a faint whimper against the barrage of bombs that rage in the skies above. But how to determine his body from the swell of body parts all about me? My nostrils fill with the smell of decay as I wipe my face.

'Kate.'

I'm getting closer; I can sense him, though I know I don't have much time. The fridges whir as I dig and dig to the bottom of the pit. Then I hear a groan and I know I'm close.

'I'm coming, Nidal,' I yell into the darkness. 'Stay there, I've almost got you.'

Deeper and deeper I dig until I see a flash of dark hair and his face, expectant and terrified all at once.

'I see you, Nidal. I see you. Now hold on to my hand.'

I feel him grip my hand tightly.

'Now pull, pull with all your strength,' I shout but my voice is obliterated as the sky explodes and we are saturated with red rain.

'Kate.'

His voice grows louder though I know that's impossible as he is deep underneath the ground.

'Kate.'

The door of the shop bursts open and a soldier stands there caked in blood and sweat and excrement, a dead body draped across his arms, its entrails hanging out in silken threads behind him.

'This what you're looking for?' he growls as he steps towards my prone body and throws the corpse on to the ground where it bursts on impact, spraying me with a fine mist of deep-red blood.

'Kate.'

The voice grows fainter as I shield my eyes from the putrid liquid and curl myself into a tiny ball.

'No,' I cry. 'No, no, no.'

I open my eyes and slowly unfold myself. My hands are shaking and my mouth tastes of foul gristle. As the bedroom comes into focus I exhale long shallow breaths to ward off the nausea that is rising in my gullet.

Two bottles of red. Why did I do it? I climb out of bed in search of water and pills.

Red wine always brings on the blood dreams. They're the ones I dread the most because they are relentless and there is no way out of them.

The room is cold. I drag my suitcase from under the bed and take out a thick wool cardigan. I put it on and step out on to the landing. As I walk down the stairs I hear a tapping sound. I pause and listen for a moment. There it is again: a muffled *tap, tap, tap*, like the sound of distant shelling.

I slowly make my way downstairs and stand in the hallway listening. The noise has stopped. It must have been the pipes spluttering out the last of the heat. Another thing in need of modernizing, I tell myself, as I wearily make my way to the kitchen.

The water is heavenly and I drink glass after glass of it, washing away both the taste of the blood dream and two more oblong pills that will ensure me a few hours of blank sleep. I turn off the tap and stand for a moment, my eyes sore from exhaustion. The noise, when it comes again, is harder, more insistent, a bang rather than a tap. It's coming from outside. I go to the back door and unlock it. What is it? The banging continues. It's coming from the garden next door.

I go to the pantry and take out the heavy rolling pin my mother kept as a prop to hold one of the shelves in place. I shudder as I hold its bulky weight in my hands and remember its former use. My father, the policeman of the house, favoured the rolling pin as truncheon in order to implement his unique brand of crowd control.

With the rolling pin in my hand I open the door and step out into the garden. The air is freezing and I pull my cardigan round my chest as I creep towards the plastic chair that is still where I left it by the fence. Easing my weight on to it, I carefully climb up and stand looking into next-door's garden. The noise has stopped and there is nothing there but an empty washing line and a pair of old wellington boots lying by an overgrown rockery. The shed is in darkness. I look to my right and see that the house seems to be locked up; the curtains in the back bedroom are closed and there is no light coming from inside.

'Hearing things again,' I tell myself as I climb down from the seat but just as my feet touch the ground the noise starts again, this time louder and more frantic.

I scramble back on to the chair and peer over. And then my heart flips inside my chest.

There, in the window of the shed, is a face, a child's face.

He is very pale, almost translucent, and his face is framed with a shock of jagged black hair. He looks so scared. He bangs his fists against the glass window of the shed.

I have to get him out.

I haul myself up and into a sitting position on the fence, as if I were on the back of a bony horse, then with one swift twist of my body I land on the grass with a thud. The rolling pin that I had wedged under my arm bounces off my knee and I wince in pain.

Pulling myself up from the ground, I look around the garden for something I can use to get back over the fence. We'll need to be quick. A rickety wooden chair lies on its side on the raised decking area by the back door. That would work but it's so close to the door I risk alerting Fida. As I stand procrastinating the boy bangs on the window again. I will have to risk it. Crouching on my haunches, I hurry across the lawn and drag the chair back to the fence.

Once it is in place I turn and head to the shed, waving my arms to let him know I am coming to help. He looks terrified. A large cloud drifts across the moon, plunging the garden into darkness. I carry on waving as I approach the window but the glass is opaque and the boy's face no longer visible. I turn the door handle, holding the rolling pin in front of me like a cumbersome compass. The door is locked but the wood is thin and half yields as I push it with my shoulder. One good shove will get it open, I reckon, and I stand back and come at the door with all my weight. It springs open and I land in a heap in the centre of the shed. It's pitch black.

'Hello,' I call out and my voice comes back at me. 'It's okay, I'm here to help you.'

My back aches as I pull myself up and look around. The moon comes out again and exposes slivers of objects: a stepladder is wedged against the window, a bulky lawnmower, a set of secateurs and, at the far end of the shed, a wall of shelves with paint pots and gardening tools neatly stacked. But no child.

'It's okay,' I call out to the shadows of the room. 'I know you're scared but you can trust me. My name is Kate. I'm staying in the house next door.'

Where is he?

I move aside some boxes. Peer behind the ladders. Nothing.

157

He was here, I tell myself. He was right here. I stand for a moment at the window, where a spider has woven a silvery web. From this angle I can see my bedroom window quite clearly though the curtains are closed. I can see a quarter of the kitchen window and can just make out the shape of the plant pots that line the patio by the back door. He could see me. He knew I was there and he wanted my help.

And I have felt his presence. Ever since I arrived at my mother's house I've had the feeling I am being watched.

A child can't just disappear, I tell myself as I fling aside more boxes and gardening tools. It just isn't possible. I didn't imagine it; I know I didn't. He was here, banging at the window.

'Please, will you just come out,' I cry, throwing aside more detritus. 'You don't need to hide from me.'

And then out of the corner of my eye I see a light. My stomach contracts. I go to the window and see that the kitchen light has come on. If Fida or her husband find me here I'll be in serious trouble.

I look around me one last time. Nothing. But as I make my way to the door I hear voices. They are coming from the garden. Shit. I leap back into the shed, close the door and crouch in the corner.

I hear the crunch of footsteps coming down the path and my heart flips in my chest. They are outside the door. They are going to come in. They are going to find me.

But after a couple of moments of terrifying silence I hear the footsteps going back towards the house. I put my hands to my mouth and exhale slowly. I was so close to being discovered. What the hell would they have said if they'd found me in here?

I give it a couple of minutes then creep towards the window and look out. The kitchen light is off. They must have gone back to bed.

After waiting a while longer I open the shed door and scurry across the garden to the fence. There's no sign of anyone. But as I climb on to the chair, all I can think about is the boy; his terrified little face.

'He was there,' I whisper, steadying myself as the chair rocks beneath my weight. 'He was right there.'

I jump down on to the stony remains of my mother's flower bed, and my bare feet sink into the soil. For some reason as I stand up and cross the lawn I think of Chris and that last trip to Venice. We were walking around a farmers' market when one of the stallholders started to yell. His grill had caught fire. People were screaming and running away but Chris went straight towards the fire and helped put it out. He always knew what to do. It was one of the things I loved about him. His resilience and strength. If only he were here now, he would find a way to help that child. He would know what to do. But he's not here and all I have is my own gut instinct. I have to trust it, I think to myself as I head back to the house. I have to be brave.

19

Shaw nods her head as she walks back into the room. We've had a ten-minute break during which I was offered a cup of coffee and a sandwich filled with orange stringy cheese. I sipped the coffee and left the sandwich untouched and now it lies congealing on the table beside me as Shaw sits down and opens up her briefcase. There's something different about her. Almost sad. She takes out a sheet of paper and places it on her lap. I see the words 'University College Hospital' and I know what is coming before she even opens her mouth.

'Can we talk about the baby, Kate?'

The room contracts as I sit looking at the last moments of my child; one solitary paragraph on a piece of paper.

'What do you want to know?' I reply. 'It seems you have it all there in front of you.'

'I'm sorry,' she says. 'It must have been devastating.'

Her voice is sorely lacking in empathy and this puts me on guard.

'Why? It happens every day, doesn't it?'

Shaw doesn't respond. She thinks I'm heartless.

I take my bag and root around for the photo. This woman thinks I'm some kind of psychopath. I have to prove to her that I have feelings, that I'm a human being; someone who cares. I take my wallet and pull out a small, square piece of paper.

'Here,' I say as I hand it to her. 'My first scan.'

Shaw takes it and I watch as she squints at the fuzzy image.

'It was a boy, apparently,' I say, taking the picture from her hand and placing it back into my bag.

'I know this is incredibly difficult, Kate,' she says, reciting the words like an automaton. 'But it will help so much if you can just share a little of what happened. I understand you miscarried the day of the altercation with Rachel Hadley.'

'Yes, I'd just left the office when it . . .'

I pause, remembering the lift plunging downwards and the blood staining my trousers. One more thing I couldn't keep alive.

'Did anyone go with you to the hospital?'

'No.'

'So you went through the whole thing alone?'

I nod my head. The sharp hospital smell still lingers in my nostrils as I try to recall the events of that even- ing. But it's all a blur. I was in so much pain I could only make out faint outlines; the doctors and nurses were just bluish wisps on the edges of my consciousness.

'How far into the pregnancy were you?'

'Four months,' I tell her. 'But according to the doctor the baby had died two weeks earlier.'

The guilt is still as raw as it was when it happened. Even knowing that he had been dead throughout it all and had nothing to do with Chris or the bottle of wine, the fact that I failed my baby gnaws away at me. I should have been strong for him and I wasn't.

'You spent the night in the hospital?'

'Yes.'

I look down at my feet as I recall the tiny room with a curtain separating me from the corridor. I was handed a cardboard potty and told to pee into that rather than the toilet so they could monitor the stages of the miscarriage. It was undignified in the extreme but I was so full of painkillers I barely registered when the nurse came in to take the potty away.

I birthed the dead baby sometime around dawn. I remember the sun was just coming up through the wire railings of the hospital car park. I was standing by the window when I felt something shift. I ran to the bathroom with the potty and watched as this tiny, grey creature slipped out. My child.

I blink my tears away as Shaw plunges into her next question.

'The baby's father?' she asks. 'Did he come to see you?'

'No,' I reply. 'He didn't know I was pregnant.'

'Why didn't he know?'

'I didn't have the chance to tell him,' I reply. 'I'd planned on telling him that day, over lunch, but before I could he told me the relationship was over.'

I see him in my mind's eye, sitting at the table waiting for me. His hands were clasped in front of him and he was staring fixedly at a picture on the wall: a Chagall print of a naked woman, hanging like a piece of fruit from a heart-shaped tree.

'That must have been hard,' says Shaw.

'Yes, it was,' I reply. 'But then part of me had been expecting it for years.'

'Why is that?'

'He was married.'

I remember walking over to his table. He looked up at me and his face was so sad. He kissed me clumsily. His lips missed my mouth and caught my cheek instead. I went to kiss him but he turned his cheek. I just thought he was tired. I never would have imagined . . .

'Married,' says Shaw, interrupting my thoughts. 'And how long had you been seeing him?'

I bristle at the term she uses. 'Seeing him' makes it sound like a casual fling when it was so much more.

'Ten years,' I reply. 'Though we'd known each other much longer.'

I want Shaw to know that it was serious. I want her to know that I am capable of loving and being loved; that I am not some messed-up crazy woman. So I tell her about him, my Chris, my love, the man I can't live without. The man I must live without.

'We met in New York just after 9/11,' I begin. 'He was a forensic anthropologist. He and his team were exhuming body parts from Ground Zero. I was reporting on the work they were doing.'

My thoughts drift and I see myself standing looking at this beautiful man, his black hair covered in dirt, his large hands clasping a shovel. He was very tall, around six three; and, though strong, his body was lean and wiry.

With his sharp cheekbones and thick beard he looked like a pioneer from the Midwest. I couldn't take my eyes off him. I was only twenty-six and it was one of my first big assignments. I was nervous but when he introduced himself in his gruff Yorkshire accent I immediately felt at ease. It was as though we had known each other before. We spoke for about an hour. He answered my questions as best he could; he was polite, professional, but I knew, we both knew, right then, that something had happened between us, something unspoken.

I look beyond Shaw's head and stare at the pockmarked wall. I see us sitting outside a wine bar in Victoria. It was three years after our first meeting that we finally got together. He'd come down to London from his home in the north to attend a conference and we'd bumped into each other in the street. He asked me out for a drink and that was it. I can see his pale blue eyes twinkle as he tells me what he wants to do when we get back to my flat later. I hear him whisper *every little bit of you*; his low voice caressing each word as he takes my hand in his and rubs the dry surface of my skin.

'Did you know he was married when you started seeing him?'

Shaw's voice brings me back to the room. I look at her, noticing a glint of gold on her wedding finger, and suddenly the pen in her hand is a weapon.

'Yes, I knew.'

'And did that bother you?'

Her voice has hardened. I have to keep her onside. I can't tell her my thoughts on marriage; how I never wanted to end up like my parents; that I didn't want anything from Chris, just the knowledge that he would always come back to me; that knowing he loved me more than he would ever love his wife was enough. Though I know now that's a lie. So I tell her what she wants to hear.

'Yes, of course it bothered me.'

'How did you feel about it? The pregnancy?'

'Shocked at first,' I tell her. 'Unprepared. But then I started to get used to the idea. Although that might have been the happy hormones kicking in.'

Shaw nods her head and looks down at her notepad. She hates me, I can tell. I am the 'other woman', the kind women like her have nightmares about. But right now I would give anything to be in her place, to live a safe, cosy existence with a husband and family. As I sit waiting for her to continue, I feel so alone it physically hurts.

'You say you'd planned this lunch to tell Chris about the baby?'

'Yes.'

The memory of his lips on my skin as he stood up from the table and greeted me burns through my body as I sit waiting for Shaw to go on.

'But he chose to end the relationship before you got the chance to tell him?'

'Yes.'

'Did he give you a reason?'

'His wife had found a message,' I say. 'And she made him tell her everything, so he did.'

My voice comes out like a croak. Chris is all around me. I can smell his cedarwood cologne, see his eyes narrow as he leans towards me, takes my hand and says: *It's Helen. She knows.*

And with those words I knew it was over. Given a choice between his dependable wife and his flighty mistress, I was always going to come away the loser.

'He agreed to break it off. Give their marriage another chance.'

'That must have been a shock,' says Shaw, looking at me intently.

'To be honest, I just felt numb,' I say.

And it's true. I did. They say emotional shock doesn't strike until long after the event and as I sat there listening to him I found myself smiling. Jesus, I even agreed with him. I didn't storm out of the restaurant or throw a glass of wine in his face or tell him that he was a bastard, I just sat there and ate my risotto and told him that, yes, this was all for the best.

'Why didn't you tell him about the baby?' asks Shaw.

'I couldn't.'

Looking back now I guess I was paralysed with grief. Yes, I could have told him about the baby, but it all felt so wrong, so tainted. He didn't want me. He wouldn't want our baby either.

'And what did you do then?'

Something tells me she knows the answer.

'I went to my club on Greek Street.'

'And is that where you drank the wine?'

'Yes.'

'How much did you drink?'

'A couple of glasses. But before then I hadn't drunk for . . . some time.'

We stare at each other for a moment, doctor and patient, both taking in the seriousness of my admission, not mentioning the big things like babies and birth defects and safe limits.

'And when you returned to the office you lost your temper with Rachel Hadley?'

'Yes,' I say. 'Can you understand it now?'

Shaw doesn't answer.

'How long did you stay in the hospital?'

'Just a night,' I reply. 'The bleeding slowed down over the course of the morning and by midday it became clear that I would be bed blocking if I stayed any longer. They prescribed me a course of strong painkillers and I left.'

'And then?'

'I walked home. I wanted to think.'

'Taking a detour by the Star cafe?'

'Yes,' I reply. 'I didn't really know where I was going though. I just needed to think.'

'When the police finished talking to you, did you go home?'

'Yes.'

I think back to that evening. The scent of the hospital clung to my canvas rucksack as I climbed the stairs. I can smell it now as I sit here. Hospitals and police cells have the same scent – a mix of chlorine and despair. When I opened the door to the flat my phone rang. It was Graham asking if I'd received the itinerary. And I pretended I was fine; that my world hadn't just fallen apart. I told him I would see him in the morning and then I curled up into bed and cried myself to sleep.

'I went to Syria the following day,' I say, looking up at Shaw. 'With Graham, my photographer.'

She looks flabbergasted.

'The next day?' she exclaims. 'Even though you'd just had a miscarriage?'

'Women lose babies every day, Dr Shaw,' I tell her. 'This is my job. People were relying on me to go out there.'

'Who was relying on you?'

'The morning of the miscarriage I'd got a message from my close friend,' I tell her. 'He's a translator I've known for years and he told me that terrible things were happening in Aleppo. I felt I needed to go back and find out what was going on. I couldn't live with myself if I didn't.'

'So apart from the translator, it was just going to be you and the photographer crossing the border into Syria?'

'Yes.'

'Did that concern you?'

'No. We'd done this many, many times before. Graham was highly experienced and we'd worked together a lot over the years.'

'And Chris? Did you let him know you were going?'

'No, I didn't tell Chris I was going. Why would I? We were over.'

'And how would you describe your mental state at this point, as you prepared to return to Syria?'

'My mental state?'

'How were you feeling?' she goes on. 'Were you happy, fearful, nervous?'

I shake my head.

'I was numb, Dr Shaw,' I say. 'Completely and utterly numb.'

20

Friday 17 April 2015

I am sitting at the table in my mother's kitchen watching Paul as he prepares lunch. I haven't mentioned last night. Part of me still isn't sure it really happened. Although the soil I found on the kitchen floor this morning tells me it must have. And even now, as I sit here with the back door open, I can smell my blood dream: a faint whisper of death.

'I've bookmarked a shortlist for you to have a look at,' Paul says, his face moistening as he stands over a vat of steaming hot soup, pulverizing the liquid with a shiny chrome blender. Apparently he got the morning off work and thought it might be nice if we spent it looking at bathroom suites. Not exactly my idea of fun, but according to him a new bathroom will make all the difference once Mum's house goes on the market.

I look at the small black laptop that sits on the table in front of me. Paul has kindly opened up the bookmarked web pages and now it is down to me to decide between the gleaming white 'Sorrel' suite, the off-white hexagonal 'Myriad', the silvery-grey 'Bartley' and, the wild card, a burnt-orange number named 'Sienna'. They all look fine to me and are similar in price. I told Paul that I would foot the bill for the bathroom. He has done so much already, it's the least I can do.

'I think we should go for the Myriad,' I say, moving the laptop to one side as he places a large bowl of vegetable soup in front of me. It smells sweet and nutty and my stomach growls with hunger. I hadn't been able to face breakfast as, no matter how much I had scrubbed, the stench of the blood dream seemed to cling to my skin.

'Are you sure the shape won't put people off?' asks Paul, taking the seat opposite me. He slices a hunk of bread from a granary loaf and places it on my plate. 'Here, I got the seeded stuff from the fancy bakery for you.'

'Thanks,' I say. 'That's really sweet of you.'

I take the bread and dip a little into the soup.

'I like the shape,' I say, putting the bread in my mouth. 'Sharp edges are good. You should see my apartment, it's one big sharp edge.'

'That doesn't surprise me,' says Paul. He pauses to slurp his soup. 'I bet it's all minimalist and white, your place.'

'Yes, it is,' I reply. 'It's my reaction against all the chintz I grew up with.'

'I'll have to see it some time, your flat,' says Paul. 'Bring Sally too,' he adds. 'Make a day of it.'

'You're more than welcome,' I reply. 'But I can't see Sally making the trip. I've lived in that flat for almost fifteen years and she hasn't visited me once.'

'Well, I'd like to see it one day,' he says. 'You can show me the sights of Soho.'

He laughs awkwardly and we sit for a few moments in uncomfortable silence.

I take a mouthful of the soup. It has cooled slightly and tepid soup makes me queasy at the best of times. I put my spoon down and play with a morsel of bread.

'Anyway, where were we?' says Paul, pulling the laptop towards him. 'The Myriad. If you're happy with it, I'm happy to trust your better judgement. I'll order it this afternoon and we can settle up later.'

'Great,' I say. 'I'll write you a cheque before you go.'

'Are you finished?' he says, gesturing to my half-empty bowl.

'Yes, thank you,' I reply, handing it to him. 'It was lovely.'

'Fancy a coffee?' he asks as he balances the bowls and plates in the crook of his arm and takes them over to the sink.

'Yes please,' I reply, pulling the laptop over to have another look at the 'Myriad' bathroom suite. I try to imagine what it would look like in my mother's bathroom. I think back to this morning when I stood in the mildewed pink bath holding the sorry excuse for a showerhead over my body with one hand while using the other hand to scrub at my skin with a sliver of carbolic soap. Yes, I think, as Paul returns to the table with the coffee pot, the 'Myriad' is a very good idea.

As we sit, Paul pulls the computer towards him and opens up Facebook. 'Just got to check my messages,' he says.

'Oh, I didn't know you were on it,' I say as he clicks on the message icon.

'It's the lads at work got me into it,' he says. 'It's okay for a bit of banter I suppose. They send me all these silly videos. You'd probably find them a bit immature but it gives us a laugh.'

Why do people bother, I ask myself, as Paul gets up again and opens the back door to take the bin out. What purpose does it serve to paste your life on a website for all to see? I think of Rachel Hadley and her burgeoning Twitter page and my stomach knots.

In the corner of the screen there is a box that reads, 'People you may know,' and I scroll through the faces, happy that I don't know any of them. Without thinking, I find myself typing a familiar name into the search bar, safe in the knowledge that the man I love would never parade himself on a site like this. But then there it is. His name. And I feel my fingers calcify as I click on it and see the life he has chosen over me.

His profile picture, taken at some sort of family gathering, shows him, suited and smart, with his arm draped round a pretty, fresh-faced woman with short blonde hair. I take a closer look. She looks rather Sloaney in her lilac pashmina, all white teeth and rosy cheeks; like a young Lady Di. I click on the image and a page full of photographs comes up. One by one they tell the story he had always been too scared to share with me.

On I go, while outside the window Paul clatters the lid of the wheelie bin. My finger becomes stiff as I click through image after interminable image. I walk beside him as he celebrates his wedding anniversary in the same restaurant in Mayfair he had taken me to when he returned from a long stint in Uganda. My skin prickles as I enlarge a photo of his wife, eyes glazed with alcohol, draped across the green banquette seats. My hand trembles as I click on another image. This one shows his wife lying on a secluded beach, holding a glass of champagne towards the camera.

'I'm not one for holidays,' he had told me as we lay naked, entwined in each other's arms, in a bombed-out Iraqi hotel. 'How can anybody want to travel for pleasure any more? How can we ever forget the things we've seen?'

His voice pierces my eardrum with its deceit. I want to rip it out and stamp on it until it expires right here on my mother's kitchen floor. He lied to me, all those years he told me he didn't love his wife; that they lived separate lives; that nobody in the world would ever understand him as well as I did. And all the time I was pining for him he was living it up in shabby-chic heaven with Helen.

Almost without thinking, I click on his wife's name — it is displayed in blue type beneath her photograph. Helen pouts moodily in a single black-and-white profile picture. Further down the page there's a link to a website called Carrington & Miller. I click on the link and discover that she co-owns a homeware shop with her best friend, Della. Images of baby-pink bunting and Union Jack sofa cushions float across the page along with toe-curling posters extolling all to 'Keep Calm and Carry On'. The whole thing drips with saccharine and I feel sick.

I close the window and return to the Facebook page. I enlarge Helen's cover photograph and my stomach lurches as I see him, champagne glass in hand, at some street party. I look closer and read the caption underneath: 'Harrogate Celebrates the Royal Wedding.' What the fuck? This is the man who sat up with me through the night lambasting the establishment and raising a toast to the republic of the future, and here he is grinning like a fool in a lurid pink party hat. I scroll further and see the interior of their smart town house; his daughters, preppy, all teeth and backcombed hair, sitting astride horses. I see his life through the eyes of his wife and I realize I have spent the last ten years making love to a stranger.

'Sorry about that, the bin was overflowing,' says Paul as he comes back in. 'Coffee should be nicely brewed now.'

The smell of the coffee clashes with the bitter taste inside my mouth: the remains of the blood dream. It burns through my skin and rises up my gullet with such violence I think I might pass out. Scraping the chair back, I run from the table, up the stairs and reach the bathroom just in time.

'Kate?'

I hear Paul's voice as I kneel on the floor and vomit it all up: the smell, the coffee, the soup, the champagne flute in Helen's hand, the daughters on their horses and the unconditional love on Chris's face as he stood beside her. I heave and heave it all up until there is nothing left but the taste of my own despair.

'Kate, are you okay?'

I feel the warmth of his hand on the base of my back and I spring to my feet before the tears can come. I need air and noise and nothingness to block out the searing pain that is coiling round my chest.

'I'm fine,' I whisper as I stagger to my feet and dab my mouth with the wedge of toilet paper that Paul has handed me. 'I just need to rest.'

'Why don't you go and have a lie-down?' he says. He is standing in the doorway, his face ashen with concern. 'I'll bring you a glass of water.'

I silently implore him to stop being nice. I can deal with anything right now except kindness. Kindness will end me.

'No, honestly, Paul,' I say, squeezing past him and making my way downstairs. 'I just need to be alone for a bit.'

I grab my bag and take out my chequebook.

'Don't be silly,' he says, following me into the kitchen. 'We can settle that later.'

'No, it's fine,' I say as I scribble out a cheque and hand it to him. 'I'll only forget if I don't do it now.'

'Are you sure you're going to be okay?' he asks, taking the cheque and putting it in his back pocket. 'I can stay a bit longer if you want to talk.'

'Please stop worrying,' I tell him as we walk to the front door. 'I'm fine.'

'Well, you know where I am if you need me,' he says. 'Call me any time.'

'Thanks,' I mumble as I open the door.

'Oh and if you're still up for it,' he says, lingering on the threshold, 'I'll meet you at Neptune's Arm tomorrow. Shall we say eleven?'

I have no idea what he is talking about. I just want him to go.

'The trip to Reculver,' he says.

'Oh, that,' I say, guiding him out of the door. 'I forgot all about it.'

He looks at me and frowns. 'Are you sure you're okay? You look so pale. I just hope I haven't poisoned you with my soup. It was a Nigella recipe as well.'

'No, no, Paul, the soup was perfect,' I say, trying with all my might to suppress the sobs that are wavering at the back of my throat. 'It's just . . . me.'

'I'll leave you to rest,' he says, patting me on my arm. 'Take care, yeah?'

He walks down the driveway and gets into his car and I watch as he drives away past the neat boxed gardens and modest semi-detached houses. This is life, I tell myself as I close the door. Not war and disease and burnt-out hotels, but men and women in their boxes with their babies and their coffee makers and their holidays, this is what real life should look like. It's what Chris's life looks like. And I am on the edge of it all, a ghost with no foundations, no roots. As I step back into my mother's dark house and close the door, I feel like the last person left on earth.

The phone lies on the floor beside me and I watch as its screen darkens on the unsent message. He still won't pick up, so all I'm left with is my own bitterness and hate. I've spent the evening trying to express it in a text message but my words are coming out wrong. The first text was a barrage of hurt and anger at his hypocrisy, his cowardice, his double standards and his appalling taste in party hats. Then I changed my mind, deleted, and started another one. And now, after the third attempt, I have given up. A text is too small a medium to relay all that I want to say to Chris. And there is dignity in silence, I think, as I pick up the phone and wipe the final text.

It's late, but I can't face my bed. The old woman waits for me there. So I take my warm sweater, wrap it round my shoulders and head downstairs. After a handful of sleeping pills I decamp to the firm green armchair. Sitting here brings me closer to my mother; its threadbare arms feel like her embrace as I sit here sinking into its folds, darkness swallowing the house.

I try not to think about Chris but he is everywhere. I can smell his skin – a mixture of sweat and cedarwood – as I curl up in the chair.

We came from such different worlds. He'd had a happy, middle-class upbringing in Yorkshire. His parents were teachers and they had brought up their four boys in a rambling farmhouse deep in the Dales. It's where Chris discovered his love of forensics. I remember him telling me the story so clearly. When he was eight years old he had found a bone sticking out of the ground. He'd pulled it out and couldn't believe the size of it. The next day he came back to the spot with his father's spade and began to dig. After a few hours he'd excavated a huge skeleton. It was later confirmed to be that of a Clydesdale horse that had been lost in a storm some fifty years previously. Over time its body had sunk back into the ground. It had fascinated Chris how a set of bones could reveal a mystery that had lain unsolved for years and the discovery changed his life. He knew then what he wanted to be when he grew up and he set about achieving it. His parents supported him through university; encouraged his dreams. And as far as I know they still do. Last I heard they were still living in the same old farmhouse. Of course, I've never met them. They don't know I exist. But I imagine their home to be full of framed photographs of their children and grandchildren; there will be a big wooden table where they all gather at Christmas and a roaring open fire to keep everyone warm.

That was Chris's childhood. Warm and secure. The total opposite of mine.

And he tried to recreate that childhood for his own kids. But then he met me and I turned everything upside down. I was his secret; his buried bones; the mystery he just had to solve.

My eyes grow heavy but as I close them Nidal is there, clutching his scrapbook.

'*Tusbih 'alá khayr*, Kate.'

'*Tusbih 'alá khayr*, Nidal. What are you doing today?'

'I'm making a book.'

'That sounds wonderful. What's it called?'

'It is called the book of smiles.'

And as I sink deeper into sleep, flimsy paper cut-outs flutter around my head: I see a beaming boy standing on a fairy-tale bridge; I see the sugary pink towers of Disneyland glistening in Technicolor sunshine and Mickey Mouse gambolling across a lush green meadow.

'I want that.'

I hear Nidal's voice but I can't see him. All I can see are his pictures.

'You want Disneyland?'

'No. I want that. To be the boy on the bridge. You help me.'

178

'I can't see you, Nidal.'

'Help me.'

'Nidal, where are you?'

His voice is closer. He's right next to me. If I reach out I can touch him.

'Help me.'

I stretch out my arms towards the voice and I feel myself falling. There's a loud bang and when I open my eyes I'm lying in a heap on the living-room floor.

'Just a dream,' I reassure myself as I haul myself up. 'Just another sodding dream.'

Sweat clings to my forehead and I wipe it with the back of my hand as I step out into the hallway. The air is salty and a breeze flutters across my bare feet. Then, as consciousness returns, I hear it: *thud, thud.*

'Who's there?'

The words come instinctively. The human body knows when it is alone, truly alone, and when another being is nearby, every nerve, every muscle reacts accordingly. As I creep down the hallway I take a cursory glance around to see if there is something I can arm myself with and I grab my mother's old wooden clock from the sideboard. It's the closest thing to hand.

If there is an intruder then one crack on the correct part of the head will be enough to disable him. Holding the clock tightly in my hands, I slowly make my way to the kitchen. The sound grows louder as I approach. *Thud, thud, thud.* It falls in step with my heart as I reach the kitchen door and prepare to launch myself at whoever is in there. I take a deep breath and slowly count to three. One, two, three —

I burst into the kitchen ready to fight. With the clock raised above my head I let out a scream of fear and relief. The room is empty, and nothing, as far as I can see, has been touched. Except the door, which is wide open. And the cool evening breeze that had drifted into the living room and tickled my feet is now blowing it open and shut. *Thud, thud, thud.*

Moving slowly towards it, I stand on the step and call out into the empty garden. 'Who's there?'

The sky is moonless and the darkness makes me feel vulnerable as I step out. I push my hair out of my eyes with the back of my hand so I can see clearly. I should have brought my torch, I tell myself, as I hear Harry's voice through the gloom. 'If you ever need a spare torch,' he used to chuckle, 'just ask Kate. She's got enough to supply a whole army.' And he was right. In my job a torch is a necessity I can't live without. I have hundreds of them. And here I am standing in the darkness with only an old wooden clock to light my way.

I put the clock down and creep towards the fence, my hands shaking as I pull myself on to the plastic chair and look into next-door's garden. Everything is still and silent. The house is in darkness and the shed just an ordinary garden shed. No noise, no movement, no face at the window.

What is happening to me?

I stand there for a few moments longer, but all is still. I have to sleep. Perhaps the stress of everything is getting to me.

I go back inside and double bolt the kitchen door.

But as I reach the stairs I catch a glimpse of myself in the hallway mirror. There's something on my face. I step forward to take a closer look. There are rusty red smears across my cheeks. What is it? I go to wipe my face and then I see that it's on my hands too. I smell it. It's blood. Dried blood. My heart starts to pound. I check for cuts or grazes – maybe I scratched it on the fence. But there's nothing.

My mind feels like it's shutting down. How can this be? I am standing here covered in someone else's blood.

21

Herne Bay Police Station

35 hours detained

'I'm sorry, Kate, but I'd really like to talk about your last visit to Syria,' says Shaw softly. 'I think it's important.'

I immediately tense. The woman won't give up. The whole interview, I realize now – these past thirty-odd hours – has been a prelude to this. Shaw doesn't care about sleeping pills. She doesn't care about Polish waitresses. What she *is* interested in is what happened in Syria. It's Syria that has sent me mad. Or at least that's what she thinks.

'I told you. I'm not going to talk about Syria.'

Shaw leans forward in her chair and looks at me.

'Kate, we *have* to talk about it if I'm to make a full assessment. Do you understand?'

I look at her. Her face is expressionless. She has no idea how hard this is for me.

'Kate, if I can't make a full assessment then the alternative is –'

'That I'm stuck in here for good?' I say, interrupting her.

'No,' she says. 'But we would need to take you to hospital for further assessment. Look, I know this is terribly distressing for you but it really is crucial for me to ask these questions.'

She's right. I know that. Still, it doesn't make it any easier.

'Okay,' I say quietly. 'Let's do it. But can we be quick about it?'

'We can take a break at any point,' says Shaw, opening her notebook. 'If you feel it's getting too much, just say and we'll pause.'

I nod my head.

'Right,' she says, her voice gentler than before. 'Can I begin by asking why you decided to return to Syria? It seems odd that you would choose to go when you were obviously in such mental and physical distress.'

'What do you mean?' I ask, trying to stay focused.

'Well,' continues Shaw, 'we've spoken about the incidents with Rachel Hadley and Rosa Dunajski and I know that you're taking some pretty strong antipsychotic medication. Surely, in such a fragile state, it would seem ill-advised to travel to a place as volatile as Syria?'

'You make it sound like I was booking a package holiday, Dr Shaw,' I reply. 'Nobody *advised* me because I'm a senior reporter. I know what I'm doing because it's my job, a job I've done without any trouble for almost twenty years.'

Shaw writes something in her notebook. I know she thinks I'm unstable. I have to stay strong; I have to show her that I'm not what she thinks.

'Can you tell me what happened on 29th March?' she asks, without looking up. 'I understand that was your last day in Aleppo?'

'Yes,' I say. 'It was.'

'And there was an incident?'

'Is that what you'd call it?' I reply, no longer able to keep the contempt from my voice.

'What happened, Kate?'

'Look,' I say firmly. 'Why are you asking me about this? You know what happened. The fucking world knows what happened.'

'I'd like you to tell me,' she says coolly, ignoring my outburst. 'As I said, I need you to tell me everything so we can complete the assessment.'

'Oh yes, the assessment,' I say drily. 'Never mind that a young boy is in serious danger, let's just carry on with our box ticking so you can make me out to be some sort of nutter.'

'Kate, talking like that isn't going to help anyone.'

I look at the clock above her head. I've been here almost two days. Who knows what they'll have done to him in this time?

'Kate?'

'Okay, Dr Shaw,' I exclaim, admitting defeat. 'Where would you like me to begin?'

'How about the morning of the 29th?'

My hands feel clammy as I clasp them together and try to gather my thoughts. There is no escape. I will have to talk about it, the event I have spent the last few weeks trying to erase from my mind. I lean forward in the chair and take a deep breath then slowly start to speak.

'Okay,' I begin, in as calm a voice as I can muster. 'As Harry told you, we were staying in a basement below a grocery store along with a Syrian family.'

'Khaled and Zaynah Safar?'

'Yes,' I reply. 'And their young son, Nidal.'

I'm trembling. I can't stop. I grip the side of the chair with both my hands as I continue.

'We'd been there a week,' I tell her. 'It was utter devastation. In the few months since my last visit the city had been reduced to dust and rubble. Electricity and water were in short supply and there were mass food shortages. The streets were no-go areas. It was hell.'

'What a terribly dangerous situation to be in,' says Shaw, her eyes widening.

'Yes,' I reply. 'But this is what ordinary people in Syria are dealing with every day. As a journalist it was my duty to witness it, to record it and let the world know what was happening.'

'But in the light of your recent ill health perhaps you weren't in the best mental state to be undertaking such a risky assignment?' suggests Shaw tentatively.

'I've told you I was fine,' I say. 'We can't all wrap ourselves in cotton wool and hide behind fucking notebooks.'

She says nothing, just flicks her pen between finger and thumb.

My chest tightens and I rub it as I stand up and walk to the window.

'You asked me to tell you about the last day,' I say, turning to look at Shaw who, I notice, has now closed her notebook. 'May I do that now?'

'Yes, of course,' she says, watching me as I return to my seat. Is that a note of excitement I detect in her voice?

'Thank you,' I say, keeping my voice calm as I sit down and try again.

'My photographer Graham and I had spent the morning in downtown Aleppo interviewing a family whose house had been bombed overnight. Graham's photographs were to lead that Sunday's dispatch. I was in the middle of writing it up when I heard a banging in the corridor outside the room. I looked out and saw Nidal. He was kicking a football at the wall.'

I close my eyes and there he is: a thin, wiry boy wearing an over-sized Brazil football shirt. I blink the image away and continue.

'I went to close the door then I heard his father's voice. They started arguing.'

'What were they arguing about?'

'Khaled was worried that Nidal was making too much noise,' I tell her. 'He was concerned that he would attract the attention of the soldiers outside. He wanted him to come back into the room.'

I close my eyes and see Khaled's tired face and Nidal's defiant one.

'Go on, Kate.'

I hold my hands in my lap, trying to control the shaking.

'I came out of my room to see if everything was all right. Nidal saw me and started to cry. He said he just wanted to play football and be normal again. He said he was sick of being kept in a prison.'

'And what did you say to him?'

'I told him to calm down. I explained that his father was tired and that he should do as he said and leave the ball game for now.'

I take a sip of water and look at the clock. My body starts to tingle all over and I realize it's been over forty hours since I last had a sleeping pill. I scratch at my injured arm. Shaw notices and looks at it disapprovingly.

'You told him to calm down,' she says. 'And did he listen to you?'

The itching becomes worse and I pull my sleeve up and scratch furiously at my mottled skin. I can smell the street dust on my clothes, in my hair, on my skin. I can hear him screaming. It's unbearable but I have to go on; I have no choice.

'No, he didn't listen,' I say, tugging down my sleeve. 'He started to yell and said that he hated his father, hated me, that we couldn't keep him locked up like this. That he wanted to leave. Then his father lost his temper.'

I hear Khaled's voice, low and ominous as he grabbed his son's collar: *You think there is time for football if you are refugee, huh? If you are refugee you are treated like vermin, like shit. Is that what you want, boy, is it?*

'I don't blame him,' I go on. 'The poor man was scared and exhausted and Nidal just wouldn't give up. Khaled went back into his room when he saw me. He thought Nidal would be safe with me. He trusted me.'

He's here again, right here in the room with me. His little face is wretched with fear and rage and disappointment. Shaw clears her throat and shuffles impatiently in

187

her chair. I continue my recollection as Nidal watches me from the corner of the room.

'It all just happened so fast,' I say, feeling his hot skin brush against my arm. 'I tried. I really tried but he was in such a state and then he . . .'

'Then he what?'

The blood pounding through my head merges with the voices. Nidal's. Khaled's. Graham's. They are so loud I can barely hear what she is saying.

'Kate.'

She leans forward in her chair and puts her hand on my arm. It's a gentle, steadying gesture and it takes me by surprise.

'Just take it slowly,' she says. 'We have plenty of time.'

I know that's not true. I know that time is running out and I have to fight against the voices and tell her what happened.

'He ran away,' I say, my voice a whisper. 'He ran out of the basement and out into the street and he was so fast I couldn't stop him. I just couldn't stop him.'

2 2

Saturday 18 April 2015

Paul is waiting by the benches on Neptune's Arm. He has dressed for the weather in a thick padded coat and hiking boots that wouldn't look out of place on the front line. He has a bulky rucksack with him, I presume packed with provisions for the day.

'I thought a picnic might be nice,' he says as he comes to greet me. 'Out on the beach.'

'It's not really the weather for picnics, though, is it?' I say doubtfully, looking up at the grey clouds gathering overhead.

'We should be okay,' he says, following my gaze. 'There's a sliver of blue sky over Reculver.'

He points towards the far end of the shoreline where the towers are peeking out from the cliffs. I can't see any blue sky. I have no idea how he can be so relentlessly optimistic.

'Come on then, let's go,' I say as we walk down the steps to the seafront.

I still feel uneasy about last night. The noise. The blood. I'd stripped off my clothes and stood in the shower, searching every inch of my body for a cut. But it was like it had come from nowhere. And once it had all washed down the plughole, how could I even be sure it had been there?

I'm tempted to tell Paul my concerns. But I don't want to worry him. He's got enough on his plate at the moment with Sally. I pause to fasten my ancient parka. Its padding feels like a blanket as the sea air whips into my face.

'God, it's freezing,' I say as I hurry to catch up with Paul. 'I'd forgotten how cold it gets by the sea.'

'We'll be fine once we get a stride on,' he says. 'Soon warm up.'

I quicken my step to keep up with him.

'You sound like my mother,' I shout, my voice a thin reed fluttering in the searing wind.

'You calling me an old woman?' he laughs as the wind almost blows his scarf away. 'Cheeky mare.'

Climbing up to the wide path that will take us towards the cliffs, we are met by a trail of bright pink mussel shells that crunch underfoot as we walk. I stop to pick one up and marvel at its fuchsia hue. Turning it over in my hands, I lay it in my palm; it looks like a tiny broken heart. I scrape the sand from its centre and place it in my pocket. As we continue up the path I put my hands inside the warm folds of material and rub the coarse shell with my fingers. It is strangely comforting.

Paul has gone striding ahead and I run to join him, the blood pumping vigorously through my body. The air is clean and I drink great gulps of it down into my lungs as I go, feeling myself opening up with every breath I take. Up ahead, I see Paul standing on a narrow wooden bridge that connects the path to the steps that lead to the clifftops.

'I remember this bit,' I say as I catch up with him and we climb up the steep steps into a narrow country lane fringed with bracken. 'It always used to scare me.'

'Why's that?' asks Paul.

He has fallen in behind me and I can hear the quick puffs of his shallow breath as he walks.

'It's just so enclosed,' I say. 'It's like, now, I can feel you behind me, but that's fine because I know it's you. But if I were here alone and felt someone walking behind it would spook me. There are too many curves, too many hiding places for people to jump out of.'

'What, you mean people like Alexandra?' says Paul, putting on a silly voice. 'Woo, woo.'

'Stop it,' I say, without looking back, 'or I'll summon her. Then you'll be sorry.'

I am relieved when the path opens up into a wide stretch of meadow and we pick up our pace. Gorse bushes cluster amongst the grass, with tiny shimmering yellow flowers dotted across their stubby fingers like jewels. In the distance a cockerel crows and I stop to listen.

'The farms,' says Paul, nodding his head to the east. 'There are loads of them beyond the hedge.'

I smile as I remember going to visit the farm with Mum. We got a guided tour from the farmer's wife and ended up having our tea there. I think Mum had been to school with her. We left with a basketful of eggs and cheese and fresh milk. Mum was so happy that day; genuinely happy, not like the pretend smile she wore when we went to the beach.

The low groan of a cow answers the cockerel's call and as we walk on I think of my mother, the country girl who had spent her life trapped in suburbia. She deserved more than what she got.

'There they are,' cries Paul.

He puts his hand out and points towards the shore-line. 'The towers. Aren't they spectacular?'

I look up and see the two towers of Reculver rising ominously out of the cliffs, the only remains of the Roman fort that had once guarded the bay from unwanted intruders.

'The sisters,' I whisper as we start to walk again with the towers as our guide. 'That's what we used to call them. I'd forgotten how beautiful they are.'

The wind pummels our faces as we walk towards the towers and I pull my hood up round my face to shield it from the biting cold. The site is heaving with day trip-pers and we have to wriggle our way through groups of tourists and harassed parents who are guiding their small children away from the edge of the cliff. It is a lot busier than it was when I was a child. Back then the only attrac-tions had been the towers and the beach below where the bouncing bomb had been tested in 1943. Now there is a visitor information centre with a shop selling T-shirts and mugs and bottles of striped humbugs, and further up the hill an ice-cream van is doing a roaring trade from the queue of small children snaking its way around the path.

Paul goes on ahead and climbs over the low wire fence heading for the side of the towers. The wind is fierce up here and I steady myself as we walk towards what would have been the main entrance of the fort. From this angle it doesn't look like a ruin but a beautiful complete building, its V-shaped facade dwarfed by the towers on either side. An optical illusion that's just as breathtaking now as it was when I first saw it. I see Paul's head darting in and out of the stones and as I walk towards him the building appears to crumble, spilling its rubble behind it like entrails hanging from a slaughtered body.

I step back to let a group of tourists past. They are following a tall man in a black trilby hat and frock coat. He speaks in a loud theatrical voice as he leads them deeper inside the ruins.

'It's been said that these towers are one of the most active sites in Kent for paranormal activity,' he booms.

The tourists follow him, open-mouthed, as he continues. 'You must agree there is a deeply disturbing presence here.' He looks at them expectantly and they nod in unison. A woman in a purple waistcoat takes a photograph but the guide puts out a gloved hand. 'Perhaps later. We don't want to disturb the inhabitants.'

Paul jumps down from the rock he is standing on and comes to join me by the information board.

'He's talking about the children,' he whispers, leaning towards me, and I shiver at the coldness of his breath on my neck.

'Oh, that old story,' I say, turning to face him. 'Are they still trotting it out?'

I remember the tales of the children that were supposedly buried alive in the foundations of the fort. The legend was that they had been offered up as a sacrifice to consecrate the building. On dark and stormy nights their screams could be heard in the grounds of the fort. It was the usual fodder designed to lure tourists to the site.

'You have to admit there is an odd feeling here, though,' says Paul as we abandon the noticeboard and walk towards the cliff edge. 'I certainly felt it as a kid. Once, I even thought I heard something.'

'What did you hear?'

I duck as a sand martin darts past my head.

'Voices. Screams. I can hear them now. Can you?'

I look at him. He is winding me up, surely? But his face is deadly serious.

'The only screams I can hear are those of the parents who've just been charged a tenner for a couple of ice creams,' I say, laughing shakily. 'I don't believe in the supernatural, Paul, and I don't believe that the Romans buried their children alive in these towers.'

'Why not? They threw Christians to the lions.' Paul grimaces. 'Can you imagine being buried alive?'

'No, I can't,' I say as a shiver flutters through me. 'Hey, Paul, speaking of children, have you managed to ask the letting agent about the people at number 44 yet? About the boy?'

'I haven't had the chance, Kate,' he says. 'Work's been mental recently and to be honest . . .' He goes quiet and shakes his head.

'What?' I ask him. 'What were you about to say?'

'It doesn't matter,' he says. 'It was nothing.'

'Please,' I say. 'Just tell me.'

'Well, it's just that . . . well, I understand,' he says. 'I mean, it's natural after all you've been through.'

'What's natural?'

'Hearing things, seeing things,' he says, lowering his voice. 'It's the grief, isn't it? I've read about it. It was a boy, wasn't it, in Syria?'

'I know what I saw, Paul,' I say, anger rising through me. 'I know it was real.'

'Look, don't get yourself upset,' he says, taking my hand. 'I'll talk to the letting agent as soon as I can, yeah? Put your mind at rest. Now, come on. How about we go down to the beach and have our picnic? I don't know about you but I'm starving.'

23

We jostle through the tourists and make our way down the steps to the beach. And as my feet sink into the sand and the smell of the sea fills the air I hear her.

Come on, girls, sandwiches!

I follow her voice to a secluded spot where Paul stands unfolding a giant tartan beach rug.

One more page, Mum, then I'll be there.

Paul opens his rucksack and brings out flasks of hot tea, sandwiches wrapped in tinfoil and a round biscuit tin full of shortbread, my favourite.

Don't be scaring yourself silly now, love. Put the book away and come and have some cake.

I sit down on the blanket, take the flask and pour myself a cup of hot tea while Paul unwraps a sandwich.

Now, let's talk about nice things.

I sip the tea and feel its goodness trickle down my throat, filling my body with wholesomeness. For once Paul is quiet, and I lie back on the rug.

The sea air is making me sleepy and I close my eyes. I can hear the waves whispering in the distance and my mother's soothing words.

See, told you it would do you good.

I have spent the last few days trying to locate my mother in that house when all along she has been here, deep amongst the ruins on Reculver beach.

As the sound of the sea lulls me to sleep I see him. He is out on the street with his football; his back to me. I pound my fists on the window.

'Look up, Nidal! For God's sake look up.'

But he is lost in his game and can't hear me.

'Look up, child. Please look up.'

A man's voice speaks over mine. Graham.

'We have to tell his parents, Kate.'

'No, wait. I can help him.'

He runs towards the ball and kicks it high into the air. It hits the ground and bounces into the road with such force that a cloud of dust rises in the air. He goes to run after it but when he looks up his face contorts. He has seen them.

'Nidal!'

He is frozen in the road, his thin arms raised above his head. He is terrified and I am here, trapped behind glass.

'Kate, help me.'

I smash my fists against the window but it won't break.

'Help me.'

Eventually the glass yields and I fall with it, down, down, on to soft sand. When I open my eyes, Paul is standing there above me.

'Come on, sleepy head, time we headed back.'

'I must have nodded off,' I say as I get to my feet. 'What time is it?'

'Almost four,' he says, his voice agitated. 'I fell asleep too. We really should go, tide's coming in. Mist too.'

I look towards the cliffs and realize I can't see them. The fog has obscured most of the route back.

My head feels thick and I wonder how long I've been asleep.

'Come on,' calls Paul as he heads up the beach. 'Quick, before the water rises.' He's soon lost in the fog.

I grab my coat and fling it round my shoulders, then stumble across the rocks in the direction Paul went in. But after a few steps I lose my footing and fall face down into the shingle. My legs are wobbly, the dream still working its effects.

'Kate!'

I can hear Paul but I can't see him. I want to call him back but my head hurts and I feel dizzy. I feel drunk. What is wrong with me? I have to stop taking those pills.

Finally I pull myself to standing and start to stumble towards where I think the path was.

Suddenly through a gap in the mist I see him.

'Get to the rocks,' yells Paul. He's on the far side of the beach, gesturing with his arms. In between us a churning sea of water has somehow appeared. 'Don't walk this way. I only just managed to get over. You need to head to your left; to the rocks.'

Then he disappears again behind a wall of mist. Sea-water laps around my ankles as the beach slowly disappears. I am trapped against the rocks.

'Climb up!' yells Paul from somewhere to my left.

The wind whips water into my face as I try to get my foot on to the rocks and I am blinded. Wiping my eyes with the back of my hands serves only to blur my vision even more as my mascara loosens off in thick black clumps. The water is rising and I know I will have to get out of here soon or risk being swept away. I grab hold of a sharp rock that's jutting out and heave my body on to it. It's no wider than my foot and won't hold me, I'm sure of it, but somehow it does and I stay there immobile while inches below me the water thrashes angrily.

A sheer cliff face rises above me, leading to the towers. I need to climb it. But as I look up, panic surges through my exhausted body. There are no ledges, just a smooth surface. There is no way I can get to the top. I think of the tourists up at the towers. Maybe if I call out one of them will hear me.

But my voice is a whisper against the surging sea and I close my eyes and try to summon my strength. Then I hear him again.

'Kate.'

Paul. I open my eyes and look up to the top of the cliff.

'Kate.'

He's far away, but it must be him. It is. I can see him, vaguely, through the mist. He is holding his hand out. I hear him telling me to climb.

'There are no ledges,' I cry. 'I won't be able to get a grip.'

'Okay, listen to me,' he yells above the howling wind. 'You need to jump down . . . tread through . . . before it gets too high. There's another way you can get up.'

I look down at the water. Even on this ledge it is almost at my knees.

'I can't,' I cry back.

'. . . have to, Kate . . . only way.'

'Tell me what to do,' I shout. My mouth fills with salty water and I spit it out on to the rocks.

'Wade through . . .' he shouts. '. . . to your left . . . boulders . . .'

His voice follows me in snatches from above as I wade into the water. It is thick with mud and I have to lift each foot high to avoid sinking into the slime. The mist enfolds me glutinously as I search for the boulders.

'There,' he shouts. Paul is running along the top of the cliff, observing my floundering.

Finally I see the boulders and trudge towards them. The water is rising and my legs feel like lead.

'Climb up . . . there's a ledge. Go on, Kate, hurry.'

The boulder is covered in saturated seaweed and at first my hand slides down it as I try to climb up. I try again, this time using my elbows too, and finally get a grip. I haul myself up and stand on the top of it, catching my breath and looking back at the rising water.

'Quick,' he shouts. 'It'll be over your head in less than a minute. Get yourself on to the ledge.'

I look up. It's so far. How will I make it?

'Come on, Kate!'

My body feels so heavy. My arm is throbbing and when I look down I see that it's bleeding in several places. I must have cut it climbing. A seagull cries overhead. Seabirds can smell blood, like the vultures in Ethiopia. I drag myself up on to the ledge. It is wide and I manage to get both feet on to it but as I stand up straight the wind almost sends me flying backwards.

'Lean into it,' shouts Paul. 'That way you'll get your balance.'

I do as he says and lean my body into the cliff face; so close I can taste seaweed.

'Now grab that ledge just above you.'

I look up into the driving rain and see a wide bit of rock jutting out. I'm terrified it won't hold my weight but I reach up and haul myself on to it.

'Good girl,' shouts Paul from somewhere above me. 'Just a couple more to go and then you'll reach the top.'

I get myself into a standing position and reach out for the next ledge. It's closer this time and more sturdy. I get myself on to it but I have to stop to catch my breath.

'Come on, you're nearly there. One more to go.'

I see the next ledge but it is so far up I'm scared I won't make it. My legs are numb with cold and if I miss my footing it's a long way down.

'Just grab it, Kate!'

His voice spurs me on and I pull myself on to the ledge.

'Good girl.'

I look up and see him.

'Now on a count of three I want you to grab my hand,' he shouts.

I look up and see his hand hanging over the edge.

'Kate. I'm going to count. Are you ready?'

'Yes,' I call. My hands are trembling.

'One.'

I wipe my shaking hand on the back of my sleeve.

'Two.'

The water below me is a raging sea. All I can do is go forward, no matter how terrifying.

'Three.'

I reach out and grab his hand and he holds me so tight I fear he will break my wrist. Soon I am flying through the air, over the cliffs, off into the ether it seems, and I close my eyes, waiting for the moment he loses his grip and I fall. But I don't. We do it. We hold on to each other and we don't let go until I'm safely on the clifftop. Paul puts his coat over me as I lie there trying to get my breath.

'I thought I'd lost you,' he cries as he pulls me towards him. 'Jesus, I really thought I'd . . .'

He buries his face in my shoulder and as I hold him close I feel his body trembling.

'Shall we go home?' I whisper into his sodden hair.

He looks up and it may be the salt in my eyes or the dense mist that hangs over the clifftop, but he looks different. His hair, battered by the wind and the rain, looks black. I watch as he pushes it out of his eyes and a familiar sensation twists inside my stomach. He looks, for a moment, like someone else.

'Yes, I think we should,' he says. We get to our feet and stand face to face, our backs against the violent coastal air. 'Come on.'

I nod my head and he takes my hand as we walk silently towards the lights of the bay.

24

Herne Bay Police Station

36 hours detained

The air has changed inside the interview room and I am finding it difficult to breathe.

'Could we open a window?' I ask Shaw. 'It's so hot in here.'

'It's the central heating,' she replies. 'It comes on automatically. I'm afraid the window only opens slightly but I can see if it helps.'

She goes to stand up but I shake my head.

'Oh, don't bother, it's fine,' I say. 'Let's just carry on.'

I take off my cardigan and drape it over the back of the chair. As I sit here in my flimsy vest and mud-splattered jeans I feel vulnerable, exposed. As though I have no dignity left.

'Okay,' says Shaw. 'Let's continue, if you can, Kate.'

She looks down and reads from her notes.

'Nidal was playing football in the hallway. His father came out of the room and they argued. Then you told the boy that he should listen to his father and stop play-ing football. The boy shouted and ran away.'

It all sounds so neat and contained, nothing like how it actually was.

'What happened then?' asks Shaw.

'I don't know,' I whisper. 'I can't remember.'

'Please just try,' says Shaw.

I don't answer. Silence seems so appealing. I feel like I have no words left.

'Perhaps if I can read you the account Graham Turner gave to Harry Vine when he returned from Aleppo,' says Shaw, her voice calm and deliberate.

'No,' I cry. 'Please don't do that.' How could Harry do this to me?

'Kate, I need to understand the conditions that led to your arrest at number 44 Smythley Road,' she says. 'And part of that is to look at what happened that day in Aleppo.'

She is holding an A4 sheet of paper. So that's all it took to sum up what happened, Graham? A few lousy paragraphs?

'Account given by Graham Turner,' Shaw begins.

As she continues I put my head in my hands and try to drown out her words with the rhythm of my breathing.

'We had been staying in downtown Aleppo for a week and during that time Kate had befriended a young Syrian boy, the son of the family we were staying with. Her behaviour went beyond the professional and I could see that she was becoming emotionally involved with the boy and his family to the detriment of our safety.'

I think of Graham Turner, my friend, my colleague, the man who'd accompanied me through hell on so many occasions, and I wonder why he has done this to me; why he felt the need to betray me like this.

Shaw clears her throat and continues:

'On the afternoon of 29th March we had been disturbed by the boy kicking a football outside our room. Kate ran out to see him and the next thing I knew she had grabbed her shoes and was making her way to the shop above to find the boy. At that time of day it was a grave mistake as the district was under heavy bombardment and the shop was in a prominent position. Alarmed for her safety, I ran after her, and when I got to the door of the shop I saw her outside on the street.'

Tears stream down my face as I sit listening to Graham's words. I can smell the dust and the petrol in my mouth as Shaw continues.

'She was talking to the boy and telling him that if he came back inside she would take him to England.'

'And I would have,' I sob. *You bastard, Graham.* 'I would have taken that child anywhere he wanted to go if it meant I could have saved him.'

Shaw waits for me to catch my breath then continues.

'I opened the door and saw them coming towards me. The boy had taken her hand and they were coming back inside.'

'No, no, no,' I wail as I feel his little hand in mine. 'Don't do this to me.'

We were nearly there; we were so close.

'They got to the door and were just about to step inside when the boy said something about his football, said he'd left it in the street. Kate told him to leave it. She said she would buy him a new one. But the boy was frantic. He was pulling at her, trying to break free from her hand. Kate lost her temper. She shouted at him. Told him that it was just a stupid football and to get back inside. Then the boy yanked his hand from hers and ran into the street. She went to run after him but I held her back. I told her not to be so reckless. The street was a no-go area and we needed to get back inside and find the boy's parents.'

My whole body is shaking. I can't do this. I need to make her stop. Please make her stop. As she continues with Graham's account, I put my hands over my ears. But I can't block out those final moments.

A series of shots. A cloud of dust rising into the air. I can't see him but I can hear his little voice:

Kate. Help me.

My legs are lead and it seems like for ever until I get to him.

'Help me!' he screams.

He's been shot in the head but it wasn't a clean shot. He's still alive.

'It hurts,' he whimpers.

'It's okay, Nidal,' I whisper. 'Help is coming. You're going to be fine.'

He struggles in my arms and I hold him tighter. Where is Graham? Why isn't he coming to help?

'That was a great match, Nidal,' I whisper. 'The captain says you've made the first team. Next stop: Brazil, eh?'

He squeezes my hand.

'Not long now and we'll get you safe,' I say. 'Keep your eyes open, Nidal. Don't close them. Stay awake, baby, stay awake.'

But his eyes are rolling to the back of his head.

'Come on, Nidal,' I shout. 'Come on. You're not dying here. You hear me? You're not dying on this street. We're going to get out of here. We're going to go to Disneyland and we'll stand on that bridge together, do you hear me? And then you can write all about it in your book of smiles. But you have to open your eyes to see it, Nidal. You have to open your eyes.'

But as I speak he goes limp in my arms.

I hear voices above me; men's voices. They try to prise him away but I won't let him go. I won't.

'Kate,' says Shaw, her voice a blade cutting through my heart. 'Kate, are you okay?'

'Stop!' I yell. 'Stop, stop, stop! What are you trying to do to me? You want me to live through all that again just so you can prove I've lost my mind; so you can tick some bloody box? He's dead. That little boy died, he was shot as he tried to get his football. And it was my fault. I shouted at him. I lost my temper and he ran off. If I'd stayed calm he might still be alive. Is that what you want to hear? That he died in my arms and that ever since that moment he won't leave me alone; that I see his face and hear his voice every minute of the day?'

'Kate,' says Shaw. 'Calm down now. Take deep breaths.'

'Fuck off, you patronizing bitch,' I shout. 'I don't need to take deep breaths. I need to tell you some hard facts. About Graham Turner. The man whose statement you're using to paint me as a mad woman – do you want to know what he did instead of helping me? He just stood there with his camera. He stood there, photographing a dead child. He's the one who should be in here being assessed, not me. This is bullshit, every word of it is bullshit.'

I hurl myself out of the seat and run at Shaw, grabbing the sheet of paper from her hands.

'Nidal,' I cry as I slump to the floor and hear Shaw's reedy voice calling for assistance. 'Nidal.'

25

Saturday 18 April 2015

It is getting dark as the taxi pulls up outside 46 Smythley Road. The journey from the seafront was short and we sat in silence, damp, cold and exhausted on the back seat while the driver ranted about migrants, raising his voice to be heard above the din of local radio.

And now we are here. There is no turning back.

'£3.20 please, folks,' says the driver as Paul fiddles with his rucksack. He pulls out his wallet from the front pocket. It is dripping with seawater.

'Sorry about that,' he says as he hands over a soggy ten-pound note. 'It's all I have.'

'No bother,' says the driver. 'It's all legal tender, wet or otherwise.'

He fiddles with his money holder as we sit waiting awkwardly.

'Listen, keep the change,' says Paul impatiently, leaning across me to open the door.

'Thanks, mate,' says the driver, folding the note into a neat square.

We step out on to the rain-soaked street and as I look up at the darkened house I feel a stab of panic. This was not my intention when I agreed to the day out. I look at Paul. He smiles, though I detect a sense of unease. Are we really going to do this? Perhaps there's still time to turn back.

'Come on,' he says, holding out his hand. 'Let's get out of these wet clothes.'

A light goes on next door in the upstairs bedroom, and I imagine Fida pulling the curtains, climbing into bed beside her brute of a husband, and suddenly I don't want to be alone any more.

So I take Paul's hand and let him lead me inside the house. I let him lay me down on the stairs, where my mother's blood still stains the carpet, and slowly remove my sodden clothes. His skin is warm against mine and as I lift my head to meet his lips my body tingles with desire. It's been such a long time.

It's different to how it was with Chris and I blink away the memories of the last, precious time I did this and yield instead to this new being, the one that is pressing against me. But there is little emotion as he turns me over and takes off my knickers, no tenderness as he thrusts himself deep inside me. A sharp pain makes me cry out and I know that I am not better yet. I shouldn't be doing this. He is heavy on me and I try to shift position but he pushes me back. He doesn't want to see me, I think, as he presses my face into the dirty carpet. If he sees me, it will ruin it all. This way we can both pretend we are with someone else and that will absolve us of our guilt. He's thinking of Sally, the girl he first met with the loud voice and the zest for life. As he comes jerkily, he yelps with a sound that falls somewhere between pleasure and pain. I lie deathly still as he pulls himself out of me.

'Well,' he says, kissing me lightly on my forehead. 'That was . . .'

'Don't,' I say as I get to my feet. 'Please don't. We shouldn't have done that.'

I reach for my clothes and stumble up the stairs to the bathroom.

I lie on the bed with the door closed. Paul is asleep beside me. I didn't really want him to stay, but he said Sally would be more suspicious if he came back late. In the end I decided better Paul than the voices.

My arm is throbbing from where I cut it on the rocks earlier. Paul bought some antiseptic cream and plasters from the chemist when we got back to the seafront. He'd applied them to my cuts while we waited for the taxi.

'There you go,' he said when he'd finished. 'All better.'

That was when I knew we were going to end up sleeping together.

As I lie here watching the moon filter through the curtains, Nidal's face floats in front of me, splintering into fragments of silver. Somewhere in the distance an owl hoots and the night grows heavy. I close my eyes and imagine the boats bobbing up and down on the water under Neptune's Arm, waiting for the sun to rise and take them out into the fertile sea. I feel the motion of the waves under my body as I drift out with them, across the estuary, to the Channel and on to France. Out, out into the wide world where nameless people live out their lives, their stories yet to be written.

Lying back in the boat, I hear the faint tap, tapping of the lifebuoy as it bobs alongside. *Tap, tap*. The sea is getting wilder and the noise intensifies. I turn on my side and cover my ears. Deep sleep is within reach and I am clinging to it with every ounce of strength. But the boat is rocking violently and the buoy crashes into the sides with a force that shakes me out of my stupor.

I sit up and look around as the boat becomes a room with a bed and a chest of drawers and a narrow wardrobe that looms in the shadow of the heavy damask curtains.

The noise brings me clean out of the bed and I stand shivering in the centre of the room. Then I hear it, a voice.

'Mummy!'

It's coming from outside but I'm too terrified to go to the window.

'Mummy!'

The voice is so wretched with fear that it dispels my own and I tentatively creep towards the window. Placing my hands on the ledge, I take a deep breath and look outside.

He is there again, sitting in my mother's flower bed. The little boy. I can see him clearly now. He's around four years old and dressed in an orange sweater and dark, loose-fitting trousers. His face is pale and framed by a mop of lank black hair. I lean forward and gently tap the window. He looks up, his eyes wide with fear, and I go cold. He has a black eye.

'Jesus,' I cry as I run back to the bed. 'What have they done to him? Paul, wake up,' I shout, tugging at his shoulder. 'Quickly, Paul. It's the boy. He's out there and he's hurt.'

'Wha—' he groans, pulling the covers up to his chin. 'Go back to sleep.'

'It's the boy, Paul,' I cry insistently. 'The one I told you about. He's out there in the garden. He's hurt. You've got to wake up. Please.'

I tug the covers clean away and Paul curls up into a fetal position. He is naked and I quickly grab a towel from the floor and throw it at him.

'Here, put this on,' I say as he opens his eyes. 'You have to come and see.'

'What time is it?' he mutters as he stumbles to his feet and wraps the towel round his middle. 'It's still dark, Kate.'

'It doesn't matter,' I say impatiently. 'Just come and look.'

I take his arm and drag him towards the window. The moon has gone behind a large black cloud and I put my face to the glass to get a better view.

'There,' I say, pulling Paul closer. 'Can you see him, by the flower bed?'

He shakes his head.

'I can't see a thing,' he says drowsily. 'Except that knackered old garden chair.'

'You're looking in the wrong place,' I say, jabbing my finger on the glass, which is quickly misting up with our breath. 'He's over there, right in the middle of the flower bed.'

'It's probably nothing, Kate,' he says, leaning over me to open the window. As he lifts the latch, I hear a noise like a flutter of wings.

'See,' says Paul, sticking his head out into the night air. 'Nothing at all. It'll have been a fox or something. Those urban foxes are huge. It would be easy to mistake one for a child.'

I push past him and put my head out of the window. The garden is still and quiet and the flower bed is empty.

'He was there,' I whisper, turning to Paul, who is standing shivering in his towel. 'I swear he was right here on the flower bed. You must have scared him when you opened the window.'

'Come back to bed,' he says gently, putting his hand out. 'It was just a bad dream. Come on, you need to rest, particularly after what happened at the beach today.'

'I don't need to rest,' I cry, slamming the window shut. 'I need to help that child. It wasn't a bad dream, it was real. I heard him shout "Mummy", then I saw him. He was there. I know he was and so does somebody else.'

I push past him and pick up my clothes from the floor.

'Kate, what are you doing?' says Paul as I pull my sweater over my head. 'You're going to get yourself into trouble.'

'No I'm not,' I say, grabbing my boots from under the bed. '*She's* going to get into trouble. What kind of mother lets her husband beat up her kid? What kind of mother lets her little boy get out of the house in the middle of the night? She's a disgrace.'

'This is crazy,' says Paul, running down the stairs after me.

'It's not crazy,' I shout. 'She's got a child in there and she's mistreating him and if the police won't help me then I'm going to have to go and search that house myself.'

Paul stops to gather his clothes that are lying in a pile by the bottom step. I flinch as I remember our desperate fuck. What was I thinking? I stand at the front door and fumble with the key while behind me Paul huffs and puffs as he pulls his clothes on.

'Kate, think about this,' he says. 'Think of the consequences. We all know what this boy is. Kate, he doesn't exist.'

'Yes he does!' I yell as the lock finally yields. 'He does exist. And he needs me.'

I pull the door open and head out into the night.

'Kate, come back,' Paul calls after me. 'If you go next door she'll have the police on to you and that's not going to help anyone.'

The air is warm outside and the sky smeared with tiny stars as I stomp up the drive and hammer on the door.

'Open this door now,' I shout. 'You hear me? Open the door.'

I stand back and look at the bedroom window. A light goes on and I return to the door, hammering harder this time. Finally, after about ten minutes of yelling and knocking, the door opens.

'What do you want?' Fida says, not looking me in the eye. 'It's the middle of the night.'

She is fully dressed, headscarf in place. Maybe that was why she took so long to answer. She was getting dressed. Conserving her modesty. Or hiding something?

'Yes, I know it's the middle of the night,' I say, my voice trembling with anger. 'And your little boy should be in bed but instead he was cowering in my garden. Now can you tell me what the hell is going on? He's a tiny little thing and he was calling for you, crying for his mummy.'

'Ms Rafter,' she says, shaking her head. 'You have to stop this. You're scaring me now.'

She looks up at me and I gasp. Her eye is swollen and there is a deep cut across the bridge of her nose.

'My God,' I exclaim, stepping towards her. 'What's happened to you? Did he do this?'

'It's nothing,' she says, brushing me away. 'I fell and hit my face yesterday, that's all.'

'Fida, listen to me,' I say, lowering my voice. What if he's there right now? 'This is serious. I know what your husband has done. You have nothing to gain from covering for him. He's an abuser and I know that because I lived with one. My mum used to end up looking like you most evenings and she made every excuse in the book. Now please, Fida, let me in so I can make sure the boy is all right.'

'There is no boy,' she yells. 'Now please will you just leave me alone.'

She goes to close the door but I put my arm inside to block it.

'Fida, I can help you,' I say. 'You don't have to go through this alone. I can get you and the boy out of here.'

She stares at me. Her hands are shaking and I see that she is terrified.

'Just go,' she whispers. 'Please go.'

And with that she closes the door.

I stand on the step wondering what to do next. The boy must be here somewhere, I think, as I walk to the side of the house and try the gate to see if it's open. I push the lever up and I'm about to go through when I hear something move behind me. I turn and see Paul walking down the drive towards me.

'Kate,' he says, his voice scared. 'That's enough now. Come on.'

'He's in there,' I cry. 'And I'm going to go and find him.'

'Please stop,' says Paul. But it's too late, I'm already running into the garden.

The shed door is open and I step inside.

'It's okay,' I call. 'I'm here now and I can help you.'

I step further inside. Where is he? Perhaps he's hiding. Then I hear something, a muffled voice. It sounds like it's coming from below the earth.

Kate.

'Nidal?' I whisper.

'Kate Rafter.'

I look up and see a desperately young police officer standing in the entrance.

'Could you tell me what you're doing?'

He steps towards me and I see Fida standing outside with another male police officer and Paul.

'Oh, thank God you're here,' I say. Fida must have seen sense and called them. I take the officer's arm and pull him into the shed. 'There's a child being abused. They're hiding him here somewhere.'

'Kate, stop this,' calls Paul. 'Just come out.'

'Ms Rafter, we've had a report of trespass from the occupier of the house,' says the officer. 'Do you mind telling us what you're doing in her shed?'

My heart sinks. She hasn't reported her husband; she's reported me.

'Isn't it obvious?' I shout. 'There is a child in grave danger. I've seen him with my own eyes. He's constantly crying for his mother and tonight he was in my flower bed.'

The officer smirks then tries to cover his amusement with his hand.

'Oh, I'm glad you find this funny,' I say, fury coursing through my body. 'But forgive me if I don't share the joke. That woman out there is a victim of domestic abuse. Look at her face. So is her child. I'm sure he had a black eye when I saw him. You need to go and search the house. They must have him locked up in there.'

'Come on, Ms Rafter,' says the officer, taking me by the arm. 'You shouldn't be in here.'

As we reach the door, Fida steps towards me.

'This is happening almost every day,' she says. 'She just won't stop. I don't have a child. I fell over, that is all. I don't deserve to be hounded like this.'

I can see in her eyes that she wants to say something. For God's sake, why won't she just tell them?

'She needs help,' she whispers to the officer nearest me. 'She's not well.'

I look at her and something inside me snaps. Her blank face is my mother's face and every bit of frustration and impotence comes hurtling to the surface. I need to make her see sense.

'Why won't you tell them, you stupid woman?' I shout, grabbing her scarf and shaking it violently. 'Why won't you just tell them where he is?'

My answer comes in the form of cold, hard metal clasped round my wrists and a male voice telling me what I can or cannot say. As they lead me back through the garden I can hear Fida sobbing and I know that this time I have gone too far.

26

Herne Bay Police Station

37.5 hours detained

Shaw has left the room and a young officer is guarding me. He's sitting by the door with his hands clasped in front of him and, like his colleagues, he looks like he is just out of nappies. How can my life be in their hands?

I told Shaw everything she wanted to know and now my fate rests with something called a Full Mental Health Act Assessment, which, somewhere in this building, she is completing.

The clock above the young man's head reads 16.01. I have been here for almost forty hours. Last night I slept in a windowless cell and dreamt of nothing. That is something at least. Perhaps the very act of recounting my nightmares to Shaw has rendered them obsolete. Who knows?

Paul has been called and informed of my detention. I was allowed to speak to him for a couple of minutes. He told me that he would do everything he could to get me out but they were empty words. The only person in the world with the power to release me is Dr Shaw and I have no idea what she is going to do.

While I have been detained in this tiny police station in a deserted backstreet, Fida's husband will have unleashed his fury on the boy, there is no doubt about it.

If I'm released I will call Harry and tell him there is a story unfolding. I will draw on my contacts in child services and use all the influence I have left to get that child out of there. But I can only do that if I'm released from my own prison. And I have no idea if that is going to happen.

The door opens and the young man jumps to his feet. Shaw enters with the officer who arrested me. In her hands she holds a wedge of papers. I scrutinize her face for an answer but it is a screen of impenetrability. My heart begins to pound against my chest and my mouth is dry. Only now, at the final moment, do I understand the enormity of my situation. The woman sitting in front of me, shuffling into her seat, has the power to incarcerate me in a mental institution. My life, my career, my whole future, has shrivelled to this room, this woman and the papers she holds in her hands.

'Kate,' begins Shaw. She pauses to clear her throat before continuing. 'I've completed the assessment form and I am satisfied that you do not pose a threat to yourself and others. Therefore I will not be recommending further detention under Section 136 of the Mental Health Act.'

My eyes water and I look down at my knees, willing myself not to cry. Not here, not in front of these people.

'However,' continues Shaw, 'from what you have told me, and the symptoms you have presented, I believe that you are suffering from severe post-traumatic stress disorder and I would like to refer you to a relevant professional for counselling. I cannot order you to do this but I would highly recommend it, particularly at this critical point where your behaviour has resulted in arrest.'

I nod my head. I will do whatever she asks me as long as I can get back to the house and help the boy.

'My work here is done,' says Shaw, placing the papers on to her knee. 'And I'll now hand you over to PC Walker to outline the outcome of your arrest.'

I look up at Walker and he raises his eyebrows. What a pathetic excuse for a police officer. There he stood, yards from an abused child, and what did he do? He arrested me.

'Do you have any questions before I go, Kate?' asks Shaw.

I have many questions. I want to ask her if she has ever seen a child die in front of her eyes. I want to ask her why she keeps taking her wedding ring off then putting it back on again. I want to ask her why she flinched when I described my father's beatings. I want to ask her if the nightmares will stop. I want to ask her if she believes me.

Instead I shake my head.

'Okay,' she says, standing up from her seat. 'I'll leave you with PC Walker.'

She nods her head and for a moment I think she is going to speak some words of comfort to me. But then she turns and walks towards the door. I am just another case to her, another form to fill in. She has no interest in my life and what I have seen. She will walk out of this room and into another one where some poor bastard will sit and unload his life to her while she neatly ticks her boxes. And I think of the countless men and women I have interviewed over the years, some whose stories stayed with me, others to whom I barely gave a second thought once the dispatch had been written, and I wonder if that is how I looked to them: a woman who had taken a piece of their soul along with their story as she walked away.

The door closes and PC Walker steps towards me.

An hour later I'm sitting in Paul's car in the train station car park with my rucksack on my knee.

'I packed everything of yours I could find,' he says, resting his arms on the steering wheel. 'I hope it's okay.'

'I'm sure it's fine,' I say. 'I didn't bring that much with me anyway.'

'You know it's probably for the best, don't you?' he says. 'And at least Fida didn't press charges.'

'Ha,' I cry as I look out into the late-afternoon gloom. 'She didn't press charges. Of course she didn't because she knows if the police delved deeper they'd find out her husband's little secret. He's an abuser, Paul, and she's covering for him.'

'Well, whatever she's doing it's none of your business now,' he sighs. 'It can't be. You heard what the copper said, if you go back to the house Fida will apply for a restraining order. Which they'll definitely approve. And then that's it, your life's over. You'll be dragged into court, your reputation will be down the toilet. It's not worth it.'

'No,' I whisper. 'So it seems I have no choice. Other than to see a shrink.'

'Well, would that be such a bad thing?' he says gently. 'Nip this PTSD in the bud before it gets worse, while you still can. Before you end up like . . . well, you know what I mean.'

'Before I end up like Sally?'

He puts his head on to the steering wheel and sighs.

'Will you tell her?' I ask. 'About us.'

He lifts his head. His face has drained of colour.

'Of course I won't,' he says. 'It would destroy her.'

'Yes,' I reply. 'But then I think Sally destroyed herself a long time ago.'

He puts his hand on my arm and strokes it tenderly.

'I do care about you, Kate,' he says. 'I always have. Perhaps in another life we might have –'

'Don't,' I say, easing my arm away. 'I think we both know that's crazy talk. The other night was just one of those things. We needed some comfort.'

He smiles and rubs his face with his hands. 'So where will you go? Back to London?'

'I'll go to my flat first but I won't be hanging around. Too many ghosts there.'

'You mean Chris?'

I flinch at the sound of his name.

'You left his Facebook page open on my laptop,' says Paul. 'Married, eh? Sounds like a bit of a shit to me.'

'Sally is very lucky,' I say as I unclip the seat belt. 'Having someone like you. I don't think she realizes it.'

He smiles but I can see it's painful.

'You said you won't be hanging around,' he says, changing the subject. 'So where will you go?'

'I'll talk to Harry,' I say. 'Get him back onside, then I'll go back to Syria. It's the only place I can be right now.'

'Are you insane? Have you seen the news?'

'I write the news, Paul,' I reply. 'It's my job.'

'But after all you've been through with the little lad in Aleppo, are you sure it's the right thing to do?'

'Yes, I'm sure.'

'Jesus, girl,' he says with a wry laugh. 'You don't do things by halves, do you? I'm going to miss you.'

He leans over and hugs me tightly and it feels so good that I almost want to stay but I know it's impossible, not just with the Fida situation but Sally too. It's best for everyone if I get as far away from here as I can.

'I'll miss you too,' I say as I ease myself out of the embrace. 'You've been a wonderful friend to me these last few days. I really appreciate it.'

'I told you, it's no bother,' he says. 'Now, you just get yourself better, you hear me?'

'I'll try,' I say. 'Oh and, Paul, I know you think it's all in my head, but would you do me a favour and keep an eye on number 44? Just for me.'

'Of course I will,' he says, his voice gravelly.

I open the door and step out into the salty air.

'Bye,' I say. 'Take care.'

'You too,' he says, wiping his eyes. 'Now go on or you'll miss your train.'

I close the door and head for the station entrance. When I get there I stand for a moment, watching the silver saloon pulling out of the car park, and as it disappears into the sprawl of the suburban housing estate I take out my phone and go over to the bench by the ticket office.

I sit down and press her number. One last try.

The call connects and I hear heavy breathing.

'Hello,' I say. 'Is that you, Sally?'

'Who's this?'

'It's me. Kate. Look, Sally, I need to tell you something.'

'You said enough last time.'

Her words are laboured. She's drunk. Dammit. Still, I need to try.

'Look, I have to be quick. I'm at the station and my train arrives in five minutes.'

'Off on your travels again, are you? I knew you wouldn't stick around for long.'

Her voice drips with venom. She'll be on to her second bottle. I can tell. The first makes her merry; the second makes her nasty.

'It's work,' I tell her. 'I'm needed back at the office.'

'Nice to be needed,' she slurs.

I'm tempted to just end the call but I know I have to try. I take a deep breath.

'Sally, I'm calling to ask you a favour,' I tell her. 'It's really important.'

'Ooh, a favour,' she says mockingly.

'Please, Sally, this is serious,' I say. 'I need you to keep an eye on the house next door to Mum's. Paul's house.'

'What you on about now?'

I take a deep breath.

'There's a little boy living there and I think he's being mistreated.'

'Little boy?'

'Yes.'

'In Mum's house?'

'No. Next door. The house Paul rents out.'

'What's that got to do with me?'

'Nothing,' I reply. 'But it would be really helpful if you could . . . maybe go and see the neighbours, check them out. I mean, after all, they are Paul's tenants.'

'Are you having a laugh?' she cries. 'You want me to go and knock on someone's door and ask them if they're bashing their kid about?'

'No, I just –' 'You never change, do you, Kate? Always sticking your nose where it isn't wanted; always telling people how to live their lives.'

'Sally, it's not like that. This child . . . he's in trouble.'

'Yeah? Isn't that what you said about Hannah? You know your problem? You're bitter.'

'Bitter? What are you talking about?'

'Bitter that you've never had kids; that you put your big-shot career first and now it's too late.'

Her words cut, but I won't let myself show it.

'Oh for God's sake, Sally, you're talking rubbish.'

'Really? Am I? Nah, I just know you too well, that's all. Truth hurts, don't it?'

'You're drunk,' I say, trying not to lose my temper. 'I don't know why I even bothered.'

'Disrespect you, did she, the woman next door? Say something you didn't like? Is that why you're making shit up about her?'

'No, it's not like that.'

'You're always making stuff up,' she says, raising her voice. 'Just can't help yourself, can you?'

As she rants, I hear my train being announced over the tannoy.

'Look, I've got to go,' I say, interrupting her. 'Thanks for nothing, Sally.'

I terminate the call and put the phone back in my pocket.

Why did I ever think that she could help? She can't even look after herself never mind anyone else.

I stand up and as I pull my rucksack on to my shoulders I try to expunge her drunken insults from my head. Time to get back to work, I tell myself, as I make my way to the train. Time to leave Herne Bay and all its misery behind me.

27

Aleppo, Syria

Two weeks later

Something has changed. *I* have changed.

I arrived in Aleppo last night. It was a terrifying journey. We were smuggled into the city by my old friend and translator Hassan. We had to walk for several miles through an abandoned sewer. Hassan led the way, a torch taped to his forehead. Rats crawled across our feet as we stepped through ankle-deep water and ancient shit. My body didn't stop shaking the whole way. Every step I asked myself why. Why did I come back? I covered my mouth with my hand as the water rose higher and my nostrils filled with the smell of excrement and chemicals. Just when I thought I would collapse we emerged into an expanse of wasteland, a disused industrial site on the outskirts of Aleppo where a makeshift camp has been set up. And as I stood there looking at the dilapidated tents I felt like running back through the sewer. I could smell death on the air and it reminded me of my baby. And as Hassan took my shaking hand and led me to my tent I asked myself again: why did I come back?

This morning I have been touring the clinic on the north side of the camp. It was set up by a couple of young medical students and is packed with terrified, bloodied people, most of them women and children. A young man in a filthy white coat rushes from bed to bed, desperately trying to stem bleeding limbs with bits of cloth. I have witnessed many scenes like this before in Gaza and Iraq but back then I was stronger. This time I feel nervous. My skin prickles at the slightest noise.

And as I step through the chaos of the clinic I feel something depart. I can't do this any more.

Yet I swallow my fear and go through the motions. I follow the young medic, who introduces himself as Halil, around the clinic and listen as he tells me what has happened.

We stop at a rickety stretcher where a young woman is lying motionless. She is barely out of her teens and she stares at the ceiling, her mouth wide open, while Halil fixes a tourniquet to the remains of her arm. I kneel down beside her, my heart pounding in my chest. I know there are no painkillers and that she will be in agony. I stroke her arm and as she turns her face to me I think of Hannah. She was close to this girl's age when I last saw her. And as I sit looking at the broken body of the young woman a searing sensation rips through my own; a memory of an old wound that I had inflicted but never tried to heal.

It happened on Hannah's tenth birthday. I had just returned from Gaza, where I had reported on the bombing of a school where hundreds of children had been killed. The experience of walking through mounds of mutilated bodies had affected me greatly and I remember thinking how lucky we were in the West, how chance dictated that some children were born into peace while others were born into conflict. Three days after I returned I was invited to Hannah's birthday party and the little girl delighted in showing me her new doll. I have no idea what came over me but seeing Hannah in her sparkly new dress, with all her presents, made me see red. I grabbed the doll and twisted its head off. 'Come on, Hannah,' I shouted as I threw the doll at her. 'Let's play Gaza.' I will never forget the look of fear and confusion on her face as she stood there above the remains of her doll. My mother and Sally were furious but they soon forgot it. Hannah, though, never forgot, and after that whenever she saw me, she flinched.

I blink away the memory and ask the girl her name. She looks at me blankly, her eyes cloudy with pain.

'She is Amira,' says Halil. 'Her house was hit while she and her family were sleeping. Her baby was blown from her arms and her little son also died.'

I turn to the girl. She seems so young and yet she has been a mother. I look at her missing arm and imagine the baby that once lay there; one minute warm and safe and suckling its mother; the next obliterated. The young woman closes her eyes and turns away, and as Halil guides me to another bed all I can see is Hannah and her broken doll and I know that it has happened; I have finally lost my nerve.

I got back to my tent an hour ago but I couldn't rest. All I could think about was that girl and her missing baby.

My heart was thudding and it felt like I was going to collapse. I needed air. So I put my rucksack on my back and walked.

I'm sitting outside now, watching the stars come out. It's quiet here away from the groans of the patients. My mind drifts to Paul and Sally back in Herne Bay. I wonder how they are. Paul will be worrying about Sally; I know he will. I wish she would do the right thing and stop drinking. I also think of my own demons. Coming back here has convinced me that I need to face up to my problem.

When I got back to London I assured Harry that I would talk to the company's occupational therapist as soon as I returned from Syria. He was dubious about letting me come out here but he knows I'm the only one who can get close to what is happening. My reports sell papers and that is enough for Harry. But perhaps I will see someone when I get back, I think to myself. Perhaps it's time.

It's getting cold. I grab my rucksack and open it up, taking out the first item to hand, a thick woollen sweater. I pull it over my head but as I put my arm into the sleeve I feel something hard. I push my hand out and a slim black object drops on to the ground.

I stoop to pick it up and shake my head as I turn it over in my hands. Mum's Dictaphone. Paul must have packed it thinking it was mine. I push the rucksack to one side and sit back on the grass. If it still works I can hear her one last time, my lovely mum. I curl up on my side and fiddle around with the buttons. It's an older model than mine and it takes me a while to get it going, but finally I hear a hiss and then the unmistakable tones of my mother:

'Testing. Testing. That's what they say, isn't it? I'm meant to speak into this thing cos I keep forgetting where I left my glasses. Kate says I'm going to get through a whole rainforest of Post-it notes if I'm not careful so she's bought me this nice new thingy. Though I told her not to bother. I'm too old for all this new-fangled nonsense.'

I smile as her voice drifts through the dusty air. She's come back for me just when I need her most. My eyes well up with tears as she carries on talking about what she needs to get from the supermarket and the Christmas bin collection dates. Silly little trivial things, but hearing her talk about them makes me feel safe. Then she stops and there is a long pause. I fast forward and hear her voice again.

'. . . the house next door.'

I rewind a bit and wait for her to start up again.

'I'm telling this to you because I know they'll all think I'm barmy but I've seen him twice now and he was as clear as the nose on my face.'

Her voice is serious and I stand up and increase the volume, my heart thudding in my chest as she continues.

'There's a little lad. Tiny little thing, can't be much more than three or four, in the house next door . . .'

It's the last thing I hear as a shaft of bright white light blinds me and I'm flung to the ground. I hear the familiar tap, tapping of an approaching shell. I cover my face and close my eyes, then all is black.

PART TWO

28

Herne Bay

Tuesday 5 May 2015

Someone is shining a light in my face. I squint and try to remember where I am. When I come to I see a man standing in front of me. From this angle he looks like a giant with great big hairy arms folded across his chest. But as my eyes focus I see that it is just Paul. My husband. And the light is the light of early morning, coming through the conservatory window.

'What do you want?' I mutter as I lie back into the folds of the armchair. My mouth is dry and my head hurts when I speak.

'Sally, I need to talk to you,' he says. His voice is low and serious.

'Well, I don't want to talk to you.'

I squint. The sunlight pouring through the window is making my head throb. I can still taste last night's wine and if I move I will throw up. I close my eyes and try to pretend he's not here. Why is he standing over me like this? He knows not to come in here; this is *my* space. I just want to go back to sleep.

'Sally, please,' he says. 'You need to wake up. We've had some bad news.'

I open my eyes and look at him. He's been crying. I go cold. It's her.

'Hannah,' I whisper. 'Is it Hannah?'

He shakes his head.

'No, it's not Hannah.'

Thank God, I think to myself, as I sink back into the chair. If it's not Hannah then I don't care what he has to say. But he's still there. I can feel him looming above me.

'What is it?' I say. 'Just tell me.'

He sits down on the edge of the table and puts his head in his hands.

'Paul, for God's sake tell me.'

'It's Kate,' he says, looking up.

'Oh, what's she done now?' I say, looking around the room for the wine. I need a quick drink just to take the edge off. 'Got herself kidnapped?'

I can't see the wine. I must have finished it last night. I stand up and head for the door.

'Sit down,' says Paul, putting his hand on my arm. 'This is serious.'

I look at him. His face is deathly pale.

'Look, whatever this is,' I say as I sit back down, 'Kate will be fine. She can look after herself. Always has done.'

'Sally, listen to me.'

'She was only here a little while ago, she seemed fine.'

My hands start shaking. I need a drink.

'Come on, love,' he says, leaning forward and taking my hands. 'Just let me speak.'

'I'm not interested,' I snap, pushing his hands away. 'Kate can look after herself.'

What does he think he's playing at, coming in here at this time of the morning wanting to have serious conversations when I haven't even had a drink?

I push past him and head into the living room, but as I get to the door I feel his hands on my shoulders.

'Sit down,' he says, guiding me towards the sofa.

'Get your hands off me,' I shout. 'I told you I'm not interested in Kate or whatever trouble she's got herself into. Get out of my way.'

'Sally, stop,' he says firmly.

'No, I won't,' I reply, struggling against him. 'You don't get to tell me what to do any more.'

'Jesus Christ, will you just listen, you stupid woman,' he yells, gripping me hard with both hands. 'She's dead. Your sister is dead.'

Everything goes black and I slump on to the floor.

'I'm sorry, love,' he's saying. 'I'm so, so sorry. I didn't want to tell you this way, but you just wouldn't listen.'

Paul picks me up gently and settles me on the sofa.

'I'll get you a glass of water,' he says as he plumps up the cushions behind my head.

'No,' I cry. 'I don't want water.'

He sits down next to me and holds my hand.

'The first I knew about it was last night,' he says. 'I was driving home with the radio on and there was a report saying that a makeshift hospital had been bombed in Syria.'

'Shut up,' I whisper, but he carries on talking.

'I took notice,' he says. 'Because it was in Aleppo and I knew she was going back there.'

'Just shut up.' I dig my nails into his hand but he doesn't pull away. He just keeps talking.

'I put the TV on this morning,' he says, rubbing my hand. 'And her photo came on the screen. The camp she was in was hit, Sal. There were no survivors.'

'I said shut up,' I yell, pushing his hands away. 'You're wrong, you bloody idiot. You don't know what you're talking about.'

I pummel his chest with my fists and he just stands there and lets me hit him, again and again. I carry on pounding his chest until I have no energy left and I collapse in a heap at his feet.

'Kate's always been fine. She can look after herself. You're wrong,' I sob.

'I'm sorry, love,' he whispers as he puts his arm underneath my head and lifts me off the floor. 'I'm so sorry.'

He kisses my cheek but I feel nothing. My body goes limp as he carries me through the room and back into the conservatory.

'She's not dead,' I tell him as he puts me down in the chair. 'If she was dead I would know.'

'It's a big shock,' he says, putting his hand on my forehead. 'A lot to take in . . .'

'I said she's not dead,' I yell, pushing him away. 'Now just piss off and leave me alone.'

'Look, Sally,' he says, 'I think I should stay with you, at least for a bit. You're in shock.'

'Didn't you hear me? I said I want to be alone.'

'Okay,' he says, stepping towards the door. 'Whatever you wish.'

'And close those bloody blinds,' I say. 'The sun's giving me a headache.'

I hear his footsteps on the wooden floor as he goes to the window.

'Is that better?' he asks as the light disappears and I nod my head, glad of the darkness.

'Shout if you need me,' he says, and as he closes the door, I think of Kate, slamming her fists on the table when Dad was having a go at Mum. It's just not right, I tell myself, as I sink back into the chair. How can she be dead and I still be here? She was the strong one, the fighter. It's just not possible. He must be wrong.

I need a drink.

I put my hand down the side of the chair and feel about in the darkness for the bottle of wine I hid last night. My hand rests on it and I pull it up. I don't have a glass but I don't need one. Unscrewing the top, I take a long glug. It's warm and slightly sour but it will do the trick. I just need to numb the pain in the pit of my stomach.

It's dark outside now. I have no idea what time it is. I've finished the wine and I would kill for another bottle. Paul has come in a couple of times to ask me if I want a cup of tea. I've told him I need a proper drink but he won't listen to me. Just keeps saying I'm in shock.

Is that what this is?

As I sit here in the dark, all I can think about is Kate. I see her with Mum, standing at the end of my bed the day Hannah was born. Mum was making a fuss about me getting the latch right and making sure I winded

Hannah properly but Kate just stood there staring at the baby. It was like she was looking at some strange creature. I knew exactly how she felt because Hannah might as well have been an alien for all I knew about babies. I was just a child myself.

Eventually I told her to sit down and while Mum went to get some tea the two of us watched Hannah as she slept in the plastic crib. At one point I turned to Kate and said: 'What do I do with it?' And she looked at me for a moment, then shrugged and said, 'Don't ask me.' And we both burst out laughing. When Mum came back in she asked what was so funny but we were too cracked up to answer her.

Three weeks later she left for university and never came back. That moment in the hospital was one of the few times we bonded. For as long as I can remember Kate had been the better sister, the clever one, the brave one, and I could never live up to her, but for a few moments as we sat looking at Hannah sleeping in her cot we were just a pair of giggly, clueless schoolgirls.

Then I remember something. She phoned me. It was just before she left for Syria. I try to piece together what was said but I can only recall snippets. I must've been drunk. I can remember she said she was at the station – or was it the airport? I vaguely remember being angry at her for leaving again. I should have just bloody listened. What was she trying to say to me? It's no use. I can't remember.

And now she's gone and I will never hear her voice again.

As I blink away the memory of the phone call my thoughts turn to Hannah. I wonder where she is. If only she would get in touch. She needs to know about her gran and now her aunt Kate. Why does she have to be so stubborn? And then I hear her voice in my head. *Just let me go, Mum.* I'm pulling at her wrist, begging her to get back in the house. And then it all goes black and I will myself to remember what happened next but I can't. I just can't.

'Sally.'

I look up. He's standing at the door in his dressing gown.

'Come on, love, it's gone midnight,' he says. 'Why don't you come up to bed?'

'I'm not tired,' I say.

'You've been in that chair all day,' he says. He steps into the room and goes to turn the lamp on.

'Leave it,' I shout, anger and grief and resentment rising up my gullet. 'Just bloody leave it, will you?'

He pauses with the cord from the lamp in his hand.

'Sitting here like this, not moving, not speaking, is not going to bring Kate back,' he says, letting the cord drop. 'If you shut me out it's only going to make things worse. We can talk about it. I'm here for you, Sally. I'm here to listen.'

'I have nothing to say to you,' I reply.

His voice is setting my nerves right on edge. I need to be alone with my memories of Kate. I need to make sense of all of this but him coming in all the time just distracts me and makes me feel like I can't breathe.

'You'll regret it in the morning,' he says. 'If you sleep in that chair you'll be stiff all over.'

'Well, that's up to me, isn't it?' I say. 'Now, please just go to bed and leave me be.'

As he closes the door, my skin prickles. I need another drink. I wait for a few minutes then get up out of the chair and creep through the living room and into the hallway. I pause by the cupboard underneath the stairs. There's no sound of Paul; he must be in bed. I carefully open the cupboard door and reach my hand inside. The bottles are still there where I left them a few days ago. My secret stash. It's the perfect hiding place. Paul never goes near this cupboard. He thinks it's full of junk and old clothes. I carefully close the door and slip back into the conservatory.

I sink into the chair clutching the bottle to my chest. Just one glass, I tell myself, one glass to calm my nerves. But as I unscrew the lid I know that will never be enough.

29

I wake up in an empty bed. My back is aching and I pull the bedclothes round my shoulders but sleep won't come. I open my eyes and lie still for a moment. The air feels different. Something happened before I went to sleep, something horrible. And then I remember. The news. Paul's face. It is real. I am alive and my sister is dead.

'Paul!' I shout. 'Paul, are you there?'

There is no reply and I climb out of the bed. The clothes I was wearing yesterday are neatly folded across the back of the chair by the window. Paul must have carried me upstairs in the middle of the night and got me into my pyjamas but I can't remember any of it.

'Paul!' I shout again, but there is still no answer.

I put on my dressing gown and go downstairs to find him.

He's left a note on the kitchen table saying that he's been called into work but will be back as soon as he can.

I put the note in the bin and walk out of the kitchen feeling a little clearer. When Paul is here I feel suffocated and my brain won't function. At least with him out of the house I can think straight.

I go straight to the cupboard under the stairs and open the door. I need a drink, just one, to ease the aching in my chest. I put my hand inside. There's nothing but old coats and boxes. Turning on the light, I push aside the junk and feel around for the bottles. But there is nothing. I step further inside and get down on my hands and knees. Where the hell are they? I put six bottles in here two days ago. There should be four left. Where have they gone? My mouth goes dry and my heart starts to pound as I search frantically through old shoeboxes and moth-eaten jackets. Then I see it, a yellow Post-it note stuck to the floor where the bottles had been.

I rip it off, my hands shaking with anger.

'It's not worth it, Sally,' he has written. 'We can get through this together . . . without the booze. I love you xxx.'

The fucking idiot. He's got rid of my wine. I run back into the kitchen and start pulling open cupboards and drawers. Where's he hidden it? I can't deal with this without a drink. It's too much; too huge.

I go into the conservatory and look behind the sofa, behind the cushions, screaming with frustration as I go. Then as I get to the chair by the window something outside catches my eye. The recycling box, ready for tomorrow morning's collection, is sitting on the patio with four empty wine bottles in it. He's poured it down the sink. I don't believe it.

I slam my fists against the window. The stupid, stupid man. Why would he do that? He's just making everything worse.

There is no way I can get through this day without a drink so I'll just have to go and get some more. 'Didn't think of that, did he?' I mutter to myself as I take off my dressing gown and throw it on the floor. What was the point of pouring my wine down the fucking sink when I can just go out and buy more? I'm a grown woman and he treats me like some stupid kid. Sod him.

I find my over-sized green puffa coat hanging on the hook in the hallway and put it on over my pyjamas. Hopefully no one will notice, I think, as I dig out my old trainers from the shoe rack, but as I bend down to put them on I catch sight of myself in the hall mirror. My eyes are bloodshot and it's been days since I last washed. My hair is limp and greasy; my skin a sickly yellow. Jesus, I think to myself, as I step away from the mirror. What must Kate have thought when she saw me? She was always immaculately turned out. Ever since she was a kid she had been fussy about her appearance. Everything had to be just so. And she was so slim and pretty. I could never compete.

I try not to think about her as I reach into my coat pocket and pull out a pair of sunglasses. It's an overcast day and I'll look silly but better that than scaring people to death.

The streets are deserted as I set off. Thankfully. I have no idea what time it is or what day, all I can see in front of me is a bottle of cold white wine and all I can feel, as I cross the road that leads to the shops, is the absence of it in my bloodstream.

I pull the hood of my coat up round my face as I walk up the narrow path to the Spar. I don't want anyone to see me. I just want to do what I need to do and get back to the house without any hassle.

As I enter the shop I'm relieved to see that it's the man working today and not his wife. She always looks

247

at me like I'm dirt when I put the wine bottles on the counter. Bitch. But her old man is pleasant enough and he smiles as I pick up a basket and head to the fridges.

The shop radio is playing 'Hey Jude' and I feel a crushing sense of sadness. It's as if I've been punched in the stomach. Kate loved this song when we were kids. She used to change the words to 'Hey You' and dance with me around the room. But that was when I was very little, before we started hating each other. I try to block out the song as I put three bottles of Pinot Grigio into the basket and make my way to the counter, but it's already wormed its way into my head and I know that it will stay there for the rest of the day unless I drink it away.

I put the wine on to the counter, making a mental note to myself to find a new hiding place; somewhere Paul will never think to look.

'Sun come out, has it?' says the man, noticing my glasses. He scans the bottles and begins to put them into a flimsy carrier bag.

I nod my head, wishing he would just hurry up.

'Spring is here,' he says with a smile. 'Makes it even more poignant, doesn't it?' He points in the direction of the newspaper rack by the door. 'She was from round here, you know.' I follow his gaze and see a mass of headlines:

WIPED OUT

NO SURVIVORS

BOMBED WHILE THEY SLEPT

'Syria,' he says, opening another bag to put the remaining bottles in. 'Never ends, does it? I mean, how much can one country take? Those poor people and that poor journalist. She was only in her thirties. They say she's officially missing but no one could survive that. Have you seen the photos? It was carnage. Makes you think, though, doesn't it? One minute you're going about your business, the next, whoosh.'

He clicks his fingers and the noise makes me jump.

I leave the counter and walk across to the newspapers. I take a copy of *The Times* and look at the picture that is splashed across the front page: a pile of body bags lying in a scorched field. My stomach twists and I drop the paper on the floor. I'm going to throw up.

'That's £27.36 when you're ready, love,' says the man as I bend down to pick the paper up. 'Are you wanting the newspaper too?'

'No,' I reply, putting it back on the shelf and returning to the counter. I grab the bags and thrust a wedge of twenty-pound notes into the man's hands; the entire contents of my purse.

'Hang on, love, that's far too much,' he says. 'Come back and get your change.'

But I'm already out of there. Clutching my stomach, I run behind the pizza shop and throw up violently. Afterwards I put my hand on to the wall to steady myself and stand there for a few moments just trying to breathe. Then, wiping my mouth, I head back to the parade. I have to get home. I have to get away from the man and the newspapers and the Beatles song that is going round and round my head. I have to get home and pour myself a small drink and then it will all be better. I'll be able to think straight.

Two hours later I'm drunk. Lying on the sofa, I close my eyes while Paul McCartney's voice flutters through the room.

Just one glass, I'd told myself, but the first glass barely registered so I had a second. That warmed me up and blunted the edges a bit but it still wasn't enough and as I poured myself a third I remembered I had Kate's records. It's got to be here somewhere, I thought, as I rummaged through the tattered sleeves. And then I found it. A twelve-inch copy of the Beatles' 'Hey Jude' and there on the back of it in black felt tip was her name: Kate Martha Rafter. I took the record out and gave it a wipe with the back of my sleeve, then, taking a big sip of wine, I put it on my ancient turntable and suddenly she was back. We were two little girls dancing around the living room.

And now, as I lie here on the sofa with the song still playing in my head, I try to picture her but all I can see is a damn body bag.

'Hey you,' I sing to the ghosts in the room. 'Dum, dum de dum.'

Slowly, my eyelids grow heavier than the words and everything goes dark.

I wake to a loud bang. I sit up and listen. The thud of heavy feet and a voice, low and muffled, calling my name. I go to stand up but I can't move. My heart pounds and I can't get my breath.

The footsteps grow closer.

'Kate?' I whisper. 'Is that you?'

I try to get up from the sofa but my legs are so heavy I can barely move.

'Oh, for God's sake!'

I look up and see him. He's standing at the door, his face like thunder.

'Sally, why did you do it?' he says as he steps inside. 'You know this isn't the answer.'

'It's nothing,' I say, flopping back on to the sofa. 'Just leave it.'

'Jesus,' he says, picking up the bottle from the floor. 'Three bottles of wine in one morning? You're going to kill yourself.'

He puts them on the table then comes and sits on the arm of the sofa.

'Drinking's not going to bring her back,' he says, taking the empty glass from my hands.

'I know that,' I say.

'In fact, it's just going to make things worse,' he says.

I bury my head in the cushion so I don't have to listen to him, but I can still hear his voice droning on.

'You're going to need a clear head to deal with this, Sally,' he says. 'To fully come to terms with her death.'

And as I lie here I remember something. One of the headlines from this morning.

'You're wrong anyway,' I say, sitting up. 'About Kate. She's not dead.'

'Oh, Sally, what are you talking about?' he sighs.

'I saw the papers in the shop,' I tell him, pointing my finger in the air. 'They said "missing" – she's *missing*, not dead. I tell you, she'll turn up right as rain in a couple of days.' I laugh loudly.

He shakes his head and his face looks so smug I want to punch him.

'What? What you shaking your head for?'

'Sally, listen to me,' he says. 'We got a call just now from the MoD. They told me that Kate had us down as her next of kin. Sally, they've confirmed it. Your sister's not missing, love, she's dead. They're sending her belongings to us.'

I stand up from the sofa, grabbing for something, anything, to hold on to.

'But the papers,' I begin. 'They said missing. Why would they say that if it isn't true?'

'I'm so sorry, Sally.'

Her face fills the room and my head starts to spin with that bloody song. *Hey you.* I hold out my arm to stop myself from falling but it's too late and I go crashing into the edge of the coffee table.

30

'I shouldn't be here,' I think to myself as I sit on a sterile white bed. Through a gap in the thin green curtain I see disembodied feet passing by, all in such a hurry but none of them stopping at my cubicle. Why won't anyone come?

The nurses cleaned me up when I arrived; stitched my head and put a monitor on my heart. Paul stayed in the waiting room while they wheeled me into Accident and Emergency. I was relieved. He kept asking me if I was all right. What did he want me to say? Yes, I'm great. I'm deliriously happy. My sister is dead and everything's fine and dandy.

As more feet pass below the curtain, not stopping, my loneliness intensifies. Everyone I love is gone: my daughter, my sister. I even miss my mother, the cantankerous old cow.

I should be dead too, I think as I place my hand on the jagged stitches that ripple along my forehead like a railway track. There is nothing left for me to live for.

Nothing.

The curtain is pulled back and Paul steps into the cubicle with a concerned smile. I start to cough. Just his presence seems to suck the oxygen out of a room. Is this what happens when a relationship dies? You drain each other to the point of collapse. I know I drain Paul.

I can see the exhaustion on his face as he closes the curtain and walks towards the bed.

'I feel like this is all my fault,' he says. 'I shouldn't have gone out. I should have stayed with you. I'm so sorry.'

'It's not your fault,' I tell him. 'I'm a big girl now.'

My head is sore and it hurts to speak. I watch as he pulls out a chair and sits down. He rolls up his sleeves and scratches at his arms. I look at the silvery scars and remember that night. Him trying to grab the bottle from my hands and then the sound of broken glass. He notices me looking and stops scratching.

'I'm sorry,' I whisper. 'I'm so sorry, Paul.'

After that night things haven't been the same between us. We sleep in separate bedrooms. We don't eat together any more. And Paul is spending more and more time at work. We're two strangers who just happen to live in the same house.

'Let's not worry about that now,' he says gently. 'You didn't know what you were doing.'

He smiles and my stomach twists. Poor Paul. The day after, he didn't even want to admit what I'd done to him.

'I didn't mean to do it.'

'I know,' he says. But I can see in his eyes he doesn't trust me.

'It's fine, honestly.' He attempts a smile. 'Anyway, the doctor said you can go home now. The car's out front, we can go whenever you're ready.'

The thought of going home makes me think about Kate again; the news.

'It just doesn't seem real,' I say, turning from him. 'That she's gone.'

'I know,' he says. 'I can't believe it either. She was an amazing woman. I just wish I hadn't left you today. I'm an idiot. Or what was it Kate used to say? A plonker.'

He laughs sadly and my heart hurts.

'She used to call me that too,' I say as I ease myself off the bed and pick up my cardigan from the chair. 'When we were kids.'

I see the two of us on Reculver beach. One of my clearest memories. I'm building a sandcastle and she's digging. She was always bloody digging. Then she stops and I look up and she's got this thing in her hands. 'Is it a fossil?' I ask as I come closer. 'Dunno,' she replies. 'But I'm going to keep it.' Next minute Mum's looming over us and then she grabs the fossil thing from Kate's hands and runs and throws it in the sea. 'What did you do that for?' Kate whines as my mother stomps back up the beach. 'That was mine.' Mum's skirt is dripping wet from the waves and she scowls at us as she settles back on to her beach towel. 'That was a bomb, Kate. You don't mess around with things like that.' And Kate nods her head, her face all serious, and carries on digging, but I can't concentrate on my sandcastle because I'm confused. 'What's a bomb?' I ask. 'Is it a kind of dinosaur egg?' And my mother and Kate roll about laughing and they look so funny I can't help but join in. 'Oh, Sally. You're such a plonker.'

I close my eyes and bury my face into the woollen folds of the cardigan. I hear my mother's voice as the tears finally come: *You don't mess around with things like that.*

'The silly, stupid fool,' I cry. 'Why did she always have to be so bloody brave? Why couldn't she just leave those people to it; let them fight their own battles?'

'Oh, Sally,' says Paul. He stands up and takes the cardigan from my hands. 'It's all right. Let it out.'

He puts the cardigan on to the bed and takes me in his arms. He smells of Paul, of fresh soap and cake mix, though he never makes bloody cakes. It's just there in his skin. It's such a comforting smell, and I bury my face into his chest and breathe him in.

'It's been a massive shock for you,' he whispers. 'But we're going to get through this. I promise you.'

'I can't,' I say, extricating myself from his arms. 'I will never get over it. Knowing that she died all alone, with nobody to comfort her in her final moments. I should have been nicer to her when she came to see me but all I could think about was everything she'd done. It was eating me up inside and now it's too late.'

'Shhh,' says Paul, picking up my cardigan. 'It's okay. You can't change the past. What's done is done. And I'm going to help you, baby. We'll get through this together. Now come on, let's go home.'

I am being held captive in my own house. Paul is determined that I won't sneak out to buy more booze so he has taken the rest of the week off work so he can stay here and play nursemaid.

He has been up to see me several times throughout the day, bringing me tea and biscuits and a pile of crappy magazines, and telling me that whenever I'm ready we can talk about Kate.

The lack of booze is making me jittery and my stomach is aching terribly. I'm going to have to find a way to sneak out and get some drink. Still, right now I feel strangely calm, though I don't know how long that will last.

Brushing the biscuit crumbs from the quilt, I turn over and lie on my side. Paul has suggested I have 'a nice bath' but I don't want to move because if I do then this all becomes real. If I lie here and think hard enough about her then maybe I can bring her back.

I close my eyes and I'm back in that house. I must've been around eight. We're sitting round the table waiting for him to come home from the pub. I'm chatting away to fill the silence but my mother and Kate are just looking at each other. I can see the fear in their eyes. I'm not stupid, despite what they think. Mum's cooked a chicken pie from scratch. It was perfect when it came out of the oven but that was three hours ago and now it sits in the middle of the table getting cold and dry.

'Oh, this is ridiculous, Mum,' cries Kate, slamming her hands on the table. 'We can't just sit here all night. It's almost nine o'clock and I have to do my history homework. Just slice the bloody thing and heat his up when he gets in.'

My mother folds her hands in her lap and bows her head. It looks like she's praying.

'You know he likes us to eat together, Kate,' she says, her voice quivering. 'Now please don't make a scene, not tonight.'

'Me make a scene?' she exclaims. 'Me? This is crazy, Mum. If he wants us all to eat together then why can't he get himself back from the pub?'

'We could watch the TV?' I suggest, but my mother frowns at me. 'There might be something nice on.'

'Oh, for goodness' sake, Sally,' she snaps. 'Don't talk nonsense.'

The iciness of her voice rips into me and my eyes start to water. I put my head back and try to keep the tear that is balancing precariously on my eyelid from falling on to my plate. Then I feel a hand on mine. A gentle squeeze, telling me that everything is going to be all right. I turn my head and see her smiling at me. My big sister. She smiles and for that moment we all feel okay. She has the ability to convey such reassurance with her smile.

But then the front door slams and we all sit erect, silent soldiers on parade. The colour drains from my mother's face and my heart begins to pound.

'Now remember, Kate,' whispers my mother. 'No antagonizing him; okay?'

Kate goes to reply but before she can he is there in the doorway, filling the room with the stench of stale cigarette smoke and whisky.

'Fuck me, it's the three witches of *Macbeth*,' he slurs as he stumbles towards the table.

He grabs hold of the corner and almost sends a plate flying.

Kate sighs dramatically and I glare at her, willing her not to provoke him.

'What you sighing at, eh?' he sneers as he slumps into the chair next to mine. 'Something wrong with your lungs?'

'Come on now, let's all be nice,' says my mother as she takes the knife and begins to slice at the pie. As always, she serves my father first. I watch as she spoons the vegetables on to his plate carefully, her hand shaking as she deposits a pile of carrots and peas next to the pie.

Kate is next, then me. Finally, she cuts a tiny sliver for herself.

'Right, tuck in,' she says. She nods at Kate as if to say 'keep quiet' but Kate is busy stuffing the food into her mouth as fast as she can. As soon as she's finished she'll be up the stairs.

I begin to eat but my throat has gone dry with the tension and as I try to swallow a piece of pastry it wedges and I start to choke. Kate thumps me on the back and I grab for my glass of water.

'Jesus Christ,' yells my father as the food finally goes down and I sit trying to get my breath back. 'What you trying to do to us?'

I look up but he is not addressing me. Instead he has his hand on my mother's wrist.

'No wonder the poor kid choked,' he snarls. 'This is fucking inedible.'

He sticks his fork into the pie and starts flicking bits of pastry across the table.

'Look at that. It's not cooked properly. And it's dry.'

Beside me I can feel Kate's temper start to rise, like heat spreading across the table.

'What do you think, sweetheart?'

He is talking to me.

'Do you think it's dry?'

I look at my mother. She is smiling at me, but her eyes are scared.

'Erm, I . . .'

'Come on, I'm asking you a question,' he slurs. 'Is it fucking dry?'

I know what will happen if I don't agree with him. He'll get even angrier and take it out on them. I just want this all to stop.

'Yes,' I whimper. 'It *is* a bit dry.'

'Oh, nice one, Sally,' yells Kate, clattering her cutlery on to her plate. 'For God's sake!'

'Come on now,' whispers my mother, putting her hand on Kate's arm. 'Don't rise to it.'

My father is silent but we all know this is bad news; the longer the silence the worse the punishment.

'You can eyeball me all you want. I'm not scared of you,' says Kate.

Oh no. I look up at her. She is sitting with her hands on the table, glaring at my father.

'You should be,' he mutters.

'What's that, Dad, I didn't hear you?'

She's goading him now. My heart is in my mouth as I wait for the explosion. One, two, three . . .

The plate misses Kate's head by inches and he leaps to his feet and grabs her by the hair.

'Stop it, Dennis,' my mother screams. 'She's just a child.'

'She's a bitch, that's what she is,' he sneers as he takes off his belt. 'A mouthy, know-it-all bitch. Get out of that chair and into the kitchen. Now.'

'Come on then, big man,' Kate yells as he drags her out of the room. 'Hit me. Make yourself feel better for being a lousy waste of space.'

'Kate, stop it,' cries my mother, gripping hold of the back of her seat. 'Don't talk back to him. Come on, Dennis, she didn't mean it.'

But he didn't hear her. He had already pushed Kate into the kitchen and all my mother and I could do was sit and listen to her screams.

I turn over in the bed and look at the darkening sky. Soon the day will be over but I am dreading the coming of morning. Another day without drink; another day without Kate.

As I lie here with my legs pulled up to my chest, my mind drifts back to that evening. When Dad came out of the kitchen there was no sign of Kate, but Mum and I were too scared to ask where she was. Mum took me up to bed while Dad sat and watched late-night TV with the volume turned right up. I lay in bed waiting to hear Kate's footsteps on the stairs but all I could hear was canned laughter. Had she run away? Had she finally had enough and made her escape? Or had he done something – but there my thoughts stopped. She'd be okay. An hour or so passed then the laughter stopped and I heard the thud of my father's footsteps on the stairs. No other footsteps, just his. I screwed up my courage and when I heard my dad on the landing I called him in and asked where she was.

'You get yourself to sleep now, love,' he said as he stood in the doorway. 'Don't be worrying about your sister. Everything's fine.' He was always kinder afterwards.

I sat up in bed, determined to do something. Perhaps he'd listen to me if I asked nicely.

'Why do you hurt them, Daddy?'

He stood there for a moment in silence then he stepped inside and closed the door.

'You wouldn't understand, sweetheart,' he said. 'Now get yourself to sleep.'

'Please, Daddy,' I said, starting to cry. 'Please stop hurting them. It's mean.'

And then he sighed and sat down on the bed next to me.

'I'm not mean, Sally,' he said. 'I'm heartbroken. There's only so much a man can take. Do you want to know something about your sister, eh? Shall I tell you a secret?'

His hoarse voice sent shivers down my spine and I can still hear it as I lie in my bed, years away from that conversation. I can smell the whisky on his breath as he whispered in my ear a secret that I have kept for more than twenty years.

I didn't want to believe him, but at the same time I knew it must be true. Why else would Mum have protected her like she did?

'Where is she?' I asked my father as he stood up to leave. 'Has she run away?'

He gestured to the window. I got out of bed, opened the curtains and looked out. There she was, in the garden. She was lying so still, curled up like a baby on the flower bed with some kind of bag wrapped round her.

'We have to let her in, she'll freeze,' I said, turning to my father who was standing with his hand on the door frame. 'Please, Daddy.'

'She's a bad person, Sally. She needs to learn her lesson,' he said. 'An hour or so out there won't kill her.'

He closed the door, leaving me by the window. And then she stirred and looked up.

'Sally!' I could see her shouting for me to let her in.

And I wanted, more than anything, to go down and help her but my father's words were ringing in my ears:

'She's dangerous, Sally. She's a bad person.'

As Kate waved her arms and begged me to let her in she suddenly looked like some wild monster. A frightening, uncontrollable thing. And for the first time in my life I was scared of her. My father is right, I thought, as I drew the curtains and blocked her out, she needs to learn her lesson.

And I thought she had. But then just a few weeks later she did something that made me change my mind. I had a school friend over to play. Jenny Richards. Kate was out and Jenny asked if we could go and look in her bedroom. We had a good root around and then we pulled out Kate's clothes and started playing dress up. It was just two little kids having a bit of fun. But then Kate came back early and found us. She went mad. I'd never seen her so angry. She dragged us out of the bedroom then slammed me up against the wall on the landing.

'Never go near my stuff again,' she yelled as she put her hand round my throat. 'Do you hear me? Never. Just keep out of my way.'

The anger in her eyes made me feel like I'd done something much worse than just try on a few of her dresses. She looked like she wanted to kill me. It was terrifying.

I was shaking as I made my way downstairs. My mum asked what the matter was but Jenny and I were too shocked to speak. When Kate came down for tea a few hours later neither of us could look her in the eye. From that moment on I did what she had asked and kept out of her way. But something inside me changed that day. I became tougher, less trusting. And I told myself that no one would hurt me like that again.

I'm sitting in the back garden waiting for the sun to come up. It must be around 5 a.m. now. My sleep was plagued with nightmares. Every time I closed my eyes I saw Kate in the flower bed staring up at me with dead eyes. I woke up an hour or so ago screaming. Paul ran in and made a big fuss. He brought me cocoa, told me everything was going to be okay, but how could it be? In the end I gave up on sleep and came out here.

The garden is slippery with dew and my feet feel damp as I sit huddled on my plastic seat. I should have put proper shoes on but my slippers were the nearest thing to hand. As I tuck my feet underneath the chair I feel something brush against my leg. I stifle a scream. But when I look down I see it's just a scrawny little seagull.

'What do you want?' I say as it slinks around my legs, like a cat in search of petting. 'Are you lost?'

I take my phone out of my dressing-gown pocket and shine its light at the bird. Its eyes are half closed and I see that it has a broken wing. Black dots, like specks of mould, are scattered along the edge of it and the flesh beneath is raw and broken. It must be in agony but I have no idea what to do. I've never tended to a sick bird before. It stares at me pathetically, like a small child looking to its mother for reassurance. Its eyes unnerve me and I shoo it away.

'Go on, you mangy thing,' I hiss. 'There's nothing I can do.'

It feebly flaps the broken wing and staggers away into the darkness.

As I watch the bird disappear I think of Hannah. I remember when she was a little girl she wanted to be a vet and she would bring half-dead birds and mice into the house that she'd rescued from next-door's cat. I would try to explain that it was kinder to let them die but she would spend hours tending to them, wrapping them in bits of cloth. When the inevitable happened we'd take the little bodies and bury them at the bottom of Mum's garden. Hannah would sob as we laid them in the soil and my mother would tell her that God was calling them back. We'd have a little wake after that with cake and lemonade but we always knew it wouldn't be long before the next casualties arrived. She would have made a wonderful vet if she'd stayed on at school. God, I miss her.

As I sit in the darkness I feel a dull pain creeping up my body. I've lived with this pain ever since she left. It's an emptiness I've filled with booze but now, with no alcohol in me, the pain is all I have. At Dad's funeral the vicar said when you lose someone you love a little piece of you dies. I didn't know what he meant until Hannah left. Then it all made sense. Without her I was no longer a mother, I was barely a wife. The Sally that had existed before then had disappeared and been replaced with the person I am now. I may look the same, and talk the same, but there is a hole inside me that can never be mended. I may as well be dead.

It would be so easy to slip away, to say that's it. I think of the many ways you could do it: a couple of bottles of champagne and a fistful of pills; a sleek pistol edged in gold leaf like a baddie in a James Bond film – both too glamorous for me, of course. Perhaps a luxuriously hot bath and a sharpened knife. I look at the bulbous blue veins that snake along my wrists and imagine myself slicing through them.

I shudder as I look up at the sky. The night is thick and heavy and I wish for the light to come and take away these thoughts. I stand up, suddenly desperate for a drink. I flick a woodlouse from my lap. My legs feel like lead as I make my way to the conservatory door and I know that I'm only going to make myself feel worse, but I need it. It's the only way I can deal with this pain.

I tiptoe across the room and grab the wine bottle from my new hiding place, an old holdall that I've kept hidden under my armchair. Paul hates coming in here so there's no danger of him finding it. I managed to sneak out of the house when he'd gone to sleep last night. I went to the all-night petrol station round the corner and bought a couple of bottles. He was still asleep when I got back, thank God.

I come back outside just as the sun breaks on the horizon. I'm desperately tired but I know what will come if I go to bed. *She'll* come; with her dead eyes watching me. I won't risk it. So instead, I sit down and drink.

I'm at the bottom of the bottle when I see it: a tiny mound of white on the grass that, as I look closer, turns into a living creature.

'Oh no,' I sigh as I stand up and go to it. 'Please no. I don't need this.'

The seagull doesn't move and I assume it must be dead. Its eyes are cloudy, its beak partially open. But as I crouch down to take a closer look it makes a gut-wrenching sound. Not a cry but a sob; this bird is coughing up its death rattle. I can't bear it.

I hear Hannah's voice in my head.

'Mummy, we need to help him.'

But he's past help now, I think, as I step over him and walk to the kitchen. From the door I can still hear it: *creee-oo, creeee-oo*. It's a pathetic sound, like a baby crying for its mum, and I know that I will have to do something. It could take hours to die.

So I go to the cupboard and take out the heaviest object in the house: the rolling pin. I think of my dad threatening Kate with Mum's rolling pin as I wrap my hand round its rough surface. I remember Kate's words in an article I read years later: *Give someone a weapon and they become a warrior.* 'Give me strength, Kate,' I whisper as I return to the garden.

The bird doesn't move as I step towards it and I pray that it's dead, that I won't have to do this, but as I bend down to check, it flinches and starts crying again. It sounds like it's coming from beneath the bird, somewhere deeper and darker. It's creeping me out. It almost sounds like a child.

'Don't look at it,' I tell myself as I raise the rolling pin above my head. I want to close my eyes but I know that I mustn't or I risk missing the target and causing it more pain. No, I need to get it over with in one clean blow.

But my hands are shaking as I bring the pin down and although I feel the crack of bones, I miss its head. The bird flounders and starts to walk away, dazed. I chase it, raining down blows again and again until the path is strewn with feathers and deep-red blood. With each strike the bird cries out and I want to block my ears but I can't. The sound reverberates through my body as I finally manage to smash its skull and it comes to rest in a heap by the side of my foot.

I stand there for a few moments, the bloodied rolling pin still raised above my head, and I look at the remains of the bird. Its pink eyes are now black with blood. I don't want to look at them any more. I just want this to be over.

I pick it up, the sharp needles of its broken wing pressing against my skin, and I slowly walk to the flower bed. Placing the bird by the side of the grass, I begin to shovel the soil with my hands. He needs a peaceful resting place, I tell myself, as the soil becomes damp under my fingertips. That's what Hannah would want. I dig and dig, deeper and deeper, through tangled roots, disturbing worms as I go, and then my hand catches on something hard.

I look down and see a sliver of gold. Brushing away the roots and soil, I pull at the sparkly thing until it yields and then I sit holding it in my hands. My heart hurts as I remember picking out the slimline gold watch for Hannah's sixteenth birthday. I turn it over and read the inscription on the inside of the strap:

To our beautiful girl on her 16th birthday. Love you always, Mum and Paul xxx

How did it end up here? Did she throw it away to punish me? But then as I sit rubbing my fingers over the cracked face I hear her voice.

Just let me go, Mum. You're hurting me.

She was going to leave me. I was angry. I'd found an internet search on her computer. She'd been trying to get back in touch with her real dad, the little shit who got me pregnant when we were both fourteen. I told her he wasn't interested, told her that his parents had moved away when they found out about the baby and told me to leave him alone. I told her that in sixteen years he'd never once tried to get in touch. I told her that Paul was her dad, that there was nothing to be gained from raking over the past, but she wouldn't listen.

Just let me go, Mum.

Until now those words have been the last thing I could remember from that night, the night she left. But as I sit here, her voice ringing in my ears, I see something more. I see her standing at the door. She's telling me I'm a drunk. I run at her, grabbing her wrists to pull her back inside.

'Just let me go, Mum.'

I pull and pull at her; tell her she's not going to leave me, that I won't let her. She's all I have. And then there's a bang. A door slamming? Me falling over? I'm holding her watch in my hand. I have Hannah's watch, but she's gone. What happened? I can't remember. I don't know if I want to remember.

I look down at the watch with its rusty strap and broken face and my stomach knots. Paul can't see this watch. He already thinks it's odd that I don't remember anything about Hannah leaving and he knows things were volatile between us. If he finds this watch he'll know by my face that something went on and then I'll have to tell him. I'm a terrible liar. And once he knows we fought that night he'll blame me for her leaving and I can't bear that. I have to get rid of it.

So I place it back in the hole I've dug and put the dead bird on top, folding its wing over its blackened eyes, then I cover them both with mound upon mound of earth until all that remains is a brown patch; an unremarkable square of soil in an unremarkable garden. Nobody would know, I tell myself, as I stumble back to the house and make for my wine stash. Nobody would know.

'What have you done?'

His voice sounds like it's coming from a great distance but I feel his hands gripping me as he hauls me up to my feet. I try to open my eyes but I can't; they're too heavy with sleep.

'What's this all over you? Is it blood? What the hell . . . What have you done to yourself?' He puts his hand on the base of my back and guides me across the room.

I hear running water then the shock of heat on my skin.

'There, it's coming away,' he says, and I feel his skin rubbing against the flesh of my hands. 'Where've you hurt yourself? Honestly, I can't leave you for a minute, can I?'

The water stops and I half open my eyes but they burn with the light. I feel his arms clasped round my waist and a surge of warmth through my body.

The bed is soft and I fall into it like a stone. I feel him behind me. I hear his breath grow shallow and then his hands are on my breasts. He's moving against me like he used to. It feels wonderful to be close to him again. I arch my back and he eases himself inside me. 'Sally,' he moans and as we begin to make love my eyes fill with tears. I've missed him so much.

32

Paul is gone when I wake though I can still trace the shape of his body on the bed where he lay beside me.

Why do my hands hurt? I lift them in front of my face and see a pattern of scratches. Grains of black dirt edge my fingernails.

Panic rises inside me. What happened last night?

I pull on my jeans and a sweater and run down the stairs, calling his name as I go, but there is no reply.

'Paul!'

I stumble into the kitchen. Nothing. I see his empty mug sitting in the sink. I slump across the counter and try to clear my head so I can work out what to do next. But it's so jumbled all I can see are broken images that don't fit together: Paul lying beside me on the bed; my fingers digging through soil. Why was I digging?

Then suddenly I'm back there. I'm standing in the garden looking down and my heart jerks so fiercely it feels like it's coming out of my chest. Bones, a string of them, tiny and intricate, rippling across the top of the soil, and a flash of gold. I can see it now but I don't want to see it. I blink my eyes to make the image go away but it stays there like a stain growing darker each time I close my eyes. I'm remembering but it's coming to me in pieces. A loud crack and a screeching noise. Hannah. *Just let me go, Mum.*

Am I going mad?

I need Paul.

I run out of the kitchen and go from room to room shouting for him but there is no reply. I need him to come and get me out of here, to rescue me and take me away. He thinks I'm losing it but he can't abandon me. I won't let him. I'll make it up to him. We can try again; book a nice holiday to Spain or somewhere, just the two of us. We can get away from everything and have a bit of peace and quiet. That will be nice. And the thought of it makes me feel calm where just moments ago I was all panicky. See, if I just keep focused and think good thoughts then it will be all right.

I walk back into the kitchen and as I go to the sink to fill the kettle I see him out of the window. He is there, standing looking at the flower bed. Relief floods through my body, but then I remember the gold watch and I run to the door.

'Paul!' I yell. 'Come inside.'

He looks up at me then back at the flower bed and I wonder what he's thinking.

'Paul, please.'

He puts his head down and shuffles towards me.

'What's going on, Sally?' He looks strange. Is he angry?

I try to peer round him but the soil looks undisturbed.

'It was a bird,' I say, looking around as though it might pop out at any moment. 'A seagull. Its wing was all mangled and I had to put it out of its misery. I buried it.'

'I thought it must have been something like that,' he says. 'I found the rolling pin just over there. It had loads of tiny bones on it.'

'Oh no,' I gasp, putting my hands over my face. 'Oh, please don't say that. I can't believe I did it but it was making the most dreadful noise and its wing was all broken and I didn't know what else to do.'

'Come on, love,' he says. 'Don't get yourself all worked up. Let's go inside and sit down.'

He walks on ahead and I follow in a daze, trying not to think of Hannah and her rescue missions. All those tiny bones.

'You go in the living room and I'll make us a drink,' he says, reaching up to the cupboard and taking down two mugs. 'Tea or coffee?'

I would give anything for a glass of wine but I don't want to give away my secret stash.

'Tea would be lovely,' I reply. 'Make it strong.'

I go into the living room and turn on the light. I see a pile of papers on the coffee table, Paul's work, and I feel bad that he has missed another day at the office on my account.

'Here we are,' he says, coming in with a mug of tea.

'Thanks, Paul,' I say as he puts it on the table in front of me.

He sits down and sips his tea while I wait for mine to cool down. Neither of us speaks, and the quiet makes me feel nervous. The bird is back. It's flying around the ceiling, making me feel dizzy. Round and round it goes, its cold dead eyes boring into me until I can't stand it any longer. I get up and grab the remote control from the shelf then switch on the TV.

'Sally, do you have to?'

I ignore Paul's protests as I sit back down in the armchair and stare at the screen. TV has a soothing effect on me when I feel like this, when the nerves spike up on the surface of my skin like tiny knives. It always has done. When I was a kid I would drown out my parents' shouting by staring at the television. In my favourite programmes the towns were green and sunny, everyone was happy and safe, nobody shouted or argued. If I put my hands over my ears I could pretend I lived there too. I was such a scared little girl but I knew that in the hours between three thirty and five in the afternoon – children's telly time – no one could hurt me.

I turn the volume up as the local news bulletin starts.

'Sally?'

'Blimey, he's been presenting this show since I was a kid,' I say, pointing at the lizard-skinned anchorman. 'Donkey's years. Surprised he hasn't been pensioned off.'

'Can we at least turn it down?' says Paul, reaching for the remote control that is still within my grip. 'I can't hear myself think.'

'No,' I say, holding it to my chest as the image on the screen changes. 'I want to hear this. He's talking about Kate.'

The presenter is saying that she grew up in the area and attended the local school.

'Oh, Kate would love this,' I say. 'She bloody hated Herne Bay Comp.'

'As far as we know, Kate Rafter is missing presumed dead,' he goes on.

I lean forward in my chair.

'See,' I say to Paul, pointing at the screen. 'He's saying it as well: missing. I told you. There's still a chance.'

'Sally, he said missing presumed dead. They –'

'Shhh,' I hiss as they cut to a scene from the place where it happened: a field full of tents and body bags.

'Oh my God,' I gasp. 'Look at that.'

'Sally, turn it off,' says Paul. 'This isn't going to help.'

The lizardy presenter is back. His face is grey and serious as he tells us that Kate's friends and colleagues are holding a vigil in some church in London. St Bride's in Fleet Street. Then he smiles and hands over to Christine for the weather.

'I've got to go,' I say, jumping to my feet.

'Go where?'

Paul grabs the remote control and turns the television off just as Christine is warning of strong westerly winds.

'Sally, breathe,' he says. 'You need to slow down or you'll have a panic attack.'

I pat my pockets, though I have no idea what I'm looking for. Keys. I always used to have car keys in my pocket though that's another thing I've lost.

'Stop,' says Paul, grabbing hold of my arms. 'Come on, love, just sit down and I'll make us another cup of tea.'

'I don't want another cup of tea,' I tell him as I rush into the hallway to get my shoes. 'I need to go to London. They're having a vigil; he just said that. I'll have to check the train times but they're pretty regular, aren't they?'

'Sally,' he yells. 'For God's sake, stop it.'

He's in front of me now, holding my arms with both his hands.

'You have got to calm down or you're going to make yourself ill,' he says. 'Nobody is going to London.

277

Okay? Nobody. You need to rest and let yourself grieve properly. You've had a huge shock and barely any sleep. I mean, for Christ's sake, you spent most of last night digging up the garden.'

'But he said –'

'Listen, it's okay,' says Paul as he takes me in his arms. 'The vigil isn't for another two days. If you promise me you'll get some sleep and eat some proper food then I'll take you to it. Now let's get you back to bed. You need to rest.'

But as I settle between the sheets and close my eyes all I can see is the bird. It presses its beak against my ear and whispers with Hannah's voice:

Just let me go, Mum.

33

I can smell burnt toast and my stomach lurches as I turn over in the bed. The streetlight filters through the white linen curtains and I can see the shadow of a bird sitting on the ledge, its beak opening and closing.

Just let me go, Mum.

I pull the covers over my head, willing myself to go back to sleep. But then the door opens.

'Hi, love,' he says. 'You must have needed that sleep. It's almost evening.'

He taps me gently on the back but I stay curled up in my cocoon.

'Sally,' he says. 'Wake up, love. I've brought you some food.'

'I don't want anything,' I mumble. I need to think. To plan what to do. How to get to Kate.

'Look, you've got to eat or you'll get ill,' he urges. 'It's just a bit of toast. You've had no lunch. Please, Sally.'

I yank the covers from my head and glare at him.

'Fine,' I snap. 'Just leave it on the side.'

He puts it on top of the chest of drawers and looks at me anxiously.

'I'll be downstairs,' he says. 'I'm cooking us something nice for dinner. Call me if you need me.'

I watch as he steps out on to the landing and closes the door, thankful that he has gone. There was a time when Paul's caring nature was a balm to me; now it feels like a straitjacket. I know I should be kinder to him. He saved me. He saved both of us.

I sit up in the bed and open the top drawer of the bedside cabinet. There, underneath a pile of old bank statements, is a silver-embossed photo album.

Our wedding album.

I pause for a second then open it. The first photo is a black-and-white shot of the three of us. Paul looks handsome in his navy suit and the pink spotty tie Hannah bought him as a wedding present. I've got a glass of champagne in my hand and I'm presentable but chubby in my ivory trouser suit. Hannah stands between us in the pistachio green bridesmaid dress she picked out a couple of weeks earlier in a little vintage shop in Whitstable. She beams at the camera and I feel a pang of guilt. She was so happy to finally have a dad. And not just any dad but a warm, loving one who helped her with her homework and took her swimming. As I stare at the photo I see that it's Paul that she is cuddling in to, not me. I'm just standing there with my drink, lost in my own world.

Paul was my route into normality. He took Hannah and me away from that house, away from Mum and her endless criticism, and he gave us a new life, one with holidays and fitted kitchens and barbecues on Sundays. It was perfect. But then it all went wrong.

I close the album and put it back into the drawer, but as I lie down and shut my eyes Hannah's face is there in front of me, twisted with rage.

'I hate you,' she yells at me. 'You have no idea what it's like living with a drunk. A pisshead.'

And I want to grab her, sit her down and tell her that I *do* know what it's like; that my dad was a drunk and that my childhood had been a battleground that nobody came through unscathed.

It started slowly, the rift between Hannah and me, and then like a disease it just spread and spread until it destroyed us. As I lie here I try to pinpoint when it all started. Was it her fourteenth birthday when she went out with her mates instead of coming to Alfredo's with me and Paul? It sounds daft but Alfredo's was a family tradition. It was an Italian restaurant in Whitstable and I'd taken her there on her birthday since she was a little kid. And it hurt when she said she'd grown out of all that; it really did. Paul didn't understand why I was so upset; he said it was only natural; that she was growing up, asserting her independence. I had no choice. So I spent the evening of her birthday sitting in front of the TV with Paul, thinking about the cake that was waiting for her in the kitchen. But when she came home she said she was too tired to blow out candles and, anyway, all that stuff was for kids.

And so it grew and grew, the divide between us. Hannah would stay out with her mates most nights; Paul had set up his new haulage business and was working late shifts to get it up and running. So that left me stuck in by myself with just the TV and my memories for company. There were no more family barbecues, no laughter, just a big empty house. Wine helped fill the gap, it soothed the loneliness and stopped me thinking about the past. I didn't know how much I was depending on it until it was too late.

Getting sacked from my job at the bank should have been a wake-up call but I just saw it as an opportunity to lock myself away and drink more. Paul was there but we were like strangers passing each other on the stairs. We were no longer intimate; all the comfort and love I needed came at the bottom of a glass. Hannah would come home from school and I would try to act sober, fuss around her, make the dinner, but she wasn't stupid and we'd end up having silly arguments over nothing. In the end she would avoid dinner altogether and come down later when she thought I'd be asleep.

After she left I started to think back to those days, tried to work out if I'd missed something. Her moods changed dramatically, I know that much. Paul said it was probably hormones but I suspected she was taking drugs. She became withdrawn and secretive. She stopped going out and started locking herself in her room for hours on end. But now I wonder if it wasn't drugs – what if it was just me?

I found the internet searches one night a few months later. She'd googled him. His name was Frankie Echevarria. Kate said it sounded like 'itch of your rear'. That always made me laugh. But the fact that it was an unusual name made the search a bit easier. Hannah had found out that he was a teacher now and living in Brighton. He had a family of his own; he was settled.

I didn't want her to get hurt, so I tried to stop her.

'He won't want you contacting him out of the blue,' I told her. 'Just leave it alone.'

'He's my father,' she yelled at me. 'I need him.'

'You don't need him,' I yelled back. 'You've got me and Paul.'

'I don't want you. I want a proper parent.'

And she looked at me so defiantly that something inside me snapped.

My words come back to me now. 'That man didn't give a damn about me and he certainly didn't give a damn about you. He wanted me to get rid of you. And I told him that I'd never do that. I told him to leave me alone and I'd deal with our mistake.'

Why did I say that word? I regretted it as soon as it left my mouth but it was too late.

'Mistake?' she said. Her voice was so bitter it scared me. 'Is that what I am? A mistake. Jesus, Mother, you really are something, aren't you?'

I turn on my side and look out of the window. I can smell garlic coming from downstairs. Paul will be cooking another meal that I won't eat. We'll sit in front of the telly and then I'll come back up here, try to sleep, then it will start all over again. Another empty day. But as I lie here I see Kate's body lying in some morgue in a foreign country. I've got to face the truth. My sister is not missing, she's dead and she needs a proper burial. I jump up from the bed. I might have let Hannah down but I still have a chance to do the right thing by Kate; give her a decent send-off. As I pull on my dressing gown and go to the bathroom, my head feels a little clearer.

It's time to bring her home.

34

Paul looks shocked when I walk into the kitchen. I've washed my hair, changed into some clean clothes, and I now smell of lavender instead of sweat and booze.

'Hello, love,' he says, kissing me on the cheek. 'I'm so glad you've come down. I've made a lasagne. Would you like some?'

'Just a little bit,' I say, pulling out a chair to sit down.

'I bet you feel better for having a bath,' he says as he flits about getting plates and cutlery together.

'I feel clean, not better,' I reply. I've only been in the room for a couple of minutes and already he's making me feel tense.

'Clean is a good start,' he says, putting a plate in front of me. 'Can I get you a drink?'

I look up quickly but he's offering fizzy water not Chardonnay. I nod my head and he pours it into my glass.

'I wanted to discuss Kate's body,' I say as he sits down in the chair opposite me. 'What do we need to do to get it back?'

'I'm not sure,' he says, drumming his fingers on the table. 'There'll be a repatriation process to go through and that could take weeks. If they find her body, that is.'

'They haven't found her body?' I say, sitting up in my chair. 'So there is still a chance she could be alive?'

'Sally,' he says, putting his hand on my arm. He always does this if I raise my voice even slightly. 'She's not alive.'

'How do you know?' I cry, pushing his hand away. 'She could be out there, injured, in need of help, and we're sitting here eating bloody lasagne.'

'There were no survivors,' he says. 'The place they were staying in took a direct hit. When they say missing . . . well, I didn't want to go into detail because it's not something you want to hear.'

'You didn't want to go into detail?' I cry. 'I'm not a bloody child, Paul. Of course I want to know what happened to my sister. Stop pussyfooting around and just tell me.'

He puts his fork down and sighs.

'Are you sure you want to know?'

'Yes,' I reply, my stomach churning.

'Well,' he says. 'The MoD said that the explosion was so huge a lot of the bodies would have been . . . obliterated.'

'What are you saying?'

'I'm saying there may not be a body to bring back.'

His words are like bullets tearing into my skin. My sister; my beautiful, brave sister. I try to imagine her final moments and hope it was quick, that she didn't suffer.

'So we can't give her a funeral?' I say as I sit watching Paul spoon a heap of meaty stodge on to my plate. 'We just have to leave her out there in . . . in bits?'

He puts the spoon down and rubs my arm again.

'You'll have your memories,' he says. 'She'll always be alive up here.' He taps his forehead and smiles and it's such a stupid, patronizing smile, I want to rip it from his face.

'You have no idea, you idiot,' I yell as I jump up from the table and run up the stairs. 'No idea at all.'

I'm back on the bed, lying in the darkness and thinking of Kate's blasted body, when he comes in and turns on the light.

'You know something, Sally, I'm getting a bit sick of this,' he says, sitting down heavily on the bed.

'Oh, will you please just go away,' I say.

'No, I will not just go away,' he shouts, grabbing my wrist. He is squeezing tightly and it hurts. 'I'm not some pest you can just click your fingers at and make disappear.'

'Paul, stop it, you're hurting me,' I say, pulling my arm free.

I look at him. I hardly ever see him angry like this. His face is contorted, his nostrils flaring.

'Look, I know you're upset,' he says. 'But I'm sick of having to hold your hand through everything. I wanted a wife, not a bloody patient.'

'My sister's just died,' I say, covering my face with my hands.

'Yes,' he shouts. 'Your sister. A woman you cut out of your life because she said something you didn't want to hear. That's what you do to everyone, Sally. If you don't like what they have to say you push them away.'

'That's not true,' I say.

Why does he always take Kate's side? Years ago I told him what she'd done and he still made excuses for her;

said it was probably an accident. I'd felt guilty for telling him but I had to; I was sick of him talking about her like she was some saint. But it made no difference.

'It *is* true,' he goes on. 'Kate and I became close when she came back here. She was devastated, in a real state over the death of a little boy out in Syria. But you'd know nothing about that, would you? As you told me when we first met, you were sick to death of hearing about Kate's wonderful job. You were so jealous of her it was eating you up inside.'

I burrow my face into the pillow but he pulls my head up.

'Don't ignore me,' he spits. 'I've had years of that, of being ignored and treated like a bloody doormat. No, you're going to listen to this. For once in your life you're going to face up to things instead of running away.'

I sit up in the bed and look at him.

'Kate told me things,' he continues. 'Like how your old man used to knock her about. No kid should have to put up with that.'

My body freezes when he mentions my father and suddenly the room is full of him.

She's dangerous, Sally . . .

I put my hands over my ears but Paul yanks them away.

'No,' he yells, 'you're not taking the easy route like you always do. Kate was worried sick about you, she tried to help you even though she was battling her own issues.'

I shake my head. My eyes are heavy with tears and I wipe them away with the back of my hand.

'She was in a really bad way,' says Paul. 'What happened in Syria had seriously affected her. She was having nightmares, hearing voices, seeing things.'

'What do you mean, seeing things?'

'She said she could see a kid in the garden next door,' he says. 'There are no kids living next door. Then I found sleeping pills in her bag, loads of them, super strength they were as well. She was taking handfuls of them every night. And she was drinking. Lots.'

'Why didn't you tell me this?'

'Because I didn't want to worry you.'

'Didn't want to worry me?' I shout. 'She's my sister for God's sake.'

'Okay, I'll be blunt, shall I?' he says. 'You were drunk and sitting about in your own filth and even if I had told you, what help would you have been? Kate was losing her mind and I had to deal with it all by myself while you sat in here drinking yourself stupid.'

'She wasn't losing her mind, don't be ridiculous.'

'That's not what the police said.'

'The police?' My head is spinning as I try to take it all in.

'She was arrested,' he says, his voice quivering. 'She'd had a set-to with the neighbours. Accusing them of things. Then she broke into their shed in the middle of the night and they called the police. I've never seen her in such a state – she was completely delirious. The police psychiatrist interviewed her. Said she's got PTSD. You know, like soldiers get.'

'What was she accusing them of?'

'Oh, something about a child. I'm sure it's to do with what happened to that boy in Aleppo –'

'Hang on,' I say. 'You said you'd never seen her in such a state before. Were you with her when she broke into the shed?'

His face flushes and he turns to the window.

'I'd popped in to see if she was all right.'

'In the middle of the night?'

'I was on my way back from a late one at the office,' he says brusquely. 'Listen, that's not the point. What matters is that your sister was arrested, she was detained under the bloody Mental Health Act, and I was the one who had to deal with it.'

Nothing about this makes sense and Paul is talking so fast it's hard to keep up.

'Kate has a mental illness?' I exclaim. 'That's not possible.'

But then I hear my father's words again: *She's dangerous, Sally.*

'You didn't see her,' Paul says. 'She was like a mad woman. The neighbours were terrified. She tried to attack one of them.'

'But when she came to see me, she was fine,' I say. 'I would have noticed if she was behaving strangely.'

'Would you?' He lets out a sound that falls between a laugh and a sigh. 'Would you really? Honestly, Sally, you're so wrapped up in your own world. You only see what you want to see, what suits you.'

'I know my sister,' I reply but even as the words come out I know they're not true. I have no idea who Kate really is. Was.

Another scrap of that last phone call comes back to me. Kate's voice, pleading: *I'm calling to ask you a favour.*

289

'They dropped the charges, thank goodness,' says Paul. 'But on the condition that Kate leave Herne Bay. They made it clear they'd take out a restraining order against her if she went near the house again.'

I think of the way Kate used to rage against my father; how she would fight back, her eyes bulging, her fists raised.

'When she was released I picked her up and gave her a lift to the train station,' Paul goes on, drumming his fingers on the window ledge. I hate it when he does this. It sets my nerves on edge. 'And that was the last time I saw her. So you see, when you say I have no idea, you're very wrong. I saw Kate deteriorate right in front of my eyes, just like I saw Hannah fall apart.'

'Don't compare Hannah to Kate,' I yell. 'Hannah didn't fall apart. She was a troubled teenager. Like you said, she was finding her way.'

'Oh Jesus, Sally, you really are unbelievable,' he shouts, slamming his fist on the window ledge. 'I said that to be kind, so I didn't upset you. Now I wish I'd just been honest and straight with you, then maybe Hannah would still be here.'

'Why are you shouting at me?'

'I'm shouting because I've had it up to here with you,' he says. 'I've cosseted and protected you ever since we met, even to the detriment of your own daughter. And I was a fool because you're right, you're not a child, you're a grown woman and you needed to know the truth.'

His hands are shaking and it's scaring me.

'What truth?' I say. 'What are you talking about?'

'When we first met, Hannah was so terrified of you, she was wetting the bed almost every night,' he says, his voice ice cold. 'But instead of telling you I covered it up, to protect you.'

'Paul, you're talking nonsense,' I say. 'Hannah never wet the bed, even when she was a toddler. She was potty trained at eighteen months and after that she was meticulous about going to the loo. If she'd started wetting the bed at the age of thirteen I would have known.'

'Well, you didn't,' he says. 'The poor kid begged me not to tell you. She was terrified of what you might do. By the time you'd woken up with your hangover I'd already changed the sheets.'

'Oh, come off it, Paul,' I say. 'I know Hannah and I had our differences but that came later, when she was well into her teens. She wasn't scared of me. That's ridiculous.'

'Oh, really?' he says. 'You know she told me once that when she was five you left her in a pub garden while you got pissed at the bar. I mean, what kind of mother does that?'

My cheeks burn at the memory.

'That was a one-off,' I say. 'It was the anniversary of my dad's death and I was in a bad state. It was wrong, I know it was, but it didn't happen again.'

'As I said, Sally, you only see what you want to see,' he says. 'How about your mother, eh? What was the name of the care home I found for her, the one she died in?'

My head is a fog. Why is he bombarding me like this?

'Erm, it was Hill something,' I stutter. 'Hill View?'

'Nice try,' he sneers. 'It was Willow Grange. I know that because I found it, I paid for it and I visited her there twice a week. When did you visit her, Sally? Oh, that's right, you didn't.'

'My mother and I had a difficult relationship,' I say.

'You've had a difficult relationship with everyone,' he yells. 'This is what is so exasperating. You blame everyone else but you're the one who causes all the bad blood. You didn't get on with your mum, you didn't get on with Kate, you didn't get on with Hannah, you can barely look at me. The only person you ever seem to have liked is your bloody father and he was a drunken mess. I guess the apple didn't fall far from the tree.'

'No,' I cry as I leap from the bed and run at him, my fingernails clawing into his face. 'Don't you dare say that. Don't you ever say that.'

He grabs my wrists and holds them tightly, and when my anger subsides I see the blood streaming down his face.

'That's it,' he says, his voice quivering. 'I'm done with you.'

'I didn't mean it,' I sob as he lets go of my wrists and storms to the door. 'I'm sorry, Paul. Please don't leave me, we can sort this out, please.'

'It's too late, Sally,' he says, wiping the blood from his face. 'It's over.'

35

I can't do this any more. Paul is gone. Without him I have nothing; just a big empty house. It's time to leave. The wine will numb me then I'll finish it off with a handful of pills. Nice and clean.

I lie back on the bed and dissolve into a white-wine haze. The Spar was just opening when I arrived and the woman shook her head as she rang through my three bottles of white.

'Bit early, isn't it?'

Usually I give her some blather about having a dinner party later but this time I couldn't be bothered making excuses. 'Yes, it *is* a bit early,' I hissed as I handed over the cash, 'but I'm giving you business so what's your problem?' I could feel her eyes on me as I left the shop. I must have looked a state in my coat and slippers but I didn't care. I'd never see her again.

When I got home part of me hoped he would be there, standing in the kitchen with that look of disapproval on his face: 'Wine, Sally, at this time of the morning? Honestly . . .' But the house was empty so I took a glass from the kitchen cupboard and made my way upstairs.

I close my eyes and my head fills with his voice. He was so angry, so bitter. It was like he hated me.

I *do* push people away. Paul was right about that. But if you spend your childhood desperately seeking your mother's approval and never getting it you grow up feeling that you're not worth anything. What's the point of letting people in when they're only going to hurt you?

The love I felt for Hannah when she was born was so huge I felt like I would die, that my heart would burst, every time I looked at her. She was so tiny, so vulnerable, and I knew that it was beyond me. So I handed her over to Mum and let her do the things I could never do, like feeding the ducks and standing pushing a swing for hours on end without becoming frustrated. That's why Hannah loved Mum so much, because she was solid, as mothers should be, where I was unpredictable; unstable. I cringe as I remember that day at the pub; her little face as I left her in the beer garden and headed inside to the bar. No child deserves a mother like me.

And now the booze is all I have left.

I drain the glass and pour another then another until the room becomes a pinkish blur. I close my eyes and the blackness feels so good I want to fall into it. As I lie back I see a tiny boy drifting out to sea. The waves crash over his head, then silence. It's over. And I think how tempting it must be to just give up; to stop breathing and fall into a long deep sleep.

It's time.

I reach over to the bedside cabinet and take out a box of sleeping tablets. Drinking plays havoc with my sleep and when I wake up in the middle of the night a quick pill is the only thing to send me back off. Now if I just increase the dose I can curl up nice and cosy. I can go and find Kate and David and all this pain will stop.

I puncture the foil and pop one in my mouth, washing it down with a mouthful of wine. There are eighteen pills left but I reckon half of that will do the trick. I push another one out of the foil but as I swallow it I hear knocking at the front door. It's Paul. He's come back. He's changed his mind.

I shove the pills back in the drawer and slam it shut.

'Paul,' I call out as I run down the stairs. 'I'm just coming.'

But my heart sinks as I see the outline of a woman through the glass. It must be nosy Sandra from next door. She's the only woman who knocks on our door and it's usually because she's got something to complain about.

'What is it this time?' I sigh as I open the door.

But it's not Sandra. It's a young woman. She looks Middle Eastern and is dressed in a beautiful blue dress and matching scarf.

'Sally?' she says.

When I hear her accent I assume she must be here about Kate. She must be from the consulate.

'Have you come about my sister?'

She nods her head.

'You'd better come in then,' I say.

My head is light with booze and the sleeping pills as I lead her inside. My stomach knots. I'm not prepared for this at all. She's going to tell me about Kate's death and I know it won't be good. I take her into the kitchen and ask if she would like a cup of tea. I could do with a stiff drink but the way she's dressed tells me she probably wouldn't approve of that.

'You must have come a long way,' I say as I fill the kettle.

'No, not very far,' she says, looking around uncertainly.

'Why don't you have a seat?' I say. 'Make yourself comfortable.'

I watch as she sits down at the table. She is very nervous. Her face twitches every so often and I wonder if this is a result of living in Syria; some sort of shell shock.

'Here you are,' I say, placing the mug of tea in front of her. 'Sugar's on the table if you want some.'

'Thank you,' she says, but as she takes a sip her hands start shaking and the tea splatters down her front.

'I'm sorry,' she says, putting the cup down. 'Clumsy.'

'Don't be silly,' I reply, handing her a tea towel. 'It was probably my fault. I over-filled it. I hope it hasn't spoiled your nice dress.'

She dabs at the damp stain, her hands still shaking, then she puts the towel on the table and cradles the half-empty cup.

'So you knew my sister,' I say, sitting down next to her.

'Yes, a little,' she says. 'We only met a couple of times but she was very kind. She wanted to help me.'

I raise my eyebrows. 'That sounds like Kate,' I say as I take a sip of tea. 'She wanted to help everybody. She was born that way.'

'I was so sorry to hear of her death,' she says.

'Yes,' I say. 'It was a huge shock. You were out there too then, were you?'

'Out where?'

'In Syria,' I say. 'You were with her?'

'Oh no,' she says. 'I'm not from Syria. I live in the house next door to your mother's. My name's Fida.'

I put my cup down, my heart thudding.

'Paul's house?'

'Yes.'

'Are you the one who had my sister arrested?'

'Yes, but that was all a big mistake.'

'A big mistake?' I spit. 'As I understand it she was forced to leave Herne Bay because you called the police. If you hadn't done that she wouldn't have gone to Aleppo. She wouldn't be dead.'

'It was a misunderstanding,' she says, looking at me pleadingly. 'If you'll let me, I can explain.'

'I don't want you to explain,' I cry, my heart pounding. 'It's too late. My sister's dead.'

'But I need to tell you something,' she says. 'I need . . . I need your help. I have –'

'I'd like you to leave,' I say, getting up from my chair.

'Please just let me speak,' she cries.

'Listen, love, I'm not interested,' I say, folding my arms. 'Now clear off.'

She stands up and I march her to the door.

'I'm sorry,' she says, turning to me, 'I just wanted to –'

'Did you not hear me?' I cry as I yank the door open. 'I said get out.'

36

I step back inside the house. I'm glad that the last thing I did was stand up for my sister. Now I can get on with it. I grab another bottle of wine in case I need it. But as I make my way up the stairs I hear a clattering noise. I turn and see a pile of post lying on the doormat.

On the top is a bulky Jiffy bag. I bend down and pick it up. It's probably something for Paul – no one sends anything to me. But then I see my name printed in capital letters and the logo of Kate's newspaper printed on the back. I tear open the parcel, wondering what it can be. Looking inside, I see a thin black object. I pull it out and hold it in my shaking hands.

A Dictaphone. It's cracked and pock-marked and the plastic casing has melted in parts but I can still make out what it is. Surely it's not . . .

There's something else in there. I put my hand back inside the Jiffy bag and ease out a piece of paper. I take it and the Dictaphone into the kitchen then sit down at the table to read.

Sally,

I want to convey my deepest condolences for the loss of your sister, Kate. She was a brave and brilliant woman and the finest journalist I have ever worked with. This Dictaphone was found by one of the rescue workers close to where she was last

*seen. It was sent to the newsroom but, on listening to the
contents, it seems it is more of a personal item than a professional one as you will hear when you play it.*

*I am working closely with the MoD and the consulate in Syria
and will be in touch as soon as I have any more news for you.*

*In the meantime, if I can be of further help to you at this
difficult time please do not hesitate to get in touch.*

*Best Wishes,
Harry Vine*

Harry Vine. I run the name over and over in my head
and then it clicks. Harry. Kate's editor. She used to talk
about him whenever she came home. It was all: 'Harry's
going to love this' or 'Wait till I tell Harry, he won't
believe it.' She was godmother to his children if I recall.
Two girls. I remember feeling envious of her connection to this Harry person and his family and wondering
why she couldn't be like that with Hannah and me.

As I fold the letter and put it on the kitchen counter,
I think back to the times when Kate would come home
for a visit. I hated it. Mum would spend days getting the
house ready and making sure we had the right food in.
And then we'd sit there poised on the sofa, waiting for
her to arrive; the favourite daughter. She'd sweep in
looking immaculate and stylish and I would feel shabby
next to her in my cheap high-street clobber. I'd sit there
looking at her wondering how she did it; how she managed to get so lucky after what she'd done. It was like
she had this invisible cloak all around her, protecting her
from harm. Whatever she touched turned to gold. Yet
me, I was the opposite.

Still, she couldn't keep the act up all the time. Sometimes we got a glimpse of the real Kate and it wasn't pretty. Like the time she came to Hannah's tenth birthday party. Hannah never got over that. None of us did. Even Mum was shocked. We knew Kate had just come back from a pretty hellish assignment in Gaza, but we didn't realize how much it had affected her. Mum had bought Hannah a Barbie doll for her birthday and she was so excited. She passed the doll round to all her friends at the party so they could brush its hair and change its clothes. It was a gorgeous day and the kids spilled out into the garden to have a play before we cut the cake. I was in the kitchen counting out the candles when Kate appeared in the doorway behind me. She was holding the doll and she had a strange look on her face.

'Western kids are so pampered, it makes me sick,' she said as she came into the kitchen. 'I mean, look at all this, it's grotesque.'

'Oh, come on, Kate, it's just a few sausage rolls and a bit of cake,' I said. 'It's not the height of luxury by any means.'

'I've spent the last few weeks talking to children who have nothing,' she said, her voice all haughty and pious. 'Not a toy, not a book; most don't even have access to running water. If you'd seen those kids, Sally, you would think twice before overindulging your own.'

'I'm not overindulging her,' I said. 'It's her birthday. Now please don't make a scene.'

'A scene?' she shrieked. 'Oh, yes, I forgot. That's all that matters to you, isn't it? Keeping quiet. Not questioning anything. Not making a bloody scene. Just like when we were kids.'

I was about to respond when Hannah came in the back door.

'Have you seen my doll?' she said, looking up at us. 'Oh, there she is. Can I have her back, Aunt Kate?'

And then Kate did something so horrible it still pains me to think about. She stepped towards Hannah with this evil look on her face and she said: 'I know, Hannah, let's play Gaza.' Then she pulled the doll's head off and threw it on the ground.

Hannah was hysterical. Her cries brought Mum and the little kids in from the garden, and Mum immediately noticed Kate's expression and swung into action, telling Hannah that we would send the doll off to the toys' hospital and she would be as good as new. Then we brought the cake out to the garden and lit the candles. But the day was ruined and when her friends left Hannah went to bed and cried herself to sleep. After that she was never the same with Kate. Her beloved aunt had become something else, something unpredictable and frightening.

But I already knew that.

I sit down at the table and take the Dictaphone in my hands, fiddling with the buttons. It feels wrong. This was Kate's and I feel like I'm intruding as I press 'play' and wait. But there's just a loud hissing noise. It must be broken. I'm not surprised, the state it's in. I press 'stop' then try again. It crackles into life and I hear a voice but it's not Kate's voice. It's Mum's.

'*Testing. Testing. That's what they say, isn't it? I'm meant to speak into this thing cos I keep forgetting where I left my glasses. Kate says I'm going to get through a whole rainforest of Post-it notes if I'm not careful so she's bought me this nice new thingy. Though I told her not to bother. I'm too old for all this new-fangled nonsense.*'

Tears run down my face as I sit there listening to my mother's voice. She sounds so old, so fragile. I hadn't been near her in those final months. I was still so angry.

'Oh, Mum,' I whisper as the voice fades out.

There's a hiss of white noise and I guess that might be the end of it. I pick up the Dictaphone and try to find the rewind button. But then she starts up again.

'*I'm telling this to you because I know they'll all think I'm barmy but I've seen him twice now and he was as clear as the nose on my face.*'

What? No, it can't be. I rewind the tape so I can hear that bit again then I let it run on.

'*There's a little lad. Tiny little thing, can't be much more than three or four, in the house next door. I see him all the time. In the garden, outside the shed, he flits about like a little pixie. And I hear his voice too, mainly at night. I hear him crying for his mummy. Paul thinks it's my mind getting slow and he might be right . . . You see, he's the absolute spit of my baby David. I miss him so much.*'

A little boy . . . I remember now what Kate said. In that last phone call.

I'm calling to ask you a favour. It's really important, Sally. I need you to keep an eye on the house next door to Mum's . . .

My head is spinning as I sit there with the device in my hands, trying to make sense of what my mother is saying. Mum may have been losing it, but she had also seen a boy. Just like Kate.

Then Fida's words come back to me. What had she been trying to tell me?

I need your help.

I put the Dictaphone down and get up from the chair. Something very odd is going on in that house. I grab my coat from the end of the stairs and head out, Kate's voice ringing in my ears.

Please, Sally.

This time I promise not to fail her.

37

The sun is just dipping when I reach Smythley Road. Mum's old house is all lit up with the orange rays from the sunset. It makes it look pretty though it's just a shabby old semi. It makes me think of those Easter Sundays when Mum would drag us off to Reculver beach to see the dancing sun.

As I walk towards the house I can see the three of us clearly. We're huddled up in a tatty beach blanket waiting for the sun to rise. 'Look at the water,' my mum shouts and it's there, the sun, like a big orange beach ball bobbing along the waves. 'It's dancing,' Kate shouts. 'It's really dancing.'

It was just an illusion; the water was moving, not the sun. I knew that and I thought the whole thing was daft; a childish folk tale passed down through the family. But Kate and my mother believed in it and would sit there mesmerized, lost in their own little fantasy world, as the sun flitted across the waves.

What if all this is a fantasy too, I think to myself, as I walk up the driveway. What if this kid is just a product of my mother and Kate's imaginations? Still, either way, I feel good for just doing *something*. Maybe this is what Kate felt like when she was out in some far-flung place following up a story.

When I get to the front door I notice it's open. Who leaves their door open at this time of night, I think to myself as I tap gently on the door frame.

'Hello?' I call. 'Is there anyone home?'

I can see through the crack that the house is in darkness. Suddenly I feel afraid. Maybe I should go and come back tomorrow in the daytime when there'll be more people around on the street. But then I think of Kate again. I need to show her that I can be strong. I take a deep breath and step inside the house.

The hallway is so dark I can barely see. My heart races as I step further inside.

And then, as my eyes adjust, I see her. She's lying at an odd angle at the bottom of the stairs, her arms over her face. Shit. What's happened? I go to her and move her arms away. Her face is dark with blood.

'Fida,' I say, trying to keep calm. 'Fida, what happened? Did you fall?'

She mutters something I can't understand.

'You need to go to the hospital,' I say. 'You might have broken something.'

I reach in my pocket but my phone is not there. In my rush to leave the house I must have forgotten to pick it up.

'Fida, do you have a phone? Or a landline?'

'Shh—' she says, pointing behind me.

'What?' I say, not daring to look.

'Shh—' she says, her eyes bulging.

I look over my shoulder into the darkness. There's nothing there.

'Where's the phone, Fida?'

'Shh–' She's trying to tell me something.

I make my way up the hallway, but I can't see a phone. There's something sticky underneath my feet. I shudder. It's blood. The house smells of it. I remember that smell. It's what my childhood smelt like. Even though Kate was always first on the scene I would hover behind her, standing on tiptoes to see what state my mother was in this time. Even though Kate tried to shoo me away, I still saw the bruises; I still smelt the blood.

I need to get her out of here. Perhaps I can get her next door to Mum's and break in somehow, then call the police from there.

'Shh–' she gasps then flops her head back on to the step.

'Sorry, love, I can't hear you,' I tell her, my heart thudding. 'Look, we're going to have to get you up.'

She shakes her head then grabs my hand. Her breath is shallow as she forces the words out.

'He's . . . gone.'

'Who's gone?' Does she mean her husband?

Her eyes roll in her head.

'Shh–' she says, wincing in pain. 'Shed.' The word falls out of her mouth like a stone.

'Shed? He's in the shed?'

I'm terrified. I just want to run. But Fida squeezes my arm tighter.

'You . . . have . . . to . . . go.' She spits out each word, squeezing my arms tighter with every syllable. 'The boy –'

She lies back, exhausted from the effort of speaking, then she lifts her head and stares at me pleadingly.

'Please . . .'

'Your little boy is in the shed?'

She nods her head.

'Help him,' she gasps.

Then her head falls back. I put my hand on her chest. She's still breathing but it looks like she's fainted.

I stand up, my heart pounding. This is too much for me. I need to call the police. But if something happens to that child while I'm away I'll never forgive myself. This is one child I can help.

I take off my coat and put it gently over Fida, then make my way through the house.

Be brave, I tell myself, as I push open the back door and step out into the shadowy garden. Be like Kate.

38

My legs feel like they are going to give way as I move across the grass towards the shed. What the hell am I doing? I feel disorientated from the wine and pills but I know I have to do this. If I can help this little boy then I'll have done something right in my thirty-five years on this earth. Then maybe Paul will be proud of me. He'll see that I can be a good person.

I reach the shed. The door is wide open. I count to three then step inside.

'Hello?' I call, my heart beating so fast it feels like it's coming out of my chest.

'Hello?' I repeat. 'It's okay. You can come out. I've come to help you.'

As my eyes adjust to the dark I can see it's just an ordinary garden shed with plant pots and old boxes. What was I expecting, a dungeon? Fida must've been delirious with the knock to her head. There's nowhere to hide a child here. He must be in the house.

I'm just about to go back when I hear it. A rustling coming from the back of the shed. I freeze.

'Hello?' I call again, my voice quivering.

I am scared, so scared. But then I see something move in the far corner. I step closer and there he is: a tiny boy crouched behind a set of ladders.

'Oh my God,' I say softly, my heart thudding against my chest.

I walk towards him and he cowers further into the corner.

'It's okay,' I whisper, sensing his fear. 'I won't hurt you.'

The boy mumbles something beneath his breath.

'What was that you said, darling?'

I get down on to my knees and gently ease myself towards him. I remember when Hannah was a little girl, she was so shy and she hated it when adults stood over her; it used to terrify her. Mum would say: 'If you make yourself small then children will trust you.'

'What's your name?' I ask him. I'm next to him now and I sit down on the floor, resting my arms on my knees.

He looks up at me fleetingly then hides his face again. His hands are so tiny.

'What are you doing in here?' I ask him. 'Playing hide and seek?'

He looks at me blankly so I try again.

'Shall we go and find Mummy?'

He nods his head then whispers something. I lean in closer, gently take his hand and pull him out of his hiding place.

'What did you say, love?'

'Find Mummy,' he says, looking at me for the first time.

'Come on then,' I say, getting to my feet. 'Let's go and see Mummy.'

I hold out my hand but he stays where he is.

'Come on,' I say.

'No,' he cries, shaking his head. 'No go out there. Bad man out there.'

The poor kid is terrified but I don't know what to do. I'm guessing the 'bad man' is his father and if he comes in here to find him we're done for. I need to get him and Fida next door to my mum's house and then I can think what to do next.

'There's no bad man,' I say, kneeling down next to him. 'He's gone now. But I know a nice place we can go. It's *my* mummy's house and I bet there'll be some bis-cuits there. You can have some while we wait for your mummy.'

'Mummy not out there,' he shouts. 'Mummy down there.'

He's pointing at the ground.

'Don't be silly,' I say. 'Your mummy's not down there.'

'She is,' he yells. 'She down there.'

He sinks to the floor and pulls a scrap of old carpet back.

'There,' he says.

I go over to him. There's a square shape cut out in the floor. I crouch down to take a closer look. It's a kind of trapdoor with a large metal bolt, built into the floor.

'What do you mean?' I ask, looking at him.

He says something but I can't hear so I lean nearer to him and accidentally dislodge an old metal bucket, which tumbles loudly across the stone floor. The noise startles the boy and he goes to run past me.

'Shh, it's okay,' I say, taking his hand. 'Don't panic. It was just a silly old bucket.'

He's terrified; his little body trembles in my arms and I rub his head gently. His hair smells musty; like it hasn't been washed in weeks.

'It's okay,' I whisper, though I'm scared too.

'Mummy,' he says again, untangling himself from my arms. 'Mummy down there.'

He steps over to the trapdoor and points at it. If this is a game then maybe I should just play it; humour him for a bit until we can get out of here.

'She's down there?' I say gently as I make my way back over to him. 'Through that door?'

He nods his head.

'You open,' he says. 'Open now.'

I crouch down and tug at the bolt. It's stiff and I have to yank at it. Finally it slides across and I pull the handle towards me. As I do, a weak trickle of light filters up and the boy squeezes past me and disappears down the hatch.

'Wait,' I call as I lean over the hole. I can see a set of steps below me. The boy has disappeared into the darkness.

I need to get him out of here. I start to climb down. The steps are made of wood, the kind you find in loft conversions, and they lead me down to a wide, airless room, dimly lit by a solitary light bulb in the centre of the ceiling.

The room smells of damp and sweat and I hold a hand to my mouth as I stand at the entrance. What the hell is this place? I can see exposed brick walls with tufts of yellow insulation poking out of the cracks. As I move forward I see a filthy single mattress draped in a thin quilt, wedged against the wall. The quilt is covered with faded cartoon characters.

I keep my hand over my mouth as I step further inside. I daren't take it away as I am scared I will throw up, the stench is so bad. My foot hits something and it skitters across the floor. I look to see what it is, my heart pounding. It's a silver pen. Something about it is vaguely familiar.

I turn to find the boy. He's over the other side of the room. There seems to be another bed pressed against the wall.

'Mummy, wake up,' he shouts as he climbs on to the bed and it's then that I see a mound lying in the middle. I go cold. There's someone in the bed. His mummy.

'Lady's here,' he cries. 'Lady help. She nice.'

He pulls the covers back and I see a tuft of dirty blonde hair. Who is this poor woman? The boy curls himself into her arms and she smothers his face with kisses.

'Er, hello,' I say. 'I'm Sally, I . . .'

The woman lifts her head. I look into her eyes and my world becomes another world.

'Mum?' she whispers.

39

'Hannah!' I gasp. 'What . . . what are you doing here?'

'David tired,' says the boy. 'Mummy hug David.'

She takes the boy in her arms and rocks him like I did with her when she was small.

'Is this your boy?' I ask. I can't think of what else to say.

She looks up and nods and my heart feels like it's been ripped out of me.

This is all too much to take in.

Then I hear steps coming from above.

'Sally?'

I swivel round at the sound of his voice and my hand drops from my face.

'Oh, thank God, you're here,' I cry.

But instead of coming to me he goes to Hannah.

'We've found her, Paul,' I sob. 'Our girl.'

I move towards them but something stops me. Paul has pulled Hannah in front of him and has his arm round her. He looks angry.

'Paul?' I say.

Then I notice it. There's something in his hand. It glints.

'What are you doing, Paul, you plonker?'

My words come out light and breezy and I have to stop myself from laughing. This is a joke, right?

'The more pertinent question, Sally,' he says, 'is what are you doing? Why are you here? Did your booze run out?'

This is not a joke. This is actually happening.

Paul is holding Hannah in between us, and she's so close I can feel her breath on my skin like when she was a baby and she would fall asleep on my shoulder. Her lovely blonde hair has been cut short and it's all tangled and greasy. She was so fussy about her hair, it was her pride and joy.

'Your hair,' I sob. 'What happened to your lovely hair?'

My beautiful, blue-eyed girl who disappeared that day more than five years ago is now a woman, an emaciated woman with hollow eyes. She stares at me, then blinks and turns away, and I feel something rise up inside of me, something that has been missing since the day she left. This is my daughter and I will do anything to get her out of here. Nothing is stronger than a mother's love.

'Hannah,' I whisper, reaching out my hand to her. 'It's okay. I'm here now.'

As I speak he pulls her backwards. My mind is still refusing to work out what's in his hand.

He laughs. 'That is the most ridiculous thing I've heard in a long time. You're here now. Isn't that nice.'

'She's my daughter, Paul,' I say, keeping my eyes on him.

'Ha,' he says. 'That's a laugh. Your daughter? You were never a proper mother to her; you were a disgrace. That's why I had to step in, give the girl some security, a bit of guidance.'

He pulls a wooden chair from the side of the room and sits on it, still holding Hannah to his chest. Why won't she speak? Why doesn't she just push him away?

'Paul, what's going on?' I say, easing myself towards them. 'Just let her go.'

He stares at me and I stare back.

'I'll let her go when I'm ready,' he says, not taking his eyes off me. 'But first I want to tell you a few things and if you try anything daft, Sally, then I will slit her throat.'

He moves his arm from beneath her ribcage and it's then I see that it's a knife clasped in his hand. He moves it up to Hannah's face.

'Paul, for fuck's sake,' I cry. 'Please. Why are you doing this?'

'Why am I doing this?' he says calmly. 'Hmm, that's a good question. I'm doing this because you left me no choice. I've always been a nurturer, a sucker for lost causes. Why do you think I ended up with you? But there came a point when I had to make a decision. I had to remove Hannah from a dangerous situation and put her into a place of safety. You were abusing your child, Sally. Someone had to get her away from it.'

I feel a familiar anger rising up inside me, a memory from a childhood spent trying to hold it in, trying to keep the peace. But if I want to get Hannah out of here I'm going to have to swallow my anger once more. Keep him talking, I tell myself, as I sit down on the floor and draw my knees up, keep him talking until the time is right.

'Thank you,' I say, trying to keep my voice steady. 'Thank you for taking such good care of her.'

Hannah frowns at me. She is confused but I nod my head at her reassuringly.

'Now if you let her go,' I continue, 'I'll tell the police what a good job you've done, giving her a safe place, away from the arguments, away from me. They'll understand. I'll tell them it was all my fault.'

'You stupid bitch,' he yells, leaping to his feet and pulling Hannah up by the throat. 'Do you think I'm a fucking idiot? None of us are getting out of here, do you understand that? None of us.'

40

I sit on the floor holding my knees to my chest, staring at the wall in front of me. There's writing on it in red pen. The one word that stands out, the one that's written over and over again, is 'mum'.

'Touching, isn't it?'

Paul is smiling. How can the bastard smile after what he's done?

I stay silent. If I answer back I'm playing into his hands.

'Look at that,' he says. 'Can you read it? It says "Help me Mum". Isn't that sweet? Crying out for her mum. But Mum never came, did she, Hannah? She was too busy getting drunk. I said to her, you can write what you like, it doesn't bother me, because one thing's for certain – your mother's not coming. Your mother couldn't give a shit. And I'm right, aren't I, Sally?'

I shake my head. My girl was crying out for me and I couldn't hear her.

David whimpers in the bed and I get up to go and comfort him.

'Leave him,' snaps Paul.

'He's scared,' I say. 'He's just a little kid.'

'I said leave him.'

He stabs the wall with his knife and I sit down again, my body numb with shock and fear.

'Whose is he?' I say, trying to block out his cries.

Paul laughs and squeezes Hannah tighter.

'Do you want to tell her or should I?' he says.

She bows her head.

'All right, I'll tell her,' he says, rolling his eyes. 'He's mine, you stupid bitch. The kid is mine. And it's your fault.'

David carries on whimpering while all around me the air gets thinner and thinner. I can't breathe as I sit here listening to the man I once loved describe how he groomed my daughter.

'You were always pissed,' he says, flexing his hands tighter across Hannah's chest. 'Do you remember when we first met, you were off the booze, said you'd seen the light and gone teetotal? Well, all it took was a little encouragement and before you knew it you were an old lush like your father. I enjoyed that. Watching you destroy yourself. And you were so stupid, so gullible and desperate for love that you actually thought it was you I was interested in, not your pretty little daughter. Before long you were in no fit state to look after Hannah. Someone needed to step in. The girl needed comforting and I was there.'

Hannah turns to look at me. Her eyes are bloated with tears. She looks like a little girl again and I reach out my arms to her.

'I'm sorry, darling,' I whisper. 'I'm so sorry.'

'She's sorry, Hannah,' he repeats my words mockingly. 'Did you hear that? Mummy's sorry. Isn't that nice?'

Hannah cowers as he speaks and I want to comfort her but the knife held firmly to her throat keeps me back.

318

'And then one night we crossed the line, didn't we, sweetheart?' He prods Hannah in the side. 'Didn't we? Shall we tell your lovely mother where you seduced me?'

Hannah keeps her head down but I can see that she's crying; her shoulders are shaking. I can't bear this.

'Gone shy, have we?' he says, putting his face into hers. 'Okay then, I'll tell her.'

I hate this man more than I have ever hated any human being in my life. He's a monster and I let him into our home. How could I have been so stupid?

I put my hands over my ears and start humming in an attempt to drown out his voice but he sees me and jumps up, dragging Hannah across the floor towards me.

'Take your fucking hands off your ears or I'll kill her,' he snarls. 'You're going to listen to what I have to tell you, okay? Try to cover your ears one more time and I swear I'll kill her, slowly, right here under your nose. Understand?'

'Yes,' I whisper. 'I understand.'

'Right,' he says, returning to his spot by the wall. 'Where was I? Oh, yeah, that was it. Summer 2009. She had just turned sixteen. Sweet sixteen. Been flirting with me for months, hadn't you?'

He yanks at the end of Hannah's hair.

'I said *hadn't you?*'

She whimpers and nods her head.

'You'd been having a go at her about trying to find her dad,' he says. 'Night after night I came home to the sound of your screaming and yelling. Like a bloody fish-wife you were, never letting up. And then there was that incident with the watch. That was it for poor Hannah; the final straw.'

A chill runs through my body.

'Thought you'd kept that secret, didn't you?' he says, shaking his head. 'Thought I wouldn't find out that you'd attacked your own daughter. But Hannah told me about it when I came home that night. She told me how you'd gone at her like a mad woman and broken her watch. She was shaking like a leaf. You'd really scared the poor girl. But, see, it was a pivotal moment, Sal. It was the moment I found out just how dangerous you could be.'

'Dangerous?' I stutter. 'I . . . I'm not dangerous. Hannah knows that.'

'Hannah was fucking terrified of you,' he shouts. 'And so was I. When she told me about that watch I knew I'd have to step up to the plate; be a responsible adult. That's when I started making plans to get Hannah out.'

'Responsible adult?' I yell. 'You're a psychopath.'

He nods his head, an evil smile creeping across his face.

'Takes one to know one,' he says. 'I tell you what, Sally, you were a lousy wife but you were an even lousier mother.'

'I just wanted her to be happy,' I say, my voice catching in my throat. 'I didn't want her to get her heart broken. I wanted her to get out and have a better life than me.'

'Well, that wouldn't be hard, would it?' he says, his eyes boring into me.

My heart hurts because he still looks the same: he's still Paul, the kind man I fell in love with, but it's like he's been possessed.

'It wouldn't be hard to do better than you,' he says, his voice thick with bitterness. 'I mean, the girl didn't really have much in the way of a role model, did she? A drunken lush and a dotty old woman.'

'She had her aunt Kate,' I reply. 'She got out. Hannah could have too.'

'Oh yes, Kate,' he says, shaking his head. 'I wondered when we'd get back to her. Kate got out of this shit-hole town because she couldn't stand you. That's why she never came home. You think she wanted all her posh London friends to know about you, her drunken mess of a sister? You were an embarrassment. She told me herself . . . just after I fucked her.'

'What?' I gasp. 'No. You're a liar.'

But then I remember what he told me about the night Kate broke into the neighbours' shed. He was with her.

'Shut up,' he says, snaking his arm round Hannah's throat. 'I don't want to talk about your dead whore of a sister. That was easy. No, I want you to hear how your daughter enticed me into her bed.'

He twists the knife in his hands. It is so close to her throat that any slip could end it all. I will him to keep it still but he carries on twisting it back and forth, back and forth. I can't stand it.

'You were out,' he says. 'God knows where, probably on another bender. I got home from work, tired and hungry, but there was no food in the house. I went upstairs and there she was, slinking around the bedroom in her underwear. And I stood in the doorway and looked at her and I thought, "Here's what I've been waiting for, here's my reward and she's handing it to me on a plate." I deserved it, after suffering for years, having to carry you home from stinking pubs, having to clean you up, having to smell your rancid booze breath in my face, having to fuck your flabby body. So I went inside and I took her hand and I pressed her up against the wall.'

'Stop it,' I yell, putting my hands over my ears. 'Why are you doing this?'

'What did I say about putting your hands over your ears?' he screams and I bring my hands down to my side, silently counting in my head, trying to drown his words in numbers.

One, two, three, four . . .

'Again and again and again,' he says. 'Up against the wall, on the floor, in the kitchen, on your bed . . .'

Five, six, seven, eight . . .

'Every time you went out she would look at me with those big blue eyes of hers and I'd be putty . . .'

Nine, ten, eleven, twelve . . .

'But then we weren't very careful, were we, Hannah?'

I stop counting and look up at him.

'We had a little accident or rather she had a little accident.'

He's stroking Hannah's face now with the back of the knife. My stomach lurches.

'A teenage mum,' he says. 'Just like you.'

My head grows tighter and tighter like there's a band wrapped round it.

'Monster.'

It's all I manage to get out of my mouth. There are no more words.

'A little boy,' he says, ignoring my outburst. 'A sweet little baby. That's why I had to get Hannah out. I needed her to be in a safe place, away from you and your drunken moods. God knows what you would have done to her if you'd found out.'

The anger I've been holding in for the last hour pours forth and I leap up, only stopping when I see the knife twitch.

'What would I have done to her?' I scream. 'I would have protected her, I would have taken her away from you. I would have fucking ripped you apart. You're a psychopath.'

He sits, eerily calm, watching me. Then he starts to laugh.

'Here she is, Hannah,' he cries. 'Here's the real Sally. A violent, unhinged old drunk. Here's what I saved you from.'

Then he calmly gets to his feet and pushes Hannah back into the chair. Holding the knife in front of him, he steps towards me.

'You know what, Hannah?' he says, staring into my eyes as I step backwards. 'I've changed my mind. I don't think it's mental torture that your mother needs, it's a bit of roughing up. You always wanted that, didn't you, Sal? Always felt left out when your dad belted your sister, didn't you?'

He grabs my hair with his hands and pounds his fist into my eye. I scream and stagger back. The pain is excruciating.

'That's why Kate goaded your old man, isn't it?' he says, standing over me as I crouch on the floor, my hands shielding my eyes. 'Because she liked it when he hit her, didn't she? She liked it because it meant she got some attention. And you were jealous because you wanted some attention too. But I think a bit of your dad's violence rubbed off on you. Remember the wine bottle? Kate really liked that one, it got her right on my side.'

I take my hands away from my face. And as I look at the deep red smears on my palms and taste the metallic blood in my mouth, I see Paul's face bearing over me that night. Him standing there with the bottle in his hands; me crouched on the floor just like I am now. And it comes back to me. Paul smashing the bottle. Drawing the edges up his arm, laughing all the time.

It wasn't me. I didn't do it.

'You're a liar,' I mumble as I stagger to my feet.

'What's that?' He steps towards me.

'I said you're a liar.'

'Oh look, Hannah,' he says, a grin spreading across his face. 'The little champ's come back for a second round. What will it be this time, Sal, fists or something stronger?'

He waves the knife at me and I try to focus on its silver blade. I'm not scared any more. I can take whatever he wants to dole out if it means keeping Hannah safe. He can kill me, I don't care, as long as she gets out of here alive.

41

I can't breathe.

He's sitting on top of me, one arm holding me down, the other pressing the knife against my throat. I can't speak, I can only listen to him as he tells me how he plans to kill me.

'What do you think, Hannah, eh?' he says. 'What does Mummy deserve? A cut or something a little slower?'

I hear whimpering on the far side of the room. It's little David. I want to call out to him, to reassure him, but Paul seems to sense this and presses harder on my chest. I'm trying to piece it all together, everything he's told me. Trying to put it into some sort of order in my head. I have to know before I die.

'What about the phone call?' I say, remembering Hannah's voice on the line, telling me she was safe. 'I spoke to her. She said she was fine.'

'Oh, yeah,' he says, leaning his face against my cheek. 'That was nice, wasn't it? We had a little day out in London, didn't we, Han? And I said, I know, let's phone your mother and tell her that you're fine. Just a little white lie so she won't be worried. But you weren't worried, were you? Any other mother would be, but you? You were happy to see the back of her.'

'That's not true.'

'Of course it's true,' he says with a mocking smile on his lips. 'What did you say to me? She's a big girl now, she can do what she likes. You fucking disgrace.'

I don't respond but I know I have to keep him talking.

'But Kate?' I go on. 'She met her in Brixton . . . She said she lived there.'

'Another little day trip,' he says. 'I've got some old friends there. Nice, wasn't it, Hannah? Some reporter Aunt Kate turned out to be, eh? Didn't even see what was right under her nose. Dumb bitch.'

'And the baby?' I ask. 'Did she have him in hospital?'

He shakes his head and smiles.

'Do you think I'm stupid?' he says. 'I wasn't going to risk hospital with all those do-gooder types. Nah, she had him in here. Fida delivered him.'

Fida. She knew that Hannah was in here. Why didn't I listen to her?

'I believe you two have met,' he says.

'How . . . how do you know that?'

'I was following her. Knew she was up to no good. I saw her through the window,' he sneers. 'Thankfully, you did the job for me. Scared her off.'

I go cold. She had been so close to telling me. If I had let her then none of this would be happening.

'She shouldn't have done that,' he goes on. 'I told her to keep her mouth shut but she disobeyed me. Still, she won't be doing much talking for a while.'

'You did that to her?' I say, thinking of Fida lying on the stairs. Why didn't I go straight next door and call an ambulance?

'She's a clever girl,' he says. 'Too clever for her own good. But she slipped up; thought I wouldn't find out that she'd called the office and asked the dozy reception-ist for my home address. Silly girl. But dirty as hell in bed. She's a bit like Hannah, the product of a broken home. A war zone. And, like Hannah, I rescued her. You could say I'm a bit like Saint Kate in that respect, eh?'

'You are nothing like my sister,' I whisper.

'What's that?' he says. 'Come on. I want to hear you.'

'I said you're nothing like my sister.'

'Well, no, I suppose I'm not cos I'm alive and she's dead. You seem to have that effect on people, don't you, Sal? Your dad, your mum, Kate, all gone.'

'Mum loved you,' I say. 'She would be devastated if she knew.'

'Can I tell you a secret?' He spits the words out and I can taste his breath. 'Hannah, I'm going to tell your mother our little secret.'

Hannah doesn't respond. He's broken her. My lovely feisty, argumentative girl has gone. She's just a shell. The old Hannah would be fighting her way out of here. Instead she's just watching, letting this go on and on.

'Okay, I'll tell her,' he says, brushing the knife across my face like a feather. 'Your mum dealt with it stoically. Better than I expected.'

'Dealt with what?' I ask. 'What are you talking about?'

'I'm talking about your mother,' he says, returning the knife to my throat. 'Your darling mother who you hated. Mouthy old girl she was, just like you. She thought the sun shone out of my behind for a time but then she started sticking her nose into my business, thought she could play games with me. Talking into her machine day and night like she was fucking Miss Marple.'

I hear my mother's voice on the Dictaphone as I close my eyes.

Tiny little thing, can't be much more than three or four, in the house next door.

'Mum knew?' I whisper. 'She knew about David?'

'She saw him in the garden a couple of times,' he says as he adjusts his weight so his elbows dig into my stomach. 'But who'd believe her? Most people thought she was off her rocker anyway. And so I did the kind thing and booked her into that care home.'

'What? Mum didn't have dementia?'

'No,' he says. 'But I had a bit of fun letting her think she did. I started moving things around, made her think she was losing it. Christ, she thought her dead kid had come back to haunt her. By the time I made that call she was practically begging to be put away.'

He shakes his head and laughs.

'You need help,' I whisper. 'You're not well.'

'That's rich, coming from a bloated alcoholic,' he says. 'Yeah, that's very good, Sal.'

'Why did you do it?' My chest is so tight now it feels like my heart will burst out of it. 'Why our lovely Hannah?'

'She wasn't *our* lovely Hannah,' he says, a smile creeping across his face. 'She was the result of a quick fumble between you and some spotty teenager.'

'She was an innocent young girl, Paul.'

'Innocent, that's a laugh,' he says. 'She's a little slag, like her mother. You'll spread your legs for anyone, won't you, Han?'

He lifts himself off me and walks over to where Hannah is sitting with David.

'Move,' he says to the boy, pushing him away. David doesn't make a fuss, just sits down on the floor. His obedience is chilling.

'As I was saying,' he continues. 'She was a proper little slag.'

I look up. Paul has his arm round Hannah's throat. He's pulled her off the bed and is leading her towards me.

'What are you doing?'

He puts his hands on her breasts.

'Stop it, Paul!' I yell. 'Stop it now.'

'All soft and pert,' he sneers. 'Like you must have been once. Shame that when we met you were already damaged goods.'

Hannah has her head down but I can see she's scared; her shoulders are trembling as his hand goes further down her body.

'Like that, do you?' he whispers.

Further and further until I can't bear it any more. I can't let this happen.

'Get your hands off my daughter,' I scream as I run at him and push Hannah out of his grasp. 'You sick bastard.'

I try to grab at the knife but he is too strong for me. He seizes my wrists and smashes my face into the wall, once, twice, three times, spitting at me as he yanks me back and forth.

'Don't. You. Ever. Learn. Bitch.'

My head flops as he pulls me back and I can taste blood in my mouth again.

'No, Paul,' I whimper as he holds my face in his hands and looks into my eyes. His face softens and for a moment I fear he is going to try to kiss me.

The blow comes out of nowhere and I cry out as my head hits the wall again.

'Stop it!'

I hear Hannah's voice somewhere on the edge of the room.

'I'm teaching her a lesson,' he says as he drags me back. 'Paying her back for all the times she treated me like a fucking dog.'

He pulls me towards his chest, his face pressed into mine. I see the blade glistening in front of my face as he tightens his grip and I close my eyes.

'Run, Hannah,' I yell. 'Take David and go and get help.'

'You don't get to tell Hannah what to do,' he says as he pushes the knife into me. 'She's mine.'

I stumble to the floor, clutching my stomach with both hands. The room spins. I pull my hands away. They're covered with blood.

'What have you done?' I whimper. He's sitting on the edge of the bed now, watching me.

'What I should have done years ago,' he says. 'Put you out of your misery.'

Hannah is standing in the middle of the room. She wants to come to me, I can tell, but he'll kill her too if she tries. I look up at her and smile. I want to reassure her. David must be asleep because he has stopped whimpering.

'I'm sorry, love,' says Paul.

He is talking to me. His voice is gentle, soothing, like the person I once knew.

'You needed to be taught a lesson,' he says, his voice growing fainter and fainter as I try to stay awake.

I can't sit up any longer. I have to rest. My body feels empty as my head hits the floor. The room turns to liquid and I find myself swimming in beautiful clear water. I hear someone call my name and I see my mother on the beach. She's waving her arms frantically, telling me that it's time to come and have our picnic. I try to call back to her but my voice won't carry. I feel myself go under.

'Sally.'

Mum's voice is frantic now. I see her wading out through the waves. She's coming to rescue me but she'll have to be quick; I can't breathe. The pressure in my lungs is intense, I'm sinking. Then I feel Mum's hand grab mine and she pulls me out of the water into dazzling light. I hang in the rays of it for a moment, whispering her name.

'Mum?'

'Sally.'

I know the voice but it isn't Mum's.

'Sally. Oh my God!'

I paddle up through the darkness, through the thick wall of pain, and as I come to I feel a pair of arms coiling round me.

'It's okay,' she says. 'We're going to get you out of here. You're going to be fine. Just stay with me.'

I open my eyes. She is here. She has come to save me.

PART THREE

42

Herne Bay

I pull my hood up so it obscures my face as I step off the train and on to the platform. My legs are throbbing where the stitches are beginning to heal and it still hurts to walk on my right knee. There's a bench by the exit stairs and I go over to it and sit down for a moment, massaging the aching joint.

The Turkish doctor managed to remove most of the shrapnel but he told me there was one sliver that was almost impossible to get to. I didn't care. I was alive; I could cope with an injured knee. The rest of the camp wasn't so lucky. The whole of the north-west side was obliterated in the blast. I had been on the southern edge of the camp by the fence, well away from the centre of the explosion. Even so, it had still lifted me off my feet and I was knocked unconscious. I remember coming to and wondering where I was. In those first few moments I was sure that I was dead and I'd somehow emerged in an apocalyptic afterlife. But as I staggered to my feet and looked around I saw that this was real and it was worse than any hell I could ever have imagined.

My knee was bleeding badly as I limped towards the remains of the camp, calling out for someone, anyone. But the silence of the dead burned like a gas and rose in smoky plumes from the centre of the camp. Body parts were scattered across the smouldering field and an emaciated dog, following the scent of fresh blood, had begun to feast on the remains of the dead. It looked like the end of the world.

I stood for a moment watching a group of men who had just arrived on the scene. They started sifting through a mound of shredded canvas – all that was left of the tents. Their faces were twisted with exhaustion as they searched for survivors.

I should have stayed. It was the right thing to do, the decent thing to do, but I knew I had to get out. I'd known it in the moments before the explosion when I heard my mother's voice. This was not my battle now. I was needed elsewhere. As I stepped across the remains of the clinic I heard a child screaming for its mother, but it wasn't coming from the camp. It was coming from inside my head, from the place where memory is lodged.

Something evil was festering in that house. I'd sensed it, heard it, seen it with my own eyes. My poor mother had done the same. And both of us thought we were going mad. I knew as I stood in that field of death that I needed to follow the child's screams and try to put things right.

Miraculously Hassan had missed the bomb too. He had been delivering aid to a district on the east side of the city when it hit. He returned and found me dazed and wandering around in circles through the dust. When I saw him walking towards me I thought he was a ghost, and I collapsed in a heap by his feet. He picked me up, put me in his car and at my insistence drove me to the Turkish border. We arrived at sunset and he took me to a medical centre where he urged me to get my leg treated. At the hospital I made Hassan promise me that if anyone asked he would tell them I'd been killed in the blast. I knew I would have to fall off the radar if I had any chance of returning to Herne Bay. I handed him a pile of my things: notes, Dictaphones, my press pass, and told him to send them on to Harry and tell him they were found in the ruins. It had to look like I was dead. Poor Hassan stared at me as though I were mad, but when I told him I was doing this to save my family, he asked no more questions. For Hassan, loyalty to friends and family is all. He got me some clothes to wear – traditional Islamic dress – and arranged for a contact of his to smuggle me back through Turkey and on into Europe.

'For now,' he said as he waved me off, 'Kate Rafter is gone. I tell them you're Rima. I give you my mother's name. For luck.'

I stand up and slowly make my way to the station exit, making sure I keep my hood low over my eyes. The place is quiet. Just a smattering of people, mainly tourists, congregate inside the ticket hall. As I pass the newspaper stand I see my photograph staring out at me. I stop and pick up a copy.

HERNE BAY REPORTER NOW PRESUMED DEAD, screams the headline. It is an odd sensation to read of your own death. My stomach feels hollow as the enormity of what I have done dawns on me.

I go into the toilet and read the piece. In it Harry is quoted as saying I was the finest foreign correspondent of my generation and even Graham bloody Turner gets a look in, describing me as 'Brilliant and brave. A reporter who never lost her nerve.'

'Bastard,' I mutter to myself as I shove it in the toilet bin and head for the exit. He wasn't saying that a few weeks ago when he went crying to Harry, saying I was a liability. His testimony could have got me incarcerated and I will never forgive him.

As I step outside I take a moment to decide what to do. I haven't thought beyond this moment – arriving in Herne Bay. If I had a key for my mother's house I could go there to wait and watch but I gave it back to Paul when I left. Part of me wants to go straight round to number 44 and confront Fida and her husband, but is that wise on my own? No, the best thing to do is to find Paul. I have to trust that he won't tell the police I'm back until we've done what we need to do. He'll probably be at work at this time of day, though, and it's miles away.

Instinctively I root around in my pocket for my phone, even though I know it's not there. I'm lost without it but I had to get rid of it. Though it survived the blast – it was tucked inside my padded waist pouch, along with my bank cards and passport – I knew that if I was to successfully carry out my plan I would have to be untraceable, so I left it in Aleppo, the SIM card crushed under my boot.

Passport control at the ferry terminal in Calais was brisk and thankfully nobody looked too closely at my name. The headlines described me as 'Kate' while my passport reads 'Catherine'. Besides, customs officials are primed to look for potential terrorists, not journalists who have faked their own deaths. I'd bought new clothes in the hypermarket and tucked my hair into a thick woollen hat, though the chances of anybody recognizing me on the way back here were slim. Unlike Rachel Hadley, I've never been one for splashing my face across my reports and now I am glad of that.

There's only one option left – I have to go to their house. Please let Paul be there, I think to myself as I make my way out of the car park, keeping my head down. Having to explain all this to a drunken Sally is the last thing I need. The more I can keep her out of this, the better.

Paul's car is not in the drive when I get to the house and my heart sinks. I stand on the doorstep and ring the bell, willing Sally to be sober. I'll have to persuade her to let me use her phone to call Paul. But there's no reply. I go to ring the bell again then think better of it and make my way round to the side of the house.

But there's no sign of Sally as I peer through the conservatory window. The room looks tidier than it was the last time I was here and there are no tell-tale bottles of wine lying about. Maybe they've gone away, I think, and then I panic. They'll have seen the news. They think I'm dead. What if it's sent Sally over the edge and she's done something stupid? My heart races as I pull the door handle. It's open.

'Sally,' I call, stepping inside. 'Sally, are you there?'

But the house is silent as I walk into the hallway. I pop my head round the kitchen door. There are two mugs on the table.

'Sally,' I call again, going upstairs. 'Are you up there?'

I have a knot in my stomach and my mouth is as dry as parchment as I reach the top of the stairs.

Something is wrong.

I cross the landing and make my way to her bedroom. The door is open and I step inside. The curtains are closed and the room smells of sweat and stale alcohol. So she *is* still drinking. But then where is she?

I go to the window and pull the curtains open, releasing a cascade of dust particles that whirl through the fetid air. I shiver as I look at the room. It's in a terrible state with clothes flung on the floor and a plate of congealing toast on top of the chest of drawers. The quilt is all tangled and looks like it hasn't been washed in weeks.

I go back down to the kitchen to call Paul. But as I lift up the receiver I can't remember his number. Shit. Perhaps it's written down somewhere. I go to open the kitchen drawer where Sally always used to keep things like that.

And then I see something on the side. A black object.

A Dictaphone. It's all battered and damaged. It can't be . . . I pick it up, my hand shaking.

There's a note lying next to it. It's from Harry. It's Mum's Dictaphone. I'd tried to find it after the explosion but it had gone. I'd assumed it had been destroyed.

I look at the Dictaphone and the cups on the table. Sally will have listened to it. Paul too. And he, more than anyone, would understand the ramifications. Now it all makes sense: the silence, the deserted house. I know exactly where they are.

43

Number 44 is in darkness when I arrive and there's no sign of Paul and Sally's car.

Maybe they walked, I think to myself as I pull my hood over my head and make my way up the driveway. The front door is open and as I stand on the step my stomach lurches.

'Fida,' I say.

She is almost unrecognizable. Her face is bloodied and swollen. She's been beaten to a pulp.

'Fida.' I shake her and her eyes open. 'What happened? Did your husband do this?'

She looks up at me and her eyes widen.

'No,' she gasps. 'No. It can't be . . . I thought you were . . .'

'It's okay,' I say in a low voice, crouching next to her so she can hear. 'I'll explain it all later. We need to get you out of here.'

She's trying to say something. I lean closer to hear her.

'Didn't . . . want . . . to hurt . . . him,' she says, almost choking on the words.

'Who?' I say quietly. 'Who didn't you want to hurt?'

She tries to lift her head but it rolls backwards.

'Don't try to sit up,' I say. 'Just take deep breaths.' I notice there's a coat draped over her. I tuck it in round her more tightly.

'It's okay, Fida. I'm going to call an ambulance.'

'You must believe me,' she whispers. 'He made me . . .'

Her voice falters and I wonder if she's delirious.

'He made me do it.'

Her eyes roll back in her head. I know I need to act fast and get her out of here before her psycho husband comes back. Then I remember I have no phone.

I scour the hallway. Nothing. I run into the kitchen. Then I see it: an old-fashioned cordless push-button phone on a shelf by the door. I grab it, punch 999 and head back to Fida.

'Ambulance, please.'

As I speak to the operator, Fida tugs on my sleeve.

'Hang on a sec,' I tell her as I give the address to the woman on the other end of the phone.

I end the call then turn to Fida. Her injuries are worse than I initially thought. I can see now why she can't speak properly. Her mouth is all cut and swollen. It must be agony.

'It's okay, the ambulance is on its way,' I tell her, praying that it will be fast. 'You're going to be fine.'

She starts to shake and I put my hand on her arm.

'Shh,' I whisper. 'It's okay. They'll look after you in the hospital. I'll make sure they know about your husband. He won't find you.'

'Not okay,' she mumbles. 'I . . . he nearly died . . . he's so tiny, I . . . I'm not a monster.'

Her words twist inside me. So he's real. I wasn't going mad.

'Fida,' I say, leaning over her. 'Tell me. Where is he?'

342

Her breath becomes shallow and for a moment I think she is going to pass out, but then she opens her eyes and grips my arm.

'Sally,' she gasps.

'Sally? My sister?' I cry. 'Is she here?'

I recognize the coat covering her. It's Sally's green puffa.

'Please, Fida. Where is she?'

'Sh . . . sh . . . shed.'

The exertion of getting that final word out is too much and she flops back on to the stairs.

'Listen, Fida,' I say, jumping to my feet. 'The ambulance is on its way. Everything's going to be fine. I'm going to go and find my sister.'

I step out into the garden. It is eerily quiet. As I close the back door, my heart thudding, something rustles in the hedge and I freeze.

'Who's that?' I call, wishing I had my torch with me. 'Sally?'

Probably just a bird, I tell myself, though my skin prickles as I make my way across the grass.

Why did Sally come here? She's usually scared of her own shadow. It's not like her to go running into danger like this.

The door is open when I get there and I step inside.

'Sally?' I call. 'Sally, are you there?'

I hear a muffled sound, like voices speaking underwater.

'Sally?' I rush forward.

I don't see the hole until it's too late.

44

I fall down some steps and land on cold concrete, winded and bruised. What the hell just happened? I slowly push myself to my knees, clutching my ribs. And that is when I see her.

She is lying on a filthy mattress, tears coursing down her face, and next to her, clinging to her chest, is the boy.

'Aunt Kate?'

'Hannah,' I exclaim, holding my hand to my chest to steady myself. 'What are you doing here? What the hell is going on?'

I stumble towards them.

The boy starts crying too and it's then I see the rope tied round Hannah's wrists. I rush to her and begin undoing it.

'Hannah,' I say, speaking quickly. 'What's going on?'

I repeat the question but she doesn't answer. The tears continue to stream down her face.

I undo the knotted rope and she rubs her wrists. The boy stares up at me, his eyes wide.

'We heard you when you were in the shed that time,' says Hannah through her tears, holding the boy to her chest. 'We thought you were coming to rescue us.'

'Rescue you?' I say. 'You mean you've been here all this time?'

She nods her head.

'But who's the boy?' I ask.

'David's mine,' she says.

David.

I stand frozen to the floor, trying to take it all in. Then I see something glinting in the half-light. My silver pen. It's lying on the ground by the bed.

Hannah sees me looking at it.

'David found it. He brings me presents to cheer me up.'

I feel numb.

'He likes sparkly things,' says Hannah.

As I bend to pick up the pen I see a little pile of marbles next to it and I remember the one I found in Mum's garden.

'Mum.'

That's Sally's voice. I turn round. There's a mound of old blankets in the corner.

'Is your mum here, Hannah?'

Her eyes are terrified, looking towards the blankets.

I run over and start pulling at them. 'Oh my God! Sally!'

She's been wrapped up, like a child in swaddling. I turn her towards me.

'Oh, Sally!' Her face is a mess. She's covered in blood. It's in her hair, all over her clothes.

'Jesus, what happened?' I cry as I gently put her in the recovery position. She moans softly.

'He had a knife,' says Hannah.

I look up. Hannah is standing above me, just staring at her mother.

'Who stabbed her?' I ask, trying to keep my voice calm so as not to alarm Sally.

'Hannah, who stabbed her?' I repeat but she doesn't answer. She just looks at me with vacant eyes.

'Mum,' murmurs Sally. 'Is that you?'

Blood is seeping through her sweater in her stomach area. I check her pulse. It's weak and she's losing blood fast.

'We need a cloth to stem the bleeding,' I say to Hannah. 'And help . . . we need to get some help.'

I look up. Hannah is still standing there, motionless.

'Hannah!' I scream. 'You have to go and get help now.'

'I can't.'

'Hannah, please.'

I feel something brush my skin and I turn and see that Sally has opened her eyes.

'It's okay,' I tell her. 'We're going to get you out of here. You're going to be fine. Just stay with me.' I press the blanket against her stomach wound.

'Kate,' she whispers. 'It can't be. You're . . .'

Her face drains of colour and I'm worried that, along with the blood loss, the shock of seeing me could send her into cardiac arrest.

'It's okay, Sally,' I say, rubbing her forehead with my fingertips like Mum used to when we were little. 'Just keep calm. Breathe in and out, just like this, in and out.'

Her eyes are wide, like a child's, and she doesn't take them off me as together we fight to keep her alive.

'Hannah, you need to go and tell someone that we need help,' I shout.

In and out. In and out.

'That's it. Good girl, Sally,' I say. 'Everything's fine.'

'Paul,' she says suddenly, grabbing my arm. 'Paul.'

'It's okay,' I say soothingly. 'Paul will be here as soon as he can. He'll be worried about you.'

She shakes her head and her breath starts to rasp.

'Shh now,' I say. 'Remember, in and out.'

She grabs my hand.

'No,' she gasps. 'Paul . . .'

'We'll call him from the hospital,' I say. 'Let's just concentrate on your breathing. It's all going to be fine.'

'No,' she cries, shaking my arm. 'Paul did this.'

'What?'

'Paul . . .' she says, her voice hoarse and shallow. 'He did this . . . kept Hannah . . . raped her when she was just –'

She lets go of my arm and clutches her chest as though trying to squeeze the words out.

'The boy,' she gasps. 'Paul . . . his dad.'

Her breath gives out and she slumps back.

'Sally, come on, we can do this,' I say, trying not to let the shock that is permeating my bones show in my face. 'Come on, in and out, in and out.'

I turn round and look at Hannah. She is sitting on the edge of the mattress now, the boy in her arms. She looks terrified.

'Is it true?' I say. 'What your mum says, is it true? In and out, Sally. Good girl.'

Hannah nods and it feels like my head is on fire.

'Where is he, Hannah?' I say, turning my head so Sally can't hear me. 'Where's Paul?'

'I don't know,' she says. 'He told me not to try to escape . . . If he comes back . . .'

'We need the police,' I say. 'You look after your mum. I'll go and call them.'

Thump.

The boy whimpers and Hannah leaps to her feet. There are footsteps overhead.

'It's him,' Hannah whispers, her face ashen with fear.

45

'You're still alive then,' he snarls. 'Christ, you must be stronger than you look.'

I watch from my hiding place underneath the mattress as Paul steps into the room and walks towards Sally. He's holding a sheet of plastic, and is wearing rubber gloves.

Hannah is sitting on the other mattress with the boy. She holds him to her chest but her eyes are on the man bearing down on her mother.

I note the position of the wooden chair lying on the floor a yard or so away.

'Well, Sally,' he says, crouching to his knees. 'I've found a lovely spot for you. I think you'll like it. Just a short car ride away.'

Sally whimpers and it takes every ounce of restraint to stop myself from going to her but I have to do this right or we're all dead.

'It's a site you know well,' he continues, kneeling next to her, stroking her hair. 'The perfect resting place. Somewhere no one will disturb you. I've made sure of that. It will be nice and quiet, Sally. After all the chaos, you'll finally have what you wanted. A bit of peace.'

Sally's breathing grows shallow as he starts to heave her on to the plastic sheet. I need to act fast. I slither out from under the mattress and crawl on my stomach along the floor behind him. I am almost at the chair when something clatters. My pen. It's fallen out of my coat pocket. Shit.

'What was that?' he says.

He jumps to his feet and turns round. There is nowhere for me to hide. His eyes widen.

'What the fuck?' he cries.

He puts his hand to his chest and I take advantage of his shock by grabbing the chair, but before I can lift it his foot is on my hand, pressing down.

'No you don't,' he says, glaring at me.

'Kate, please,' whispers Sally. 'Just leave it. Don't fight him.'

But I have to. I'll fight this man with every bit of strength I have left. I yank my hand away and get to my feet, kicking the chair away. I don't need it. He doesn't seem to have a weapon. He must have thought he didn't need one any more.

'You don't scare me,' I say as I stare into his eyes. 'Because I'm not a little girl. And that's your thing, isn't it? Little girls?'

Sally lets out a sob and I am aching to go to her, to reassure her that we're going to get out of here, that everything will be fine.

'Get out of my way, you mad bitch,' he growls, grabbing my hair and throwing me on to the floor. 'You're supposed to be dead.'

I scramble to my feet and as he comes at me again I try to kick him in the groin. But I miss and he grabs me and throws me down hard.

'I'll say this for you, Kate,' he says, kneeling on my chest and putting his hands round my neck. 'You're a hard one to get rid of. Those bloody pills weren't strong enough.'

'Pills?' I whisper as his hands tighten round my throat.

'Yeah, you like pills, don't you?' he says. 'All those ones I found in your bag. Proper little druggie, aren't you? Your body must be used to them, that's all I can say.'

'What do you mean?' I croak out as I grab at his hands with my fingers.

'Remember that time in the pub,' he says, pressing his face against mine, 'when you went crazy out on the street? Then the cosy night in we had with the bottle of red wine, that nice flask of tea on the beach? I must say, for a hotshot journalist you're a bit stupid when it comes to leaving your drinks lying around.'

'You drugged me?' I gasp as I frantically try to prise his hands from my neck.

'You didn't give me any choice,' he says. 'Sticking your nose in where it wasn't wanted. I tried to stop you but you must have the constitution of an ox. Still, you'd have to be a tough bitch to do what you did.'

'What are you talking about?'

He nods his head and smiles.

'Sally told me,' he says, pressing his mouth against my cheek. The pressure on my throat releases a bit. 'What happened when you were a kid. The big family secret.'

'Paul, no,' groans Sally from the corner of the room. 'Please, no.'

'Shut up, bitch,' he hisses. 'You were the one who told me. You were the one who fucking hated her for what she'd done.'

'What did I do?' I say, holding his gaze. I want him to know I'm not scared of him. 'Tell me, eh? What did I do?'

He tightens his grip round my throat again then pushes his face in mine.

'You killed your little brother,' he hisses. 'Your dad told Sally all about it when she was a kid. It wasn't an accident. It was you. You held him under the water until he drowned. Evil bitch.'

No. It's not true. He's making it up. I yank one of my hands away from him.

'You're lying, you sick fuck,' I scream, raising my free arm to his face.

But he's quicker than me and he grabs my head and smashes it into the floor. My entire body goes limp.

'You bitch, you fucking murdering bitch,' he yells.

I can taste blood in my mouth as my head hits the concrete again and I close my eyes, waiting for the next blow. But it doesn't come. Instead, a heavy weight crashes down on top of me and I feel his grip loosen.

I open my eyes as Paul rolls to the floor and see her standing there, the wooden chair raised above her head.

'Hannah,' I cry.

'I'm sorry,' she says, her lip trembling. 'I'm so sorry.'

Paul isn't moving.

'It's okay,' I say, getting to my feet. 'You have nothing to be sorry for, darling. It's over now. It's all over.'

I feel dazed as I look at his slumped body. He's not moving but when I lean over him I can hear the faint sound of breath. Good. I want him to pay for what he's done. I grab the rope that was tying Hannah, and bind his hands.

'Kate.'

Sally. I stumble over to her and as I take her hand I hear footsteps overhead and relief floods through my body.

'It's okay,' I say. 'The ambulance is here now. You're going to get seen to and then you'll be all better.'

'No,' she gasps, taking my hand and squeezing it. 'Can't breathe.'

Her eyelids are drooping and her skin feels so cold.

'Yes you can,' I say, stroking her hands to warm them. 'He's gone, Sally. You're safe now. I promise.'

She stares up at me. Her eyes are clouding over. I know that look. I saw it on Nidal's face when I picked him up off the pavement.

'No, Sally,' I shout, rubbing frantically at her hands. 'Don't do this. The ambulance is here now. Hannah's here and you've got the most beautiful grandson. You have so much to live for.'

'I'm . . . sorry,' she says, smiling up at me. 'I'm so . . . sorry.'

'Sorry for what?' I say gently. 'You have nothing to be sorry for.'

'I should have let you in,' she says, her voice rattling in her chest. 'That time in the garden . . . should have let you in . . . He said . . . I'm sorry.'

'It's okay,' I tell her. 'It doesn't matter any more.'

And I mean it. Suddenly all the hurt and resentment I have felt towards Sally over the years is meaningless. We were both victims of my father in different ways. How did I not see this until now?

'Is there anyone down there?'

A voice. Female. Coming from above.

'Yes,' I call. 'Down the steps. Quick.'

'The ambulance is here, Sally,' I say, turning back to her. 'Sally?'

She is still. So very still.

I grab her body and shake it.

'Sally, wake up!' I yell. 'Please wake up. The ambulance is here.'

I hear footsteps coming down the wooden steps.

'No,' I cry. 'You can't do this. You have to wake up.'

'Miss, you'll have to stand back,' says a female voice behind me. 'You'll have to let her go.'

I do as she says and watch as the paramedics surround her body. But the resuscitation kit they have brought with them lies redundant on the floor. They look at one another and then at me. And with that look comes confirmation and I start to scream and the sound of my grief fills the room, the garden, the whole wretched town.

46

I'm sitting in a hospital corridor waiting for the doctors to finish examining Hannah and David. When the police arrived David started shaking and didn't stop, all the way to the hospital. He and Hannah were taken into a private room and a stream of doctors and social workers have been in and out of there throughout the night. The nurses have brought me tea and asked if I would like to get my forehead looked at but I have refused. This pain is my penance. I should have protected her but I failed and the guilt will live with me for ever.

Somewhere in this hospital my sister is lying in a sterile box. Her life needlessly snuffed out by a psychopath who duped us all. I hear a clicking of heels coming up the corridor and I turn, half expecting to see her, arms outstretched, chattering nineteen to the dozen, asking what the hell just happened. But it's not her, it's a nurse, and as she walks past I feel something depart, something warm and glowing. In its place is a black hole; a dark, sister-shaped void.

She is gone.

'Ms Rafter.'

I look up and see two figures coming towards me: a woman in a long tweed overcoat and a uniformed police officer.

'DI Lipton,' says the woman, extending her hand. 'And this is PC Walker.'

'Yes, I know who he is,' I reply bitterly, recognizing the young man. 'I tried to tell you what was happening in that house and you did nothing. Well, actually you did do something. You arrested me.'

He twitches and DI Lipton looks at him and frowns.

'If you had taken me seriously that night, PC Walker, then my sister would still be alive. Instead she is lying in some lousy morgue.'

It's all too much for me, all of it, and the tears that have been threatening for the last few hours come rushing forth.

'I'm so sorry, Ms Rafter,' says Lipton.

She pulls out a chair and sits down next to me. Walker remains standing.

'This must have been a terrifying ordeal for you.'

I wipe my eyes and look at Lipton.

'Is he alive?' I ask. 'Paul Cheverell; the man who did this to us. Have you got him?'

She nods her head.

'Good,' I say, clenching my fists.

I am glad he is alive because I want him to suffer like my sister suffered in her final moments. I want him to never know peace again for as long as he lives.

'He's in police custody,' says Lipton. 'We've obtained some information from Fida Rahmani and we'll need to speak to you and Hannah too once you're ready.'

'Fida Rahmani,' I spit. 'She was part of all this. She needs locking up with him.'

'From what we've gathered, it seems Miss Rahmani was as much a victim of Cheverell as your niece and sister,' says Lipton. 'We believe that Miss Rahmani was trafficked into the UK, and somehow Cheverell took advantage of her situation.'

'What? I don't understand.'

'We're still trying to find out the details,' says Lipton. 'But your sister's neighbour told us that a woman of Miss Rahmani's description went to see your sister yesterday, perhaps to tell her what was going on. We think Cheverell must have found out somehow, and attacked her. We found a cricket bat with blood on it in the garden.'

'Right now I don't care about Fida Rahmani,' I say bitterly. 'She had ample opportunity to tell me what was going on in that house. But she didn't and now my sister is dead.'

'She told us that Cheverell threatened to kill her and the boy if she spoke out,' says Lipton. 'He kept them all separated. Hannah was held in the shed and the rule was that David was to be kept away from her in case he got too attached. She just did what he said. It's common that women like her grow to be dependent on their captors.'

I can't believe the evil of this man.

'Why didn't I see it?' I say to Lipton, tears running down my face. 'I've reported on enough cases of this kind of abuse.'

'I suppose it's not something you'd expect to find right under your nose,' says Lipton. 'And in such a quiet residential street. I know it's taken us by surprise.'

She looks up at Walker and smiles, perhaps hoping to exonerate him from his negligence.

'Well it shouldn't,' I say abruptly.

She doesn't know how wrong she is. We're all of us, every day, just a hair's breadth away from evil. If I've learned anything from over fifteen years of reporting, it's that. But I couldn't expect these people to understand.

I stand up.

'Listen, we'll be in touch, Ms Rafter, but in the meantime we've arranged for a social worker from Kent Child Services to come and speak to you. They can go through your options.'

'Options?'

'For the care of Hannah and David,' she says. 'They'll be able to talk through the next steps. Temporary accommodation, counselling, possible foster care for the boy.'

'That won't be necessary,' I say briskly. 'I'll be looking after Hannah and David now. It's what Sally would have wanted.'

Lipton nods. 'Well, the help is there if you need it,' she says. 'Hannah and David will need a lot of support and counselling to help them recover from this.'

'I understand,' I say, David's cries still ringing in my ears.

'And if there's anything else you need,' says Lipton, handing me a card, 'please don't hesitate to get in touch. You'll find my direct number there and the contact details for your liaison officer at Kent Child Services.'

'Thank you,' I say, taking the card.

'Oh, and there's just one more thing,' says Lipton. 'Fida Rahmani has asked to see you.'

I shake my head furiously.

'No,' I say. 'I don't want to see her.'

'She said she had something to tell you,' says Lipton. 'She's in Ward Three. It's up to you. Whatever you feel is best. Goodbye, Ms Rafter. We'll be in touch.'

She's lying in the bed while a female police officer sits on a plastic chair by the door. The police officer nods as I walk in and Fida looks up. Her face has been cleaned up but she still doesn't look good.

'Hello,' I say as I reach the bed.

She nods her head drowsily.

'Thank you for coming,' she says. 'Sit down.'

'I'm not staying long,' I reply.

'Please,' she says, gesturing to a chair.

'Okay, just for a few minutes,' I say, sitting down.

'I'm sorry about your sister,' she says.

'Are you?'

'Of course,' she says. 'I should never have got her involved. I should have just called the police.'

'Why didn't you tell me?' I say. 'I begged and pleaded with you to tell me. I could have helped you.'

'I wanted to,' she says, wiping her eyes with the thin blanket. 'And I almost did. But then one night Paul came to the house. He said you'd told him I'd been speaking to you. He beat me. Little David tried to stop him and he ended up getting a fist in his face. It was terrifying. I thought he was going to kill us.'

She stops and blows her nose with a tissue.

'Later that night,' continues Fida, 'when Paul had left, I told David to go and find you; to ask for your help. He

359

was scared but I told him to be brave, that you weren't a monster. Paul used to tell him the world was full of evil people, to stop him running away. But I told him you were kind. That your name was Kate and you'd help us.'

'But he couldn't find me?'

'No, he did,' she says. 'But he said you were asleep in a chair and when he tried to wake you, you screamed at him. He was so scared he ran away.'

I shiver as I recall the blood on my hands and face. Little David's blood. Why did I take those stupid pills? If I hadn't been so reliant on them then Sally would still be here. I remember Fida coming to the door with a cut on her face the following night, the night I was arrested. And David staring up at me from the rose patch with a black eye. All because I'd asked Paul about his tenants.

I stand up from the chair. I need to get out of here now. I need to mourn my sister properly.

'I'm sorry, Fida,' I say. 'For everything you've been through.'

I take a notepad and pen out of my bag and scribble my phone number on to it.

'Here,' I say, handing it to her. 'If you need me for anything at all, call me on this number.'

Her eyes fill with tears as she holds the paper to her chest.

'Oh,' she gasps. 'Oh, that would be . . .'

She starts to sob.

'Shh,' I whisper. 'It's all over now. He can't hurt you any more. You'll get through this, okay?'

She looks up at me and nods.

'I'm sorry, Kate,' she says. 'I'm so sorry.'

'I know you are.'

I nod to the policewoman and make my way out. When I get to the door I look back. Fida has curled up on her side. She is still holding the piece of paper, clutching it to her chest like a sleeping child.

47

My head feels like it will burst as I make my way down the corridor. The artificial heat in the hospital clings to my skin. I need to breathe fresh air for just a few moments before I go back and find Hannah and David.

I walk through the hospital reception area towards the exit. Light is coming, the muted, marine light of dawn, and I damn the sun as it slowly emerges beyond the wide glass automatic doors.

I stand outside for a moment, wishing I was a smoker so that I could do something with my trembling hands. And then I see him, a dark figure, waving his arms as he weaves through parked cars.

'No,' I whisper as his face comes into focus.

He can't be here. It is impossible.

'Kate.'

I blink my eyes to make sure this isn't another of my visitations but he is real.

He is here.

'Chris.'

He comes towards me and holds my hand.

'Oh, Kate,' he says. 'I'm so happy to see you.'

'What are you doing here?' I ask as we stand motion-less, two damaged souls in front of a hospital full of hundreds more.

I feel his breath on my face, inhale his cedarwood scent, and it's all I can do to stop myself from grabbing hold of his arms and losing myself completely in him. But instead I allow him to kiss my cheek before breaking away and standing as before. Two people, two separate lives.

'I saw it on the news,' he says, putting his hands into the pockets of his smart woollen coat. 'And I couldn't believe it. I had to see for myself. I've been beside myself . . . and then suddenly there you were. It was like . . . a miracle.'

'My sister is dead,' I tell him. 'I couldn't save her.'

'I know,' he says quietly. 'It's all over the news. I'm so sorry, Kate.'

'Sorry for what?' I say as I look deep into his eyes. 'My sister's death or the fact that you're an arsehole?'

I can't help it. Seeing him brings it all back: the restaurant, the lies, the baby. Our poor dead baby.

'I deserve that,' he says. 'What I did, the way I did it, was cowardly. I know that now.'

'I need to sit down,' I say, walking back towards the strip-lit entrance. 'There's a cafe somewhere in this godforsaken place. We can get a coffee.'

We walk in silence through corridor after corridor. I can sense him behind me, his tall, reassuring frame.

'Here we are,' I say as we approach a set of garish orange doors. 'You get the drinks. I'll find us a table.'

I walk through the deserted cafe and sit down by the window, looking out as an ambulance pulls into the car park below. I flinch as I remember the paramedics lifting Sally's lifeless body off the floor.

I'm sorry, I think as I look out into the expanse of concrete. *I'm so sorry, Sally.*

'Here we are.'

I look up as he places a plastic cup of coffee on the table in front of me. His face glows in the borrowed rays of the morning sun, making his eyes a sharper blue. Everything I love about him is magnified and for a moment I allow myself to imagine a different life. We could live together in some sleepy Yorkshire village, buy a dog and take it for a walk each morning. I could bake cakes and every night I would go to sleep entwined in his arms. In the morning I would wake first and watch him sleep, the sunlight bathing his face in gold just like it is now, and I would whisper thanks to whatever God we believed in that day for sending this man to me.

But the dream dissolves and scatters across the cafe as he takes off his coat and sits down opposite me.

'Why have you come, Chris?'

'I needed to see you,' he says, wrapping his long fingers round the coffee cup. 'And after all you've been through I reckoned you could do with a friend.'

'Oh, is that what you are now?' I snap. 'Sorry, I can't keep up.'

'You know we're more than that, Kate,' he says, leaning forward and touching my arm. 'Much more.'

'Then I must have dreamt the bit where you took me out to lunch and told me it was over,' I say bitterly. 'I've seen your wife, Chris. I know what kind of life you lead when I'm not around.'

'Kate, I'm so sorry.' He looks at me sheepishly.

I look out of the window as he sits opposite me. I see his reflection in the glass: his hands clasped together, hiding the gold wedding band with his thumb. I have to tell him. It has to be now otherwise I'll lose my nerve. But I keep my eyes on the knotted wilderness of cars outside as I speak. I don't want to see his face as he hears it; that would be the end of me.

'I was pregnant, Chris,' I say, my eyes fixed on those cars. 'I wanted to tell you that day in the restaurant but you got your announcement in first.'

I hear him take a breath but I need to get the rest out.

'The baby died a few hours later,' I say coldly. 'So, don't worry, there's no mess for you to deal with.'

His silence fills the huge space and I turn to see if he's still there. He is. He sits with his head in his hands, staring at his coffee cup.

'Chris?'

He looks up and his eyes are swollen with tears.

'Oh God, Kate,' he whispers. 'I'm so sorry. You deserved so much better than me. You're right, I *am* an arsehole. It should be me who got punished, not you.'

I nod my head and look into his eyes. Here in the bright light of the cafe I can see him properly for the first time. Our whole relationship had been conducted in near darkness; sneaking into bed in the early hours of the morning, clandestine meetings on hotel balconies as the sun went down. We were a pair of vampires who sucked the life out of each other. Now, looking at him in the white glare of the strip lights, I realize that I have no idea who he is. The man who I made love to, who caused me to tremble with lust and desire, who kissed my forehead as I lay in his arms, was a shadow, a figment of my imagination. He bears no resemblance whatsoever to the man sitting opposite me now in his expensive suit.

The cafe doors open and a family with two young children come inside. One of the children, a girl, has her arm in a sling and the parents look exhausted as they navigate their charges towards a vacant table.

'It was callous of me,' says Chris, leaning in to let the family pass. 'Cowardly. And believe me, Kate, I have gone over that last conversation in my head countless times since then, wondering if I could have done it differently.'

I look at the little girl with the bandaged arm as she settles into her seat and suddenly this whole conversation with Chris seems utterly futile. I want him to go now so I can be with Hannah and David. So I can find some redemption for all of it: for my brother, Nidal, Sally.

'Chris,' I say, folding my arms across my chest, 'what's the point of all this? We're over. Whatever we had is over. Your wife and daughters need your undivided attention. I understand that.'

'You're being remarkably calm, Kate,' he says, smiling nervously.

'Oh, for fuck's sake,' I yell. 'What do you want to hear? That you ripped my heart to shreds?'

A polite silence descends upon the cafe, broken only by the high-pitched chatter of the children at the table behind us.

But I'm angry now and I want to unsettle him, want him to feel the pain that is invading every inch of my body.

'Your wife,' I say, raising my voice slightly. 'She's not at all how I imagined. But, hey, you were always full of surprises.'

He puts his head in his hands and I turn away. This is pathetic. I'm being pathetic. But I can't stop myself.

'I needed you,' he says. 'Not once did I lie. You knew from the beginning that I was married.'

'Yes, I did.'

'And you said that you didn't want commitment,' he continues. 'What with your father and everything, the idea of marriage repulsed you. You told me that when we first met, before anything had happened.'

'And you said your wife repulsed you, if I remember correctly,' I say, my voice catching.

His shoulders sag.

'I love you, Kate,' he says.

Big fat tears well in my eyes. Why won't he just stop?

'I love you so much it scares me. But we could never work. We've seen the same horrors; we have the same nightmares. I read what your cameraman, Graham, said in the paper about that child in Aleppo and I knew what you'd gone through because I've hauled bodies like his from shallow graves, sometimes up to ten of them a day. I've cradled them in my arms and they looked just like my children sleeping.'

His face is puffy with tears and I can't help but lean across and wipe his cheek gently. He catches my wrist and kisses it.

'When I close my eyes at night I see those dead children,' he says. 'There's a darkness that sits up here and won't go away.' He taps his forehead with my hand.

'That's why I need Helen. I need her because she has no idea what I've seen. I can go home and forget everything. I can wash away the smells and replace the images. The house, the girls, Helen, they're untainted.'

'And I'm damaged goods,' I say, releasing my hand from his grasp.

'No, Kate,' he says. 'You are beautiful and clever and brave, the most amazing woman I've ever met. And if this world was good and just, well, who knows what would have happened.'

'Happy ever after,' I say ruefully. 'You know that doesn't exist, Chris, and it wasn't what I was looking for.'

'Then what was it?' He leans forward and stares at me. 'What made you stay with me all those years?'

'While I was with you the nightmares stopped,' I say. I meet his gaze for a moment then turn and look out of the window.

Another ambulance has pulled into the car park and as it sits waiting to dispatch its patient I feel the engine vibrate beneath my feet. I can sense that Chris wants to continue the conversation but I am tired, tired of trying to resurrect something that had no right to live in the first place.

I press closer to the glass and as the landscape fragments into a series of dots I see my past flickering in front of me. I see my father standing on the doorstep, his arms folded, a broken man in a broken house; I see my mother running towards the waves; David's face as we collected pink seashells; Hannah wriggling in her plastic cot. I see Nidal's football lying in the street and Sally's smile as she closed her eyes. The cafe is full of ghosts and as Chris holds my hand I close my eyes and try to brush them all away but they remain lodged inside my brain like tumours feeding off each other.

I look at Chris and I can see in his face that we have said all that needs to be said. This is it; the end of the line.

Silently we stand up and make our way out of the cafe, through the labyrinthine corridors and out into the vast concrete car park.

As the air hits my face, my muscles contract with exhaustion. A cab toots its horn and a group of hospital workers bustle past as we stand inertly on the kerb, neither wanting to be the first to say goodbye.

'You're right,' he says finally. 'Happy ever after doesn't exist. But we can try, Kate, we can hope. Because at the end of it all surely it's not wishful thinking to dream of a happy life?'

'Of course it isn't,' I tell him, thinking of Hannah and David and the long journey ahead. 'I couldn't do my job if I didn't believe that. As long as I can believe that human beings can love as well as hate, then I can go on living.'

'And the nightmares?' He looks at me pleadingly, as if he is hanging from a precipice and I am his only hope of salvation. 'Do we just live with them too?'

'I'm going to work on it,' I tell him. 'Maybe go and see a therapist, I don't know.'

'Well, if it works, give them my number, eh?'

I smile. Here we are, two shattered people standing on the threshold of a new life, both reticent to take the first step.

'So,' I say. 'Where are you headed?'

'I . . . I'm not sure,' he says. 'What did you have in mind?'

'Me? I'm going to go back in there and find my family,' I tell him. 'And I think you should too. Go home, Chris.'

He nods his head and frowns. 'And then what?'

'Then who knows?'

'Yes,' says Chris. 'Look, I'm going to get a cab and let you . . .'

He leaves the sentence trailing as I pull him towards me and kiss his cheek. I feel his body relax into mine like it always did and for a moment I almost succumb; almost let him back in.

'Goodbye, Chris,' I say as we peel apart.

His eyes glint in the reflected light of the hospital entrance as he presses a finger to his lips then places it on my mouth.

Then, turning, he walks towards the row of cabs and I watch as he opens a door and climbs inside. I watch as the taxi pulls away and the back of his head grows smaller and smaller, until it's just a dot quivering on the edge of the watery horizon.

48

It is almost 2 p.m. when I arrive at the seafront. The fishing boats are moored and a group of men stand on the beach untangling their nets. I cross the road and head towards the boats, reading their names as I go: *Castaway*; *Star of the Sea*; *Merlin*; *Captain's Mate*. And then I see it: *The Acheron*, with its ominous black and white stripes. But there is no sign of him as I walk along the shingle crunching mussel shells with my boots.

It's my last day here and, though I'm scared, I know that I have to ask him before I go.

The men look up from their nets as I approach. They smell of sweat and salt.

'Excuse me,' I call out above the growling waves. 'Is Ray around?'

'He's on his break,' says one of them, a young man in his late teens. He stands looking at me; his eyes narrowed.

'Oh,' I say as the wind pummels my face. 'Do you know when he'll be back?'

'You'll find Ray at the cafe over there on the corner, love,' says an older man, stepping forward. He pushes the younger one aside. 'Sorry about this one; he has no manners.'

I thank the men and as I walk back across the road I can feel their eyes on me. It's like they know.

The cafe smells of egg and chips. I step inside and look around. Then I see him. He's sitting at a table by the window looking out to sea; a big mug of tea in his hand.

As I walk towards the table he looks up.

'Kate,' he says, getting to his feet. 'I saw it all on the news. Poor wee Sally. I'm so sorry.'

'I need to know, Ray,' I say as I sit down at the table. 'About David's death. And this time you have to tell me the truth.'

He looks at me, his eyes full of pain, then he gestures to the waitress.

'I'll get you a warm drink first,' he says.

We sit in silence while the waitress places a mug of steaming hot tea in front of me. When she leaves I lean forward and put my hand on Ray's.

'Ray, please. Is it true?' I ask him. 'Did I kill my brother? I need to know.'

His eyes widen.

'It wasn't like that,' he says, shaking his head.

'According to Paul it was,' I say, Paul's words still ringing in my ears. 'He said Sally told him that I . . . I drowned David.'

'Oh Jesus,' says Ray, putting his head in his hands.

'Ray, please,' I say, squeezing his arm. 'You have to tell me what happened.'

He lifts his head and looks out of the window. His voice quivers as he starts to speak.

'I was in my boat,' he says. 'Moored up just by the rocks. I had a day of fishing ahead of me and I was just setting up my line when I heard children's voices. Happy

372

voices. I looked over towards the beach and I saw a little girl with black hair. You.'

My heart is pounding and I can taste the saltwater in my mouth as he continues.

'Your brother was with you,' he says. 'Tiny little thing he was, with a mop of dark hair. I smiled as I sat there casting my line, watching the two of you playing. You were holding hands and jumping the waves. And all the time I could hear your laughter. It was such a lovely sound.'

His voice catches and he gulps then goes on.

'I got a bite,' he says. 'I could feel it tugging on the end of my line and I started to reel it in. But just as I was about to bring it overboard something made me look up. You see, the voices had stopped.'

'Voices?'

'Yours and your brother's,' he says, clutching his teacup. 'It was silent. Oddly silent. I could see you on the shore. You were bending down to pick something up though I couldn't see what.'

As he speaks a shiver ripples through my body and I'm back there. I can see it as clearly as if it were yesterday. I'm bending down in the shingle to pick up the pink heart-shaped shells that clustered on the beach. Years later I would see those shells and feel an odd sensation, a fearful feeling, yet I never knew why. I do now.

'Shells,' I murmur. 'I was collecting shells.'

I look up at Ray. His mouth is open. We pause for a moment to take in the fact that I have remembered something.

'Yes,' he says finally. 'I think you were.'

I nod my head. I can still feel the rough shell in my hands as Ray continues.

'But as I watched you my heart froze,' he says, his eyes widening. 'You were alone. There was no sign of the littl'un. Something was wrong. I dropped my line and stood up in the boat to get a better look. That's when I saw him.'

He stops and takes a breath.

'I'm sorry,' he says. 'It's just . . . it's still so fresh in my mind.'

'You said you saw him,' I say gently. 'Where was he?'

'He was . . . he was floating face down in the water about ten feet from where you were,' says Ray. 'When I saw him I rowed like the clappers. I looked up at the beach and saw your mum running towards you. You put your hand out to her. I think you were showing her your shell.'

Mummy, look . . . it's heart-shaped.

The memory burns in my chest as I sit at this sticky table waiting to hear what comes next.

'Your mum called out David's name and I looked up,' says Ray. 'I was expecting to see her running but she was just standing there, stock-still, looking out on to the water.'

Mummy, look . . . look at the shell.

I see my mother standing looking out to sea. Something's the matter. Why is she not moving? She's like a statue. I follow her gaze and see my brother floating on the surface of the water. And I remember now the sense of urgency that has stayed with me my whole life, the feeling that someone is in danger and I have to go and help.

'It was you that ran,' says Ray, interrupting my thoughts. 'Not your mum. As I rowed I could see you running through the waves, trying to get to your brother. Your mother stayed where she was. It was like she was in a trance.'

Mummy, look . . .

'When I got near I couldn't see the little lad any more. It was just you sitting in the shallows. I jumped out of the boat and ran to you and that's . . . that's when I saw . . .'

'What?' I cry, my hands trembling. 'What did you see, Ray?'

Tears are coursing down his cheeks and he swipes his gnarled red hand across his face.

'He was in your arms,' he whispers. 'And when you saw me you said . . .'

He pauses to wipe his eyes again.

'You said: "I'm trying to keep him warm."'

He takes my hand and squeezes it tightly.

'You thought you'd saved him.'

My body goes cold.

'So it's not true then?' I stammer. 'I – I didn't drown my brother?'

'No, Kate,' he says, looking at me clear in the eyes. 'You never drowned him. I had a view of it all and I saw him face down in that water minutes before you got to him. You didn't drown him, love, you brought him back to shore.'

I nod my head as the enormity of his words begins to sink in.

'Then why?' I say. 'Why would my father tell Sally that I did?'

Ray shakes his head.

'I don't know,' he says. 'I told your old man exactly what happened. I told him about your mum standing frozen on the beach – we found out later she was in deep shock, it can do that you know, make you immobile – and I told him that you'd run through the waves and got to David first. I told him how you had him in your arms and that you said you were keeping him warm. But your dad, he was a troubled man, Kate. Your brother's death was senseless and he needed someone to blame. He took what I'd told him and it got all jumbled and warped in his mind, I guess.'

'So Dad chose to believe that I drowned David while Mum just stood and watched,' I say, shivering as I remember the venom on my father's face whenever he looked at Mum or me.

'As I said,' says Ray softly, 'he was a troubled man.'

We sit for a moment, not speaking, barely breathing, as the past flutters then settles around us.

'Thank you, Ray,' I say, puncturing the silence. 'Thank you for being there.'

'You don't have to thank me,' he says. 'All I want is to see you happy; to put all this heartache behind you and go and live your life. There's been too much pain in your family. Make it end, eh?'

I nod my head and we sit in silence for what seems like a lifetime.

'I'd better go,' I say finally as I get up from the table. 'I'm leaving with Sally's daughter and grandson.'

'Good,' he says, smiling warmly. 'A new start is what you all need. But before you go I want to say something.'

'Okay,' I say, sitting down again.

'What happened that day at the beach was the worst thing I have ever lived through. Laying your little brother out in my boat and desperately trying to revive him . . . I had nightmares for months afterwards. Horrible nightmares that wouldn't leave me alone.'

He has had the nightmares too. I understand.

'But do you know what eased them?' he says, pressing his hand into mine. 'Do you know what got me through?'

I shake my head.

'It was the memory of those few minutes,' he says. 'When the sun was shining and I'd just set up my line and I heard the sound of laughter. And it reassured me to know that in his final moments David was happy; he was playing in the waves with his big sister.'

Tears run down my face as I stand up from the table.

Ray gets up and hugs me. He hugs me like my father should have all those years ago.

'They will stop,' he whispers. 'The nightmares. I promise you they will.'

I leave Ray in the cafe and make my way out. But before I head back to the hospital I stand for a moment on the shingle and look out to sea. And as I breathe the last of the day's air into my lungs and listen to the faint moan of the seabirds I feel something leave me. It is subtle, barely discernible, like the tickle of a feather across a sleeper's face, but I know what it is as I turn to go. My brother, the boy I tried to save, has said goodbye.

Epilogue

The little boy squeals as the plane begins its descent and I lean across the seat and take his hand.

'This is exciting, isn't it, David?'

He nods his head and smiles a beautiful, beaming smile. When Sally was a child we used to say that her smile was like the sun coming out and as I sit holding her little grandson's hand I feel something of her spirit around us. She will live on through this little boy.

Hannah opens the blind and looks out.

'Just a few moments and we'll see it,' she says.

David lets go of my hand and presses his face to the window, waiting for the clouds to part so he can get his first glimpse of our new life.

A woman in the seat across the aisle looks at us and smiles and a deep sense of contentment stirs in my bones. Here we are, a little family, broken at the edges but slowly piecing ourselves back together.

We spent the last few months in London living in a rented house while I finalized the sale of my Soho flat. A safe house you could call it, though Hannah blanched when the family liaison officer used that name to describe it, as that was how Paul had referred to the shed: their 'safe house'. So I suggested we call it our holiday home; a place to stay for a while until we were ready to face the world again.

It wasn't easy. Hannah and David had to attend twice-weekly counselling sessions where the horrors of what they had endured were dredged up, sifted through and analysed. There were some days when I thought we wouldn't make it and I worried that I'd made a terrible mistake in agreeing to look after them. But then light began to break through the darkness, slowly, tentatively, like snowdrops through hard frost. David still wakes up screaming some nights but I'm learning how to help him. I'm learning how to be a mother; to dispense hugs and kisses liberally and check for monsters under the bed.

As for my nightmares, they still come. I guess they always will. The hallucinations have lessened though there are still times when I have to ask myself if what I'm seeing is real life or just a strange trick of the eye. But I'm talking to someone – a counsellor who specializes in PTSD – and things are starting, slowly, to get better. Instead of running from my memories and trying to blot them out with sleeping pills and booze, I now face them head on. And like most monsters, once you stand up to them you find that they are not as powerful as you thought.

The real monster, Cheverell, is in prison now. I don't know which one and I don't want to know. After the trial we found out that he had been in prison before for raping and beating his first wife. He had just been released when he returned to Herne Bay to claim his parents' house. According to the psychiatric reports, he saw himself as a messiah figure, preying on any vulnerable woman who crossed his path. I think of Sally waving to him across the garden fence that day and how her fragility must have reeled him in. She always saw the good in people and it was her downfall.

But I made a vow as I saw him being sentenced to life imprisonment that I would rebuild what he had tried to destroy. Bit by bit, Hannah and David are recovering and I am determined that we will live without fear.

'Will we see her soon?' cries David, his face still pressed against the glass.

'Very soon,' I tell him as the city skyline looms on the edge of the horizon.

Harry thought the change of scene would do me good and I think he might be right. There was a time when the thought of a desk job would have signalled the end of the world for me but I have a family to think about now and, anyway, 'New York correspondent' has a nice ring to it.

'Now, David,' I say. 'Get ready to say hello to your new home.'

We huddle around the window then Hannah jumps back.

'Mum needs to be part of this too,' she says.

I watch as she lifts the porcelain container out of her hand luggage. We have planned to scatter Sally's ashes when we get there and I know that it's almost time to say goodbye.

'I see her, I see her,' David shouts. And suddenly there she is, rising up into the sky, a beacon of hope and freedom.

'She's huge,' he exclaims. 'Like an angel.'

I lean back in my seat, letting Hannah and David take in the Statue of Liberty while I close my eyes. He is there as always, holding up his book of smiles.

'*Tusbih 'alá khayr*, Kate.'

I wrote one last article before I left. I wrote about a small Syrian boy who loved football and dreamt of a better life. I wrote about my sister, Sally, who just wanted to feel safe. I wrote about Layla, Hassan and Khaled, all the people who gave me something of their lives and who will stay with me always.

I think about my final words, the words I'd hurriedly typed as I prepared to leave the newsroom for the last time.

'It's a peculiar way to earn a living,' I'd written. 'Hurling yourself time and time again into the eye of the storm. People think we're fearless because we go towards the battle rather than run away, but I could never call myself brave. For me, being a journalist is about giving a voice to those who have been silenced; to tell their stories and show the world the true human cost of war.'

And as Nidal's face begins to fade I think of the inscription on the statue: *Give me your tired, your poor, your huddled masses yearning to breathe free. The wretched refuse of your teeming shore. Send these, the homeless, tempest-tossed to me. I lift my lamp beside the golden door.* And I weep for the man he would have become; the life he could have had.

'*Tusbih 'alá khayr*, Nidal,' I whisper as the plane touches down.

Acknowledgements

I would like to thank the following people for their help and encouragement as I wrote *My Sister's Bones*:

Katy Loftus at Viking for being such a wonderful and inspiring editor. Your intelligence and insight have truly helped bring *My Sister's Bones* to life.

The whole team at Viking Penguin.

My agent Madeleine Milburn for your belief in this novel from the start.

Cara Lee Simpson and all the team at the Madeleine Milburn Literary, TV & Film Agency. You are wonderful people and I really appreciate all your support.

Arts Council England for giving me the time and space to immerse myself in the research for this novel.

Dr Anthony Feinstein (Professor of Psychiatry at the University of Toronto and author of *Journalists under Fire: The Psychological Hazards of Covering War*). Thank you for taking the time to answer my questions, for shedding light on the impact of trauma on journalists around the world and outlining the stark realities of PTSD.

Hayley Vale for giving me an invaluable insight into the daily life of a forensic psychologist.

Mark Starbuck for your brilliant design work on the booklet as I documented the research phase of the novel.

Rowan Coleman, Carolyn Jess-Cooke and Cally Taylor for your words of encouragement when I needed it most. You are wonderful writers and I admire you all so much.

My family and friends. Thank you Fiona, Adam, Daniel and all my nieces and nephews for your love and encouragement.

My sister, Siobhan Kerr. Thank you for sharing your experiences of life as a journalist, the highs and lows, the procedures, the spine-tingling feeling when a story is unfolding. I will never forget election night 1997 when I came to sit with you in the newsroom and watched history being made as the new government swept to victory. I knew then why you loved the job so much and you inspired Kate Rafter in lots of ways.

Mam. You're my best friend and I couldn't do any of this without you. Thank you for listening to lengthy, unedited chapters over the phone and crying at the sad bits!

Dad: a brilliant journalist with a command of language I can only aspire to. Quite simply, you're my hero and this book would not exist without you. 'Words have value,' you once told me. 'Do them justice.' I hope I have.

Luke. My beautiful, big-hearted boy. You inspire and delight me on a daily basis. Thank you for giving me the strength to write this novel. Everything I do is for you.

Nick. Thank you for bringing the story of *My Sister's Bones* to life with your beautiful reportage drawings as part of the research process and for cheering me on to the end. The stories you shared of life in a refugee camp in Calais will stay with me for ever and I am so proud of the work you do.

To the memory of Marie Colvin, a fearless and gifted journalist who always sought the human story within the chaos of war and whose bravery inspired this novel.

Finally, though the character of Nidal is fictional there are many, many children like him currently trapped and suffering in conflict zones around the world. If this novel does anything I hope that it highlights, in some small way, the pressing need to do what we can to help them and, to paraphrase the legendary war reporter Martha Gellhorn, 'to make an angry sound against injustice'.